A Daughter's Journey

lyn
andrews

A Daughter's Journey

headline

First published in 2008
by HEADLINE PUBLISHING GROUP

1

Cataloguing in Publication Data is available from the British Library

Demy cased 978 0 7553 4607 3
Royal paperback 978 0 7553 4834 3

Typeset in Janson by Avon DataSet Ltd,
Bidford-on-Avon, Warwickshire

Printed in the UK by CPI Mackays, Chatham, ME5 8TD

Headline's policy is to use papers that are natural, renewable and
recyclable products and made from wood grown in sustainable forests.
The logging and manufacturing processes are expected to conform to
the environmental regulations of the country of origin.

HEADLINE PUBLISHING GROUP
An Hachette Livre UK Company
338 Euston Road
London NW1 3BH

www.headline.co.uk
www.hachettelivre.co.uk

For my cousin by marriage, the other Lyn Andrews, who has a far better memory of the fashions we wore in the 1960s and the prices we paid for them than I have and has therefore been a great help with my research.

Lyn Andrews
Tullamore 2008

Part I

Part I

Chapter One

Offaly, 1952

'THERE'S NO HELP FOR it, Maura, she's going to have to go to Mary and Liam. There's nothing else we can do. We're going to have to give her over to them. We're desperate, ye know that. There's not enough money, there's never enough and now what bit of work there was through the summer months is finished and winter coming and with another baby on the way, what can we do . . . ?' Martin O'Rourke shook his head and ran his hands through his rapidly thinning brownish-red hair in a gesture of utter despair. He felt defeated. His thin shoulders were hunched and bent beneath a patched and greasy tweed jacket that had seen better days, a slightly more affluent man's cast-off, no longer good enough even for everyday use but Martin O'Rourke had been grateful for it. He was only forty but looked like a man in his sixties. Constant unemployment, poverty, malnutrition and the worry of providing for his ever-increasing family had taken their toll.

Maura reached out and put her arm around her husband's shoulder, her heart heavy. 'Ah, Martin, I'd thought it was the end of the babies. I thought I was after getting too old and too worn out. I thought that Angela was the last, it's been over six years, but . . .' She bit her lip. It seemed she'd been wrong and now God had seen fit to send them an eighth child. She was weary and heartsore as she thought of the future. Of the long months that stretched ahead when she would be so tired, her back aching at the end of each exhausting day, constantly beset with the worry of how to feed and clothe her family and with no one to turn to for help. She, too, was pale and thin. All the delicate softness of her youth, the clear translucent complexion, the sparkle in her hazel eyes, the shine on her golden-brown hair had gone, to be replaced by sallow lined cheeks, haunted eyes and lustreless, lank hair pulled back in a knot.

She glanced around the small kitchen of the run-down, single-storeyed cottage which was all they could afford – and even then there were times when the rent went unpaid. They were fortunate in having a patient landlord. It was a poor home. The floor was flagged and uneven, the walls lime-washed and bare. There was very little in the way of comforts, she thought sadly. No curtains, no bright cushions or rugs, no trinkets, ornaments or even pictures – save the one of the Blessed Virgin that hung by the door; it had been a wedding present. All they had were the bare essentials: a table, a dresser with a very few pieces of delft, a couple of chairs, a narrow wooden bench and three stools, and the woven basket that held the turf for the range. The cottage, which was at the end of a narrow, overgrown bohreen that led to a coppice of ash and willow and then the flat brown scarred bog land that stretched away into the distance for miles, comprised just two rooms and an outside privy.

Two rooms for nine people and now another baby on the way. There was no running water; a pump and a stone trough stood in the tiny yard in front of the cottage. Like all the houses in the parish the cottage had been wired up for the electricity but they couldn't afford to use it. They still used candles or oil lamps while most of their neighbours had the comfort and convenience the electricity provided. It made her life so much harder.

Ireland was still a poor country and Offaly was one of the least affluent of the twenty-six counties, but the O'Rourkes were the poorest of the poor. Martin did his best; he'd work at anything if it brought in a few shillings but often there was no work to be had, and when there was and he did spend the occasional shilling on drink she didn't have the heart to complain. Things hadn't been too bad for them in the early days but as the number of children had increased it had become harder and harder to make ends meet. She had long ago resigned herself to the fact that she was raising her children only to see them emigrate. There was no other choice for either them or herself but she'd never before had to resort to what had now been decided for Angela, her youngest daughter. She had cried so many bitter tears as she'd discussed it with Martin but in her heart she knew it had to be done.

'Mary and Liam can give her a decent home, Maura,' Martin urged. 'Hasn't he a steady job with Bord na Móna and a grand little house with every comfort – electricity, hot water, even a bathroom?'

She nodded miserably. It wouldn't be possible to give the new baby to Mary, she wouldn't be able to cope with it and besides she believed that a baby thrived on its mother's milk. Her sister and her husband lived in what could only be described as luxury compared to their circumstances. Liam worked at the turf-fired power station and their small neat house on the edge of the little town of Edenderry had electricity, hot and cold running water and even a tiny bathroom. Of course all that could not hope to compensate for the great sorrow of not having been blessed with children. Poor Mary had said countless novenas, she had gone on a pilgrimage to Knock, she had climbed Croagh Patrick, the holy mountain in Mayo, in her bare feet but heaven remained deaf to all her entreaties. Maura often pondered why poor Mary was childless when she herself had seven and her other sisters had a dozen between them. Martin wondered was it Liam or Mary who was at fault but Father Kenny often said that no blame should be apportioned for 'Who are we to question the ways of Almighty God?'

Martin took her hand and squeezed it. 'Think of all the good things, Maura. She'll be well fed and have decent clothes on her back. She'll not grow up bold or ignorant, with no learning or manners on her at all. She'll not be after having to take the emigrant ship either, ye can be certain of that. Won't they want to keep her with them to mind them in their old age? Sure, there'll be no one left to mind us, Maura, they'll all have gone to England or America,' he pointed out.

She couldn't argue with him, everything he'd said was true, but it broke her heart to have to literally give her child away because they just couldn't afford to feed and clothe her. She'd come to look on Angela as the baby of the family and once Mary and Liam took her she would become theirs. She would see little of her daughter. Edenderry was twenty miles away, too far for visiting as they had no transport of any kind and train fares were well beyond their means. In future she'd see her little daughter no more than once or twice a year and then only if Mary and Liam brought her to visit. Still, the alternative didn't bear thinking about. It would have killed her to have put Angela into an institution, she'd heard that life was fierce harsh in those places, even though it was what Sister Imelda up at the convent had suggested, and for Martin it would be the greatest humiliation of all. Mary was her oldest sister, her own flesh and blood, she would take good care of Angela, hadn't she said so in her letter? No, Maura wouldn't let her child go amongst strangers, even though they were almost destitute.

'I'll get her few bits together tomorrow and I'll tell her first thing in the morning,' she said dejectedly, already dreading trying to find the words.

'I'll go above to the church and ask Father Kenny if he can get us a ride with someone, even if it's only for part of the way. Ah, I know it's hard, Maura, and we'll all miss her but . . . but 'tis for the best. 'Tis better than an institution and in years to come she'll thank us, so she will.'

Angela stood rigid with shock, her blue eyes wide with fear and hurt above chalk-white cheeks framed with long dark curly hair. She bit hard into her thumb, then she slowly and silently turned away from the crack in the door through which she'd heard her parents' conversation. Oh, how she wanted to throw open the door, run into the kitchen and fling herself into her Mammy's arms and cry that she didn't want to go and live with Aunt Mary and Uncle Liam – ever! She didn't want to go all the way to Edenderry and probably never see Mammy and Daddy or her brothers and sisters again. This new baby was the cause of her being sent away and they must love it more than they loved her otherwise why did *she* have to go? Mammy had always called her 'the baby' but now there was to be another one and already she *hated* it! She wouldn't mind not having enough to eat or warm clothes or even the fact that sometimes she couldn't go to school because she had no shoes. She wouldn't mind not having book learning and manners or even taking the emigrant ship when she was older, if only she could stay here *now*.

A huge sob filled her chest and she stuffed her fist into her mouth to stop it rising up and escaping. Big, salty tears ran down her thin cheeks and instead of going back to the bed she shared with her siblings she sank down on the floor behind the door, sobbing quietly.

Aunt Mary was old, much older than Mammy, and she had never seen her smile or laugh. In fact she'd only ever seen her a couple of times that she could remember. And Uncle Liam looked even older. She didn't care if their house had the electricity or hot water or a bathroom – whatever that was – she wanted to stay *here*!

'What are ye snivelling for and why are ye sitting on the floor? Come here to me before ye have Mammy in on top of us and we all get clattered!' came the hissed instruction from her sister Aoife.

Angela rubbed her eyes with the back of her hand and sniffed. Aoife was sitting up at the end of the bed, an old coat clutched around her.

'What is it? What has ye in that state?' Aoife persisted in a loud whisper.

Angela crept towards the bed and Aoife unceremoniously shoved aside one of her sleeping sisters and drew the shivering child to her.

'Ye'll take a cold, so ye will. What's wrong?'

Between stifled sobs Angela told her what she'd heard.

Aoife was a little mystified. 'Is that all? Wouldn't I only be delighted to go and live with them? To have a bed of me own with thick blankets and a quilt, maybe even a whole room to meself! And plenty to eat, grand clothes and not having to walk miles and miles to school in all weathers and with the cold and wet squelching in through the holes in me shoes.'

Angela looked up at her in some astonishment. 'But I don't *want* any of that! I don't want to go and leave Mammy and Daddy and all of youse.'

This turn of events wasn't a complete surprise for Aoife had heard snatches of the discussions – there was very little privacy in this house – although when she'd commented she'd been swiftly silenced. ('Aren't ye a bold brat?' 'Little jugs have big ears!') Yet she was at a loss to understand her sister's attitude to what she thought of a a stroke of luck.

'Are ye mad, Angela O'Rourke? Ye'd sooner stay here where we're all crammed like sardines in a tin, with empty bellies and barely a shoe to our foot and no chance of getting anything better at all until we're old enough to leave? And having half the parish making a mock and a jeer of us because we're poor and ignorant?'

Angela lifted her chin defiantly and the light of determination filled her blue eyes, which still swam with tears. 'Then I'll tell Mammy that ye'll go and live with them instead. I want to stay here. I'll tell them that that *baby* isn't going to push me out.'

Aoife shook her head slowly. 'Sure, they won't have me, I heard Mammy say so. I'm thirteen, I'm too old. I'd be too much of a trial to them and too bold by half and, besides, I help Mammy all I can. Ye are too small to be much help.'

'But I'll *try* and I'll grow, I will!' Angela was emphatic.

Aoife sighed and drew the thin, shivering little figure into her arms. At thirteen years of age she was already acutely aware that life wasn't always fair but that there was little anyone could do about it. ''Tis no use, Angela, they've made up their minds. It's not because they don't love you, they do!

They just think it will be best for you. Da just doesn't earn enough money to keep us all.'

'But he's enough for this other baby!' Angela protested, still heart-broken, the tears again threatening to overwhelm her.

'Ah, there's nothing they can do about the baby. Don't you just have to accept what God sends you and be thankful. It's all part of Mammy's duty as a Catholic wife and mother. That's what Sister Agnes is always telling us,' Aoife parroted. 'Now, don't start crying again. Pull this bit of a blanket around you and snuggle up to me and go to sleep.'

Angela lay down sandwiched between Aoife and Caitlin her second oldest sister who was breathing noisily. She stared into the darkness, which was pierced by a beam of moonlight filtering in through the uncurtained window. Soon she would have to go far away to that house in Edenderry and maybe have to sleep in a room on her own. All alone in a strange bed, in a strange room, in a strange house and with an aunt and uncle who were virtually strangers. The prospect frightened her and tears again slid down her cheeks. Her safe, secure, familiar little world was bounded by these two rooms, the yard, the bohreen, the bog and the fields across which she walked to school and to church and now it was crashing around her. She would have to go to a different school with children she wouldn't know and who might torment her. She would have to attend a different church where everyone would stare at her with curiosity and maybe pity. There would be no Mammy to scold her or pet her, no sisters or brothers to play and laugh or fight and cry with. And all because God was sending Mammy another baby. She was almost certain that Mammy didn't really *want* another baby, she didn't seem very happy about it and after all *she'd* been Mammy's baby for six whole years. Never mind what

Sister Agnes said, why couldn't Mammy tell God that she didn't want this baby and would He please take it back? It all seemed perfectly simple to her and yet, overcome as she was by misery, she knew in her heart that nothing was going to alter the fact that she was to be given away to her Aunt Mary and Uncle Liam. Her da had mentioned an institution but she knew he hadn't really meant *that*. Your mammy and daddy had to be dead for the orphanage to take you and she could hear hers still chatting quietly in the next room. Were they still discussing her or was all the talk now of this hateful new baby that would take her place? It was a long while before, utterly exhausted, she slipped into a restless, dream-filled sleep.

Chapter Two

———◦═◦═◦———

ANGELA FELT AS THOUGH she had no more tears left to cry when, next morning, her mother in a falsely cheerful yet slightly unsteady voice told her she was to go and live with her aunt and uncle and that it was a great opportunity, that she'd have plenty of good food, nice warm clothes and live in a house with every comfort. Her brothers and sisters crowded around and, taking their lead from Aoife, all exclaimed how lucky she was, how they wished they were to have this wonderful chance in life instead of her.

Angela found it all very puzzling and confusing. 'But won't ye all miss me? Will ye be *glad* I've gone?' she asked in a whisper as they stood around her in a circle. Maura watched with a heavy heart as she sorted through the pitifully few, shabby clothes that Angela possessed.

'Of course we'll miss ye and we *won't* be glad ye've gone, but wouldn't we be a desperate lot of begrudgers if we all begged and pleaded with Mammy to let ye stay?' Aoife as usual was trying to be sensible.

13

Angela bit her lip but said nothing in reply; she wasn't entirely convinced.

'I wish it was me that was going. I bet the first thing herself does is to take ye out and buy ye some new clothes for Mass,' Caitlin said enviously, plucking at the hem of the ragged old cardigan she wore over a faded dress that had been handed down from Aoife. It was too long and hung on her like a curtain.

'I bet she'll take ye out and buy ye some sweeties to stop ye fretting,' Jimmy, who was a year younger than Aoife, added rather tactlessly.

'Oh, trust ye, Jimmy O'Rourke, to be always thinking of sweeties!' Aoife snapped, glaring at her brother as Angela's lip had begun to tremble at the word 'fretting'.

'Now, that's enough out of all of ye. Ye'd best get yourselves off or ye'll be late for school and I've chores to attend to,' Maura instructed firmly. As she watched them straggle across the yard, Angela's hand held firmly by Aoife, she uttered a quick prayer of thanks that there had been no tantrums. The child was pale and quiet but seemed more bemused rather than upset.

It was late afternoon, and the light was already fading and a chill was creeping into the air when Martin came home accompanied by the parish priest.

Maura greeted him with deference. 'You're very welcome, Father, will ye have a cup of tea? 'Tis a raw day.'

The priest shook his head, knowing only too well their circumstances and noting the small, spluttering fire in the range that did nothing to dispel the chilly dampness of the room. He doubted that she had milk and probably no sugar either but knew she would go without a hot drink herself to meet the convention of hospitality that his visit demanded.

'Thank you but no, Maura. I've come over to tell you that I've arranged for Martin and Angela to go to Edenderry with old Mr Devaney. He has a bit of business to attend to there.'

Maura nodded. John Devaney was a substantial bachelor farmer and one of the few people in the entire parish who owned a motor car. 'Oh, that's good of him, Father. He won't feel inconvenienced by having to call at Mary's?'

'Not a bit of it, wasn't he only delighted to be of help? I'm taking the opportunity to go over myself to call on Father Dwyer and then John will bring both myself and Martin back here. Can you have the child ready for half past six?'

She hadn't expected Angela to go today, she'd thought perhaps tomorrow or the day after, but she nodded slowly.

Father Kenny was a kind man who felt deeply for all his parishioners, knowing how they all struggled to make a living, especially those like the O'Rourkes who had no land or property, no skills or learning and little hope of any improvement in their lot. It wasn't in his nature, however, to question the teachings of the Church to which he'd dedicated his life; all he could do was try to ease things for them. He reached out and patted Maura on the shoulder. 'I know it's hard on you, but I'm sure it's for the best. She'll be well cared for and she'll have opportunities she'd never have if she stayed here. I'm not criticising, Maura, I know you do your best for all of them. I know you have little in the way of material things but you give your children as good a Catholic home as you can provide and isn't that all Our Lord asks? You'll have your reward in heaven.'

Maura managed a weak smile as she nodded. 'Thank you, Father. It *is* hard to let her go but . . . but I know she'll be grand with Mary, once she's settled in.'

'That's the spirit. It's not as if she's off to Liverpool, London or New York or Boston. I'm sure your sister will be after bringing her over to visit. Edenderry isn't that far away,' he reminded her, trying to bolster her spirits.

'But it's too far for any of us to walk,' she replied a little dejectedly, 'and I can't be expecting Mary to bring the child all the long miles here very often.'

'Ah, maybe when Angela is older they might get her a bicycle so she could come to visit?' he suggested and was relieved to see that his words cheered her. 'All right so, I'll be back at half past six. God bless you both.'

When he'd gone Maura once again took Angela's few clothes and laid them out on the table, then she refolded them and wrapped them in a piece of old newspaper and tied it with some twine. In the pocket of her apron she had the little set of rosary beads that she'd begged from Sister Patrick who worked in the convent kitchen and was kind and generous. She had been going to give them to Caitlin when she made her First Holy Communion, but now they would be given to Angela, the first and probably the last gift she would ever have from her mother. As she put on the pan of potatoes – all they had for the supper – her tears fell unchecked into the boiling water.

By the time the children came in from school, all cold, tired and hungry, Maura had pulled herself together. At least there would be something more substantial than potatoes on Mary's table for when Angela came home from school, she thought resolutely.

'Sit down with ye all and don't be snatching and grabbing like savages!' she commanded. 'I won't have Mary thinking I've put no manners on you at all, Angela.'

Aoife's sharp eyes had noted the parcel lying on the dresser. 'Is it all arranged then, Mammy?' she questioned as Maura divided out the potatoes, slapping down the eager little hands that tried to hurry the process.

Maura nodded and smiled encouragingly at Angela. 'Isn't your da going to take ye this very evening with Father Kenny himself and won't ye be going in the height of style in Mr Devaney's motor car, no less.'

Her words were met with cries and gasps. None of them had ever been in a motor car in their lives; they counted themselves fortunate if they got the occasional ride on an ass cart or on the crossbar of someone's bicycle.

'It's not *fair*! She's after getting *everything* and us getting *nothing*!' Caitlin protested, her eyes flashing with jealousy.

Angela said nothing. She pushed the potatoes around on her plate, her appetite suddenly deserting her. There had been times during the day when she'd actually managed to forget that she was going to have to go and live with Aunt Mary but now all the fear and anguish were back. She didn't care that Caitlin was eaten up with jealousy or that Aoife was protesting that she was being spoiled rotten. She hadn't expected to have to go so soon, this very night! She looked up pleadingly at her mother. 'Mammy . . . Mammy do I really *have* to go?' she begged.

'Now, Angela, Mammy explained everything this morning,' Martin answered firmly, seeing his wife's shoulders slump and trying to head off a scene. 'And don't be after being so ungrateful when Father Kenny has gone to great trouble to arrange for us to go all the way in the car. Eat up your food now, there's a good girl.'

Angela pushed her plate away. She couldn't eat another bit, she felt it would choke her, and she was fighting as hard as she could to stem the tears. 'I . . . I'm not hungry any more,' she stammered.

Instantly Jimmy snatched the potatoes from her plate and was admonished by his father to 'put them back this instant, ye little blackguard!'

Maura leaned across the table. 'Ah, try to eat a bit, child. Ye can't go all that way with no food inside ye,' she coaxed.

Angela shook her head and returned the potatoes to Jimmy's plate. They were quickly devoured before they could be removed again.

Maura sighed heavily. 'Well then, go and sit beside the fire, you look perished.'

The rest of the meal was eaten in silence and as Aoife, Caitlin and Carmel collected up the plates and Jimmy, Declan and Peter went to bring in more turf Maura pulled up a three-legged stool beside her daughter. 'Carmel, pass over the hairbrush, child. We'll have to do something with this mop of hair of yours, Angela. Make you nice and tidy.'

Carmel duly passed over the brush from the top of the dresser and Maura began to try to smooth down the child's tangled mop of dark curls, resolutely pushing away the thought that this would be the last time she would do this. 'Now, will I tie it back or shall we try and plait it?'

Angela shrugged listlessly.

Maura tied it neatly back with a piece of twine. 'There now, that's better. If you give your hands and face a bit of a wash you'll look grand.'

As Angela got to her feet Maura delved into her apron pocket. 'This is especially for you, Angela. Will ye promise me that ye'll be a good girl, work hard at school and say your prayers?' She pressed the rosary into the child's hand.

Angela's fingers closed over it and she managed to nod. She'd never had a gift of any kind before and she should feel happy and grateful but somehow it made her feel worse. Mammy was only giving her this little gift because she was sending her away. Hot tears pricked her eyes and her heart felt like a lump of lead in her chest.

The gift of the rosary caused another outburst from

Caitlin and when Aoife tried her best to defend her mother's gesture a full-scale row between the two sisters erupted.

By the time everything had been sorted out and Aoife had been forced to apologise for all the names she'd called her sister and Caitlin had said sorry for slapping Aoife, the dishes washed and put away and the fire banked up, the sound of a car could be heard coming slowly up the bohreen.

Angela was hugged by every one of her brothers and sisters as her father shrugged on his old jacket and looked hastily around for his cap. Now that the moment had come Maura steeled herself, nailing a smile to her face as she took her youngest child in her arms.

'Sit nice and still in Mr Devaney's fine car. Your da will see to your parcel and be a good girl for Aunty Mary.' She gently stroked the child's pale cheek. 'Don't forget to say a prayer for your mammy every night, Angela, and remember we all love you. Goodbye, darlin'.'

Angela clung to her, her face buried in the coarse apron. She couldn't speak, her throat felt as though it had closed over.

Father Kenny strode into the room and took the situation in hand. 'Come along now, child. Mr Devaney is turning the car around in the yard and I've telephoned the post office nearest to your aunt's house and they'll get word to her so she'll be expecting you.' Gently but firmly he drew the child away from her mother, for lingering would help no one. 'Don't you be worrying over her, Maura.'

'I . . . I'll try not to, Father.' Maura couldn't keep the tremor out of her voice.

In a daze Angela let herself be led out to the car. Under any other circumstances she would have been completely overawed by the prospect of a journey in this new shiny black vehicle. Her father climbed in and she followed, turning her head to look through the window at her brothers and sisters who were all crowded in the doorway of the cottage, waving madly. Behind them, in shadow so she couldn't see her face, stood her mother.

'Give them all a wave, Angela,' her father urged, so like a little automaton she raised her hand in a gesture of farewell. That bitter little scene was to remain for ever in her mind. She didn't know if she would ever be able to forgive her mother for sending her away.

Chapter Three

———◆———

A NGELA HAD CRIED HERSELF to sleep halfway through the journey and it was dark when they finally arrived at Mary's house.

Gently Martin shook her awake. 'Come on now, pet, we're here and here's your Aunt Mary coming out to meet us.'

Angela rubbed her eyes sleepily. She was confused. Where was she and why was Aunt Mary here? There was her da but who were the other two shadowy figures? Then, as her father helped her out of the car, she remembered: Mr Devaney and Father Kenny.

They were in what seemed to be a small narrow street. Facing them was a row of houses, all with lights in the windows, and the street was quite brightly lit too. She blinked rapidly in all this unaccustomed light. Her aunt was coming across the pavement towards them, a coat thrown around her shoulders. She was plumper than Mammy and smaller. Her dark hair was cut short and set in tight, rigid curls and waves. She wore a black and white tweed skirt and a black jumper. There was a string of beads around her neck and she was smiling.

Martin propelled Angela gently by the shoulders towards his sister-in-law. 'Here we are, Mary, thanks be to God and the goodness of Father Kenny and Mr Devaney.'

Mary's expression remained the same; her smile didn't widen. She didn't have much time for Martin O'Rourke whom she considered to be something of a feckless waster. She had never understood what Maura had seen in him and he had certainly not proved to be any kind of a good provider. 'You'd better come inside then.' She turned to the priest. 'Thank you, Father, for having the consideration to get word to me. It's a blessing it isn't my night for the Confraternity meeting.'

'Sure, it was the least I could do, Mrs Murphy. It was all arranged in a bit of a hurry. Now, I'll leave Martin and Angela with you. John here is dropping me off to visit Father Dwyer while he attends to some business, we'll be back in an hour or two to take Martin back.'

Mary nodded curtly and held out her hand to the child but Angela clung tightly to her father's arm. He looked helplessly at Mary and shrugged, passing over the small parcel of his daughter's belongings.

Without a word Mary took it and turned back towards the house and they followed as the car drew away.

Angela gazed around her as they entered the narrow hallway. There was a brown and cream rug on the floor and a strip of brown carpet ran up the stairs, secured on each step with a highly polished brass rod. A frosted glass shade covered the electric lightbulb and there were pictures on the walls. At the bottom of the stairs was a little table covered with a clean white cloth. On this stood a statue of the Sacred Heart, with a little candle burning in a red glass bowl at its foot. Mammy didn't have a room like this; they didn't have a staircase or carpet or a rug or statues. And it smelled different, fresh and clean with no trace of cooking. She was ushered into another room and Uncle Liam got up from the chair by the fire and smiled at Father, holding out his hand. He was a big, ruddy-faced man with brown hair neatly brushed back. To Angela he looked much older than her da.

'So here you are then, Martin. Sit yourself down, man, it's a fair auld journey on a raw evening like this, so it is.'

Martin sat down and Angela stood by the side of the chair, still gripping his arm. 'Ah, didn't we come over in style, Liam? You'd hardly notice the time passing with all the comfort.'

Mary had hung up her coat and bustled into the room. 'I'll put on the kettle and Angela, child, you can come and help me with the cups then you'll be after knowing where things are.' She firmly detached Angela's hand from Martin's jacket sleeve and steered her towards the tiny kitchen. Even though she had little time for her brother-in-law, Mary wouldn't let it be said that she hadn't shown him hospitality and she *was* pleased that the child had come to them. It would make a huge difference in their lives to have a child in the house for she had given up hope of ever having any of her own.

'Now then, get out the cups and saucers from that press there and put them on this tray while I put on the kettle to boil. I'll see to the teapot and the milk jug but you can put these buns on the plate for me; that will be a great help, Angela. Then after we've had our tea we'll go and see the lovely little room I have for you and we'll put your things in the press that's in there,' she said kindly.

Angela nodded but she was glad of the distraction of finding the cups and saucers and placing them on the tray, it meant her aunt didn't see the tears that had started to prick her eyes at the mention of the 'little room'. As she placed the freshly baked little cakes on the plate she suddenly felt very hungry and had to force herself not to snatch a cake and cram it into her mouth. They never had things like buns or pies or the biscuits with pink icing that her aunt was putting out on another plate. They didn't have delicate cups and saucers with red and yellow roses painted on them either. In fact Aunt Mary seemed to have a great many things that Mammy didn't have.

Mary watched her, thinking how thin and pale she was. Her clothes were obviously hand-me-downs and her hair was tied back with a piece of string. Not for the first time did she reflect how utterly unfair it was that she and Liam, who could provide a good, comfortable home for them, were denied children while Martin and Maura, who could provide virtually nothing, managed to produce babies at the drop of a hat. She pushed the thought aside as she made the tea. Angela was looking up at her with what looked like trepidation. Poor child, she thought. It must be hard for her to have to leave her mother and all those bold brats of sisters and brothers but it wasn't going to be easy for herself either. She had standards and what little she'd seen of the manners and behaviour of her nieces and nephews left much to be desired. Well, to all intents and purposes Angela was *her* child now and she was not going to have her grow up like a little savage. She smiled down at the wan little face with the huge blue eyes. She was quite a pretty little thing – or she would be with some flesh on her bones, decent clothes on her back and that hair cut into a manageable style.

'Now, do you think you can hold open the door for me while I take in the tray?'

Angela nodded and held the door wide, then followed her aunt into the other room. Her father and Uncle Liam were chatting together amiably and she noted that they were both smoking cigarettes, something she'd rarely seen her da do before.

Mary instructed her to sit at the table and a cup of tea and a small plate was put before her. On to the plate her aunt placed two buns and two biscuits and she ate them in rapid succession before lifting the cup carefully with both hands and taking a gulp of the hot sweet liquid.

'Have you not had your supper, Angela?' Mary enquired, glancing at Martin.

She shook her head but then, trying to be fair to Mammy, she'd informed her aunt that she had been given potatoes but hadn't been able to eat them so Jimmy had had them.

'Sure, she was upset,' Martin explained.

Mary nodded. 'Now then, Angela, we'll leave these men to their chat. Bring your parcel with you and we'll go up and see your room.'

Angela glanced fearfully at her father. 'Will ye still be here when I come down, Daddy?'

'Of course he will! And we don't say "ye", we say "*you*", it sounds so much . . . nicer,' Mary added, taking her hand and leading her from the room.

Even though she still felt utterly miserable Angela couldn't help but marvel at her aunt's house. Every room had bright, shiny lino on the floor and rugs. The rooms had plenty of furniture too, all nicely polished, and there were pretty little vases and china candlesticks and pictures on the walls. There were curtains at every window: two sets, one white lace, the other heavy material. In their room her aunt and uncle had a big brass bed with a green bedspread and matching eiderdown and in the room that she was to have there was a smaller brass bed with a yellow and white checked bedspread. There were yellow curtains and a press for her clothes. Everything was very neat and tidy.

She was astonished by what her aunt called 'the bathroom'. She'd never seen the like before. She'd never seen a proper bath. At home they had an old tin tub that was filled with hot water once a week in which they were bathed one after the other. This bath was big and white with shiny brass taps and stood on little legs, and there was a white basin too, where Aunt Mary said she must wash her hands and face. The toilet was in the bathroom too, not outside in the yard, and that too was white. There were big fluffy towels on a stand and soap that smelled of flowers in a little dish on the washbasin.

'Won't it be grand not to have to get up in the night and go out into the cold and wet to the toilet? You'll just have to take a few steps from your own room. Won't you have every comfort here, Angela?' Mary enthused, noting the astonishment in the child's wide blue eyes.

'I will so, Aunt, but . . .'

'But what?' Mary pressed.

'But won't I be very lonely all on my own in that bed?'

Mary smiled kindly at the serious little face. 'Won't I be in the very room next door and you'll soon get used to getting a good night's sleep without elbows and knees being jammed into you all the time.' Mary well remembered her own childhood, having to share a bed with her sister, never enough to eat, never enough decent clothes. Thank goodness she had managed to leave all that behind. 'Ah, Angela, I know you're going to be happy here. We're going to love having you live with us and you'll make new friends at school,' she said, trying to reassure the child.

Angela tried to smile back; she knew she should be grateful.

'Now, let's put your things away, shall we? Then we'll go

back down and wash up those dishes and before you go to bed I'll make you a big sandwich so you won't be hungry in the night.'

Angela cheered up a little at the thought of the big sandwich and began to pull the twine off the parcel.

Mary shook her head and tutted at the condition of the few clothes the child had brought. First thing in the morning she would have to go to the drapery in town. There was nothing remotely decent in that parcel that she could send the child to school in and she would have to have a good pair of shoes, a warm coat, proper underwear and socks. It was fortunate that she had a few pounds put by. After Martin had gone she determined that she would give the child a bath and wash her hair and then she'd have to put her in one of her own nightdresses; never mind that it would be far too big. She would start as she meant to go on for in her mind there was great truth in the saying 'cleanliness is next to godliness'.

Martin had settled comfortably in the chair by the fire and was greatly relishing the drop of Jameson's Liam had produced 'for the day that was in it'. Liam had said he wasn't to think he was losing a daughter, they were just 'sharing' Angela. Circumstances couldn't be helped and look at all the comforts and benefits the child would have. She'd a grand life ahead of her. His words helped Martin to convince himself that it really was for the best and when Angela came down with her aunt he thought the child looked a little less lost and unhappy.

'She's delighted with her little room and now she's going to help me with the dishes and then we're going to get some things together for you to take back to Maura for the dinner tomorrow,' Mary informed him, having decided that she couldn't in all conscience let him go back to a house where

27

there was nothing but potatoes to eat when she had plenty of food in her larder.

'Ah, 'tis a saint ye are, Mary. She'll be delighted, so she will,' Martin replied as his glass was refilled.

Before going into the kitchen Mary shot a warning look at her husband. There was no call to be overdoing the hospitality and sending the man home reeking of drink. What would Father Kenny and your man with the motor car be thinking of them? And she was certain that her poor sister had enough to contend with this night without a husband with drink taken. These days she often thought that Liam Murphy was getting altogether too fond of a 'drop'. It was a habit she had every intention of nipping in the bud; you only had to look around this town to see examples of where it led.

The moment Angela had been dreading finally arrived when Father Kenny was ushered in and her da reluctantly stood up. 'Ah, there ye are Father. I suppose we'd better be getting on our way then.'

The priest smiled down at the child. 'We had indeed. Isn't this a fine house, Angela? And has your aunt settled you in?'

Angela nodded, trying hard to be brave as a feeling of panic began to creep over her.

'And she's been a good help to me, Father, too. See, we've put some things in a basket for her da to take back. Won't that be a nice surprise?' Mary kept her tone light and cheerful. The last thing any of them wanted now was tears and demands to be taken home. *This* was the child's home now.

Father Kenny nodded his approval as he took the basket from Mary. 'Would you like me to tell Mammy that this is a little present from you and Aunt Mary, Angela? I'm sure she'll be very pleased.'

Mary took Angela's hand. 'She will indeed. Now, I don't

want to rush you but we have to get Angela a bite of supper and then get her ready for bed. We've a busy day tomorrow, lots of nice things to do.'

Martin bent down and hugged his little daughter. Her welfare was one less worry off his mind. She would be happy here, he was certain of it. They were good, generous people.

Angela buried her face in the rough tweed of his jacket that smelled of turf and cigarette smoke and whiskey. ''Bye, Da,' she whispered, fighting down the sobs.

Gently he disentangled her arms from around his neck and stood up and Mary quickly put her arm around the child's shoulder. It was best not to prolong the moment. She nodded in a curt gesture of both farewell and dismissal and held the child close to her, feeling the tremors that ran through the thin little body as Liam ushered Martin and the priest from the room. The child would quickly come to think of this as her home and would be grateful that she hadn't been condemned to grow up in dire poverty and ignorance. There would be no sense at all in taking her back to that hovel to visit. That would only make things harder for them all.

Part II

Chapter Four

Offaly, 1961

A S SHE SAT BY THE window that looked down on the street
that straggled away at the bottom end towards the fields
and open countryside at the edge of town, Angela
remembered that evening and the days and nights that had
followed. She had lived with Aunt Mary for almost ten years
and now she was accustomed to her ways but she had been
utterly miserable and confused in those early weeks. Her
aunt had so many rules. There were so many things she must
remember to do or not to do. Life here was an entire world
away from Mammy's house at the top of the bohreen. Her
cheeks still flushed pink as she remembered the horror and
embarrassment that had filled her when she realised that she
had wet the bed that first night. But it had been as nothing
compared to the rage of her aunt. How could she, a big girl
of six and going to school, do such a thing? She wasn't a baby.
There was no excuse at all, wasn't there a bathroom right
next to her room? Was she just too lazy and idle to get out of
bed? Had she been in the habit of doing it at her old home
and if so it was something that must stop, right now! It was
disgusting. *She* was disgusting and there was to be absolutely

no repeat of such behaviour. Mary wasn't going to stand for it, ruining good bedding to say nothing of the mattress. Nor would she have the house stinking like a midden. But to Angela's shame the bed-wetting had continued and she had had to lie on a rubber sheet and be woken up late at night and taken to the toilet before her aunt went to bed.

Gradually she had grown out of it but the humiliation remained. As did the bitterness she felt whenever she thought of her parents. She had learned that she had another sister but she hadn't seen either her mammy or da since the day she'd been brought here. At first she had plagued her aunt with questions as to when they might go and visit and if she could write a letter to them, begging them to try and come to visit her. Mary had firmly discouraged such notions and gradually she had realised that there would be no visiting. In fairness to her aunt she knew she had a much better life here than she would ever have had with her parents, but she still missed them and her brothers and sisters. True, she was never cold or hungry. She had better manners and spoke with less heavy a brogue. She was well dressed and she'd had a fairly decent education and she had been happy. She had to help her aunt with the chores but she had plenty of leisure time too, most of which she spent with her friend Emer or listening to Lonnie Donnegan, Tommy Steele, Billy Fury, Cliff Richard and all the other pop stars on Radio Luxembourg on the small transistor set she had here in her bedroom – last year's Christmas present, which had cost an astronomical amount of money, according to her aunt. Uncle Liam had insisted she must have it but she now knew there was a very good reason for his generosity.

She glanced across at the radio on the table beside the narrow bed with its plain white bedspread that had replaced the original yellow and white one. She couldn't deny that it was a pretty little room. At her aunt's insistence her uncle had covered the walls in a new paper with pink roses on it and her aunt had had new pink curtains made. It had been done for her sixteenth birthday last month. She herself had made the little pink cushion for the bed from scraps of leftover curtain material. The nuns in the National School had taught them to sew and she had a natural aptitude for it, or so Sister Mary Francis had said. There was a press against the opposite wall that held her clothes and she knew she was fortunate to have so many. She had made some of them herself under the guidance of Mrs Mannion, a seamstress friend of her aunt. She loved clothes and was avidly interested in the latest fashions. She begged the old copies of magazines from friends who had relatives in England and America who sent over such luxuries and she had often taken ideas from them. She frequently found herself adding trimmings to her existing clothes or making a new skirt or blouse.

Mary's voice interrupted her thoughts. 'Angela, will you come down? Young Emer is coming along the street.'

Angela leaned forward and glanced out of the window. Emer Cassidy, her best friend, was walking down the narrow pavement, her progress slowed by stopping to chat with the neighbours. Angela smiled; Emer had been the first person to befriend her on her first day at the new school. She had been nervous that day despite the new clothes her aunt had bought her and the packet of sandwiches and biscuits she had for her lunch, a previously unheard-of luxury, wrapped in greaseproof paper and stored safely in her new schoolbag. She'd hung back when she'd been taken in and introduced to her new classmates. Sister Oliver, who had been informed of Angela's circumstances, had wisely placed her beside Emer, who had instantly viewed her with great interest and curiosity. When Angela had shared the meat paste sandwiches and biscuits with Emer, who confided that her mammy had had nothing at all to give her for lunch – something she herself had all too often experienced in the past – they had become friends.

She glanced quickly at her reflection in the mirror on the wall. Her dark curly hair was worn in a very short 'elfin' cut which everyone said suited her. She and Emer had saved up and bought between them a Pond's lipstick in Sari Peach and a block of Max Factor's black mascara. They used both only sparingly, but putting mascara on her eyelashes made her eyes look much larger and more luminous. Her skin wasn't bad so, fortunately, she didn't need foundation, which would have definitely branded her 'a painted hussy' in her aunt's eyes and caused a huge row. Snatching up her cardigan from the bed she ran lightly down the stairs and into the kitchen.

'Come on in with you, child!' Mary called as Emer politely knocked on the open back door. Mary, whose tightly permed hair was beginning to go grey, was enveloped in a large white apron. She was up to her elbows in flour and the kitchen showed all the signs of the twice-weekly baking session.

'Aren't you always cooking, Mrs Murphy?' Emer commented, grinning at Angela who had appeared in the doorway.

'Ah, Mr Murphy is a great man for his food. There's a good deal of truth in the old saying "The way to a man's heart is through his stomach". You'd do well to remember that, both of you. I hear you're all set to go off to Dinny and his wife on Monday, Emer?' Mary added, transferring the lump of pastry from the brown earthenware mixing bowl to the floured surface of the kitchen table that had been scrubbed to a degree of whiteness that almost matched her apron. Angela was to start work on Monday, up at the doctor's house helping the housekeeper with domestic chores, a fact she was greatly relieved about. Decent work was hard to come by.

The grin faded from Emer's face and she nodded.

Angela's smile too disappeared as she remembered that there wasn't much time left now for her to spend with her friend. 'Is it all right if we walk down the fields a bit, Aunt?' she asked.

Mary nodded. 'Just take care you don't go snagging your skirt on those brambles, and change your shoes. There's bound to be puddles after the rain last night and don't forget you've to be back here in time for Confession.'

As Angela slipped off her tan leather shoes with the tiny heel and replaced them with the pair of old flat black ones she had worn for school, Mary smiled at them both with some satisfaction. 'You look as fresh as a pair of daisies in those summer dresses, so you do.'

Some of Emer's good humour returned. 'Mam said I could wear this today as long as I keep it clean and decent; I can't wear it for Mass tomorrow as it's got no sleeves. Then she'll give it a bit of a press before it's packed although I told her not to bother, won't it be creased to bits by the time I arrive?'

'She just wants to see you go off with everything looking well. I have to say it does suit you, Emer. It makes you look more grown up.' The pale blue and white flowered dress did suit the girl's fair complexion. The blue seemed to deepen the colour of her eyes and the shawl collar and full skirt gave her some semblance of curves. It would have looked better if she had had the layers of net and paper nylon petticoats beneath the skirt as Angela had but she also knew how hard it was for Peg Cassidy to find the money to dress the girl with any kind of style at all. It was the very reason Emer was being dispatched to live with her oldest brother and his wife in America. There were no opportunities here for young Emer. Dinny had sent the fare for even that was beyond the Cassidys' budget.

'We'll be back by a quarter to four, Aunt, in plenty of time to get to the church,' Angela promised as both girls made for the back door.

'Does it really make me look grown up?' Emer asked when they were outside.

'It does and she wouldn't have said so if she hadn't meant it, she's not a one for idle compliments,' Angela replied, linking her arm through her friend's as they crossed the road heading towards the gate that led to the narrow track that ran beside the fields.

'I just wish I had a few more like it instead of all those old things that are no better than rags that I have to take with me.'

'Will you stop giving out about that, Emer! You have a couple of new blouses and we both dyed our school skirts seeing as we don't need them any more and you know your mam has been paying off that dress for ages, ever since you saw it in the drapery window. She wanted you to have it to take with you.'

Emer shrugged. 'I know but I have the feeling that I'll look very streelish and old-fashioned when I get to Dinny's. I bet everyone over there is dressed in the height of style, don't they have some of the biggest pop stars? I wish my hair was long so I could put it up in a ponytail and wear Capri pants and lovely tops like Connie Francis does, but Mam says these new fashions aren't a bit ladylike and you'd be going around dressed like a tomboy,' she finished glumly.

'Well, maybe Dinny's wife won't be so old fashioned and will let you wear what you like. And just think, you'll get to

38

hear all the new records as soon as they come out, you won't have to wait ages and ages. You could even get your own Dansette record player and they'll have a television and, who knows, you might even get to see Ritchie Valance or the Big Bopper, which is more than I'll do. Maybe even Elvis!'

Emer looked excited but then rolled her eyes. 'You know what Mam's views on *him* are!'

Angela nodded. 'The same as Aunt Mary's.'

'She's probably already written to Dinny and told him I'm never to be let near a rock-and-roll concert in case it "corrupts" me.'

Angela sighed. 'It's all so exciting for you but I'm going to miss you. You'll get a grand job and have a fabulous time while I'm stuck here helping out up at the doctor's house. That's going to be desperate dull, especially with Herself virtually an invalid, and on what they're to pay me I certainly won't be able to afford many new clothes, even if there was anywhere to go to wear them. Aunt Mary won't hear of letting me go to a dance until I'm at least eighteen. *Eighteen!* It won't be the same going down to the coffee bar without you.'

Emer shrugged. 'I wouldn't mind staying here and working up at the doctor's.' Angela's enthusiasm for life in America hadn't really had much of an impact on her. Emer was very apprehensive about the whole thing even though her mam said it was a huge opportunity for her, especially now that the country was being run by President Kennedy and him an Irish-American Catholic. 'At least I wouldn't have to go amongst strangers,' Emer added.

'You won't *be* amongst strangers. He's your brother, for heaven's sake!'

'But he's the eldest and he's been gone so long I hardly remember him and I've never even met the wife. No one could afford to go to the wedding and they couldn't afford to come over here to visit and besides . . .' She fell silent and broke off a stalk of cow parsley and idly trailed it along the grass at the foot of the hedgerow.

'Besides what?'

'I'll be worrying about you and . . . and . . .'

Angela gave a little shiver; it was as though the sun had suddenly dipped from the sky. 'Sometimes I wish I'd never confided in you, Emer.'

Emer looked at her in confusion. 'But who else could you tell? Aren't I your best friend, don't we tell each other everything? Besides, as Mam says, "A trouble shared is a trouble halved."'

Angela nodded. 'But I don't want you to be worrying about me.'

'Has . . . has he . . . ?' Emer asked tentatively, biting her lip. She didn't want to upset her friend by dragging it all up again but she *was* worried. Oh, anyone seeing them strolling along arm in arm, chatting, would think that neither of them had a care in the world but that wasn't true. She had this huge change in her life to face and Angela had *him* to contend with.

Angela shook her head. She tried not to think too much about the incident that had cast a dark shadow over her life. It had all happened just before last Christmas. She had had her bath and was in the bedroom drying herself when her uncle had surprised her by coming into the room. He'd often helped give her her weekly bath when she'd been younger but when she'd reached her tenth birthday her aunt had said she was getting far too old for all that splashing about, she wasn't a six-year-old now and from then on had supervised bathtime herself. On that Saturday night her aunt had been summoned to a neighbour's house urgently and Angela had thought nothing of her absence until he had appeared behind her. She had been so surprised that she had dropped the towel. At the look on his face the blood had rushed to her cheeks and she'd scrambled to retrieve it and cover herself. He'd reached out and touched her small breast and she'd gone cold and rigid with panic. She could smell the whiskey on his breath.

'Haven't you grown up, Angela? You're a fine girl now; I'll be beating the lads from the door soon, that I will,' he'd said. 'Here, give me that towel and I'll help you dry yourself, you'll be after taking a cold standing there shivering. Didn't I always used to dry you when you were a wee girl?'

In an agony of fear and embarrassment she'd submitted to being dried, his hands frequently brushing her in intimate places. At last she'd dragged her nightdress over her head and pulled on her dressing gown.

'I . . . I think I heard Aunt Mary coming in,' she'd stammered, pushing past him towards the door. He hadn't followed her downstairs and she'd been very relieved for it had been a while later when her aunt had returned. She'd said nothing, feeling ashamed as if it had been her fault, as if she had somehow encouraged him.

All that week she had been quiet and subdued. Finally, racked with fear and guilt, she had broken down and told Father Dwyer in Confession the following Saturday. His response had totally shocked her. He had more or less called her a liar, castigating her for her ingratitude to a good, God-fearing, generous man who had taken her in and given her a good home. He asked her how she could even think that such a man would sink so low into sin and bring such humiliation and hurt to a wife he cherished. At best it was all a figment of her disgusting, lewd imagination. At worst it was an evil and deliberate attempt to vilify a man who had shown her nothing but kindness. She should be mortally ashamed of herself; she had let herself be dragged down into sin by all these modern songs with their vile sentiments. There had been much of the same until at last she had fled in tears. Only to Emer had she unburdened herself. Emer had been very sympathetic but strangely not shocked. She had told her about Trish Molloy, a girl she knew who had suffered similar treatment at the hands of an uncle. 'She didn't tell the priest but she did tell her mam,' she'd finished.

'And what did her mam do?' Angela had asked, thinking bitterly that her own mother didn't know or care what happened to her daughter.

'She told her to tell no one, not even the priest. You see the old uncle was the one in the family with the bit of money and land and if there was a huge row then they'd be left nothing in his will.'

She'd been appalled. 'What did she do? Did . . . did she just have to put up with it?' she'd asked in horror.

Emer had shaken her head. 'She went off and got herself a job up in Dublin.'

After that Angela had made sure she was never alone in the house with Uncle Liam and she always locked the bathroom door. She wished she could have asked for a lock to be put on her bedroom door but she knew her aunt would want to know why and she couldn't think of a good enough reason.

Emer gave her arm a squeeze. 'Maybe Father Dwyer *did* have a word with him after all, you never know.'

Angela shook her head. She was sure he hadn't but she didn't want to waste the time she had left with Emer thinking about Uncle Liam. She resolutely put the whole horrible affair out of her mind. 'Don't you go worrying about me, I can take care of myself. I'll be up at the doctor's house all day and I'll go with Aunt Mary to her novenas and her Confraternities.' In the past she had always gone to Emer's house on the nights that her aunt went to these religious services and meetings.

Emer pulled a face. 'That won't be much fun.'

'But it will be better than staying in on my own with him. Oh, I wish I was coming with you.'

'I wish you were too. It wouldn't seem half as bad.'

'You will write to me often and send photos?' Angela urged.

Emer nodded. 'I promise and if I ever get to earn pots of money I'll come back and see you and we'll go up to Dublin and stay in the Shelbourne Hotel and go shopping in all the smart shops!'

Angela managed a smile. 'And if Dr Leahy dies and leaves me – his faithful servant – his house and all his money, I'll come over and see you and we'll stay in the Waldorf Astoria and go shopping on Fifth Avenue!'

Emer laughed. 'Sure, and pigs might fly for the both of us!'

Chapter Five

———◦•◦•◦———

EARLY ON MONDAY MORNING Angela had called in to say a final goodbye to Emer. They had spent a few hours together on Sunday afternoon and Angela had given her the little red vanity case she'd bought as a going-away present. Emer had admired it when they'd seen it in the hardware store, which also stocked suitcases and bags, for there were always people leaving Edenderry. Angela had saved up the deposit and had begged her aunt to pay the rest. Emer had been delighted but had then exclaimed she had nothing to give in return.

'Aren't you the eejit, Emer Cassidy! I'm not the one who needs a going-away present!' Angela had laughed.

The Cassidy house was in uproar as Emer's mother tried to get Emer's younger brothers and sister ready for school and herself ready to see her daughter off at the station. Mr Cassidy, who was to escort Emer to Dublin on the first leg of her journey, was trying to find a strap with which to secure her case. Emer herself, dressed in a pair of navy cotton trousers, a pink sleeveless blouse, navy cardigan and flat shoes, looked pale and nervous.

Angela looked anxiously at her friend. 'I just called in on my way up to Dr Leahy's. Are you all right?'

Emer nodded, holding back the tears. Now that the time had actually arrived she was feeling far from all right. She'd never been on such a long journey in her life and she had to face it on her own. Even the thought of finding her way around Dublin Airport was becoming increasingly daunting.

Angela hugged her, sensing her fear. 'You'll be just grand. Sure, you've a tongue in your head. If you're not exactly sure where you should go, *ask*. And Dinny is going to meet you, isn't he?'

Emer nodded, not trusting herself to speak.

'He's got the flight number and the time it's to arrive. Just think, Emer, this time tomorrow you'll be there and Dinny said in his last letter that the weather is grand, really hot. Won't that be a change from what passes for summer in this country?' Mrs Cassidy was trying to bolster her daughter's spirits and her own. She prayed the girl would do well and also that she would be the last child she would have to see emigrate. Please God, things in Ireland would have improved by the time Declan was old enough to leave school.

'Well, I'd best get off now or I'll be late and then Aunt Mary will be giving out to me, it being my first day.'

Mrs Cassidy smiled at her. 'Wasn't it the blessing of God that Mary was able to get you that bit of a job up there? Ah, Tess Dunne is getting on now and is not able for all the work and looking after poor Mrs Leahy too. It's time she had a bit of help, you'll be well able for it, Angela.'

'I suppose it's better than some of the other things that were suggested,' Angela replied, although she would have preferred to work with someone more her own age rather than the middle-aged housekeeper, whom she'd heard was a bit set in her ways. And of course both the doctor and his wife were far from young.

'I'll write as soon as I get there and tell you all about the journey,' Emer promised and Angela hugged her again before leaving to make her way up to the large house at the end of town.

She greeted all the shopkeepers and the people she met on the street as she walked, wondering what lay ahead of her. She pondered, too, on the wisdom of asking Dr Leahy, after she had been there a while, about trying for nursing. She had no chance at teaching or the Civil Service, or even of becoming a woman police officer or Ban Garda as they were called: they were all the best professions; but surely nursing wasn't out of the question? She hadn't done too badly at school and lots of Irish girls became nurses. With Emer gone she realised that she didn't want to stay in Edenderry all her life. She couldn't go home. They didn't want her, she thought bitterly. They'd made that plain by their silence over the years. And there was even less chance of any kind of a decent job back there. But she could go to Dublin, there were plenty of hospitals up there. Of course it would look bad if she were to start asking all sorts of questions now when the doctor been good enough to give her a job. She'd wait a few months and try to save, it would be something to look forward to and it would put her well out of Uncle Liam's way, for that fear constantly haunted her.

The house was set back off the road behind a small walled garden. There was an entrance to the surgery and another around the side that boasted a small glass-sided porch. She pressed the bell, noting the large plant in a gleaming brass pot, the spotlessly clean black and white tiled floor, the small shelf attached to the wall – presumably for the post – and the framed picture of one of the Aran Islands. She knew that her duties would include polishing the brass and mopping the tiles.

Miss Dunne opened the door to her and her heart sank a little. The housekeeper was a tall thin woman with angular features and a prim and slightly suspicious attitude, who cultivated an air of stiff formality and discretion. Never in all the years she had been with the doctor and his wife had one word about the domestic arrangements, the furnishings, the financial situation or the doctor's trips to Dublin to the dinners held by the College of Physicians been uttered by her. To all enquiries as to the health and wellbeing of her employers she gave the same, stock answers, all rounded off with the words 'thanks be to God'. Angela wondered if she ever smiled or laughed. She was certainly not a one for gossip of any kind.

She frowned at the young girl standing before her. 'I expected you fifteen minutes ago. Surgery will be starting in half an hour and Doctor likes a cup of tea before he starts and there's always tidying up to be done in the waiting room.'

'I'm sorry, Miss Dunne, but I called in to see my friend Emer Cassidy, she's off to America this morning,' Angela replied apologetically.

Miss Dunne pursed her lips. 'Well, come along inside with you. I'll overlook it this once. "Punctuality is the courtesy of princes": you'd do well to remember that.'

Angela followed her down the hallway and into the large kitchen at the back of the house, which she remembered from her visit here with her aunt a few weeks ago. Her aunt had marvelled all the way home at the great labour-saving appliances there were in that house. Her duties had been listed for her that day and it had been stressed emphatically that there was to be no talk of *anything* concerning this house or its occupants to anyone other than Miss Dunne herself.

'Take off your jacket and hang it up on the peg on the wall, then put on this apron and go and tidy the magazines in the surgery. Straighten the chairs and give everywhere a good dusting.' Miss Dunne sniffed. In her opinion the place did need to be clean and tidy but she had always thought that sick people did not need magazines to look at while they waited. Surely their time would be better spent thinking how best to describe their symptoms and therefore not waste her employer's precious time with long, rambling tales of woe. 'I'll make the doctor's tea and set a tray for Mrs Leahy which you can take up when Himself starts surgery,' she continued. 'Miss Johnson will be arriving in a few minutes to sort out the appointments.'

Angela nodded, thinking that from her tone the housekeeper didn't approve of Cecelia Johnson much either.

To her relief the morning went quickly. She was certainly kept busy. She'd known Dr Leahy for years; he was a kindly man with a shock of iron grey hair and dark eyes that missed little. He had infinite patience and sympathy providing you really were sick, but he could be abrupt and sharp with those Miss Dunne scathingly referred to as 'hypochondriacs and time-wasters'. She had never seen his wife, who was always referred to by her aunt as 'poor Mrs Leahy'; she knew she had been incapacitated for years but exactly what was wrong with her Angela didn't know. The Leahys had no children and that, according to her aunt, was partly to blame for the poor woman's affliction.

When she'd taken the tray up to the large airy bedroom that overlooked the large garden at the back of the house she'd been quite astonished by the richness of the

49

furnishings. She'd never seen a room like it before. The floor was covered by a thick carpet patterned with pink roses on a pale green background. The furniture was of highly polished wood and the curtains came right down to the floor. All the lampshades were of pleated pale green chiffon trimmed with pink fringed braid and matched the lovely quilted silk bedspread. On one wall was a large mirror in an ornate gilt frame, on another two prints in matching frames and on the third a picture of Our Lady of Lourdes. A large vase of fresh flowers stood on the broad window ledge.

Mrs Leahy had been sitting in a small brocade-covered chair by the window and Angela was surprised to realise that she must once have been a beautiful woman. There was still an aura of that beauty in the delicacy of her pale skin, her wide grey eyes and light brown hair that fell in soft waves around her cheeks. There were dark shadows beneath her eyes and she looked tired and of course she was very thin beneath the cream silk dressing gown, but she'd smiled encouragingly.

'So you are Angela, Miss Dunne's new assistant. I hear you are Mrs Murphy's daughter?'

Angela set the tray down on a small polished table inlaid with mother-of-pearl that stood beside Mrs Leahy's chair. 'I'm her niece, ma'am. I started this morning.'

Dolores Leahy raised an eyebrow, then smiled. 'Well, I hope you will be happy here, Angela. Doctor and I are not too demanding, I hope.'

'Oh, I'm sure you are not, ma'am. Shall I pour the tea?'

Mrs Leahy had nodded and she'd poured the tea, praying she wouldn't slop any in the saucer and 'make a holy show' of herself as Aunt Mary would put it.

'Thank you, child.'

She'd relaxed a little and had smiled. 'Is there anything else I can do, ma'am?'

'Could you please pass me that little bottle of tablets from the bedside table?'

Angela had passed her the small brown bottle and wondered what they were for.

As she'd gone back down the carpeted stairs Angela had glanced around her. It was a fine house with every comfort but it was very quiet. Miss Dunne had the radio on in the kitchen but you couldn't hear it from here. There seemed to be thick carpets everywhere and good furniture. She wondered how many rooms there were in all and then thought how sad it was that there should only be two people living here for Miss Dunne had her own little house to which she returned each night. This was a big family house with plenty of space for children. She caught a glimpse of a grand piano in one of the rooms and wondered had Mrs Leahy played when she'd been well? The doctor didn't look like a man who would play the piano; he struck her as a man who would prefer more active hobbies. In fact she knew he enjoyed a round of golf and sometimes a game of tennis in the summer. Maybe poor Mrs Leahy had also played tennis when she'd been young? She would have looked good in a white dress with a white silk scarf holding back her hair, she'd thought.

As the clock in the hallway struck the hour she'd realised that she had been dawdling and had bitten her lip. She didn't want to give Miss Dunne reason for complaint for she'd begun to realise that she would enjoy working here, despite the housekeeper's somewhat dour ways. Tomorrow she would perhaps tell Mrs Leahy about Emer and her new life in America. Maybe she would find that interesting? She would also ask Miss Dunne if she might have the magazines that had become too tatty even for the surgery. Even though her health was poor, Mrs Leahy must still take an interest in fashion and society for the magazines were obviously ones she had finished with. Angela would love to read them, she was always looking for ideas to keep her wardrobe up to date.

Chapter Six

—◆—

MARY WAS WAITING FOR her when she arrived home that evening and one look at her aunt's face told Angela that she was bursting to know how the day had gone and possibly glean a few bits of 'inside' information, for Mary was certain that Tess Dunne hadn't really included herself when she'd said Angela must tell no one about how the doctor's household was run. The woman was altogether too secretive, in Mary's opinion.

'So here you are home and how did it all go? Was Herself pleased with you?' Mary poured out two cups of tea and then sat at the table, looking expectantly at her niece as Angela took off her jacket and hung it up.

'I was a bit late getting there, I called in to see Emer before she left, but she didn't really give out to me. She's not bad, a bit strict and starchy.' Angela sipped her tea, deliberately misunderstanding Mary.

Mary tutted. 'I didn't mean Miss Dunne, I meant Mrs Leahy. Did you not get to see her at all then?'

Angela smiled. 'I did so but haven't I been sworn to

secrecy about everything that goes on in that house?'

Mary tutted again. 'I'm sure she didn't mean you have to keep everything from *me*. Am I asking you to divulge some kind of state secret? Wasn't I only asking after the poor woman?'

Angela relented. 'I did see her and she's very nice. She's quiet and she looks tired and of course she's very thin. I took her tea up to her.'

'Did she not come down the stairs at all?' Mary pressed.

'No. I don't think she does much. You can see she must have been lovely once though.' Angela helped herself to a biscuit, determined not to divulge too much.

'Ah, that she was, so I do hear tell. It was before I came to live here myself but old Mrs Murphy, your Uncle Liam's ma, said that when she came here as a young bride she made heads turn. People actually stopped to look at her. And of course he was terribly proud of her. Such a desperate shame it was.' Mary shook her head sadly.

'What was? What *is* the matter with her, Aunt, do you know? I was tempted to ask Miss Dunne but I was after thinking she'd bite the head off me.' The thought had indeed crossed her mind for she was curious to know what was wrong with her employer but she felt that it would be viewed as impertinence, she only just having started working there.

Mary looked thoughtful and toyed with her teaspoon. Angela was only sixteen and there were certain things girls of her age really didn't need to know. When she was older and maybe thinking about getting married was time enough.

'Do you know or do people just sort of speculate?' Angela probed.

Mary put down the teaspoon. 'I heard she lost a baby and that there were complications.'

'What kind of complications?

'Nothing you need bother your head about but she had to have an operation and it went wrong. These things sometimes happen, only the good Lord knows why.'

'And that's why they don't have any children?'

Mary nodded and stood up to clear away the cups. She knew how heartbreaking *that* was. Apart from the constant disappointment and the terrible yearning to hold your own child in your arms, society pitied you. You were *different* to other women, women like her own sisters. It was as though you were a failure – she knew that Liam believed it was her fault not his and he'd wanted a son desperately. Even though she now looked on Angela as her own she knew Liam held the fact that she was barren against her. It had driven a wedge between them and these last few years he had taken to going to the pub more often. At least Dr Leahy didn't do that; he might take a drink at home, of course, she would never know. At least she, Mary, had her health and that poor woman did not. She sighed heavily. 'I wouldn't go asking Tess Dunne too much about poor Mrs Leahy's state of health, Angela. I don't want that one thinking we do nothing but gossip.'

Angela nodded. She felt even sorrier now for her employer. It must be terrible to have your health ruined and never to be able to have children. She glanced with affection at her aunt who was bent over the sink washing up. She must know only too well how Mrs Leahy felt about the lack of children but at least Mary had good health. 'I'll finish those, you go and sit down for five minutes.'

Mary smiled at her. 'Ah, you're not the worst, Angela. So, do you think you'll settle well enough above with Miss Dunne and the Leahys?'

Angela nodded slowly; she didn't want to confide in her aunt that she didn't intend to stay in Edenderry for ever. Her options were fairly limited and if she were truthful she really didn't know what she might like to do. She decided to change the subject. 'Is Uncle Liam not in from his work yet?'

Mary's smile vanished and she frowned. 'He is not. He'll have called in to Dempsey's – again! Well, 'tis no matter. We'll have our supper and I'll leave his in the oven. I'm away to sit with Maria Maher's mother this evening while Maria goes off to see their Bernadette. The old lady's getting frail now.'

The familiar wave of unease crept over Angela. 'I'll come with you.'

Mary raised her eyebrows in surprise. 'Why would a young one like you want to be doing that? Listening to us women chatting about things that don't interest you one bit? Wouldn't you be better off going down to that coffee bar with all the others?'

'It's no fun going out now without Emer and I can hold the knitting yarn for you while you roll it into balls. Didn't you say you wanted to get started on that cardigan?'

Mary thought she understood. Angela and young Emer had been almost inseparable. 'All right so, come along with me if you want to. I expect Emer will have arrived by now and will be finding it all a great excitement, though I dare say she'll be tired.'

Angela bit her lip. She was missing her friend already. As she'd walked home she'd thought how much she missed telling Emer all about her first day at work. They'd have spent hours chatting about it. She really didn't want to have to spend the evening listening to Maria Maher's old mother rambling on about how hard things had been when she'd been young and how the young ones today didn't know how lucky they were, but there was no way she was staying here on her own. Dejectedly she wondered how many more such boring evenings lay ahead of her.

*

The following morning when she took up Mrs Leahy's tea she found her looking brighter.

'You don't look as tired this morning, ma'am, if you don't mind me saying so?' Angela ventured with a smile, setting down the tray.

Dolores Leahy smiled back. 'Thank you, Angela, that's because I had a good night's sleep – for a change. And did you have a pleasant evening?'

Angela tried not to grimace. 'I went with my aunt to sit with an old lady.'

Dolores raised an eyebrow. 'That was a very charitable thing to do. I thought you would have been out with your friends?'

'I used to be, ma'am, but my best friend went off to live in America yesterday.'

The older woman sipped her tea while Angela told her about Emer. From time to time Dolores nodded; it was an all-too-familiar story, but when the girl had finished she smiled sympathetically at her. 'I'm sure you'll keep in touch being such great friends, and even though she might not think so now, it *is* a great opportunity for her. I went there myself when I was young, before I married Dr Leahy.'

Angela was surprised. 'And did you not like it enough to stay, ma'am?'

Dolores laughed. 'Oh, there was never any question of me staying permanently. It was just a visit. I have cousins who live in Vermont.'

'Imagine, going all that way to visit!'

'People do, you know, Angela. I expect that the fare is less expensive these days. You might even go out to see Emer one day yourself.'

Angela shook her head. 'There's not much chance of that, ma'am. Wouldn't I have to earn a fortune and, besides, who would help Miss Dunne out here?'

Dolores could have kicked herself for being so insensitive. She came from a privileged background. Her father had been a prominent Dublin solicitor and her mother had been a teacher before her marriage. They had both considered her completely mad to accompany James Leahy (of whom they approved) to a town they considered to be in 'the back of beyond'. There was indeed little chance that young Angela O'Rourke would ever go to visit her friend. There was very little likelihood of the girl ever leaving Edenderry, but she wondered did she have any ambitions? Or was her main aim in life to get married?

'Is there anything you would really like to do, Angela, if you had the opportunity?'

'I . . . I don't think so, ma'am. Haven't I a great life here? Aunt Mary is very good to me and I have this grand job.' She put on a bright smile; she wasn't going to mention that she was interested in nursing and she certainly wasn't going to say a single word about her uncle. 'Will I give these flowers a change of water, they're looking a bit sort of wilted?' she asked to change the subject.

Dolores nodded. Maybe the girl really was thankful for the life she had and did not harbour any ambitions to either obtain a more rewarding and fulfilling occupation or travel. In a way she was relieved. She liked her and wanted her to stay.

'I'll let you know how Emer is getting on when she writes to me,' Angela offered as, picking up the vase, she made for the door.

'I'd like that, Angela. News from abroad is always interesting.'

When she returned to the kitchen Miss Dunne looked at her with some suspicion. 'What kept you so long up there?'

'I was just telling her about Emer.'

Miss Dunne sniffed with annoyance. 'There's no need to be tiring the poor woman with all that idle chat when there's a list of chores to be done.'

'Sure, she didn't mind. She was interested and she looks much brighter this morning. She said she'd had a good night.'

'Thanks be to God for that, she has few enough of them. Now fetch the mop and bucket and make a start on this floor. It's a disgrace, that's what it is. Didn't that delivery lad from the butcher's come trailing sawdust from the floor of the shop in all over it. And when that's done you've the brasses to clean.'

Angela nodded and went for the mop and bucket. If Miss Dunne had her way there would be no conversations with Mrs Leahy at all.

As she walked down the street towards home she was surprised to see Mrs Cassidy standing at her door, waving. Angela hurried her steps.

'Is there something wrong?' she asked worriedly as she came within speaking distance of Emer's mother.

'Ah, not at all. Wasn't I just hoping to see you to tell you that she's arrived safe and sound, thanks be to God?'

Angela stared at her bemused. 'How do you know?'

'Didn't Dinny telephone the post office earlier and didn't Pat Kinnade come all the way down to tell me. Dinny knew I was worried about her going so far on her own and she being a bit of an eejit. He said she looked a bit sort of lost when she arrived but she's grand. Tired, of course, but she'll be fine when she's had a sleep. He said he'll make sure she writes.'

Angela smiled with relief. For one terrible moment she had thought some disaster had befallen Emer. 'I knew she'd be all right, she's not that much of an eejit. I was telling Mrs Leahy all about her this morning.'

Mrs Cassidy folded her arms in anticipation of an interesting conversation and maybe the odd bit of news. 'And how is the poor woman?'

'She's very nice, Mrs Cassidy. A real lady, so she is. But I only see her for a few minutes, Miss Dunne keeps me busy.'

'Ah, that one would,' commented Emer's mother darkly.

'Well, I'd best be off home. I'm delighted Emer arrived safely. I'm going to write to her tonight and post it in the morning.'

Mrs Cassidy face fell with disappointment as Angela walked briskly away. You could see they had her well trained already, she thought. She'd learned nothing that she didn't know already.

Angela smiled to herself as she walked on. She fully intended to tell Emer every detail but she knew her friend would not relay anything back to her mother. Emer had that much sense. Her aunt wouldn't be going out tonight, she had ascertained that before she'd left for work this morning, so she had all evening to write her letter. She looked up and caught sight of her uncle walking towards her from the opposite end of the street. Obviously he hadn't stopped off at the pub tonight. He seldom went to Dempsey's after supper for it always caused a row. She thrust her hands into the pockets of her jacket, wondering just how long she should wait before approaching Dr Leahy for his advice on nursing. Maybe she should have taken the opportunity to mention it this morning when his wife had asked was there anything she really wanted to do but she'd felt it was just too soon. If she could wait until, say, November, she would have been with the Leahy's five months by then and was bound to know them better. But that was five whole months of having to go with her aunt to all her boring meetings. Life was looking increasingly dull and miserable. She was already wishing that Emer hadn't gone. Would she ever find another friend like Emer? she wondered. One to whom she could confide all her hopes and dreams and her fears? She doubted it.

She had reached the door and so had her uncle. She couldn't avoid him.

'And how did it go today up at the doctor's house?' Liam asked jovially.

Too jovially, Angela thought. She shrugged. 'Much the same as yesterday.'

He looked down at her and then looked away. 'And I suppose you're off out again tonight?'

She shot him a suspicious look. 'No. I'm writing to Emer. Aunt Mary is going to start knitting her cardigan and there's a programme on the radio she wants to listen to.'

'So I suppose you'll be up in your room with your transistor on listening to all that caterwauling these young fellers call "music"?'

'I will not. I'll be down in the kitchen,' Angela replied quickly.

He shrugged. 'Then I might as well go down to Dempsey's for an hour or so and have a few jars with the lads.'

Angela pushed open the door. 'There'll be a row if you do. There always is,' she reminded him quietly.

'Sure, I wouldn't have thought the pair of you would even notice I'd gone!' came the curt reply.

Angela arranged her features in a smile as Mary looked up from setting the table.

'Here you both are nice and early,' Mary greeted them,

61

thankful that Liam had come straight home tonight, knowing nothing of his intentions for later that evening.

'I'd have been a bit earlier but Mrs Cassidy wanted to chat.'

'And I can guess what about. Did you have much to say to her?' Mary demanded.

Angela grinned as she took off her jacket. 'I did not. Sure, Miss Dunne would have been proud of me.'

Liam looked at them both and scowled. These days they seemed to exclude him from even the simplest of conversations. What joy or comfort did he get out of life? he wondered. He worked hard to keep them both and little thanks, never mind any small bit of affection, did the pair of them offer him. Well, they could keep each other company this night. He would find a more convivial atmosphere with the lads down at Dempsey's and to hell with the fact that it would cause a row!

Chapter Seven

THE WEEKS OF SUMMER slipped by and Angela settled into the routine of work at the doctor's house. She received regular letters from Emer in America, letters which at first she looked forward to reading. Emer had settled in well and seemed to be having a great life. She loved her brother's apartment and all the labour-saving appliances they had which made life so much easier. She had a job in a department store which paid more than she could ever have hoped to earn in Ireland (had there been such a thing as a department store in Edenderry) and there were great prospects too. She also got a discount on everything she purchased and had made friends with some of the girls she worked with and went out with them. Of course she paid something towards her keep and tried to save a bit to send home but she still had money left, which she spent on clothes and make-up, of which there was a much greater selection. Joy, her American sister-in-law, had a very modern outlook on life and consequently she had far more freedom than she had been allowed at home. Dinny seemed to work very long hours and was tired when he got home and so he wasn't too interested in what she got up to. Angela read with envy of the dances, the trips to the cinema, the coffee bars, diners and soda parlours. Of the Independence Day celebrations and the Labor Day picnic. Emer was certainly living her new life to the full and she had access to luxuries unheard of in her previous life. For the next big celebration – Thanksgiving – Joy had promised that she should pay a visit to their local beauty parlour and have her hair cut in a more flattering style and her nails manicured. Angela had read this with feelings of pure envy.

Summer faded and autumn came in with strong winds that rattled all the window frames, sent clouds of turf smoke billowing out into the living room instead of up the chimney – to her aunt's annoyance – and tore the leaves from the trees. Heavy showers of cold rain turned them into a slippery sodden mass on the streets and pavements and the evenings grew darker and Angela began to feel that life was passing her by entirely.

Each morning she went up to the doctor's house and helped Miss Dunne with the cleaning and cooking. Most evenings she stayed in listening to the radio and replying to Emer's letters, although lately she had to admit that this depressed her somewhat as she contrasted her life to that of her friend. She had asked her aunt could they not have a television set, which she was certain would have livened up the evenings – she could have watched *Top of the Pops* and *Juke Box Jury* – but this request had been met with something akin to shock and outrage and the demand to know did she think her uncle was made of money? She doggedly accompanied her aunt on the evenings she went out, a fact that seemed often to irritate Mary, and she went regularly to Confession on Saturday and Mass on Sunday.

Occasionally she went to the coffee bar and to the cinema but not very often. Because she and Emer had been so close and had more or less shunned the company of their former classmates, she now seemed to be left on the fringe of the group of girls who frequented the town's only coffee bar and she felt that she didn't really belong. Nor was it any fun going to the cinema alone; besides she was trying to save up. It was becoming increasingly important that she get away from Edenderry for there had been another far more disturbing incident with her uncle.

She had gone to the bathroom one night, she guessed it must have been well after midnight, and had been half asleep when she had almost bumped into Liam on the landing, which had jolted her wide awake with shock. He hadn't arrived home from the pub when she'd gone to bed and she could smell the sour odour of drink on his breath. He had said nothing but had lurched toward her, making a grab at her. Terrified, she had backed away.

'Touch me and I'll scream the house down, so I will! And then I'll tell Aunt Mary and she'll kill you!' she'd hissed. She'd meant it. If he laid one finger on her she would raise the entire street with her screams. He had backed away and she had fled to her room, wishing there was some kind of lock on the door. As the terrible realisation that he could come into her room at any time during the night when she was asleep swept over her she shivered in horror. She'd got very little sleep that night and now she never rested easy in her bed.

Mrs Leahy was always interested in what Emer was doing and sometimes Angela would read bits of her friend's letters out to her employer. They discussed what it was like living in a modern society like America's and often Mrs Leahy would recount details of her trip to Vermont all those years ago.

After Angela had read out Emer's intentions to buy some warm boots, a heavy coat with a fake-fur collar she had her eye on, gloves and a set of fake-fur earmuffs to match the coat, which apparently were all the rage, Mrs Leahy said she though that Emer was being very sensible.

'She'll need them. The winters are far colder than anything we get here. Sometimes the temperature falls well below freezing, even during the day, and they have heavy snow. My cousins often went skiing and skating.'

'She does say that when it gets really cold she's going ice-skating with her friends. Well, that's something she's never done before but I expect she'll enjoy it,' Angela replied, thinking of her aunt's comments when she had read out her friend's plans. 'That girl seems to have completely lost the run of herself since she went over there!' Mary had said darkly.

Dolores Leahy had become fond of Angela and she thought she detected a note of dejection in the girl's voice. 'They do have a lot more to entertain them through the winter months over there. You must find life here very quiet compared to Emer's.'

Angela managed a smile as she switched on the lights and drew the curtains against the dismal late autumn evening and took the teacup and saucer and placed it on the tray. 'Oh, I really don't mind, ma'am, and Christmas will be here before we know it. That's something to look forward to.'

Dolores nodded, thinking how much quieter and with far less sparkle and glamour Angela's Christmas would be compared to her friend's.

'Would you not like to take a day off in a week or so's time and go up to Dublin on the bus to do some Christmas shopping? I'm sure Miss Dunne wouldn't mind coping for just one day without you,' she offered.

Angela considered it and then shook her head. 'Thank you, ma'am, but I'll get what few things I intend to buy here in the town.'

Dolores smiled at her. The girl probably couldn't afford the prices they charged in Dublin. She made a mental note to ask James to look for something a bit special for young Angela O'Rourke as a Christmas gift. She was a pleasant girl, always cheerful and obliging. The child she'd lost and which had cost her her health would have been about the same age, perhaps a bit older, she thought sadly. Maybe a little bottle of perfume or some scented soap and bubble bath? What did the young girls these days like? she wondered. She really didn't have much of an idea and it was certainly no use asking Miss Dunne. She'd ask James to seek the advice of Mrs Dolan in the chemist; she'd know what the young girls spent their money on.

After Angela had washed up she went through into the library. Miss Dunne had told her that once a year all the doctor's books had to be taken from the shelves, the covers given a good wipe and the shelves dusted and the books replaced in the exact order they'd originally been displayed in. That was most important. She was to make a start as soon as possible.

It was a small room to warrant such a grand title, she'd always thought. It was at the side of the house and only had one little window, so didn't get much light. Three of the walls were entirely covered with bookshelves, the other had framed prints and cartoons from old newspapers above the fireplace. Beside the hearth there was a large brown leather button-backed chair, the leather creased and worn with age and use. Beside this was a table on which there was a reading lamp and a stack of medical journals and papers which she had been warned not to touch. A heavy fringed rug of an oriental design covered the floor and thick brocade curtains hung at the window and kept out most of the draughts.

She sighed and switched on the main light. It was rather a dismal room, she thought as she stared at what seemed like the hundreds of books on the bookshelves. She glanced at the gilt carriage clock on the mantelpiece. There was an evening surgery at six for people who worked and it was now just turned four o'clock. She was aware that Dr Leahy sometimes came in here for an hour before he started surgery, presumably to read or make reference to his journals, and she didn't want him to find the place in chaos so it was no use taking down too many books. They'd have to be left in piles on the floor and no doubt Miss Dunne would have some comment about that.

She removed all the books from the bottom shelf and sat down on the floor and began to give them a wipe over with the damp cloth she'd brought in with her. They were mainly medical books and after she'd done half a dozen she decided to open one. It seemed to be a textbook with diagrams of the organs of the human body. Maybe it would give her some kind of insight into what she would have to learn if she got a place as a student nurse, she thought, and began to slowly read the text appertaining to the functions of the heart. There were many words she didn't know how to pronounce let alone understand, but she persevered, wondering was there such a thing as a medical dictionary that she could buy to help her?

She was concentrating so hard that she didn't hear the door open or see the doctor standing in the doorway watching her with a bemused smile hovering on his lips.

'So, Angela, is it a career in medicine that you have planned for the future?' he asked quietly.

Angela was so startled she nearly dropped the volume.

'Oh, sir! I . . . I didn't hear you! I didn't think you'd be after coming in here yet. I'm supposed to be giving the books a good dusting and I just opened one to see . . .'

He smiled at her kindly. 'Now don't be getting yourself all flustered, child. I didn't intend to startle you. I just came in for my most recent copy of the *Lancet*.'

Angela had struggled to her feet, still holding the book she had been trying to make sense of.

'What is it you have there?'

Angela held out the volume feeling like a child caught out in a misdeed.

He grimaced then grinned at her. 'This is a bit heavy for someone of your age. Could you make head or tail of it at all?'

She shook her head, twisting the cloth awkwardly between her hands.

'I don't wonder. What made you open it? Were you just curious to see what an old man like me reads in his spare time?'

He wasn't annoyed with her, she could see that, and from his tone she also realised that he wasn't teasing her. She took a deep breath. Maybe now was just the right time to ask him about nursing. 'I . . . I was interested.'

He looked at her closely. She was a quiet girl but not without intelligence and maybe ambition, which was something he had hitherto not suspected. 'Interested in medicine?' he probed.

'More . . . more in nursing. Sure, I don't have the education and I'm not clever enough to be a doctor.'

He sat down in the easy chair. 'Nursing is a very worthy vocation, Angela. Demanding and certainly not easy. It involves a great deal of dedication, hard physical work and study.'

She nodded. 'I realise that, so I do, but . . . but it's something I would really like to have a chance to do. Not that

I'm ungrateful, sir, for the position I have here. It's a grand job and I get on very well with Miss Dunne and Mrs Leahy.'

'I know you do. My wife speaks highly of you and we'd hate to lose you but if you really want to train to be a nurse it would be both selfish and churlish of us to deny you that opportunity. You realise that you would have to go up to Dublin or even to England? They are always short of nurses in England, it's a much bigger country – more sick people – and they have the free Health Service. How would you feel about having to leave home?'

Angela wondered briefly if he was trying to put her off, but maybe he was just pointing things out. 'I wouldn't mind that at all, so I wouldn't. And I'd work hard at my studies,' she replied enthusiastically and truthfully. He could have no idea of how the shadow of Uncle Liam hung over her constantly or the fact that she felt as though she were being stifled here in Edenderry.

He nodded slowly and got to his feet. 'Have you mentioned this to your aunt and uncle?'

She shook her head. 'I . . . I don't think they'd understand. They think I've done well to have this job and shouldn't ask for anything else. Aunt Mary's always telling me to count my blessings and be thankful for everything I have. It's a lot more than many have.'

That he could understand for he knew them both. They were simple people without ambition, content to live their lives in this small town, particularly Mary who had had her fair share of disappointment in life. Naturally she would want to keep the girl with her, hadn't she brought her up as her own? Taken her from a desperately poor home where there were too many children and not enough money to feed them and given her what was a comfortable life by many people's standards? But it was not a life that

A Daughter's Journey

had nurtured any kind of hopes or ambitions.

'Well, we'll say nothing for the moment to anyone. I'll sort out some books which I think might be useful and far easier for you to understand and you can take them home and have a look at them. Then we can discuss it all again in a few weeks' time. Perhaps after Christmas when you've had time to give it more thought.'

Angela beamed at him. Oh, she was so thankful now that she had mentioned it to him and he wasn't going to go telling her aunt or Miss Dunne about it either. 'Oh, thank you! Aren't you the kindest man I ever met?'

'Well, I don't know about that. Come and see me after surgery is over tomorrow morning. Now, I'd better leave you to get on or I'll have Miss Dunne accusing me of encouraging you to shirk your duties.'

He picked up the copy of the magazine he had come in for and handed her back the heavy volume she had been trying to read.

Angela took it from him and as he left she hugged it to her. It didn't matter that the contents had been far above her understanding, it had proved to be the means by which she might possibly escape from this town, the constant dark shadow of her uncle and the boredom that was beginning to overtake her life. Life in Dublin or even England wouldn't be as exciting or glamorous as life in America but it would be far, far better than staying here. She returned to her task with an enthusiasm that had been absent when she had started it. She wouldn't mind any of the chores she had to do now, she thought. The only reason she would be sorry to leave here would be to leave Mrs Leahy and the doctor, and her aunt of course. Mary had been good to her. She'd write to Emer tonight and tell her all about her plans.

Chapter Eight

Tʀᴜᴇ ᴛᴏ ʜɪs ᴡᴏʀᴅ, the following morning when Angela went to see him after surgery, as he'd instructed, Dr Leahy had handed her three books.

'If you make a start on these, Angela, it will give you an insight into just what will be facing you.'

She'd taken them from him and thanked him. 'I'll start on them tonight,' she'd promised, her eyes shining with enthusiasm.

She had expected his wife to make some comment about her desire to go into nursing but Mrs Leahy didn't mention it so Angela assumed that the doctor hadn't wanted to worry or upset her by informing her that they might well be losing the services of Angela O'Rourke in the not-too-distant future. Thankfully Miss Dunne had not been in the kitchen and she had been able to put the books in a carrier bag which she hung on the peg under her coat. She had smuggled the books into her aunt and uncle's house under her coat and had placed them beneath her underclothes in the bottom drawer of the press in her bedroom. Aunt Mary insisted that she keep her own room clean and tidy and left the clean clothes on the bed for her to put away so there would be no chance of them being discovered.

Over the next weeks she read them from cover to cover, quite often struggling with the unfamiliar words, a circumstance she mentioned to the doctor one afternoon when she took him a cup of tea in the library.

'Now I know what we can get you for Christmas, Angela. We've been wondering exactly what you would like. A medical dictionary will be just the thing. You'll find it a great help.'

Angela had flushed. 'Sure, that's very good of you, but I didn't expect anything at all for Christmas and . . . and I didn't think Mrs Leahy knew about . . . it all.'

'I only told her a few days ago. I thought it best to leave it a while.'

She nodded her agreement.

'I take it you haven't mentioned the subject to your aunt yet?'

'No, not yet. I thought that maybe after I've applied and hopefully been accepted, I'd tell her.'

He smiled at her. 'Ah, I see. Present her with a fait accompli?'

Angela was puzzled.

'An accomplished fate or fact. Once you've been accepted there will be little she can say about it. Is that the way of it?'

Angela nodded again. 'Do you think I should write to somewhere soon? The Mater in Dublin, maybe?'

He leaned back in his chair and looked thoughtful. 'So you are getting impatient? I can understand that. I have to be honest with you, Angela, I think the chances of getting accepted in a Dublin hospital are very slim. Most Irish girls who want to join the nursing profession want to do their training in Dublin, there's fierce competition for places. Only those with the best qualifications get accepted. Let me write to a friend of mine in Liverpool. He's a doctor at Walton Hospital; they have accommodation for student nurses there in a special block. You won't have to find lodgings, which can sometimes prove to be a bit daunting in a strange city. I take it you won't mind going to Liverpool?'

'That's really very good of you, I don't mind where I go and I do appreciate it. I'll bring back the books I've finished.'

'Ah, you keep them, child, you'll have need of them for future reference.'

Knowing how expensive they must have been Angela was quite overcome by his generosity. 'If there is anything at all I can do to repay you, sir . . .' she stammered.

'Another pot of tea would be nice and we'll get the letter in the post this evening. Hopefully there will be some news for you just after Christmas.'

As she went back to the kitchen to get a fresh pot of tea Angela felt like skipping along the hall. Christmas was only a week away now, perhaps in a month's time she would be on her way to a new life in Liverpool. It was a big city, not a small backwater like Edenderry. A New Year and a new life, wouldn't that be just *great*? She would write and tell Emer.

Preparations for Christmas became more feverish as the days passed. Although it was spent quietly in both Aunt Mary's house and that of Dr and Mrs Leahy, compared to many homes, there was still a good deal of cleaning and baking to be done and decorations to be put up. Angela had bought gifts for both her aunt and uncle although she had bitterly resented spending any of her hard-earned money on him. With Mrs Mannion's guidance and the help of a pattern, she had made a lovely nightdress case in pink and green taffeta, trimmed with pink ribbon, for Mrs Leahy and with the leftover bits, a handkerchief case for Miss Dunne. It had been a puzzle what to buy the doctor for she had dearly wanted to show her appreciation for all his kindness. In the end she had purchased a boxed set of white linen handkerchiefs embroidered with the initial 'J' in dark blue from the gentlemen's outfitters in town. She felt it wasn't really very special but she had no idea what kind of a tie he would like and the likes of socks or braces seemed a bit too personal. She had wondered to Mr Kinehan, who owned the shop, would perhaps a hat be suitable but had been told firmly that gentlemen much preferred to choose their own.

Under Miss Dunne's supervision she had put up the decorations in the front lounge. These were very smart garlands of artificial greenery, dusted with white frosting to resemble snow, to which were attached baubles in red, gold and silver.

'They're just gorgeous! They must be the smartest in the entire place,' Angela exclaimed as she carefully unwrapped them from the tissue paper in which they'd been packed away.

'They came from Herself's cousins in America some years ago. Be careful with those glass balls or they'll shatter and then we'll be picking the bits out of the carpet for months! It's a miracle they survived the post at all,' Miss Dunne warned.

They were carefully draped across the top of the mantelpiece and the curtain poles and then the tree was brought in and decorated. Red candles were inserted into the silver candlesticks that stood on either end of the mantelpiece and into the smaller holders on top of the display cabinet. Miss Dunne placed the cards that had already arrived on various surfaces around the room and then they stood back to admire their handiwork. It all looked very tasteful and festive, Angela thought. Very different from the multicoloured paper chains strung across Aunt Mary's ceiling and the rather tacky-looking red and green paper bell that hung above their fireplace. They did have a tree, a small one compared to this, but she wondered whether the Leahys felt a little sad that there were only the two of them to appreciate how cosy and delightful the room now looked.

In past years she had always loved Christmas when Emer had been in and out of the house and in the weeks before the holiday they'd gone on so many excursions around the town, choosing what they would buy and what they would also like to receive. They all then went to Midnight Mass and when they got home Aunt Mary let them each have a small glass of sweet sherry, but just one. Then there would be the excitement of opening the presents on Christmas morning, the big meal at lunchtime and sometimes someone had a party on Christmas Night or St Stephen's Day. Yes, it had been a delightful time – until last year when her uncle had destroyed all that and now there was no Emer to share it with. Well, hopefully she would be spending next Christmas with friends in Liverpool.

'What's wrong with you, miss? Haven't you a great puss on your face?'

Miss Dunne's voice brought her out of her reverie and she realised she must have let her feelings show on her face. 'Nothing, Miss Dunne. I was just thinking that perhaps it's a bit of a sad time for them both. All this and no one to share it with.'

Tess Dunne sniffed. 'I'm sure they don't think like that at all, Angela. They enjoy each other's company and Mrs Leahy always comes downstairs for a while on Christmas Day. Father Dwyer comes in after morning Mass for a celebratory drink and then they have a lovely meal. I come in especially to cook and serve it, and then friends call to see them. Don't they have a grand day? Now, get all this tissue paper put away in the boxes and take the boxes back up to the attic while I give this carpet a good going over with the vacuum cleaner.'

'Will I be needed to come in and help on Christmas Day?' Angela asked. Nothing had been mentioned about this so far but she wouldn't have minded.

'Not at all, I can manage perfectly well on my own. I have done for years,' Miss Dunne replied curtly.

'Sure, I meant no harm. I just thought that if I was needed it would be a chance to bring in the little gifts I have and give them on the day itself instead of giving them on Christmas Eve.'

The older woman's attitude softened. 'You spend the day with your aunt and uncle, Angela, but it's good of you to offer.'

'Then I'll be in early in the morning of Christmas Eve and prepare all the vegetables and potatoes. I can leave them in cold water in the larder. It will be one less job for you to do,' she said obligingly.

She arrived at seven o'clock on the twenty-fourth, walking quickly through the cold, dark streets with her head bent against the icy wind. She carried a small shopping bag in which there were the carefully wrapped gifts. She helped the housekeeper with the breakfast and then started on the morning's chores. After lunch was over she made a start on the vegetables and potatoes while Miss Dunne made the stuffing for the turkey which reposed in cold and naked splendour on a platter on the marble slab in the larder, Miss Dunne having plucked and drawn it and washed it out thoroughly the day before. Mr Hickey, the butcher, would have been only too glad to have done this for her but she resolutely refused the offer. She liked to see that these things were done properly, she insisted, men never took the same care women did and she wasn't going to run the risk of being accused of giving the doctor and his wife an upset stomach, she stated ominously.

When it was time for Mrs Leahy's afternoon tea Angela dried her hands and asked should she take up the gifts she had?

'You can but don't go expecting anything in return. Isn't it enough that you're to have an extra week's money?'

'Oh, 'tis more than enough, Miss Dunne. I wouldn't expect more. Here, this is for you.' Angela held out the handkerchief case, wrapped in Christmas paper.

The housekeeper looked startled as she took it. 'For me?'

'It's nothing expensive. I made it myself.' Angela was surprised to see Miss Dunne's thin features soften and a smile of genuine surprise and pleasure crossed her face as she carefully took off the paper.

'It's beautiful, Angela. Thank you. And you made it yourself?' Miss Dunne turned the little pink and green purse decorated with the pink ribbon bows over in her hands.

'I did so. It's just to keep your handkerchiefs in.'

'You never said you could sew, Angela.'

'The nuns taught us and Mrs Mannion lent me the paper patterns.'

Miss Dunne placed it carefully down on the dresser. 'I . . . I've nothing for you.'

'Sure, I didn't expect anything, truly I didn't. It's just as a little thank you.'

'What for?'

Angela was at a bit of a loss. She didn't want to say, I wanted to give you something as it's Christmas and I might well be leaving soon. 'Well . . . for all the things you've helped me with since I've been here.'

'You're not the worst. You are at least diligent and obliging and not a bit bold, which is more than can be said for a lot of young ones these days. Now, take up Herself's tray before that tea gets cold.'

Mrs Leahy was sitting propped up in the bed by a mountain of pillows. She hadn't felt at all well these last few days and she was conserving her strength for tomorrow. She smiled tiredly as Angela came in and put down the magazine she had been leafing through.

'Ah, tea. Maybe that will revive me a little.'

Angela dutifully poured the tea and placed the cup on the bedside table. Then she held out her gifts.

'These are for you and the doctor, ma'am.'

Dolores Leahy was surprised and touched. She knew the girl had little money and was saving up. 'That's very kind, Angela.'

'The smaller one is for the doctor, ma'am. It's not very original, I'm afraid. Just handkerchiefs.'

'It's the thought that counts, Angela, not the originality or the cost and they are very useful. He'll be delighted.'

'And what is it that will delight me?' Dr Leahy asked, coming into the room bearing another cup and saucer. 'I thought I'd come and take my tea with you, Dolores, this afternoon. Just the thing to warm me up after all those cold trips on my rounds.'

His wife held out Angela's small parcel while Angela busied herself pouring him a cup of tea, feeling a little self-conscious.

'Angela has very kindly brought us both gifts,' Dolores informed him as she carefully opened her parcel.

'I was just saying that I'm afraid what I got for you isn't

very original, sir. And I made the nightdress case myself, ma'am.'

Dolores examined it carefully. 'That was very clever of you, Angela. The stitching is so neat and you've used the colours to great effect. Look, James, they match all the furnishings. You've gone to great trouble, Angela. Thank you, thank you so much. I shall treasure it, especially as you may be leaving us.'

Angela bit her lip, not knowing what to say.

'Ah, now, we mustn't go pressuring the child, Dolores,' the doctor chided gently, seeing Angela's confusion.

'James, you know I had no intention of doing so. I'd like to see you get on in life and have a good career, Angela, I really would. You are a thoroughly nice girl but I will miss you. Now, James, have you the things I wrapped up?'

He smiled down at his wife and then went to the drawer in a tall chest that stood beside the window. 'We decided that these would be of great use to you, child, and we both wish you every success.'

Angela shyly took the parcel and unwrapped it. Inside were two books. A medical dictionary and a brand-new copy of *Gray's Anatomy*.

'Oh, this is very, very kind of you. Haven't you already given me an extra week's wages and the other books?'

'That's what we always give at Christmas but we felt we had to give you something extra to help you along the way. I'm expecting to hear something after the holiday, so enjoy your time with your aunt and uncle. It might well be the last Christmas you'll spend with them for quite a few years.'

Angela smiled at them both, thinking if she never had to spend another Christmas under the same roof as Uncle Liam it would be a blessing.

Chapter Nine

IT WAS TWO DAYS AFTER the New Year when the letter arrived and for Angela it was a huge relief. Christmas had been a none-too-happy affair in their house as Uncle Liam had seemed to spend most of it in Dempsey's pub, which had caused constant rows and a distinctly cold atmosphere. When she was not castigating her husband Mary went about with a scowl on her face and her lips compressed in a thin line of disapproval and nothing Angela did seemed to please her. She had kept determinedly out of his way but she sometimes caught him watching her closely and the look in his eyes made her shiver. To add to the mood in the first days of January people started to fall ill with influenza and the doctor's surgery was packed; he also spent many hours visiting people who were too ill to come to him.

'He'll put himself in an early grave, so he will, if he goes on like this. Out half the night he was with someone way out in the country,' Miss Dunne informed Angela, shaking her head dolefully.

'Can he not get help?' Angela asked.

'There is a locum due to come down from Dublin but he can't get here until the end of the week. He'll be staying here so that will mean more work for us,' Miss Dunne had informed her.

'I won't mind that if it helps to ease things for Dr Leahy,' Angela had replied.

'And Herself isn't at all well this morning, probably worrying about the doctor wearing himself to a shadow, although I pray to God she isn't going down with it. Sure, a good blast of wind would knock her over she's that thin and what with everyone coming in here coughing and sneezing, well . . .' She shook her head in disapproval of people bringing germs anywhere near poor Mrs Leahy.

'I don't suppose that can be helped but I'll make sure she has everything she needs to make her comfortable,' Angela promised.

The doctor called her into the dining room after he'd finished his lunch and she thought how tired he looked. His eyes were bloodshot with lack of sleep.

'I have to go out again this afternoon, Angela, but I thought I'd let you know that the letter we've been waiting for has finally arrived.'

She held her breath. Oh, please let there be a hope of being accepted, she prayed.

'You are to write to Matron at Walton Hospital giving details of your education and the reasons why you want to take up this vocation and then if she finds all that satisfactory, which I'm sure she will, they'll accept you. If I had the time, child, I'd sit with you while you wrote the letter but sadly I don't. But make sure you say that you have already started on your studies. In my original letter to Dr Morrissey I told him I would give you a reference and I'm sure he'll vouch for you too, so there should be no problem there.' He ran his hands through his shock of grey hair as if trying to think if there was anything else he should advise her of.

Angela couldn't hide her delight and gratitude. 'I'll write this very night and I'm very, very grateful for all your help.'

He smiled at her tiredly. 'You'll do well, Angela, I know you will. And I think it's probably time you mentioned all this to your aunt.'

Angela nodded slowly. She wasn't too sure about that. Not with the mood Aunt Mary had been in lately. 'What about Miss Dunne? Do I tell her?' With so much sickness in the town and the locum arriving soon she wouldn't be entirely delighted that she would be losing Angela's help.

Dr Leahy considered this. 'Would you prefer me to tell her?'

'I . . . I think so. If you don't mind?'

He nodded. He understood her reluctance. 'And of course Miss Dunne is the very soul of discretion so she will say nothing to anyone. There will be no need to worry that your aunt will find out before you have had chance to tell her.' He got to his feet. 'Well now, I'd better be going. I'll just go up and see that my wife is all right.'

All the way home Angela debated whether or not to tell her aunt. She knew not a word would pass Miss Dunne's lips but was it really fair that the woman should know before her aunt? She had the piece of paper with the hospital's address written on it safely in her bag. She would write tonight, post it tomorrow and surely there would be a reply next week? A little shiver ran through her as she glanced at the still brightly lit windows of the shops on the main street. Oh, it was so important that she be accepted, it was her only way out. She prayed that it would only be a matter of weeks now before she would be leaving Edenderry for good. In the end she decided to leave it a few more days before telling Mary.

Maybe Uncle Liam would cut down his visits to Dempsey's now the festive season was over. Most men found the money for drink to celebrate the holiday but many were now having to count the pennies. Maybe the atmosphere at home would improve as things got back to normal?

She was relieved when she arrived home to find her uncle seated beside the fire reading the newspaper and her aunt about to put the meal on the table. Obviously he had come straight home. There didn't seem to be much conversation between them but at least Mary's face had lost its permanent scowl.

'Come up to the table now, the pair of you. There's nothing worse than lamb that's after being half cold,' Mary instructed.

Over the meal Angela told them of the increase in the number of people going down with influenza and the demands it made on the doctor. 'He's after wearing himself out with it all. He's working day and night, but at least there's a locum coming at the end of the week,' she informed them, helping herself to more mashed potato.

'That influenza has the place destroyed! Isn't Maria Maher's mother very poorly with it and old Mr Dooley and half a dozen other of the old folk.' Mary shook her head ominously.

'Shouldn't we be thankful 'tis only the influenza. I was reading that they've had people die from smallpox over in England,' Liam interjected.

Mary was horrified. 'Mother of God! I thought they'd stamped that out years ago with the vaccinations. Oh, that's desperate news altogether.'

'It's only a small outbreak. It was supposed to have been brought in by people coming from Pakistan.'

'Wouldn't you think they'd stay where they are and not go

bringing all these nasty diseases to places where they've been stamped out?'

Liam shrugged. 'You can't blame them for wanting to move for a better life. Isn't it what we Irish having been doing for years?'

'And it's about time it stopped. Things are bound to get better here sooner or later,' Mary said firmly.

Angela said nothing, feeling a little guilty about keeping her plans to find a better life from her aunt.

She took hours and great pains to compose the letter but finally she had been satisfied and she posted it on her way to work the next morning. When she arrived her feeling of elation dimmed, however, for Miss Dunne told her that Mrs Leahy was not feeling better, in fact she seemed worse and the doctor was worried that she had indeed caught the influenza.

'And Himself rushed off his feet and not able to give her the attention she needs,' the housekeeper finished in a tone that managed to imply that people had no consideration at all to be falling ill.

'She won't have to go to the hospital, will she?' Angela asked.

'She will not be going into *that* place! The doctor knows my views on hospitals. We'll nurse her here in her own good, clean, comfortable home,' Miss Dunne replied emphatically. She had a great mistrust of all hospitals, no matter how well run they were. 'She'll stand a far better chance of recovering here. She'll need extra care, she being frail to start with. He's left medicine to bring down her temperature. She's to keep warm and drink plenty of fluids. She eats like a bird at the best of times but he said not to worry as long as she drinks. You can make up another jug of barley water, she has one up there already but it won't last the day. I'll be glad when this

Dr Emmet arrives, so I will. It will help to take the workload off Dr Leahy, although I don't know how long he will stay. They are usually only called in at times like this, but 'tis my opinion that he should be asked to stay on permanently. Himself is not getting any younger.'

'Thank God we don't have the smallpox here, like they do in England. It was in the newspaper last night. There's six dead of it up to now.'

Miss Dunne looked at her sharply. 'Then I'd be after thinking a bit harder about wanting to go over there and work in a hospital.'

Angela bit her lip. So, Dr Leahy had told her.

Dr Emmet arrived on Friday morning and Angela immediately liked him. He was originally from Galway and had not long qualified but Miss Dunne commented tartly that she supposed he knew enough to treat coughs, colds and influenza and that if he stayed long enough he might learn to cope with other more serious things as well. Dr Leahy had a wealth of experience and would be a fine mentor but he wasn't getting any younger and having someone younger in the practice would take the pressure off him.

'I think she looks on me as being barely out of the university and not fit to be let loose on people,' he confided with a mischievous twinkle in his eye to Angela when she'd shown him his room.

'Ah, she's not the worst. Her bark is worse than her bite. You get used to her,' she'd whispered back. 'But she's glad you've come just the same what with all the extra work the doctor has to cope with and Mrs Leahy being sick too and me hoping to go to Liverpool to start nursing very soon. I'm just waiting to hear if I've been accepted.'

'Is that so? Which hospital?'

'Walton. The reply will come here as there might be a bit of a problem about it at home.'

'Well, good luck to you,' he'd said warmly as she'd left him to unpack.

Mrs Leahy was showing no signs of recovering and when Angela left that evening both Miss Dunne and the two doctors were worried.

'They're afraid it will turn to pneumonia and she so weak already,' Miss Dunne said, biting her lip.

'Aunt Mary is making the nine Fridays so I'll go up with her to the church this evening and pray to the Sacred Heart that she'll get well,' Angela promised. She didn't really want to accompany her aunt this evening. She wanted to start making her plans for as soon as she had news but then she remembered that her uncle always called into Dempsey's on a Friday night.

The evening went quietly. As she'd expected there had been no sign of her uncle when she got home and they left his supper in the oven and walked up to the church, her aunt in none too good a mood. After the devotions were over Mary chatted for a while to some friends and Angela had a brief conversation with Mrs Cassidy. When they arrived back home the dirty dishes were still on the table and her uncle was sprawled in the chair, snoring loudly.

'Would you look at the state of that great eejit that I had the misfortune to marry! God give me the patience to put up with him! That will be a pound or two wasted out of the wages he picked up this night!' Mary's voice was sharp with anger and frustration. Didn't the great fool know how fortunate he was to have a steady job! If he went on like this he'd be in danger of losing it and then where would they be?

'Ah, leave him sleep it off, Aunt. If we wake him he'll only start roaring,' Angela advised. She wanted to go and make her plans, not try to mediate between her rowing relations.

Mary had taken off her coat and hat and had started to clear away the dishes. 'If you ever do anything as foolish as getting married, Angela – and believe me it's not all it's cracked up to be – make sure the fellow is a Pioneer and has sworn never to take a drink! That way at least you'll be sure he won't be after giving all his hard-earned money to some gobdaw of a publican and falling in the door every payday!'

Angela smiled at her. 'That's the last thing I have on my mind – getting married. Here, I'll do those for you. Didn't you say you wanted to look out those recipes you promised Mrs O'Hanlon?'

Mary sighed. 'Thanks, and when I've done that I think I'll have a hot toddy and a couple of aspirins and go off to my bed and get some sleep before that great amadan comes up and disturbs me. I feel shivery myself this night.'

Angela glanced at her. 'You don't think you're coming down with the influenza, do you?'

Mary crossed herself. 'Please God I'm not. Isn't that all I'd need?'

Angela too hoped not. If she was going to Liverpool soon she didn't want to leave her aunt in poor health.

Chapter Ten

———◆———

A NGELA FOUND A PAD and a pen and started to make a list of the things she thought she would need to buy. She had almost twelve pounds saved up, the result of hardly spending anything during the time she had been working. It would pay her fare and for the items of uniform she would certainly be required to provide. There would of course be books and other expenses and she was aware that the amount she would be paid while training would be very small, but at least she wouldn't have to spend money on lodgings. She'd found out that the nurses' home was in a building adjacent to the hospital, so there would be no travelling expenses either. There wouldn't be much left over but she had always been frugal.

When she'd finished she lay on her bed, still fully dressed as the room wasn't particularly warm, with the radio on low so as not to disturb her aunt who was sleeping in the next room, and pondered how she was to tell Mary that she would be leaving for Liverpool in the very near future. It was going to be a shock, she was well aware of that, and not an altogether pleasant one for her aunt either. She couldn't care less about her uncle, the sooner she saw the last of him the better, she thought. But his drinking wasn't making things easy for Mary. It was eating into the housekeeping and causing great friction between them.

It hadn't been like this when she'd first come to live here, she thought. They had seemed happy enough but gradually over the years things seemed to have turned sour. Maybe she hadn't in reality made up for the lack of a child of their own, but that was something she couldn't help. She gazed up to where the lampshade threw a pattern on the ceiling and thought of her mother and father and her brothers and sisters. Probably Aoife, Caitlin and Carmel had by now gone to England or maybe even America, like Emer. What kind of lives did they have? And where were Jimmy, Declan and Peter? What did they all look like now? She would never know. She wouldn't even allow herself to think of the sister whom she blamed for driving her from her home. She felt the wave of bitterness rise up. To all intents and purposes she was a privileged only child but sometimes, despite all the material things she had, she felt lonely. She missed them all. She thought about the night she had learned she was to be given away. She'd been so young and naive, thinking that Mammy could just tell God she didn't want the baby and that that would have solved everything. Now she realised just how desperate they must have been but surely, surely there must have been another way? And why had there never been a single attempt to contact her or visit in all the years she'd been here? That was what hurt the most. That was what caused most of the bitterness. They had simply forgotten all about her. Sent her here, handed her over and put her out of their minds.

The tears welled up in her eyes and slid down her cheeks

and she dashed them away with the back of her hand. How could they have done that? Did they really care nothing for her? Her sisters' and brothers' behaviour she could in part understand. They had all been young; they had no way or means of contacting her without the help of their parents and in time no doubt she would just have become a memory. Life wouldn't have got any better for them. Everything would have been a struggle and they had probably been glad when they had the chance to escape. Thoughts of a younger sister wouldn't have been uppermost in their minds. Their lives were all about survival. She still had the little rosary Mammy had given her but it had never been used. It was in the little china trinket bowl on the top of the press. When she'd made her First Communion Aunt Mary had given her a beautiful one of white pearlised beads that had come from Lourdes along with a leather-bound missal. Her mother wouldn't even know that she was going to be a nurse for she was certain that her aunt wouldn't write and tell her. To her knowledge Mary had never written. There was a card sent at Christmas but none came in return. She didn't even intend to take Mammy's only gift with her when she left here. She could never forgive her.

She turned over and faced the wall. She would put it all out of her mind and concentrate on her future. She heard the creak of the floorboards on the landing and wished she'd switched off the light. She sat up, holding her breath. The step was too heavy to be that of her aunt going to the bathroom. She swung her legs to the floor and quickly switched off the radio as she watched the handle of the door turn. She backed away. What little time she had left here was not going to be spoilt by *him*! She wasn't going to submit to his disgusting advances. She wasn't going to suffer in silence. She was thankful now that she hadn't got undressed. She didn't want to have to scream and wake her aunt but if he tried anything then this time it wouldn't be Father Dwyer she told, it would be Dr Leahy. He was bound to believe her. She didn't want Mary to know about *him*, but she was sure the doctor would try to keep the knowledge from her aunt whilst making sure that her uncle was fully aware that he knew what had gone on. But she was afraid. Very afraid.

Liam peered into the room, bleary-eyed and blinking in the bright light, something he hadn't bargained on. She was a sly little madam, always avoiding him. Couldn't she have shown him some bit of affection and gratitude? It wasn't much to ask, was it? He got neither from Mary these days either.

'I thought you'd have been asleep by now,' he muttered, moving towards her a little unsteadily.

'Is that what you were hoping for? So . . . so you could surprise me and not get much resistance? What did you intend to do? Put your hand over my mouth so I couldn't scream?' She was shaking but more from fear than anger.

He moved towards her and she took another step backwards.

'Ah, now, Angela, you have it all wrong. I'd not hurt you. I just want some . . . affection. Can't you come and give your uncle a goodnight kiss?'

She backed away from him but then felt the edge of the press at her back and her panic rose. She was trapped. He was between her and the door. A scream rose in her throat but she fought it down.

'Get away from me, you filthy, disgusting old man!' she hissed.

Anger contorted his face. 'Disgusting now, is it? Me that's fed you and clothed you all these years? You'll show some gratitude!'

Before she could stop him he grabbed her and she felt his wet lips on her mouth and his work-roughened hand on her breast. With all the strength she possessed she tried to jerk her head backwards and push him away but he was too strong for her. He was tearing at her blouse and she felt sick. She couldn't scream but she fought frantically to get one arm free. She *wasn't* going to let this happen to her. She clawed at his face with her free hand, then grabbed a handful of his hair and yanked it hard. He uttered a curse and she kicked him hard on the shin. With another cry of pain he stepped back a pace. It was all she needed. She wrenched herself free and stood clutching the door handle, shaking violently.

'I'm not going to tell Aunt Mary because in a couple of weeks you won't be able to touch me ever again! I'm leaving here and I'm never coming back!'

He glowered at her, his face scratched and bleeding, and lunged at her again. 'You're going nowhere!'

She wrenched open the door and fled on to the landing. She quickly realised that he was following her. She half fell down the stairs and at the bottom she dragged her coat from the hook. She couldn't stay here, she *wouldn't*. She didn't care now if her aunt woke and wanted to know what was going on.

She heard his laboured breathing behind her. 'Come here, you ungrateful little bitch!'

She fumbled frantically with the lock on the front door and then felt a sharp pain as he caught her by the shoulder.

'Get off me! I'm going for Dr Leahy and then he'll go for the Guards!' Somehow she managed to get free and pull open the door. The cold night air stung her cheeks but she ran as though all the fiends of hell were after her.

When she reached the top of the street she realised he

wasn't following her but she didn't slow her pace. Her breath was coming in painful gasps but fear and revulsion drove her on. Up through the town she ran, her coat flying open, and only when she reached the road where Dr Leahy's house stood did she stop. She leaned against a garden wall, shivering, sobbing and trying to catch her breath. She had a sharp pain in her side but she was too upset to let it bother her a great deal. Why hadn't her aunt woken? The noise she had made crashing down the stairs, the way she had yelled at him that she was coming here should have woken Mary. Then she remembered the hot toddy and the aspirins. She fastened her coat with fingers that still shook. She wasn't going back there. She just *couldn't*!

As she drew close to the house she was thankful to see that there were still lights on. Someone was still up; she wouldn't have to rouse the household by hammering on the door.

To her surprise it was Miss Dunne who opened the door to her. The woman usually went home at eight o'clock.

'Angela! Whatever is the matter, child? Have you run all the way? Come inside with you.'

Angela let herself be drawn into the kitchen. She knew she must look a terrible sight. Tears streaked her face, her hair was standing on end from the wind and her blouse was torn. To her horror she saw young Dr Emmet sitting at the kitchen table clutching a small glass of whiskey.

'Angela! What's happened?' he asked, getting to his feet.

Miss Dunne gently eased her into a chair and the young man pressed his glass into her hands. 'Speak slowly now, child. Is it your aunt?' Miss Dunne urged.

Angela shook her head and took a sip and immediately the spirits caught the back of her throat and she began to cough.

'I . . . I had to . . . come . . . here. Nowhere else to go . . .' she choked, but beginning to feel a little calmer.

'Has there been a fight? Is it to do with you going to Liverpool?' Dr Emmet asked.

Angela shook her head. She suddenly felt terribly embarrassed and self-conscious. How could she tell this young man who was virtually a stranger and Miss Dunne who was a strait-laced spinster what had happened? 'Can . . . can I see Dr Leahy, please?' she begged.

They exchanged glances and Miss Dunne bit her lip and shook her head.

Dr Emmet looked down at her and spoke sadly. 'Angela, I'm terribly sorry but Mrs Leahy died half an hour ago. He . . . he's with her still.'

This shocking and totally unexpected news on top of everything else that had happened that night made Angela's head swim. Suddenly a grey fog was enveloping her. Dimly she heard Dr Emmet cry to Miss Dunne to take the glass from her and then everything went black.

When she came around she was still sitting on the chair but her head was down below the level of her knees.

'Slowly, come up very slowly now, Angela. That's it, nice and easy.'

The room was gradually coming into focus. Miss Dunne was dabbing at her eyes with a handkerchief and looked upset and concerned.

'She'll be fine now. It was the shock,' Dr Emmet said.

Angela looked up at him. 'But . . . but she . . .?'

'She got worse very quickly. It was pneumonia and she had no strength left. We did everything we possibly could. I'm so sorry.'

She couldn't take it in. She knew Mrs Leahy had been very sick, that was why she'd gone with her aunt to church, but she'd never imagined that she would *die*!

'What happened at home that brought you up here in

such a state?' Dr Emmet pressed. Despite his own feelings of shock and grief he knew that something had really upset the girl.

Angela looked at them both and with dawning horror realised she could never tell them about Uncle Liam, not now when poor Dolores Leahy was lying upstairs barely cold. 'Just . . . just a row. I . . . I got upset and ran out. I . . . I didn't know where else to go.' She felt overcome by utter despair. Now she would be forced to go back to that house.

'Ah, I'm sure it will all get sorted out. These things happen in all families. Now, sit there for a while. You've had a shock; we all have. I'll make some strong, sweet tea. Perhaps you shouldn't have had the whiskey, you're not used to it,' Miss Dunne said, putting on the kettle.

Dr Emmet nodded. It must have been a desperate row altogether, he thought. Obviously there'd been slaps and blows involved; the girl's blouse was torn. Of course he didn't know the family very well but maybe it was best that she was off to Liverpool in the near future.

'When you've had your tea and are feeling better, I'll walk you home, Angela. Don't you think that would be best, Miss Dunne? We can't have her going back on her own, not after just finding out about poor Mrs Leahy.'

Miss Dunne nodded. There were many things that had to be done before either herself or this young man got to bed this night, but it wouldn't take him long.

Chapter Eleven

———◆◆◆———

IT WAS VERY LATE WHEN she walked through the dark and silent streets with Dr Emmet and she said little. The fears flew round and round in her head. What would she do if he was still up and waiting for her? Should she ask Dr Emmet to come in with her? What if her aunt was up and demanded to know why she had run off up to the doctor's house so late at night? What if by some terrible chance she was not to be accepted and had to stay here? She couldn't. She just couldn't! And, running through everything, was the thought that poor Dolores Leahy was dead and that the doctor was overcome with grief.

'Well, it looks as if everyone has gone to bed. Shall I come in with you?' Dr Emmet asked as they reached the house.

Angela nodded. 'I'd be very grateful if you would.' The house was in darkness but Liam might still be up and waiting for her. She switched on the light in the hall and went through to the kitchen. Dr Emmet followed her, noticing the look of relief that crossed her face as she realised that the room was empty.

'Did you expect someone to still be up?' he asked quietly.

Slowly Angela nodded and sank into an armchair.

He didn't want to pry but he knew she had been very upset even before she'd learned of Dolores' death. 'Was it a desperate row? Are you afraid it will start up again? Are you afraid of . . . someone?'

Angela didn't reply. What could she say to him? How could she tell this nice young man the horrible truth? What would he think of her?

'Shall I stay for a bit longer?' he offered. He was certain that she really was afraid.

Angela made an effort to pull herself together. 'I'll . . . I'll just go on up and make sure I've not disturbed anyone, that's if you don't mind waiting?'

He smiled at her. 'Ah, not at all.'

She crept up the stairs praying her uncle wouldn't be waiting on the landing. He wasn't and when she stood outside the bedroom door and listened intently she breathed a huge shuddering sigh of relief as she heard the sound of muffled snoring. She went back down to the kitchen and managed to give Dr Emmet a weak smile.

'Everyone is fast asleep so I'll go on up now too. Thank you for . . . for everything. I'll be just grand now. Shall I come in in the morning as usual?'

'It will keep your mind occupied, Angela, which is no bad thing,' he said before bidding her goodnight.

When Angela got up next morning she totally ignored her uncle. As Mary seemed not to know that she had been absent from the house at all the previous night, she wondered if she should inform her aunt that Mrs Leahy had died or should she, when the news was known (as it quickly would be) feign shock and surprise? She felt too drained to put on such a charade. So she decided to tell Mary part of the truth.

'Dr Emmet called late last night, Aunt, but I didn't want to wake you. Poor Mrs Leahy has died. It was pneumonia; she wasn't strong enough to get over it. He . . . they thought I should know.'

Mary stopped buttering the toast and crossed herself. 'Ah, the poor woman! May God have mercy on her soul! Did you hear that, Liam? The young locum called last night to tell Angela. Wasn't that considerate of him? We'll have to go to the removal. Will it be today?'

Liam said nothing, wondering whether Angela had gone up to the house or had bumped into the young doctor en route. In either case, just what had she told him? He had heard them come in, heard them talking quietly and then the drink had definitely overtaken him. He shot her a quick glance but he could tell nothing from her face, except that she was upset. He felt the stirrings of guilt.

'It will be later today, I expect. Father Dwyer will know,' Angela answered.

Mary nodded. Liam was strangely quiet but then she supposed he had a hangover. It served him right. 'I'll go up and see Peg Cassidy, she'll know. That woman manages to get to know everything almost as soon as it happens. There will be plenty to do up there, Angela, with people in and out all day.'

Angela nodded as she sipped her tea. She wasn't looking forward to it. The place just wouldn't be the same without Mrs Leahy.

She was indeed kept so busy that when Miss Dunne told her that the letter she had been waiting for had arrived, she simply stuffed it into her apron pocket. All day people called to pay their respects and then at four o'clock the church bell started to toll and the coffin was closed. They assembled behind the family to walk to the church where Dolores Leahy would lie overnight, watched over by two of the sisters from the convent. She would be buried next morning after the Requiem Mass. During the church service Angela caught sight of her aunt and uncle and wondered how he had the gall to sit there as if he had done nothing. She felt in her pocket for the letter that she had not yet opened and renewed her prayers not only for the soul of Dolores Leahy but that the letter would contain good news.

After she'd gone back and helped Miss Dunne to clean up she took it from her pocket and turned it over slowly in her hand.

'Have you not opened that yet, child?' Miss Dunne commented.

'There hasn't been the time,' she replied, tearing open the envelope.

'Well?' the older woman asked, thinking the girl looked almost afraid to read it and wondering was she now having second thoughts?

Angela let out her breath slowly as a wave of relief washed over her. She had been accepted. She was to go early next week and there was a list of things she would need to take with her. 'They've accepted me.'

'You don't look entirely delighted.' Miss Dunne put more turf into the range and poked it vigorously before closing the door. It had been a long and exhausting day and she was looking forward to sitting down with a cup of tea.

'If . . . if it was any other day I'd be dancing around with delight, but . . .'

'I understand, Angela, but I know she wanted you to make something of yourself, she told me so, God rest her.'

Angela nodded. 'I'll miss her.'

'We all will, child, but especially Himself.'

'I'm sorry to be leaving you at such a time.'

Miss Dunne shook her head. 'We'll manage and with Herself gone, well . . .'

'Will you find someone else? There will still be the two doctors to see to.' Despite the feeling of relief Angela felt a little guilty.

'I don't know. We'll see how things go. Dr Emmet might not stay. I hope he does, for surely this outbreak of influenza will convince Himself he needs a partner. God knows, there's enough work in the practice for two of them these days. Now you'd best be off home, don't forget to write to your friend Emer about our sad loss. Mrs Leahy was always interested in her goings-on.'

Angela promised and left and knew that somehow she was going to have to break the news to Aunt Mary now for there wasn't much time left at all.

They were both in when she arrived home, her aunt still wearing the black skirt and jumper she'd worn under her dark coat. Her uncle was sitting reading the newspaper and didn't look up.

'How are things up there?' Mary asked sympathetically, getting up to put on the kettle. Angela looked pale and tired. She knew how much her niece had liked poor Mrs Leahy and it had been a great shock, but as Peg Cassidy had remarked, 'Who knows when the good Lord will call any of us?'

'I left the two doctors in the sitting room, talking, and Miss Dunne was going to have a cup of tea before leaving them a bit of supper. We know Dr Leahy won't feel like much but Dr Emmet has to do the calls.'

Mary sighed. 'Life – and sickness – goes on.'

Liam rattled the paper, usually a sign that he was restless and preparing to go out.

Mary turned on him. 'Don't think you're after going to Dempsey's again tonight, Liam Murphy! Have some bit of respect and don't go showing us all up in front of the entire town! That young doctor was decent enough to come out into the bitter cold of the night to tell Angela the sad news and I'll not have him thinking that she comes from a family with no manners on them at all.'

Angela shot him a surreptitious glance. He was glaring at his wife but he made no attempt to answer her. She felt a dart of pity for her aunt, wondering if she really knew what kind of a man she was married to. Well, she wanted him to hear what she had to say.

'There's something I have to tell you both. I know it's not a good time but . . .'

Mary looked concerned. 'What? They've not told you you're no longer needed up there now, have they?'

Angela shook her head and withdrew the letter from her pocket. 'No, nothing like that. I . . . I got this today. Before Christmas Dr Leahy wrote to a friend in a hospital in Liverpool, about me. I want to be a nurse and he . . . he encouraged me. So did she, God bless her. I had to write to the Matron and . . . and well . . .' She passed the letter over to her aunt.

Mary took it without a word, the colour having drained from her face. She read it slowly and then shook her head. 'I . . . Angela, I don't know what to say? I . . . we thought you were content working above.'

Angela got up and went and put her arm around her. 'I was, at first, but then I wanted to do something . . . more. Oh, please, please don't think I'm ungrateful!'

Liam had thrown down the paper and was on his feet,

furious that not only had his trip to the pub been thwarted but that she had outwitted him. He seized on her last words. 'That's just what you are! An ungrateful brat! After everything we've done for you – given you! I tell you, Mary, it's all those letters from that brat Emer that have unsettled her. Didn't we take her from that hovel when she hadn't a decent rag to her back and give her a great, comfortable life? Hasn't she had everything she ever wanted? Didn't we pay a fortune for that radio she has upstairs and now . . . now she's . . .'

Angela faced him squarely. 'I'm *not* an ungrateful brat! Emer hasn't unsettled me. I want to make something of myself. I don't want to be a skivvy all my life. Dr Leahy knew that and he thought it was a good thing.'

'Aye, he would! He wasn't the one who put food in your belly and clothes on your back!'

Mary wiped away a tear. 'That's enough of that, Liam! It . . . it's the shock of it. Angela, why didn't you say something? Why didn't you tell me this was what you wanted?' She had never realised that Angela had ambition. She had truly thought her content with her life here. She had envisaged her eventually meeting someone and getting married and settling down here in the town, or at least somewhere in the vicinity.

'I suppose I didn't want to upset you. I didn't want you to think that I *am* ungrateful. You've been so good to me. I know you've given me everything *they* couldn't.' Angela was really sorry that Mary was so upset.

'By God, it's a true saying "Blood will out"!' Liam fulminated. 'And if ever there were a pair of fecking ungrateful wasters it's Martin and Maura O'Rourke! Weren't they happy enough to shove their responsibilities on to us?'

Despite her feelings Mary glared at him. 'I'll not have you

talk like that about my sister. The only foolish thing she did was to marry him and we all make mistakes like that!'

Liam glared back. So she was saying she'd made a mistake in marrying him? Well, he'd got no bargain either. 'Ah, to hell with the pair of you both! I'm going out!'

Mary got to her feet, the light of battle in her eyes, but Angela tightened her grip on the older woman.

'Please, Aunt, let him go. We . . . we can talk about this much better without him roaring and throwing insults at everyone.' She was surprised that it had hurt and angered her to hear her parents described as 'fecking ungrateful wasters'.

Before his wife could comment further, Liam snatched up his jacket and cap and slammed from the room.

Mary sank wearily back into the chair and passed a hand over her eyes. 'I declare before Almighty God I don't know what's got into him lately. They do say when men get to a certain age they become . . . unmanageable.'

'He'll get over it,' Angela said quietly. She was well aware why he was so angry.

Mary sighed. 'I hope so or life will go from bad to worse, especially with you gone. Oh, Angela, I'd thought that in time you'd get married and settle hereabouts and that I'd have all the pleasure of grandchildren.' She wiped away a tear with the corner of her apron.

Angela hugged her feeling guilty, knowing it wasn't just Uncle Liam that was the root cause of her wanting to get away. She didn't want the kind of life her aunt had planned for her. She didn't want to stay in this backwater. She wanted something more exciting, more rewarding.

'Maybe one day I will get married and have children, you never know, and you could come and visit. But I'm only young yet, Aunt Mary. Too young to be thinking of settling down.'

Mary sniffed. 'Too young to be going off to a big city like that where you know not a living soul.'

'Emer went much further and look how well she's doing. I'll be just grand. I'll be living in the nurses' home, I'm bound to make friends quickly.'

The initial shock was wearing off and Mary was slowly getting used to the idea. 'At least it will be safer than living in some desperate bedsit in a kip of a house full of strangers.'

Angela smiled at her, thankful that she was warming to the idea. 'I think they are quite strict too. There seem to be lots of rules and regulations. Dr Leahy said it will be hard work and there will be a good deal of studying too.'

'And he really encouraged you and wrote to this friend of his?' Mary was finding this quite astonishing.

Angela nodded. It looked as if the worst was over. She went and put on the kettle and got out a packet of biscuits.

'Imagine him doing that. He must have a lot of faith in you, Angela. Make sure you don't go letting him down.' She had always thought that her niece was a great girl altogether and obviously Dr Leahy thought so too. It was indeed a great opportunity for her. Of course she'd miss her terribly but when all was said and done wasn't it a great thing to have this child that she'd reared as her own become a nurse – maybe even one day a ward sister? It was something she had never imagined Angela to be capable of. It was certainly far better than being a mere shop assistant like Emer Cassidy was, no matter how big and modern the department store. Thanks to Dr Leahy's interest and assistance Angela would do far better than most of her schoolfriends.

Angela put the cup of tea and plate of biscuits down beside her aunt and then sat down opposite her.

Mary at once became businesslike. 'Now, we don't have a great deal of time. We'd better sort out what you are going to need. Will we be after having to go up to Dublin for things, do you think?'

Angela smiled at her and reached out and took her hand. 'No. What I can't get here I'll get in Liverpool. I will be sad to leave you, Aunt Mary, you *have* been so good to me. I don't know how I'll ever be able to thank you enough. I'll write often and let you know how everything is going.'

Mary managed a smile. 'Work hard and mind yourself and it will be thanks enough. I . . . I'm proud of you, Angela. That ignorant gobdaw can't see any further than his nose but he'll come around in time. We'll both be proud of you. He'll be off boasting to the lads above in Dempsey's how well you've done for yourself, that he will.'

Angela knew that that would be far from the case but she said nothing; she had dismissed him from her mind. She wasn't going to waste a single moment of her future thinking about him. She had determined that she was never going to be a victim. Now she could look forward to a great future.

Chapter Twelve

A NGELA COULDN'T BELIEVE HOW quickly events moved after that day. As she stood on the deck of the ferry as it prepared to sail from Dublin, watching the deck hands as they pulled in the hawsers the shore gang had slipped from the bollards, leaving the hull floating free of the quayside, she pulled the collar of her coat higher around her neck. It was a clear, still night. The stars were very bright and there was a milky white ring around the moon which foretold of a heavy frost, but at least there was no wind. Beyond the docks she could see the lights of Dublin. There hadn't been much time after her train got in but she had spent half an hour in Cleary's in O'Connell Street looking at the latest fashions. She was thankful for the new scarf and matching beret Aunt Mary had bought her; they were both practical and smart. At her feet was her suitcase which contained almost everything she owned in the way of clothes, and her bag, slung by its strap over her shoulder, contained her money and all the documents she needed.

She gave a little sigh of relief as she thought of the

whirlwind pace of the last few days. They had all attended Mrs Leahy's funeral and then in the afternoon she had gone to take her farewells of Miss Dunne and the two doctors.

Dr Leahy had looked tired and old and a little haggard but he had wished her well and thanked her for all her help during the last few painful days. She had promised she would let him know how she was progressing. Dr Emmet told her to enjoy her new life for it would be entirely different to what she had experienced up to now. He'd said he knew from experience that young nurses had great social lives, but urged her not to neglect her studies. Miss Dunne had also thanked her and wished her well and to her surprise had given her a holy picture of St Maria Goretti, the very young Italian girl martyred rather than lose her virginity, and she wondered was there some underlying message or warning here from the housekeeper? Still, she'd thanked her and said she would keep it carefully in the front of her missal.

She had helped her aunt as they had washed and ironed and started to pack and she had accompanied her as they shopped for the things Angela would need. It had amused and pleased her to see how much pride and pleasure Mary derived from telling all the shopkeepers, and many other people, of her new career and the fact that Dr Leahy had been instrumental in guiding and encouraging her.

'Well, who would have thought it? Both you and Emer gone from here in less than a year,' Mrs Cassidy had commented after she had imparted the news to Emer's mother.

'It hasn't been the same here at all without her, Mrs Cassidy,' Angela had confided.

'When you young ones go it's not the same for us either, you leave a big gap in our lives. Mary will miss you.'

'Well, I'm not as far away as Emer, perhaps she will come

and visit me one day,' Angela had said, thinking that Mrs Cassidy was right regarding Aunt Mary – but not her mother. She was certain Maura O'Rourke hadn't found her daughter's absence to be 'a big gap' in her life.

'Perhaps,' Mrs Cassidy had said but without much conviction in her tone.

Her uncle had said nothing more on the subject at all and as both she and Aunt Mary were utterly absorbed in her imminent departure he spent most evenings at Dempsey's complaining to anyone who would listen about how he was being ignored and how ungrateful Angela was.

Mary had wanted to go to Dublin with her to see her safely on to the ferry but Angela had persuaded her against it. It would make the parting harder for Mary and she needed to stand on her own two feet. She had promised her aunt that she would attend Mass as regularly as she could, and Confession and Communion, and that she would behave herself and not bring any shame or disgrace on them.

'Don't you go taking any notice of the things these young lads tell you, Angela. All they are interested in is themselves and what they can get and they'll have no respect for you once you give in to their . . . demands,' Mary had warned.

'I won't, I promise. I'm not interested in anything . . . like that and besides I'll have so much else to occupy me,' she had replied, thinking that Uncle Liam's disgusting behaviour would be enough to put anyone off.

The ferry was under way now and heading towards Dublin Bay and she at last turned away from the rail and picked up her case and went down into the public saloon. It wasn't too crowded and she found a seat and tried to get comfortable. Some men were drinking at the bar but the stewards were keeping their eye on them and so she closed her eyes and gradually dropped off to sleep.

She was cramped and stiff when she awoke and, stretching, she decided to go up on deck where it wouldn't be so stuffy. Most people had managed to sleep but were now waking and beginning to gather up their belongings so she assumed it wouldn't be too long before they docked. She felt grubby and untidy and went first to the Ladies where she washed her face and hands and combed her hair, replacing her beret at what she hoped was a jaunty angle over her short dark hair.

It was only just beginning to get light and she shivered as the cold frosty morning air hit her. The estuary was wide and she could barely see the lights from the buildings on the shoreline. There were other ships in the river, some moving slowly, some seemingly at anchor, their lights reflecting on the calm dark water. The wash from those that were under way looked like slender silver ribbons. Gradually, as they drew closer to the city and the river narrowed, she could make out the lights on both banks.

'I'd go around ter the other side, miss, the gangway's on the port side.'

She looked around and saw a lad of about her own age heavily muffled against the cold in a thick navy blue sweater and duffel coat. 'Thanks. I just came up for some fresh air.'

He grinned at her. 'This yer first trip ter Liverpool?'

'I'm moving here to live. Well, I'm going into nursing.'

He winked. 'Oh, I've 'eard all about youse nurses! Well, yer'll 'ave a great time 'ere. 'Ave yer 'eard of the Merseybeat?'

Angela shook her head. 'Is it a pop group?'

He laughed good-naturedly. 'It's sort of the sound made by lots of groups. Liverpool groups. It's the "Mersey" sound.'

'You mean the Beatles?'

'Yeah an' the Swingin' Blue Jeans an' Gerry and the

112

Pacemakers an' loads of others. There's great clubs here ter go and 'ear them. There's the Mardi Gras an' the Cavern but of course if yer more sophisticated, like, there's places like the Pink Parrot and the Blue Angel. Then there's all the coffee bars. Me favourite is the El Cabala in Bold Street, yer get some crackin' lookin' birds in there, an' there's 'undreds of pubs. I 'eard youse nurses like a good time.'

'Sure, I'll only just be after starting my training. I'll hardly have time to be going out to those places and I won't have the money either.' It all sounded very exciting and a far cry from Edenderry but she had to be realistic. 'Can you tell me how I get to Walton Hospital? That's where I'm to go.'

'Yeah. When yer ger off 'ere walk up ter the Landing Stage an' yer'll see a line of buses. Yer can get the number thirty or the twenty or twenty-two. Ask the fella ter put yer off at Walton 'Ossie. Yer can't miss it though. Big owld building with a clock tower. Parts of it used ter be the owld work'ouse. Are yer stayin' in the nurses' 'ome?'

She nodded, making a mental note of the numbers of the buses he'd quoted.

'That's just a bit further down, like. In the 'ossie grounds though. Ask the fella on the gate, 'e'll direct yer.'

'Thanks. I'd better get around to the other side now.'

He grinned at her again. 'Good luck! Yer might well need it, me Aunty Flo was in there once an' she said the Matron is a birrof a tartar, like. " 'Oly bloody terror" were 'er exact words. Tarrah then.'

Angela thanked him again and headed for the stairway, his words concerning Matron momentarily dampening her excited anticipation at finally setting foot in the city that was to be her new home.

It was daylight when she got off the bus. The sky above was a clear blue without a cloud and the sun shone brightly, making the frost that still adhered to the pavements and the iron railings that surrounded the hospital grounds glisten and sparkle as though encrusted with jewels. Across the road were streets of terraced houses with small shops on their corners and further down was a cinema and a large pub and the entrance to a factory with the name 'Dunlops' in big letters across the gateway. That would be very handy, she thought, having a cinema and shops so close.

The hospital itself was set in extensive grounds and at the end of what appeared to be the main drive she could see the clock tower. She made enquiries at the gate as she'd been instructed to do and was told she was to go first to Matron's office.

The walk up the long avenue towards the main building seemed endless and with each step she took her trepidation grew. Wasn't this what she had wanted – prayed for? she asked herself. She had escaped from Edenderry and from the unwelcome attentions of her uncle. This was the start of her new life but was she really cut out to be a nurse or had it just been a means of escape? Had she deluded herself? Would it all be too difficult for her to cope with? Dr Leahy hadn't thought so, she told herself firmly. She wasn't going to let nerves be her downfall now.

She was shown into a very neat and tidy office. Through the large sash window the sunlight streamed, making the cream and pale green painted walls look clean and bright. Matron was a stout woman in a plain, severely cut dark dress, her light brown hair taken back from her face and covered with a small starched white cap.

'Angela O'Rourke? Please sit down,' came the clipped, well-modulated voice.

Angela sat, folding her hands in her lap and trying not to look nervous and edgy.

'So, you are Dr Morrissey's protégée.' Matron referred to some notes in a manila folder on the desk in front of her.

Angela chose her words carefully. 'Dr Leahy wrote to Dr Morrissey on my behalf, ma'am.'

'Matron. You will call me "Matron" not "ma'am", Student Nurse O'Rourke.'

'Yes, Matron,' Angela replied, thinking how formal and strange it sounded being called 'Student Nurse O'Rourke', but after that there was little time for reflection on anything as Matron went through the seemingly endless list of duties and instructions and rules and regulations until she felt her head was swimming and that she hadn't taken so much as a fraction of it all in properly.

At last the interview appeared to be over as Matron stood up and closed the folder. 'I will now hand you over to Sister Tutor who will check that you have all the items on the list that was provided and inform you of your timetable of tutorials. She will then pass you over to someone who will take you across to the nurses' home and see you settled in. You will find me strict but fair and I wish you success in your vocation. We have a reputation for training excellent nurses here, don't disappoint me.'

'I won't, and thank you, Matron,' Angela replied before leaving the office.

After being conducted down a maze of corridors and enduring another lecture by Sister Tutor, she was finally introduced to Nurse Collins, a girl of about eighteen with short auburn hair and hazel eyes who walked with her across to the newer square red-brick building that was the nurses' home.

'Don't let them put the fear of God in you with all the lectures and instructions and regulations, it's not *that* bad. It just seems like it when you first start.' Nurse Collins grinned. 'Did you just arrive this morning? You look worn out.'

'I did so but I'm not too bad. I'm starving though.'

'Well, we'll get you unpacked and then we'll go to the canteen and get you something to eat. What's your name? I can't call you Student Nurse O'Rourke.'

'Angela. What's yours?'

'Sheila. I come from Preston but I didn't want to do my training there otherwise I'd have had to have lived at home and had Mam watching me like a hawk all the time. There'd have been precious little freedom. Liverpool is a great place and it's not bad living here in the home, there's always someone to talk to and have a laugh with. You'll find you can borrow most things too, nearly all the girls are great. There's a couple who can be real pains but not many. Don't take too much notice of all the rules and regulations, we have ways and means of getting around most of them. And there's always plenty to do on your days off.'

'I met a lad on the ferry and he told me all about the clubs and coffee bars but I won't be able to afford to be going out.'

Sheila Collins laughed. 'Ah, don't be such a misery! You'll find the money, or you'll find someone to take you and pay for you. You can't spend all your free time with your head stuck in your books. If you don't want to spend a fortune there's always a hop on a Sunday night at the Blessed Sacrament. Well, in the hall around the corner to the church, that is. It doesn't cost much, they don't have a group, they just play records but they have all the latest and some of the fellows aren't bad. It's cheaper and nearer than going into town. I'm going with two of the other girls on Sunday. Do you want to come with us?'

Angela thought about it and the very small amount that was left of her savings and the fact that she wouldn't get paid until the end of next week, having to work what was termed 'a week in hand'. It did seem churlish to refuse Sheila's offer and she did want to start enjoying herself but maybe she'd better take things a bit cautiously to start with. She shook her head. 'I'd better get settled in first, find my feet, but thanks. Maybe if you are going again later on this month I could come with you?'

'OK, suit yourself, but the offer is there if you change your mind. Wait until you've had a week on the ward with everyone from Sister Tutor, Sister Williams and Staff Nurse Jones breathing down your neck and the patients moaning and complaining, and then slogging away at your books, to say nothing of doing your washing and ironing, you'll be dying to get out and have a bit of fun.'

Angela nodded, glancing at her companion, who didn't look as if she was at all offended by her refusal, and wondering if after all that work she would have the energy to go dancing. As they had reached the nurses' home, however, she turned her mind to the task of getting herself settled in.

Part III

Chapter Thirteen

Liverpool, 1963

ANGELA STUFFED HER FINGERS in her ears and tried to block out the sound of Elvis belting out 'Jailhouse Rock'. She was struggling to decipher the notes she had made on the functions of the liver and if she didn't have them learned by her next tutorial then she would be in deep trouble. She had been in Liverpool for eighteen months now and had only just scraped through her first year exams. Sister Tutor had already told her she had to work harder as she was in danger of falling behind again. How some people could actually study with the radio on full blast she didn't know, she was certainly not one of them, she thought irritably. The sun was beating in through the window and her head was beginning to ache. Giving up, she closed her books and glanced out of the window. At the cinema across the road they were showing *Lawrence of Arabia* with Peter O'Toole. Sheila and a couple of others had gone last night and said it was terrific but she'd been on duty and it was just too hot to go this evening. Besides, she had no one to go with. Only Sarah Payne was off this evening and she didn't really like the girl, she was always making sarcastic comments about everyone.

The music had changed to 'Stranger on the Shore', which was at least not so lively or frenetic, but she still didn't reopen her books. She was into her second year as a student nurse and she was slowly coming to the conclusion that she wasn't enjoying it. Far from it. The hours were long, the work hard and demanding and Sister Williams always seemed to be finding fault with whatever she did. Then there was the studying. She hadn't realised that it would be so hard or take up so much time. Of course she had said nothing of this to any of the others, they all complained but she was sure it was just grumbling, they weren't as dissatisfied as she was. If she was brutally honest with herself she knew that deep down it wasn't what she wanted to do for the rest of her life. She just didn't have the dedication. But what did she want to do? She'd asked herself that question so many times and the answer was that she didn't really *know*. She had wanted to leave Ireland so much that she had grasped at any straw and that straw had been nursing, but it just wasn't working out. She hated the thought of letting down her aunt and Dr Leahy; if she gave it up they would be disappointed in her, but if she didn't stick at it what else could she do? Working in a shop or an office didn't carry the same status for people like her aunt and anyway she wasn't at all sure that she wanted to do either.

She pushed the books away and stood up as Polly James stuck her head around the door. Polly was in her second year.

'Do you want a cuppa, Angela? I've just made one.'

Angela smiled at the girl who was in fact the owner of the radio that had been instrumental in curtailing her studies. 'Thanks, Polly, that would be grand. I'm after getting a headache from trying to read these notes.'

'I'd give it a rest for today, you've been stuck there for

hours. Why don't you go out and get a bit of fresh air, clear your head?'

'Sure, the air out there is far from fresh. It's heavy and sultry.'

'Well, it is August and I suppose we should be grateful for the heat, we'll be back to the cold days before we know where we are. Is that a letter from your friend in America?' Polly had noticed the blue airmail envelope on Angela's desk.

'Emer. Yes, she's been to some place in upstate New York with her sister-in-law on what she calls a "vacation", lucky thing. There's not much chance of me getting any kind of a holiday.'

Polly handed her a mug of tea and sipped her own, looking thoughtful. 'I wouldn't have minded a week at a Butlins holiday camp. My cousin and some of her mates saved up and went to the one in North Wales and they had a riot. Did you not fancy going home to Ireland?'

Angela shook her head. She had no wish to go back to Edenderry. She wrote as regularly as she could to Aunt Mary and from time to time to Dr Leahy, but what little money she earned she spent on clothes and make-up and trips to the cinema and local hops, with the occasional trip into Liverpool with Sheila to hear one of their favourite groups. She had made friends here but there wasn't anyone who was as close as Emer had been and she missed that. Sometimes she felt almost lonely.

Polly finished her tea. 'Well, I've got to get some ironing done or I'll run out of clothes. Go for a walk. It's really too nice to be stuck in here slaving over your books, especially on your day off.'

When she'd gone Angela looked around the small room she shared with Kate Aitkins, who was in her first year. There were two single beds, a wardrobe and a chest of drawers and the desk-cum-dressing-table under the window which they both shared. Kate seemed to have no trouble at all with her studies and nursing was all she'd ever wanted to do since she was a small girl. She even got on well with Sister Williams, the ward sister, who was a demon.

The room was hot and stuffy and so she decided to take Polly's advice and go out. She changed into a short white pleated skirt and a bright turquoise top with short sleeves and a scoop neckline and slipped on her flat white shoes. She combed her hair, put on some lipstick and gathered up her bag, wondering where to go. She could get a bus from outside the hospital entrance to either Walton Hall Park or Walton Park or even down to the Pier Head where it would at least be a bit cooler, but that would mean a trip on a crowded, stuffy bus and it really wasn't much fun going anywhere on your own. The city centre would also be hot and stuffy and she could only afford to window shop. There was a recreation ground off Rice Lane near Hornby Road so she decided to walk to that and there were some shops on the way which would prove to be a diversion. At least it would kill an hour or two.

She'd walked as far as the library at Stalmine Rd when she decided to cross over for the 'rec', as it was called locally, wasn't too far now. As she stood on the pavement waiting for a gap in the traffic a bus pulled up and a few people alighted, amongst them a very tall slim girl who was laden down with bags and parcels. As she stepped off the platform, she missed her footing, tripped and fell sprawling on the pavement. A couple of people immediately began to help gather up the girl's scattered belongings but Angela went over to help her up.

'Are you all right? Have you hurt yourself?'

'God, I feel such a fool! Fancy falling flat on my face like that, it's these damned heels!'

Angela looked down at the black patent leather shoes with the pointed toes and high stiletto heels and then back up at the girl, who didn't seem to be hurt and was in fact grinning ruefully. She would be head and shoulders over her even without the heels.

'Mam will say, "I told you you'd break your neck in those shoes."'

'So, you've not hurt yourself?' Angela pressed.

The girl looked down. 'Just grazed my knees, ruined my stockings and put a big dent in my pride.'

'Do you live near here? I could help you home if you like. You're a bit laden down with all this stuff and you should get those cuts washed.'

'Thanks. Can you manage these bags?'

Angela took some of the carrier bags and was startled to see the girl reach down and take off the offending shoes. 'Sure, you're never going to walk home without them?'

The girl grinned. 'Well, I'm not going to risk getting a heel stuck in a crack between the paving stones and going down flat on my face again! You're Irish, aren't you?'

'I am so.' Angela instantly liked her. She had a mane of long light brown hair that had been streaked by the sun and wide grey-green eyes fringed with incredibly long lashes. She wore a shift dress of bright tangerine trimmed with black braid and big black plastic hoop earrings. The black patent stilettos which she now carried matched a large black patent handbag. She was very stylish, Angela thought.

'My mam's family comes originally from somewhere in Cork. I'm Roz, by the way. Roz Henderson.'

'I'm Angela O'Rourke. I'm a student nurse at Walton but I come from Edenderry, it's in Offaly.'

'I've never heard of that county.'

Angela smiled, thinking it was a common response. 'It's in the Irish midlands. Where do you live?'

Roz tossed back her hair. 'Just around the corner in Yew Tree Road, it's not far. I take it you're off duty?'

Angela nodded, looking around as they turned into the road. She hadn't realised that the houses here were quite so big. The street was quite wide and tree-lined and there were cars parked outside some of the houses. They must be quite affluent, she thought. 'Have you always lived here?'

'For as long as I can remember but our Sal says she remembers living in Lancaster Street, that's up past the hospital. There's a cop shop at the bottom of it. A police station,' she added, seeing the look of mystification on Angela's face. 'My dad has a haulage business, quite a big one now, but he started off in a small way. My two older brothers work for him.'

So, they were well off, Angela surmised. 'Do you have many brothers and sisters?' she had come to realise it was unusual for people to have large families over here.

'There's the two lads, our Sarah – Sal –, then Elizabeth – Lizzie – and then me.'

'And is your name Rosalind?' Angela asked, thinking Roz must be an abbreviation of something.

Roz pulled a face and shook her head. 'No, just plain old-fashioned Rose, which I hate! Mam says she thinks it's a lovely name and she can't understand me wanting to call myself Roz but I ask you?' She cast her eyes in the direction of the sky. 'Well, here we are.'

They had reached a substantial Victorian terrace with bay windows, dark blue front door and small, neat garden. Angela followed Roz up the path.

The door was opened by a plump jovial-looking woman

with light brown hair that was twisted up in curling papers. Over her floral printed dress she wore a light cardigan.

'Mam, for heaven's sake, you've still got your curlers in and it must be nearly three o'clock!'

'I was just going up to take them out. I was about to nip down to the shops for some cakes, our Sal's bringing that lad she's keen on home tonight. What happened to you and who's this?' Mrs Henderson finally noticed that her daughter was carrying her shoes and that she was not alone.

'I caught my heel and tripped getting off the bus and don't say "I told you so". This is Angela, she helped me get home. She's a nurse at Walton.'

'Well, come in the pair of you. I see you've been spending all your wages again,' came the tart comment as the door was held open for them.

The hallway was large and there was a cloakroom to one side, the door to which had stained-glass panels. The staircase was wide and quite imposing and everywhere was decorated in cream embossed wallpaper and the carpet was of a brown, cream and russet design.

'Come through into the kitchen and let me see what damage you've done to yourself,' Mrs Henderson instructed, leading the way down the hall.

There were mahogany doors that led off the hall but they went into a room which Angela would have described as a living room, not a kitchen. There was a modern, tiled fireplace, two easy chairs, a table with dining chairs pushed under it, a dresser covered with a great deal of clutter including ornaments, dishes and papers, and a clothes rack, festooned with garments, was suspended from the ceiling. The actual kitchen led off this room, Angela noticed.

Mrs Henderson fussed around the two girls. 'Angela, give those bags here to me. She can sort all the stuff she's bought out later. Well, you've made a nice mess of your knees, Rose. Sit down while I get some cotton wool and Dettol.'

'Oh, Mam, can't you just bathe them with warm water? That stuff stings like mad!' Roz protested, gingerly examining the grazes on both her knees.

'They'll really need some antiseptic on them or they could indeed turn septic,' Angela ventured, thinking that Roz seemed to have a very easy-going relationship with her mother, something she hadn't shared with her aunt.

Mrs Henderson had taken the bags from Angela and thrown them carelessly on the table. 'Now you listen to her, she's a nurse and she knows what she's talking about. You'll have those knees bathed with Dettol, then we'll all have a nice cup of tea and some fruit cake. Hasn't Angela been good enough to get you home? Sometimes I think you're not fit to be let out on your own – especially not in those damned shoes. She's a slave to the latest fashion is this one, Angela. I said to her dad she'd go out in just her knickers if she read in *Vogue* it was the latest trend.'

'Oh, Mam! I'm not *that* bad! What will Angela think, you going on like that?' Roz again rolled her eyes and her mother tutted and went in search of the Dettol and cotton wool.

Angela smiled at her. 'Ah, I bet she doesn't really mean it.'

'She does! And next she'll start on again about me spending all my wages. Honestly, both our Sal and Lizzie buy as many clothes as I do.'

'What do you do – for a job, I mean?'

'I'm a receptionist in a big hairdressing salon in town. It's not bad, I get my hair and nails done for free, but I don't earn a fortune, although to hear Mam you'd think I did. It's my half-day today so I went shopping before I came home. I have to look smart and trendy for work. I don't have to wear an overall like the rest of them.'

'Your hair is really great,' Angela ventured, wishing her own hair was long and straight like Roz's.

'So is yours but you could get tips done. You know, get just the ends bleached? I have mine streaked. It makes it more interesting than just being left mousy-brown.'

'I thought the sun had lightened it.'

Roz laughed. 'Fat chance! But honestly, you should come in to the salon.'

'Not on what they pay me.'

Mrs Henderson returned and Roz submitted to having her knees bathed while Angela thought how open and disarmingly friendly this girl was. They seemed to get on really well. She had only just met her but she could chat to her as easily as if she'd known her for years.

Chapter Fourteen

ANGELA HAD HAD A great day with Roz. They had had tea and home-made fruit cake and when Mrs Henderson had finally taken out her curlers, brushed her hair and gone to the shops Angela had helped Roz take her shopping up to her bedroom. She had exclaimed with delight over the pretty room; it reminded her of Mrs Leahy's bedroom except that it was more modern and all the furniture was white. There was a single bed covered with a lilac and white flowered bedspread with curtains that matched, two double wardrobes and a kidney-shaped dressing table with white frilly drapes around it. There was even a small sofa in lilac with purple cushions. Roz had removed the dresses, skirt, tops and shoes from the bags and laid them out on the bed but when she had opened the wardrobe Angela had been stunned by the amount of clothes she already had.

'Haven't you enough clothes to wear a different outfit each day for months and months!'

Roz had shrugged. 'I suppose I have and some of them I've hardly worn at all. I suppose I'm really lucky too. Mam has accounts at some of the best shops in Liverpool and I'm allowed to keep all my wages.'

'I wish I had enough to be able to wear something different each week for Mass.'

'That outfit you've got on really suits you,' Roz had said, whilst holding against her a pale blue pinafore dress that had broad bands of white set into the hem, wondering if it really did suit her or was it a bit wishy-washy? Of course she could wear a white polo under it when the weather got cooler but would that then not look too 'summery'? Maybe she'd take it back.

'I've got a few summer dresses but I didn't realise how out of fashion they were. They've all got full skirts that need yards and yards of net underskirts under them and that look has gone out now and I do like to be in fashion. It's something I've always been interested in.'

'Could you alter them? Do you sew? Our Lizzie does and she's got lots of paper patterns. She'd lend you some.' Roz had discarded the dress and had sat down on the bed.

'I do but it would take ages to unpick, recut them and sew them by hand and I don't get that much spare time.'

Roz had smiled at her. 'Mam's got a sewing machine. She'd let you use that. You'd get them done in no time.'

'But she really doesn't know me. I mean, I'm a stranger to you all.'

Roz had grinned at her. 'No, you're not. You're my friend. Didn't you pick me up, dust me down and get me home? And in your time off duty. What's that if it's not friendship?'

After that they had gone through Lizzie's patterns and Roz had said she thought Lizzie was mad to spend hours making things when she could go out and buy them but that Lizzie said it gave you great satisfaction to wear something you'd made yourself; there was a huge range of materials to choose from so you never saw someone else wearing exactly the same thing, a risk you took when buying from a shop.

The time had flown by, Angela had thought, as they'd listened to records and Roz persuaded her to try some eyeliner on her eyelids and confided that she wore false eyelashes and they really weren't too fiddly to get on, once you got the knack. Of course occasionally, if you didn't put enough glue on them, one fell off and looked like a spider climbing on you. They'd both giggled at this and then she'd tried on some of Roz's incredibly high-heeled shoes and had tottered around the room which had convulsed them with laughter. Then Mrs Henderson had called to them to come down and get something to eat as 'the girls' were home from work, and she'd met Sal and Lizzie and then Mr Henderson and Tom and George. The other girls were shorter then Roz; Lizzie had dark straight hair and was very stylishly dressed. Sal was fairer with a peaches and cream complexion and was dressed in a less flamboyant style than her two sisters. They had all made her very welcome and when finally she had said she really must go, Mrs Henderson had said she must come again whenever she felt like it, it was no imposition, and she was more than welcome to come and do her cutting out in the dining room as Lizzie did, and use the sewing machine too.

Roz had walked with her as far as the bus stop. It was only a couple of stops to the hospital but it was getting late and Mrs Henderson had insisted she get the bus.

'At least that way you won't run the risk of bumping into any of *that* lot that come staggering out of the pub!' she'd said.

'I've had a really great day, Roz, thanks,' Angela had said sincerely.

'Everyone's friends are always welcome in our house.

Mam likes to see who we're mixing with. When will you come again?'

'Next time I get some time off and I'll bring a couple of dresses to unpick.'

Roz had nodded and then pointed to the bus that was approaching. 'Here's a number thirty. That will do you. See you next week then.'

Angela went again the following week and as they'd sat unpicking a full-skirted white cotton dress over-printed with large red poppies, Angela told her new friend all about her life in Ireland, leaving out any mention of Uncle Liam's behaviour, about Emer and why she had thought nursing would be the ideal career.

'And you've never seen your parents or brothers and sisters since you went to live with your aunt?' Roz thought this very sad.

Angela shook her head. 'I . . . I suppose it was for the best, in a way. They couldn't have given me all the things Aunt Mary gave me and I wouldn't have had the opportunities I've had, but I missed them, my sisters and brothers.' Having been made so welcome by Roz and her family had made her realise just how much she had missed them.

Roz nodded but she looked puzzled. 'I can understand there being no work for your father and it must have been awful for your mother trying to manage with no money, but why did they have so many children if they couldn't afford them?'

Angela looked at her blankly. She knew the Hendersons were also Catholics; they attended the Church of the Blessed Sacrament as she did. 'It's God's will.'

Roz's eyebrows rose. 'No it's not. It's just men's "carnal desires", as they were always calling them at school and when they warned us against them. You can go to the Family

Planning Clinics and get contraceptives. You still have to put up with the "carnal desires" but you don't have to keep on having children.'

'There are no Family Planning Clinics in Ireland, the Church forbids anything like that,' Angela said firmly.

'I know but you don't have to slavishly follow everything the Church dictates. Even Mam said she'd had enough after me. She said she was getting too old and too tired to keep on having babies and it would affect the time and care she could give to the rest of us. She said it was a matter between herself and God, nothing to do with the priests or bishops or even the Pope himself. They're all men, what do they know about childbirth or being worn out with looking after them and half out of your mind with the worry of making ends meet? Mind you, she doesn't believe you should sleep with a lad before you're married, that's definitely not right.'

Angela stared at her in total shock. She had never in her life known anyone who had questioned the teachings of the Church like this. Aunt Mary would have had a heart attack if she'd heard this heresy.

'Don't look so shocked. A lot of people think like that now. It's a matter between your conscience and God and personally I think it's more of a sin to bring children into the world that you can't feed or clothe or give a chance of a decent life to.'

Angela finally found her voice. 'Have you told all this to the priest?'

Roz shook her head. 'He'd have ten fits but Mam did and she had a terrible row with him over it.'

'And?' Angela asked, even more taken aback to hear this. Mrs Henderson was of her aunt's generation and she was astonished that she had such 'modern' views and openly argued with a priest.

'She still goes to church. She just won't go to Confession because she knows he won't give her absolution but she believes that God won't deny her her place in heaven because she only wanted to do the best for her family. Anyway, I'm sure she and Dad are past all that sort of thing now. They're so old!' Seeing the doubt and misgiving on Angela's face she hurried on, 'Oh, let's change the subject. I can see you don't agree so let's not fall out over it.'

Angela had been relieved to drop the subject and they had turned the conversation to Roz's life at work and the styles and prices in the salon and the fact that all the 'stylists', as the hairdressers were called, had what Roz called 'professional' names. Alice was 'Alicia', David was 'Darius' and the lad Roz had her eye on was 'Stefan', originally Stephen, and she had great hopes that he would ask her out soon. It was a myth that all male hairdressers were 'like that'. Roz had made an exaggeratedly effeminate gesture with her hand. Of course some were, but not all.

By the time Angela went back to the nurses' home the white cotton had been unpicked, pressed, pinned and cut out in a new shift style. She'd left it with Roz for she had no time to tack it, she was behind with her studies again.

Over the next few days she thought a great deal about what Roz had said. Mrs Henderson was a good woman who genuinely cared for her family and she must have had her husband's consent in the matter of contraception. They didn't seem to be people who would take a decision like that lightly and she began to wonder if it was so wrong. Had her mother taken the same stand life would have been very different – but then she would probably not have been born. Throughout her upbringing she had been taught that she must adhere rigidly to the teachings of the Church without question yet she knew many who professed to be Catholics failed to do so. The Church did not look tolerantly on drunkenness or wife beating or adultery but there were countless men who ignored that. Nor did the Church condone what her uncle had wanted to do to her (despite Father Dwyer refusing to believe her), and yet Liam had continued to go to Mass and to Confession and Communion. She wondered if she was having a crisis of faith, but then immediately tried to put it from her mind. She had enough to worry about trying to decide if she should continue with her career?

As the weeks and months passed she spent all her spare time at the Hendersons until she began to look on it as 'a second home' as Roz commented. Her friend was very generous giving her handbags and shoes to match the dresses she'd made and as the cooler weather approached found a very stylish black and white tweed coat trimmed with black leather at the back of her wardrobe which she swore looked terrible on her but which would be great on Angela (particularly if they could find a black leather cap to match it). She looked forward to her visits; there was always great chat and laughter in the house with friends of Roz's brothers and sisters dropping in. She felt she was part of a real family again. Mrs Henderson always fussed over her, saying she needed feeding up because everyone knew that young girls never ate properly, especially nurses who were always run off their feet. She insisted that Angela bring all her washing and ironing for she had a brand-new twin-tub washing machine and what were a few more bits to iron along with the rest? The latest irons made light work of it all. The purchase tax had been greatly reduced on such items lately and she was coaxing Mr Henderson to buy a new television set. You could get them with much bigger screens now that didn't need a magnifying glass over them to make the picture larger. Sal, Lizzie and Roz had all complained that you couldn't get a good view of the Beatles when they had appeared at the London Palladium and would it be possible to have the new set before they were top of the bill at the Royal Variety Performance?

Lizzie, who was even more of what her mother called 'a fashion plate' than Roz, but who was more serious than her sister, although just as generous, helped her with the more complicated bits of the patterns, like sleeves and pleating. Sal, who was by far the quietest of the trio and was a secretary, promised to teach Angela shorthand, which would help her to get her notes down more quickly. Apparently the whole thing about shorthand was to be able to get it down reasonably fast and then be able to read it back accurately. Sal had trained at one of Liverpool's best commercial colleges, where they had been mad keen on speed, so she'd said, but what was the point of that if you couldn't read it back? Angela wouldn't need to have impressive dictation speed, just enough to be useful. Looking at the strange signs of Sal's demonstration, Angela felt this was one offer she wasn't going to take up.

They were all shocked and stunned when on 22 November President Kennedy was assassinated.

Angela and Roz were discussing which of the songs on the Beatles first LP *Please, Please Me* was best while Mrs Henderson was preparing the evening meal when Lizzie burst in. It was a moment none of then would ever forget.

'Mam! Mam, switch the telly on! President Kennedy has been shot!'

Mrs Henderson dropped a plate in shock and Roz switched on the television. None of them could believe it. It just didn't seem possible that the man who had been mobbed when he'd visited Ireland just a few months ago was *dead*, Angela had thought dazedly. Aunt Mary had written her a long and detailed letter about the trip she'd made to Dublin especially to see him. Half the population of Edenderry had gone.

'Oh, the poor man and God help her!' Mrs Henderson had crossed herself devoutly and they'd all wept as they'd watched the footage from Dallas.

It had dominated the news for weeks and there had been prayers and tributes in every church in many countries around the world.

Christmas once again was approaching. Angela was now looked on as an honorary member of the family and Roz had some great outings planned. She informed Angela that they always had a great party on Christmas Night to which friends, relations and neighbours were invited.

'I'll probably be working,' Angela replied glumly. Angela had already written to her aunt informing her that she again wouldn't be able to go back for the holiday. There was the time and expense of travelling and she had learned that she would be expected to work. Mary hadn't been too disappointed, she understood and had written saying that even though Liverpool wasn't as far away as America or Australia, it wasn't expected of those who had emigrated to find work to make the journey home very often, if indeed at all. Didn't they still occasionally have 'American wakes' for those emigrating, even though there had been no such party for Emer?

'You won't be working all night, surely?' Roz had asked. 'Come when you've finished, no one goes home. People sleep on the sofas or the floor. You can share with me. Mam cooks everyone breakfast on Boxing Day, or St Stephen's Day as you call it.'

139

'I'd be killed if I stayed out all night!'

'Mam will give you a letter if you want, to say you're staying with us.' Roz pulled a face. 'It's like being at school.'

'They're responsible for our welfare, you see, as we're under twenty-one and "live in", so to speak.'

'Oh, you'll have to come. It's Christmas and Stefan is coming and he's going to bring a mate. You just might fancy him!'

Angela laughed. 'I don't know about that but I'm dying to see this Stefan.'

'Mam will show me up by insisting on calling him Stephen – or worse, Steve – and you know what she's like about calling me Rose.' She sighed. 'I don't suppose it will matter all that much. Now, what shall we wear?' Roz instantly dragged half a dozen dresses out of the wardrobe and threw them on the bed.

'I'm not getting anything new. I can't afford it. I've books to buy for next year and they cost an arm and a leg, and I want to send Aunt Mary and Emer some little gifts and there are other things to buy,' Angela said resolutely.

Roz looked thoughtful. 'I know Mam's got some black velvet material she bought in the Bon Marché ages ago but our Lizzie put her off it by saying it would make her look "matronly" and "dumpy" and was only fit for a funeral. I bet she'd let you have it. Black velvet would make a terrific evening dress for you.'

'I couldn't ask her for it!' Angela cried, aghast.

'Then I will. It's only lying in a drawer somewhere.'

'Oh, Roz, I'd feel awful, I would. You're all so good to me.'

Roz had ignored her protests and had enlisted Lizzie's aid.

'Mam, anything you had made up in that stuff would make you look like an old dowager duchess, I told you that.

It's only lying there and you'll end up throwing it out,' Lizzie said calmly and candidly. She believed in plain speaking on such matters.

Mrs Henderson had needed no further persuading and the material was unearthed and handed over.

'It's gorgeous. And sure, there's enough of it to make me a dress and your mam a skirt,' Angela said, stroking the rich fabric.

'And I've got a great pair of long diamante earrings you can borrow, they'll set it off,' Roz offered. 'Now, all I've got to do is find something equally gorgeous to wear.' She looked at Angela thoughtfully. 'You said you've always been interested in fashion and you *can* sew. Why don't you design and make things in your spare time?'

Angela shook her head. 'I don't really have enough spare time for a hobby. It's hard enough keeping up with my studies. I've already been warned by Sister Tutor about my work and besides I'm not good enough.'

'You *are*! You could do them for me and for our Sal.'

Angela laughed. 'Haven't the pair of you enough clothes to stock a shop already?' She became serious as Lizzie went off to find the appropriate pattern. 'I'll have to stick at nursing, Roz. I couldn't disappoint everyone and the pay will increase in time and I won't always have to live in. Sure, I should be thankful for what I've got and make the best of it.'

Chapter Fifteen

———◆◆◆———

I T WAS THE BEST CHRISTMAS Angela had ever spent. They had decorated the ward; they even had a tree donated by a local greengrocer; and everyone was cheerful and more relaxed. Even Sister Williams seemed to have caught the spirit of the season. In the Hendersons' house the air was heavy with the smells of baking and full of suppressed excitement and anticipation. The girls had decorated the huge tree that stood in the hall and Mr Henderson and the boys had brought home armfuls of holly and mistletoe. Angela had called on Christmas Eve and had found a frenzy of activity. The dining-room table was being set with Mrs Henderson's best china and glass, Roz was sorting the music rolls for the pianola in the front lounge and Mrs Henderson was preparing an enormous turkey, surrounded by bowls of vegetables and potatoes and the ingredients for the stuffing. Mr Henderson and the two boys were fiddling with the new television set that had been delivered that afternoon and marvelling at the size of the screen.

'We'll be able to get a good view of Her Majesty

tomorrow afternoon now without it being distorted by that damned magnifier,' Mr Henderson had said cheerfully as the choir of Coventry Cathedral filled the screen.

'Leave that on, Bernard, it makes a nice change from all those pop groups,' his wife had instructed.

Angela had received gifts from Roz, Lizzie and Sal and from Mr and Mrs Henderson too. She was very thankful that she had dipped into her meagre savings to get them all something in return or she would have been terribly embarrassed.

She had had to work on Christmas Day but they'd had a great lunch with all the trimmings in the canteen and the Salvation Army Band had come and played carols in the ward. They had all pinned bits of tinsel to their starched caps, even Sister Williams. In the evening when she'd come off duty she'd changed out of her uniform and into the velvet dress with the lace sleeves. As she put on the earrings and then tweaked a few curls forward on to her cheeks Sheila Collins remarked that she looked like a model from a fashion magazine. Angela had laughed and said she was not tall or slim enough but that Roz wouldn't look out of place on the cover of *Vogue*.

'She's five foot ten in her stockinged feet and she always wears four-inch heels. She's got this gorgeous short red chiffon dress with floating panels at the back and black evening sandals and long jet earrings. She's her hair up and it makes her look a million dollars. It's all arranged in those loopy curls that are just coming into fashion,' she'd informed an avidly curious Sheila.

'Well, you look a million dollars yourself. Lucky you, staying out at a party all night. Not like us flaming Cinderallas. Have a great time. I hope the fellers come up to expectation – and don't do anything I wouldn't do!'

Angela had laughed. 'Even if I wanted to – and I don't – won't we have Mrs H. watching us like hawks?'

She did have a great time and Mike, the lad Stefan had brought with him, had danced with her all night and been very attentive. She'd liked him, they'd found lots to talk about, but she hadn't felt there was anything special about him and when he'd suggested they meet again she had politely refused, saying she had to cram for her exams which were in the New Year. She wasn't lying, she'd thought. She was trying not to think of all the work ahead of her.

During the first weeks of the January the weather turned bitterly cold. It snowed heavily and then froze making conditions underfoot and on the roads very dangerous. The ward filled up with patients who had suffered broken bones as the result of falls or road accidents and there hardly seemed enough hours in the day to fit everything in. She had only had time to visit Roz once and her friend had been sitting by the fire in her dressing gown, sneezing and shivering.

'Don't go too near her, Angela. The last thing you need is to catch the cold she has. If she'd have listened to me and wrapped up sensibly against the weather instead of insisting on going out in a light dress under her coat and without a hat and scarf and good warm boots then she might not have caught it,' Mrs Henderson said, shaking her head at the obstinate folly of her youngest daughter.

'It's the heating in work, Mam. The place is like a greenhouse and if I wore thick, heavy jumpers I'd pass out. Everyone's got colds and we've had loads of cancellations,' Roz had replied croakily.

'I just called to say we're very busy and I have so much

studying to do that I won't be able to visit as often as I have been doing.'

Mrs Henderson had reassured her. 'Don't you worry about that. Wait until the weather gets better and your exams are over. Besides, it's not fit for man or beast to be out. The pavements are death-traps!'

Angela found the exams extremely hard and realised too late that she should have taken notice of Sister Tutor's warnings that she needed to study twice as hard as some of her contemporaries. There were questions she just didn't understand and others where she struggled to give any kind of coherent answer and it was with extreme trepidation that she awaited the results.

She was summoned to Matron's office a week later.

'Sit down, Nurse O'Rourke,' Matron said quietly.

Angela could read nothing from either her expression or her tone of voice as she opened the folder in front of her. She had butterflies in her stomach and she clasped her hands tightly together in her lap.

'Well, I'm afraid these results are not good. Not good at all,' Matron announced.

Angela bit her lip, her heart sinking. It was just as she'd feared. 'I . . . I'm sorry, Matron. I really did work hard.'

'Not hard enough, although Sister Williams gives you a good report. I have discussed the matter with Sister Tutor in some depth and we have decided that you will have to do your second year again. You have many good practical attributes, Nurse O'Rourke, but your medical knowledge is just not up to a standard to allow you to progress to your third year. You *must* have a solid foundation on which to build otherwise there could well be problems in the future. Sister Tutor is willing to give you extra tutorials, which is extremely generous of her, but you must be willing to give more time to your studies. I encourage all my nurses to take time for relaxation – it's necessary for a balanced lifestyle – but you will have to forgo such things as trips to the cinema and dances if you want to succeed.'

Angela felt her heart drop like a stone. She was going to have to do it all again and worse, every spare moment she had would have to be spent studying. There would be no time for any diversions and no time to spend with Roz and her family. The year stretched ahead of her bleak and utterly depressing.

Matron was an astute judge of character, she'd had many years experience dealing with her staff, and she had noted the look of horror followed by despair in Angela's eyes. It was as she had suspected. The girl's heart was just not in it. The strength, determination and dedication needed to repeat a year's training and study, without any kind of relaxation or diversion, was simply not there.

'I want you to go away and think very carefully about your future, nurse. Talk to Sister Williams and to Sister Tutor; you will find them both helpful and sympathetic. Not everyone has the temperament or the stamina for this career and it is better to realise it sooner rather than later. There is no shame at all in admitting you have made a mistake, you are still very young. You may find you will be happier and more successful in another field. Now, off you go and come back to see me in two or three days when you've had time to reflect.'

Angela got to her feet, fighting back the tears of disappointment and dejection. Matron obviously didn't think she was capable or clever enough. She wasn't dismissing her but in a roundabout way she was asking her to give up and find something else. 'Thank you, Matron,' she managed to get out before she turned for the door.

'Nurse O'Rourke, my door is always open should you

want advice. I take the welfare of my nurses very seriously.'

Angela nodded and left, closing the door quietly behind her.

Despite the cold and the icy conditions, as soon as she had finished her shift she pulled her heavy cape around her and headed for the hospital gates. She caught a bus and even though the conductor cheerfully asked her what the hurry was seeing that she'd come out in such weather with just her cape, she could find no words to answer him.

Mrs Henderson opened the door to her. 'Angela! You'll get pneumonia coming out like that. Get into the kitchen to the fire!' She gently propelled the girl down the hall, realising that something was terribly wrong.

Roz and Lizzie were both in, leafing through fashion magazines and half-heartedly watching the news on the television. Roz flung her magazine down and jumped up and Lizzie switched off the set.

'Angela, what's wrong?' Roz demanded.

Mrs Henderson pushed her down in the chair near the fire and went to put the kettle on, instructing Lizzie to go and fetch the whiskey bottle. What the girl needed was a hot toddy to warm her up, she was shivering with the cold and if she wasn't mistaken she'd been crying. Well, they'd soon get this sorted out. Probably that dragon of a Sister Williams had upset her.

'You got your exam results, didn't you?' Roz guessed accurately, kneeling down beside her friend.

Angela could only nod miserably.

Lizzie returned and caught her sister's eye and quickly shook her head. Best let Angela get warm and calm down a little, she thought.

Roz patted her arm. 'Never mind. When you've had a toddy to warm you up, you'll feel better.'

148

The hot whiskey and sugar did warm her and she began to feel a little calmer. 'I didn't know where else to go,' she said, brushing the tears from her cheek with the back of her hand.

'Well, you were right to come but you should have put something warmer on,' Mrs Henderson chided gently. 'Now, what's all this about, luv?'

Slowly Angela told them about her interview with Matron and its implications and the three women listened in silence until she'd finished.

'Oh, God, that's such a disappointment! Will it drive you mad to have to do it all again?' Roz asked, feeling very sorry for her friend.

Mrs Henderson looked meaningfully at Lizzie. They had both realised that Matron had placed the ball very firmly in Angela's court. It wasn't just a matter of doing an extra year, it was whether indeed Angela wanted to continue at all and Mrs Henderson understood that Matron was probably of the opinion that Angela would not make a nurse.

'What she is asking you, Angela, is do you really *want* to go on? Would you be happier doing something else?' she said quietly. Roz looked at her questioningly but her mother shook her head warningly.

Angela nodded slowly. 'I know and I know it's my decision but . . . but I don't want to let Aunt Mary and Dr Leahy down. They had such faith, such high hopes for me.'

'You can't live your life for others, Angela. You can't spend your life trying to live up to expectations that are just too high for you. All you'll do is make your life a misery and would your aunt want that? I'm sure she wouldn't. And I think the good doctor would understand that you just don't have the dedication that's needed. As Matron said, you are still very young, you've your life ahead of you. Plenty of time to change your mind.'

'You'll make yourself ill, Angela, worrying about exams all the time. It's just not worth it. Not everyone is blessed with a great brain but there are other things you're good at,' Lizzie advised.

'But what can I do if I give up? I'll have to get some kind of a job and I'll have to find somewhere to live,' Angela wailed, but beneath the worry was relief that now the possibility of her giving up nursing had actually been voiced and brought into the open. Mrs Henderson hadn't told her to pull herself together and stick at it; she had offered sound advice. She *couldn't* spend her life trying and failing in a career just to please other people. And it certainly wouldn't make her any kind of a competent nurse.

'We can solve one of those problems quite easily. You can come and live here. There's the small spare room. I'll get the lads to clear out the rubbish that's in there; it's only ever been used as a junk room. And one extra will make no difference in this house,' Mrs Henderson said firmly. She was fond of Angela and thought she had had enough to contend with in life, effectively being given away by her parents and then having to leave Ireland to find a decent job. Roz had told her all about Angela's early life and how she missed her siblings and her friend Emer. Now that the girl was faced with the prospect of no job and no home she felt it was the least she could do. She couldn't in all conscience see the girl without a decent roof over her head and what she needed was to be part of a family again.

'Oh, Mam, that's great!' Roz cried delightedly.

Tears of gratitude and relief welled up in Angela's eyes. 'How . . . how can I ever thank you? But . . . but I can't expect you to keep me for nothing?'

'We'll discuss all that later, when you've told the starched aprons up there that you'll be leaving and when we've sorted you out with a job. I'm sure our Sal could do something. She's quite well thought of in that place, maybe there's something you could do in the general office and failing that Mr Henderson's got a lot of contacts and there are a few favours he's owed that he could call in. He'll be in soon and when you're ready to go back he can run you there in the car. You're not going out in this weather again with just that cape and those flimsy shoes to keep out the cold.' Mrs Henderson got to her feet. 'Rose, you take Angela up and show her the room. You'll have to use your imagination as to what it will look like when it's emptied and done up a bit.'

Impulsively Angela threw her arms around the older woman and clung to her tightly. It was as if a great weight had been lifted from her. She didn't have to struggle on doing something she had no heart for and somehow she would find the words to impart this to Aunt Mary and Dr Leahy. She didn't mind what kind of a job she got to start with as long as she could pay Mrs Henderson something towards her keep. For the first time in years she felt that she really and truly belonged, that she once again had a family. Yes, Aunt Mary had given her a home but there had been a dark shadow over it and it had never been a home like this where such warmth and generosity were extended by everyone.

Chapter Sixteen

———◆·◆———

Angela had gone to Matron and told her of her decision and she had been aware that her news was not unexpected, but Matron had been sympathetic. 'I am certain you have made the correct decision. There is no sense at all in continuing with something that will only make you unhappy. Your patients would suffer and that is some-thing neither of us would wish to happen. So, I wish you every success for the future, Angela.' She had smiled warmly and shaken Angela's hand and when she had left the office Angela had felt a great sense of freedom. Until that moment she hadn't realised how stressful life had been these last months.

She had packed her belongings and said goodbye to the girls she had shared the home with. A few of them were quite astonished that she was giving up but others said they thought she had made the right decision if she wasn't happy. Kate Aitking, her room-mate, couldn't understand at all.

'It's different for you, Kate. It's all you've ever wanted to do and you're much cleverer than me. You just sail through your studies. It would be years and years of struggling for me,' she'd said.

Kate had nodded. 'Well, I hope you do well but I'll miss you. We got on great together.'

Angela hadn't said that quite often she'd felt lonely even though she had been surrounded by people. She didn't think Kate would understand.

Mrs Henderson had had the spare room cleared out and given a fresh coat of paint. She had found curtains and furniture had been purloined from other rooms. Roz had willingly parted with a chest of drawers and a pretty bedside lamp. Lizzie had given the white sheepskin rug that had been beside her bed, and Sal had donated a very colourful poster of Paris in the spring. Her boss had brought it back from a holiday for her but she said it would make the room look more cheerful. When Angela had unpacked and arranged her bits and pieces on the top of the dressing table she had thought it was far more cosy and homely than the room she'd shared in the nurses' home with Kate. It had surprised her to find that there was a second staircase that ran from the landing outside her door down into the kitchen. It was very narrow and dark and Mrs Henderson informed her that when the house had been built it would have been used by the maid who would have slept in what was now Angela's room, so she wouldn't have to use the front stairs like the family.

'Imagine that! The people who lived here all those years ago having a maid,' she'd exclaimed.

'Well, they paid them next to nothing and expected them to run the entire house,' had been the terse reply.

She couldn't wait to write and tell Emer about everything that had happened but it was going to be infinitely harder to write to her aunt and Dr Leahy. And it was something she couldn't put off any longer.

To her relief Mrs Henderson said she too would write to Mary.

'I don't want her to think we have influenced you in any way and I want to reassure her that you are being well looked after and assure her that Bernard and I will be responsible for your welfare, morally and spiritually. She'll want to know that you're going to church and are not staying out half the night or mixing with "undesirables".'

Angela had nodded. She did keep up with her faith, albeit in a more low-key way than she had in Ireland. 'What will I tell her about me getting work?' she had asked.

'Tell her we've got that in hand and she's not to worry. We'll not have you working in some factory,' had been the firm reply.

'I'll be only too glad to help around the house as much as possible until I do get work,' Angela had offered.

To her relief her aunt's reply hadn't been full of recriminations or demands that she return instantly to Ireland. Mary did seem disappointed but there was a note of resignation in the tone of her letter. She was very thankful that Angela had found lodgings with a good Catholic family, she had been impressed by Mrs Henderson's letter, and Angela was to keep her aunt informed of all future developments. Dr Leahy's letter had been sympathetic; he'd wondered had he pressured her and if that had been the case, then he apologised. Life was too short to be made miserable, he'd said. And he was sure that she would make a success of whatever career she now embarked on. The letter she had received from Emer had been full of concern. Sure, she had known Angela wasn't really happy doing nursing and it was great that she'd decided to give it up but what would she do now? The Hendersons had been goodness itself and she was glad Angela had somewhere nice to live with people who were fond of her but she knew from experience that sometimes it wasn't easy living in someone else's home. Hadn't she had a couple of rows with Dinny and even Joy? (Especially over the current boyfriend.) But she sincerely hoped everything would work out well for her friend and she'd find the right career, if indeed a career was what she wanted.

It wasn't exactly a 'career', Angela thought as she walked home from the bus stop on a miserable February evening. The pavements glistened with the cold dampness that seemed to seep into everything and the streetlights were wreathed in mist. Angela pulled the collar of the black and white tweed coat up around her ears and hoped the mist would not become one of the dense choking smogs. The black leather 'baker boy' cap she wore was stylish and kept the damp air from making her hair curl tightly but it didn't cover her ears. She thrust her hands deeper into the pockets of her coat as she hurried her steps towards home.

Miss Henderson, as Sal was called at work, had had 'a word' with her boss and Angela had been interviewed for the position of clerk in the general office of the shipping company where Sal was employed as a secretary. She had been taken on but her wage was not much more than she had received as a student nurse. Still, it was a job, a start, she'd told herself firmly. Her duties consisted of helping to open and sort the post, taking her turn at making the tea and then dealing with the endless amount of filing, which she was finding increasingly boring. It was a busy office and there were other girls and women who worked in it, most of whom could type. She didn't see Sal during working hours as she had her own little office, but often they met up and wandered around the shops in their lunch hour. Sal was a far more restful type of person than her sisters, Angela often thought. They usually came home together, but not tonight. Sal had promised to work a bit later as there was some panic on.

Angela had called into the salon where Roz worked at lunchtime and she had shown her the latest magazines that had come in. 'I'm going to have my hair cut like this and maybe tinted black,' Roz had confided, showing her a picture of Elizabeth Taylor as Cleopatra, a film that was highly popular. Both Miss Taylor's hair and make-up and the style of dress she wore in the film had become all the rage.

'Your mam will kill you if you have it dyed black!' Angela had warned. She couldn't see what was wrong with her friend's hair the way it was.

Roz had frowned, knowing there would be strong words from her mother about her intentions. 'Don't go saying "dyed", it sounds terrible. "Tinted" sounds better, it sort of implies that it will wash out. I'm going to try doing my eyes like that tonight.'

'It's a bit heavy. I mean it looks grand on her but she *is* a film star and she is playing a part in a film.'

Roz had studied the picture closely and had then looked at Angela. 'You know that style would suit you and your hair is naturally dark. You could let it grow. Stefan would trim it into shape as it grows.'

'My hair is curly and that's dead straight. I'd be destroyed altogether trying to keep it from curling up.'

'You could have it straightened,' Roz had suggested.

Angela thought about this now as she walked up the street. It would cost a fortune and would be almost impossible to keep in weather like this. No, she would stick with the short 'elfin' cut. It was more manageable and didn't cost too much to have trimmed in a local hairdresser's.

'Did our Sal say how late she would be?' Mrs Henderson asked as Angela came into the kitchen. Mr Henderson and the lads were both in, as was Lizzie. It was the salon's late night so Roz would also be late.

'She said she'd probably be in with Roz,' Angela replied, tying on an apron and preparing to help the older woman serve the meal. Mrs Henderson insisted on only taking a nominal amount for her keep, saying she had fares and lunches and other expenses to find out of her few pounds, so she tried to do as much as she could to help in the house.

When the meal was over Lizzie and Angela volunteered to wash up.

'I heard today that there's going to be a big St Valentine's Night dance at the Grafton,' Lizzie informed her. 'We should all go.'

Angela nodded. 'I could save up, providing the tickets aren't too expensive.'

'We'll all chip in. It will be a good night,' Lizzie offered.

'I was talking to Roz at lunchtime and she wants to have her hair cut in that Cleopatra style and she was talking about having it dyed black like Elizabeth Taylor's.'

Lizzie cast her eyes in the direction of the ceiling and shook her head. 'She'll look a sight. She's too fair to take that colour. She'll look like death warmed up.'

Angela frowned. 'Sure, I'm not going to tell her that.'

'I will. She'll look fine with her hair cut into that style but definitely not *that* colour.' Lizzie was always forthright.

'She was on at me to let my hair grow into that style too but it's too curly and I don't want to have to spend hours backcombing it all and plastering it with gallons of hair lacquer to keep it straight.'

Lizzie nodded. 'You'd ruin it. It's great the way it is. It's bit like the style that Mary Quant has, except that hers is straight, of course. I love the designs she's bringing out. I read somewhere that she said we don't want to wear the same style of clothes as our mothers. She's dead right there.' Lizzie dried the last plate, folded the tea towel and looked closely at Angela. 'Why don't you design something for us all to wear for this dance? Something "mod"? We'd all stand out. You made a good job of that black dress.'

Angela looked doubtful. 'I could try, but we haven't got much time and besides, Roz and Sal might want to buy something.'

Lizzie shrugged. 'Let them if they're set on it. You and I will set the trend.'

Angela gazed thoughtfully at Lizzie. They were about the same height and build and they both had dark hair, but Lizzie's was long and straight and held back with a wide bandeau. They would suit the same colours. 'We wouldn't be wanting something identical . . .'

'Similar. We don't want to look like twins. Think about it and maybe have a look at some material.'

Angela nodded. 'I'll see what ideas I can come up with and what the other two say.'

Lizzie was twisting a strand of hair around her finger. 'I think I'll have it cut. Sometimes it drives me mad, it's so thick and heavy. I'll have it cut short à la Mary Quant.'

'Are you sure about that? If you hate it it will take ages to grow again.'

'I'll go into Roz's salon. It will be expensive but it will be worth it.'

Mrs Henderson called that *Double Your Money* was just starting on the television if they wanted to watch it so they both went into the other room, Angela wondering whether she could cope with designing at least two dresses, if not four.

Roz thought it was a terrific idea and although Sal was a

little dubious to start with her sister's enthusiasm soon changed her mind.

'You get sick of seeing the same old styles in the shops. I've got great faith in you, Angela. Make the skirts much shorter and we'll look really trendy,' Roz enthused.

'You won't if you go having your hair dyed black. You'll look positively ill,' Lizzie remarked.

'And Mam will kill you,' Sal added. She was a little more conservative in her style than either Lizzie or Roz.

Roz stuck out her tongue at both of them and then grinned. 'Actually I mentioned it to Stefan and he said the same thing. My skin is too fair to take it, but I'm having it cut in that style though. Next week.'

'And I'm going to have mine cut like Mary Quant's,' Lizzie announced.

Sal raised her eyes to the ceiling. 'There's certainly going to be some changes around here. I wonder what Mam will have to say about it all?'

'Well, she can't say too much if we all dress in the same sort of things,' Roz declared firmly. 'You have to move with the times and as Liverpool is leading the country on the music scene I don't see why we can't be as trendy on the fashion scene.' She smiled widely at Angela. 'And you never know, we just might have our own answer to Mary Quant right here.'

Angela shook her head. 'Sure, I don't know about that. I do love fashion but your one went to art college and I certainly didn't. Doesn't she live in London and hasn't she people making the clothes for her to sell in her "boutique"? How can the likes of me from a little country town in Ireland do anything like that?'

'You don't know until you try! And I bet she had to start in a small way,' Roz enthused.

Lizzie was more practical. 'Leave Angela alone, Roz. Don't go getting carried away and bullying her into something she might not want to do.'

'I'm not! I was just trying to give her some confidence,' Roz protested.

Angela smiled at her. 'I don't mind trying to design something just for us. But don't blame me if what I think up doesn't meet with your expectations. I've not got the training.'

'You'll think up something really great, Angela, I just *know* you will!' Roz said firmly.

Chapter Seventeen

———◆◆◆◆———

ANGELA SOON BEGAN TO wonder just what she had let herself in for. She had four dresses to design and make and only two weeks in which to do it. Roz was completely carried away with the idea and insisted on meeting her each lunchtime when they trawled the department stores looking at materials. With Roz and her sisters money was no object but for Angela it was.

'Oh, we'll all chip in for your dress,' Roz had said airily when Angela had broached the subject of cost.

Angela had shaken her head. 'I can't do that, it wouldn't be fair.'

'Yes, it is. You're the one who is doing the hard part, the designing and the making, and we're not paying you to do it. Look on the material for your dress as a sort of payment,' Roz had said firmly.

After three evenings of making dozens of rough sketches she finally had four slightly different designs on one main theme. They were all straight shift-style dresses but two had short sleeves and two were sleeveless. One had a scoop neckline, another square, a third had a 'keyhole' set into the front of a halter-style neck and the fourth had what Angela described as a boat-shaped neckline. What was so unusual about them all was that the hemlines of the skirts finished three inches above the knee and they were all trimmed with asymmetrical bands in contrasting colours. Roz and Sal's were to be made in black and white while Lizzie and Angela's were to be in plain bright yellow and black.

'They'll be fabulous!' Roz enthused when Angela finally showed the designs to the girls.

Lizzie scrutinised them carefully. 'Just plain block colours, no pattern or stripes?'

Angela nodded. 'I thought the black and white would look good on both Roz and Sal and you and I both have dark hair so the yellow and black will be different.'

Lizzie nodded. 'They shouldn't be too hard to do, except for the keyhole and the trimming and all the contrasts will have to be cut on the cross to form the bias.'

'I was after thinking that for around the sleeve edges and necklines we could use ready-made bias binding. We should be able to get it in black and it will be easier to use,' Angela suggested. Lizzie nodded her agreement while Roz was already deciding that she would buy some big white daisy earrings and some wide white and black plastic bangles.

Sal was looking a bit anxious. 'The skirts are very short. Mam won't be happy about that.'

'Honestly, Sal Henderson, do you want to be trendy or not? You can't have your skirt longer than ours, it will ruin the whole effect, and it will make you look dowdy,' Roz remonstrated with her elder sister. 'And Mam can't moan too much if we all have short skirts.'

Angela said nothing but Lizzie agreed with Roz and finally Sal agreed.

'I'll give you a hand; you can't hope to get them all done by yourself,' Lizzie offered.

'And tomorrow we'll go and get the material,' Roz said firmly.

They had gone to Lewis's in the end as Angela had said both George Henry Lee and the Bon Marché were too expensive. They had four dress lengths to buy, plus contrast material and cottons, zips and bias binding. Roz had seen both earrings and bangles in Owen Owen in Clayton Square and a pair of shoes in Saxone on Church Street but Angela had insisted they get the materials first.

In every spare moment she and Lizzie had they pinned and cut out. Sal had been coerced into helping to tack but Lizzie had said it was no use at all asking Roz, she couldn't thread a needle nor could she keep her mind on the task. Her head was too full of what she was going to buy for accessories. The keyhole taxed both Angela and Lizzie's patience but in the end they got it right. When all the dresses had been tacked, they had a fitting, and Roz said she could see how they would look when finished, every bit as good as anything you'd get in a London boutique. Mrs Henderson had remarked that she'd never known there to be so much fuss over an outfit to go to a dance but at least it was keeping them all quiet so there were no arguments over who was going to watch what on the television.

To Angela's great relief the four dresses were finished two days before the Valentine's Night dance. Roz insisted they all try them on with the accessories they were going to wear, so as to get the whole effect. Both she and Lizzie had had their hair cut and everyone agreed that Lizzie's new short bob really suited her. Roz said she was still trying to decide whether her new style was a success; she was certain it would have looked better had it been tinted black.

They all congregated in Sal's bedroom, which was the largest, and Roz was almost jumping up and down with delight. 'Oh, we look *fantastic!*' she exclaimed, doing a few dance steps as she looked at her reflection in the long mirror on the door of the wardrobe. 'What's that saying you have, Angela? We'll take the sight from the eyes of everyone!'

Angela grinned at her. Now that she could see the results of her work she was really, really pleased. She felt a glow of satisfaction. These were *her* ideas. Granted, Lizzie had helped with the making but the designs were hers. Was it really something she could do? She who had no special training, no artistic flair.? She said this aloud and Roz looked at her in astonishment.

'Of course you've got artistic flair! You have to have, none of us could come up with designs like this. You haven't got the formal training but does that matter?'

'It might do with more complicated designs.'

'Worry about that when you want to do more complicated designs,' Lizzie advised. 'I think Roz is right. You certainly do have the flair.'

'Sal, will you stop trying to pull your skirt down,' Roz chided her sister.

'I'm just a bit worried that they're too short,' Sal confided.

'Well, let's see what Mam has to say and get it over with,' Roz replied and before anyone could stop her she had gone on to the landing and had shouted down for her mother to come and have a look at the new outfits.

Angela felt a little apprehensive for she didn't want there to be an argument. She would feel very responsible.

'Well, Mam? What do you think? Don't we all look great?' Roz demanded of her mother.

Mrs Henderson was taken aback. 'Mother of God! You don't intend to go to a dance with skirts that short? If you bend over everyone will see not only the tops of your stockings but your knickers as well!'

'Oh, Mam! We won't be bending over and they are the very latest fashion,' Roz protested.

'What about when you sit down? They'll ride up! I don't know about this at all.'

Angela bit her lip, feeling a little deflated. What if other people thought like this? What if they were not going to be a success?

Roz, however, was not going to be deterred. 'Go and get the lads and see what they say.'

'I wasn't sure myself,' Sal put in and both Lizzie and Roz glared at her.

'See what opinion the lads have,' Lizzie urged her mother, praying that all their hard work hadn't been wasted. If her mam really got a bee in her bonnet about this she would bring Dad into the argument and that would be the end of that. If their father forbade them to wear the dresses there would be nothing any of them could do. It would be wear something else or not go to the dance at all.

George and Tom were duly summoned and to the girls' relief pronounced that the dresses were really great and that they all looked terrific and should cause quite a sensation.

'That's what I was afraid of. You don't think they're too short then?' Mrs Henderson asked, still unconvinced.

'No. If you've got a good pair of legs you might as well show them off, that's the way I look at it,' George said.

'They're certainly doing that,' his mother replied cuttingly.

'Mam, you'd think we were going out half naked the way you're carrying on. They are only a couple of inches shorter and everyone will be wearing them like this soon, you wait and see,' Roz urged.

'Mam, you have to move with the times,' Tom added.

Mrs Henderson sighed. 'I can see I'm flogging a dead horse here. Oh, wear them but don't come moaning to me if you catch your death of cold!'

Angela let out a sigh of relief as Roz gave her mother a quick hug before she followed the boys downstairs.

The Grafton was one of the city's larger and more popular dance halls, or 'ballroom' to give it its official title, although as Roz had remarked to Angela there were not many proper 'balls' held there these days. When her parents had been young it had been expensive and people wore evening dress but times had changed. The dance had been widely advertised and was obviously going to be well attended, Angela thought as they joined the crowds going in. It had been decorated for the occasion with hundreds of red balloons and large red paper hearts. They handed in their coats and received a ticket in return and then went to the cloakroom. It was crowded with girls all applying more lipstick or mascara or titivating their hair.

Lizzie and Angela both wanted to repair the damage the wind had done to their hairstyles but Roz had sprayed her hair with hair lacquer. However she decided to apply more mascara to the false eyelashes she always wore and as she was much taller than nearly everyone else didn't have to jostle for place in front of the big mirror that covered almost the whole of one wall. They were all aware of the glances they were receiving but Roz had said they should appear 'nonchalant', as if they wore styles like this every day.

When they walked into the ballroom they did cause a stir and Roz pinched Angela's arm in delight. People glanced at them and then quickly did a 'double-take'. A few even pointed, which Sal thought was very rude. There were whispers of admiration and envy as they found a table and sat down. The group were belting out a poor imitation of the Beatles hit 'She Loves You' and the floor was already crowded.

'Pity they couldn't have got the Beatles themselves,' Lizzie commented, pulling a face.

'They're too famous now. They'd charge a fortune and they'd be mobbed. You wouldn't be able to move, let alone dance. This lot are not that bad,' Roz replied, looking around. 'The fellers aren't bad either.'

They were all asked up for every dance and as the evening wore on quite a few girls came up to them and said how great they thought their outfits were. They asked where they'd been bought, to which the Hendersons all replied that they hadn't been bought but that Angela had designed and made them.

Angela had been dancing to the twist with a tall, gangly lad whose legs seemed to be made of rubber when a girl who was dancing next to them asked where she bought her dress.

'I made it,' she replied, smiling.

'Gerroff! Well, where did you get the pattern? It's fantastic. It makes this thing I've got on look like something me granny would wear.'

Angela laughed. 'You look nothing like a granny but I didn't have a pattern. I designed it myself and I did the other three as well.'

'It must be great to go to the art school and have all these ideas.'

'I don't. I'm a clerk in a shipping office.'

'Never! Would you design something like that for me? I'd pay you, I work for Vernon's Pools and the wages aren't bad at all.'

'I don't know if I could. You see I've never really done it before. This was just for tonight.'

169

'I'd be dead grateful if you would. Give me your name and are you on the phone?'

Angela nodded. 'Well, it's the people I stay with really. It's Aintree 4669, their name is Henderson, mine is Angela. Angela O'Rourke.'

The girl nodded and, as the dance finished, borrowed a Biro from her partner and wrote the number on the back of her hand. 'I'll give you a ring. I'm Mel by the way. Mel Taylor.'

When she got back to the table Angela took a big gulp of lager and lime and sat down. The others had also returned.

'That girl has just taken the phone number, I hope it's all right. She wants me to make her a dress like this. I told her I didn't know if I could.'

'I've been asked by at least six girls where we bought our dresses,' Roz said. 'You could make a fortune.'

'Everyone wants to know where we got them. You know you *could* think about it, Angela,' Lizzie urged.

Angela nodded slowly. It would at least bring in some much needed extra money. 'Will we talk about it when we get home? It's too noisy in here to have a serious discussion.'

'And there won't be time either. Here comes the next lot of lads wanting to dance. The last fellow I danced with told me I looked fabulous and that I should be a model. Stefan's been telling me that for ages but I took no notice. Maybe I'll think about it and ask Mam can I can take a course at Lucy Clayton's in Bold Street,' Roz confided before she was escorted on to the dance floor again.

Lizzie grinned impishly at Angela. 'See what you've started? You could be about to change all our lives.'

Angela shook her head but before she could reply a lad reached down and touched her arm.

'Can I get you up to dance before anyone else muscles in?'

She looked up and smiled. He was tall and slim with fair hair and laughing blue eyes. 'Thanks.' She let him lead her on to the dance floor where they were playing 'I Love You Because' which was quite slow so they did a sort of slow waltz.

'I've been trying to get a dance half the night but I haven't been quick enough. You and your sisters look sensational. What's your name?'

'Angela and they're not my sisters. Well, *they* are sisters but I'm just a friend,' she replied. She liked him. He was well dressed in a grey Beatles-style suit with a lilac-coloured shirt and a darker mauve tie.

'Really? You all look quite alike, except that the one in the black and white is so tall. I haven't seen you around the clubs. Where do you live?'

'In Walton and I don't go to the clubs very often. I'm only a clerk and that doesn't pay a fortune.'

He smiled down at her. 'It seems to pay enough for you to dress in the latest gear and I think you're the best-looking girl here.'

She blushed. 'Sure, I don't know about that. What's your name?'

'Danny. Danny Fielding. Do you work in town?'
She nodded.

'Maybe I could meet you after you've finished work one night? I live in Faulkner Square.'

She wasn't sure, thinking about how little spare time she would have if she did agree to make Mel Taylor a dress.

'Oh, go on. I'd take you somewhere decent, promise. I'm in business for myself.'

'Really? What do you do?' She'd never met anyone of his age, which she judged to be about twenty or twenty-one, who had their own business.

He shrugged. 'Oh, you know. Marketing.'

'You mean you have a stall on a market?' She was disappointed in him, he was just talking big to impress her.

He grimaced. 'God no! I buy and sell things. Sort of import–export. I've got my own flat.'

'What sort of things?' she pressed, thinking he must be successful if he had a place of his own.

'Just about everything. You don't half ask a lot of questions.' He was smiling down at her again and she smiled back.

'It's just that I might be after thinking of starting in business myself. In a small way.'

'Start small and get bigger, that's my motto. I like a girl with ambition. What kind of business?'

She told him about the dresses she had designed and made and of the interest in them and he listened intently, nodding approval.

'You could be on to a good thing there. You can make a lot of money in the fashion business. I'd say chuck the job as a clerk and have a go at it. You've certainly got a lot of go about you. Now, what about me seeing you again?'

She smiled at him but she'd made her decision. 'Well, if I do take your advice I won't have much time to be going out on the town, so I'll have to refuse, but thanks all the same.'

The dance had finished and he reached into his pocket and handed her a small white card. 'If you change your mind that's where you can find me.'

It was a business card with his name and address printed in fancy script. 'I'll keep it – just in case,' she promised as he walked her back to the table.

Chapter Eighteen

———◆———

S HE HADN'T HAD TIME to think much about Danny Fielding for the following evening Mel Taylor had phoned and begged her to make not only a dress for her but for six other girls she knew who had all been at the Valentine's dance too. She had promised she would let her know the following day and had gone to impart the news to Roz.

'That's fantastic! You will do it? You've got to start somewhere Angela,' Roz cried.

'But . . . but *seven* dresses! How will I have time? Where will I work, that's an awful lot of material and other stuff to have scattered around the place and how will I know what to charge? And, more to the point, where will I get the money to buy the materials in the first place?'

Roz frowned with impatience. It all seemed plain to her. 'Lizzie will help you, you can use the dining room, I'm sure Mam will agree to lend you the money for materials and we can easily work out how much to charge.'

Angela shook her head. It was taking too much for granted. 'Oh, I just don't know, Roz.'

'Oh, Angela, for heaven's sake, you've just *got* to try!' Roz insisted.

'What are you bullying Angela over now?' Mrs Henderson asked, catching her daughter's last words as she came in from the kitchen.

With great enthusiasm Roz told her and begged her to persuade Angela to try it and see how it worked out. 'Mam, she really could make a success of this!' she finished.

Mrs Henderson nodded slowly. 'I think you'd better have a chat with Bernard about this, Angela. He's the one with the head for business, not me.'

'And he started in a small way, didn't he, Mam?' Roz added.

'He started with a horse and cart then progressed to a lorry and built it up from that,' Mrs Henderson agreed. 'Mind you, he worked all the hours God sent for years and you'd have to do the same.'

Angela didn't know what to think. She wanted to give it a try but she wasn't sure about asking so many other people for their help and relying on their generosity. In the end, however, she agreed to discuss it with Mr Henderson.

'I think our Lizzie should sit in with you too. She's got more idea of just how much work it will involve than our Rose,' Mrs Henderson suggested. 'Rose's got me mithered to death with this mad idea of wanting to go to Lucy Clayton's to do a modelling course. I don't know what's wrong with the job she's got.'

Between them Angela and Lizzie explained the situation to Bernard Henderson who listened closely and asked questions and jotted down some notes.

'You'll need to cost the whole thing out, Angela. The cost of materials and labour and even advertising, if you want to make it a going concern. And, ideally, you would need a workroom,' he said seriously.

Angela was horrified. 'Sure, I wouldn't be able to do that!'

'Don't get into a state about it. I know it all seems very daunting but I could help you with the costing. It would be more practical to buy from wholesalers, but we can sort that out.'

'I'd help, Dad, with the "labour" side of it,' Lizzie offered, 'I'm fed up working in that office, I'd much sooner work with Angela.'

Her father frowned. 'There is no point in anyone giving up their jobs. You'd both have to see how things go, how successful – or not – it proves to be. Could you both manage to do this first order between you in your spare time?'

'I think so,' Angela replied hesitantly. It all did seem daunting, there was far more to it than she had envisaged.

'We'll have a good try, Dad,' Lizzie added.

'Right then. If you give me an idea of how much material you'll need and its approximate cost, the price of trimmings, and how much you think you should charge for your work, by the hour, I'll come up with an estimate for each dress.' He looked thoughtful. 'There's a storeroom at the back of the yard that you could use as a workroom, rather than have your mother complaining about you cluttering up the dining room. I'll get it cleaned up and get the sewing machine taken over there. I'll also look into the matter of wholesale suppliers and we'll take it from there.'

Angela was so grateful she couldn't speak; there was a lump in her throat.

Lizzie jumped up and hugged him. 'We'll make a success of it, Dad! You'll see!'

Lizzie's enthusiasm was catching and for the first time Angela felt a glimmer of confidence in her abilities. She *could* make a success of this. 'We will so. I'll work very hard, I promise. Dr Leahy was the only one who ever thought I could do better than being just a skivvy and I didn't live up to the hopes he had for me, but this is something I really feel I *can* do, that I will enjoy doing and make a success of. And now you're giving me so much help. I can't thank you enough for . . . everything.'

He smiled kindly at her. 'I'd love to see you succeed, Angela, I really would. Everyone deserves a chance to make a better life for themselves.'

She phoned Mel Taylor the following evening and Mel and her friends agreed to meet her and Lizzie the following Friday at the workroom at the haulage yard. Angela then went to work on the designs and once again trawled the department stores looking at materials. This time she made notes of the exact type of fabric, colours, prices and even plucked up courage to ask for small swatches of those she thought suitable. The storeroom was cleared out and cleaned and the sewing machine and two trestle tables, to be used for cutting out, were duly installed, plus a portable gas heater. In an outhouse Mrs Henderson found an old chest with four shallow drawers once used for storing sheet music, which she said would be ideal for reels of cotton and trimmings and other things they'd need. Sal had agreed to do the tacking up and had promised to teach Roz how to tack if it was the last thing she ever did.

Angela's designs and suggested colours and materials had met with enthusiastic approval by her first potential customers and Mr Henderson had costed each dress at twenty-two shillings.

'I know you can get dresses cheaper in C & A Modes, especially in their basement, but not like these. We've tried to keep the price as low as we can,' Angela had informed them, seeing that some of the girls looked a bit taken aback.

Eventually they had agreed, saying it was worth it as there was nothing like them in any of the big shops yet. And then things had become quite frenetic. Mr Henderson had arranged for them to go and purchase the materials and trimmings from a supplier and all four girls worked on the order every evening and at the weekend. Mel and her friends came for a fitting and were delighted and when the garments were finally finished, picked up and paid for Lizzie had grabbed Angela around the waist and they had danced around the cramped workroom.

'Your first real earnings as a fashion designer!' Lizzie had shrieked.

Angela had laughed delightedly until she remembered that she had to start to pay Mr Henderson back at the agreed rate for his outlay.

In the weeks that followed enquiries, followed by orders, came in rapidly as Mel and her friends sang Angela's praises to all their friends and relations and Roz insisted on wearing the dress Angela had made for her every day to work for a week and gave Angela's name and their telephone number to everyone who complimented her on her outfit. Roz had even suggested to the owner of the salon that he should consider having Angela design and make a special uniform for all his female staff. It would certainly look more classy and modern than the different styles of pink overalls they now wore, even though the shade of pink was virtually the same. To her surprise he had thought it a good idea and said he would like Angela to come in so they could discuss it.

By the end of March it had become apparent that some serious decisions were going to have to be made and one very blustery evening, after the meal was over, Mrs Henderson cleared the table and her husband got a large pad, a pen and his Ready Reckoner.

'Right then, I think it's time we had a serious discussion about what you girls are going to do in the future,' he announced as his wife ushered Lizzie and Angela to the table.

'Can't Sal and I join in?' Roz asked.

'As long as you come up with constructive ideas and not hare-brained schemes,' her father stated seriously. He'd kept a close eye on the progress of this fledgling enterprise and had been impressed by both Angela and Lizzie's hard work, enthusiasm and flair. He knew from experience with his own family that young people were prepared to spend their wages on fashionable clothes and he'd also done a bit of what was being called 'market research' and had realised that there was a gap in the market for the type of clothes that the girls were designing and making. They were particularly appealing to girls in their teens and early twenties and they were colourful, stylish and original. He was an astute businessman and he'd given the matter some thought before discussing it with his wife but they'd both agreed that it was a venture worth investing in.

'It's obvious that you can make a success of this with the right investment and some practical planning—' he announced.

'I said we could, so can I now give in my notice and work with Angela?' Lizzie interrupted.

'What I suggest is that you both give up your jobs and concentrate on this full time but I have some suggestions to make as to how this business should be run.'

Angela looked at him intently; she trusted his judgement entirely. He'd built his own business from virtually nothing to one that was thriving and continually expanding. She'd also learned that in addition to the haulage business he owned quite a lot of property which he rented out.

'What I suggest is this. You can't design and make clothes for individual girls. It's just not feasible for everyone to be measured and fitted. It's too time-consuming. You will have to make clothes in standard sizes, the way they are sold in the shops, and you will have to produce enough to hold "in stock".'

Lizzie frowned. 'But, Dad, how will we be able to manage that?'

'You'll have to employ people. Machinists, cutters and the like. We can negotiate rates with suppliers for regular orders and you will have to have bigger premises.'

Angela was trying to concentrate but she was beginning to feel a bit overwhelmed. 'All that is going to cost a lot of money.'

'I've estimated the initial outlay and I'm prepared to invest it but I will expect a percentage of the profits in return. That's fair, isn't it?'

'It is indeed,' Angela agreed, not even daring to try to estimate just how much he was going to have to lay out. 'And I think we'll need to employ someone who knows how to make patterns. So far we've just used bits and pieces from patterns Lizzie has bought but, sure, we can't go on doing that. It's no use me designing something if neither of us can make a pattern for it.'

'You'll need a professional pattern-cutter. You'll have to advertise,' Mrs Henderson suggested.

'I suggest that Angela sticks entirely to designing, that we both discuss materials and trimmings but that I take charge of the ordering and the workroom. Make sure everything runs smoothly and maybe do the finishing-off myself,' Lizzie put in.

Her father nodded. 'That sounds practical. It will leave you more time, Angela.'

Angela nodded her agreement.

'How are they going to be sold? Will you sell them from here or will you try to get one of the department stores to take them and sell them for you?' Roz asked, for once giving the matter some serious thought.

'They'll want to make their profit on them which would mean we would have no control over the price they sold them for and that might well price us out of the market,' Mr Henderson replied. 'No. I suggest we find some premises of our own. In fact I have somewhere in mind.'

'Open a boutique? Dad, that's a great idea! There isn't one in Liverpool yet. It wouldn't need to be very big and you could sell things like earrings, necklaces and bangles to match. Cheaply, of course,' Roz suggested, entering wholeheartedly into the project.

'Let's just start with clothes before branching out into other things,' her father warned cautiously.

Roz's imagination had taken a firm hold. 'Angela, why don't you do a "collection" like the big fashion houses do and put on a proper fashion show? I'd help.'

'I said constructive ideas, not hare-brained schemes, Rose!' her father reminded her impatiently.

'No, wait, Dad. She might just be right,' Lizzie interrupted. 'It needn't be a big collection. Just a basic range so people can see what we are offering. What do you think, Angela?'

Angela had been thinking about it all. It *did* make sense. They had to start on a proper footing. They had to make standard sizes and sell them at prices young people could afford. They had to show just what they *were* selling to attract customers. They were not going to be doing this on a part-time basis, as a sort of hobby now. It was to be a business and she was determined it would succeed. 'I think it would work. If we had, say, a dozen designs to be modelled, mainly dresses but some skirts, trousers and tops too, it would show our customers what they can buy in the shop and how much they will have to pay.'

'We could invite people from the *Echo* and from that magazine *Merseybeat* to take photographs, and advertise in the clubs and coffee bars and all the colleges. Aim it at young people,' Sal suggested.

Mr Henderson was nodding his approval. 'It would be a good form of advertising, better than just word of mouth, although that will help too.'

Roz had been thinking ahead. 'I'll have a word in the salon and see if we can advertise it and maybe we could do all the hairstyles. They're important too, you can't have trendy clothes and old-fashioned hairstyles. I can't see that they'd object, it would be good for our business as well.'

Mrs Henderson was studying her youngest daughter thoughtfully. 'Maybe a course at Lucy Clayton's wouldn't be such a bad idea after all. You've certainly got the height and the figure to show these designs off.'

Roz grinned delightedly. 'I could be one of the models then and I'd be able to see which of the other girls would be suitable.'

Mr Henderson became businesslike. 'Then I suggest we get down to the nitty-gritty things now, like suggestions for workroom premises, finding staff and equipment and suppliers.'

'And a name for the business, that's important, Dad. A name for both the design label and the boutique,' Lizzie added.

Everyone looked at Angela.

'They're your designs, Angela,' Mrs Henderson reminded her.

Angela hadn't thought this far, her mind was already in a whirl thinking about the fashion show and the boutique.

It was Lizzie who came up with the idea. 'What about "The Green Angel Boutique"? After all, Angela's Irish.'

Angela flushed with pleasure. 'I think that sounds just grand.'

Chapter Nineteen

⬥◦⬥◦⬥

A NGELA COULDN'T GET TO sleep, her mind was so full of
plans for the future. They had sat for hours and made
long lists of everything that needed to be done, from giving
in their notices to finding a venue for the fashion show.
Everyone had their list of instructions and tasks. Mr
Henderson was to find the premises for the workrooms and
order the sewing machines, cutting tables and all the other
equipment needed. He owned the ground floor of a small
warehouse in Mathew Street, quite near to the Cavern Club,
which was in the city centre and would be ideal for the
boutique both in size and location but would need planning
permission for such a change, something he was confident
he could sort out quickly. Then it would need clearing,
cleaning, decorating and fitting out. He was to be in charge
of all the expenditure, accounts and wages, and of procuring
wholesalers and suppliers and negotiating terms. Lizzie and
her mother were to find and interview their potential
employees and were also in charge of what they termed the
'publicity' for both the boutique and the fashion show. Lizzie

had said that timing was very important. The boutique had to be ready, stocked and open at least a few days before the show and they should think about inviting the press to the opening of that. Sal had been given the task of organising the advertising in as many places where young people congregated as possible. Roz was to go to Lucy Clayton's, which was both a modelling school and an agency, to take a course and make enquiries about obtaining other models and exactly how a show was organised. She was to see the owner of the salon about hair and make-up. Their top stylists always entered for the prestigious Hairdressing Awards, so there would be no shortage of ideas for hairstyles and colours. That left Angela with the major job of designing the collection, which she wanted to be the most outstanding and innovative she could think of.

As she lay staring into the darkness, wide awake and with excitement bubbling up in her, she began to envisage designs for dresses, skirts and tops, blouses, jackets, trouser suits and maybe even coats. Nothing was impossible now, not with a professional pattern-cutter and a team of machinists. She still couldn't believe it was all happening. She, Angela O'Rourke, whose family had been so poor that they'd had to give her away to her aunt to bring up, who'd been nothing more than a skivvy in Dr Leahy's house, was going to start her own business, have her own fashion label and boutique. She was going to be the 'Green Angel' and she was going to make it a huge success. She had failed as a nurse but it hadn't been what she really wanted to do, her heart hadn't been in it and she'd had no confidence in herself, but she wasn't going to fail at this and her confidence was growing by the minute. Both Aunt Mary and Dr Leahy *would* be proud of what she was going to achieve, with the help of the Hendersons. Dr Leahy had planted the seeds of ambition in her mind, shown her that she had choices in life, and now Mr Henderson was giving her the means and the encouragement to make all her hopes and dreams become reality. When she had left Edenderry she had been looking forward to a new life but never in a million years could she have dreamed that this was what life could hold for her. She remembered the lad she had met that morning on the ferry, who'd told her all about the new ideas and sounds that were sweeping this city. He'd been right and she was certain that this was exactly the right time for someone like herself, brimful of ideas, to start out in the fashion business.

Somehow in the hectic days ahead of her she would find the time to write to Emer and to her aunt. For an instant she wondered should she write to her mother and father and tell them about these wonderful opportunities that had opened up for her but she dismissed it. They wouldn't be interested. They had never been interested to know what her life was like or what she was doing. From the day she'd gone to her aunt she'd been just one fewer worry for them.

The days of April sped by so fast that the month was drawing to its close and the weather was gradually getting warmer before Angela had a reply from Emer. Mary had written saying it was hard to take it all in and she hoped Angela wasn't taking on too much and raising people's hopes and expectations, for after all she'd had no formal training in anything like this and it could end in huge disappointment for everyone concerned. She wasn't being a begrudger but look what had happened with the nursing. Indeed she hoped Angela hadn't lost the run of herself entirely with these design notions, but she supposed Mr Henderson knew what he was about, him being successful in business already, and she was to take notice of everything he said and be guided by him and work hard to repay his generosity. It wasn't exactly the type of letter Angela had wanted. There wasn't much in the way of congratulations or encouragement, it was more about being cautious and grateful. It was as if Mary couldn't really envisage her being capable of doing anything but the most simple and mundane of jobs.

When Emer's letter arrived Angela hoped that she wasn't going to echo her aunt's doubts and fears but it couldn't have been more different in tone.

Dear Angela,

*I just couldn't believe what I was reading! I had to pinch myself and then read it over again. You having your own business, with work premises and employing people and a shop too! You will have to explain to me what kind of a shop this 'boutique' will be for I haven't heard of the like before. Will it be big or small and will you just sell clothes and will you be in it yourself or will you have staff? I'm **so** delighted for you and it will be a huge success, I know, that's for sure and for certain, especially if Himself is putting all that money into it. And having a fashion show! Oh, I wish I could be there! Please send me some photos. Isn't it great altogether that you are doing so well? We never thought when we left the National School in Edenderry that you'd have such a terrific career ahead of you – how could we, the pair of eejits we were then? I still can't believe that you are so talented and clever, wouldn't you have been wasting your time as a nurse? I think 'The Green Angel' is just the right name, an inspiration, and Joy thinks so too. She said to tell you 'good luck'. Everyone here in America, well the young ones anyway, are going wild about the Beatles and the type of clothes they wear and their hairstyles, in fact all the new fashions that are coming across from over there. It makes all the styles we have look old-fashioned and streelish. If I send* *you some dollars will you send me one of your 'creations' and then I'll have all the girls green with envy? Do you remember before I came over here we said that if you ever made a fortune you'd come over and visit and stay in the Waldorf and shop on 5th Avenue? Well, it might not be such a far-fetched notion now and wouldn't I be so proud of you? Sure, I'd introduce you as my friend 'the fashion designer'. Please, please write and let me know how everything is going and send me lots of photos if you can.*

She went on to give all her news, which she said was very boring and dull beside Angela's but Angela read it with interest anyway. She had smiled at the bit about her going to New York; she would probably never be able to afford the time. Not the way things were going. She would, however, send Emer a couple of dresses and there was definitely no need for her friend to pay her. If Emer insisted then she'd tell her she would just give the money to a charity so she had better keep it.

The fashion show had been arranged for the end of May and was proving to be a huge headache for everyone except Roz who, with her natural exuberance and enthusiasm, was enjoying every minute. She had arranged for two of their top stylists to create the hairstyles and had thrown herself wholeheartedly into her modelling course which she did mainly in the evenings but also on her day off. She had spent a whole morning in the office discussing the fashion show and had been very pleased with herself when she arrived home to inform everyone that she now had contacts for venues, lighting and music and that the agency would provide the models at the usual fee, and that Helena, who had a great deal of experience, would be willing to compere the show. Angela would have to give her the description and price of each garment in the order in which it was to be modelled.

Angela was beginning to panic, thinking she had left herself too little time in which to design and oversee the making of a collection and also the interior of the boutique and to attend to the dozens of other details connected with the fashion show. With his usual efficiency Mr Henderson had resolved the problem of the boutique. He had gone to the Liverpool College of Art and had spoken to the principal and the outcome of that was that two of the art students who were interested in interior design had taken on the project.

Angela had been very relieved. 'Sure, it's a weight off my mind but haven't you enough to do with your own business without running around after me?'

'The two lads can see that things keep running smoothly; it will do them both good to gain the experience and take responsibility. I don't intend to keep working until I drop. I intend to retire at some stage and then they'll have to take over,' he'd replied firmly.

Lizzie and her mother had proved to be very efficient in recruiting machinists and cutters: particularly Evvie who was in her forties and who wasn't particularly impressed by what she termed 'these new-fangled outfits' but who was a very talented pattern-cutter. Angela had been astounded by the fact that she could give Evvie a rough drawing and the woman would produce a pattern for the cutters to work from. Lizzie, too, was proving to be a treasure. She had a good eye for colour and fabric and was particularly impressed with the new synthetic materials that were now becoming available: Terylene, Courtelle jersey, Dacron, Bri-nylon, Crimplene and faux suede and shiny plastic-coated cotton, which she said would be fantastic for jackets and macs.

'Of course we'll still be using things like gabardine and

wool and tartan, especially for winter, but Terylene and Crimplene don't crease, drape well and have stretch and Courtelle jersey will be fantastic for trousers. They can be washed and dry easily, there's no need for dry cleaning,' she'd enthused, showing Angela the samples she'd acquired. 'And the range of colours is good too,' she'd added.

She had proved that she could supervise as well; she got on very well with all the girls and women and had great respect for Evvie. A problem had arisen with the white cotton piqué that had been ordered and Lizzie had spent an hour on the phone to the supplier being very firm and businesslike and the matter had been resolved quickly. Her father had been impressed when Angela had relayed the incident to him and had agreed that all the ordering should in future be done by Lizzie.

Lizzie had been pleased. 'It was really just a case of making them understand that we won't accept sub-standard material. We are paying for decent quality and that's what we expect and we expect it on time. We can't afford to be sending stuff back and then having to wait for a replacement. We have deadlines to meet. They aren't the only suppliers, we can go elsewhere and I made that perfectly clear.'

'Very true. I expect they thought they'd get away with it you being a young girl and in a new business to boot,' her father replied.

'I really enjoy what I'm doing now, Dad. It's all such a challenge and it's so exciting.'

'Let's hope you still think like that in a couple of years' time – all of you.'

'I just hope we can have everything ready on time and that enough people turn up. I worry that something awful will go wrong and we'll have a half-empty venue and then no customers for the boutique,' Angela said anxiously. She had begun to lose sleep worrying about all the things that could go wrong.

Roz wasn't at all negative. 'The place will be packed out! Sal's done a fantastic job on the advertising. There are posters plastered all over the city and the press have shown great interest and promised to do full-length features with photos. In fact I was thinking we should have two shows.'

Angela had stared at her aghast. '*Two* shows! Won't we all be destroyed entirely getting *one* done successfully and two shows would cost double the amount.'

Roz had perched on the edge of the table and scrutinised the list Angela had in front of her. They all had to agree that Roz had acquired far more poise and elegance since she'd started her course. Her hair was swept up in large loose curls and she wore a white tunic dress with short sleeves and a half belt at the back which showed off her long legs. Around her neck she wore a heavy necklace made of rows and rows of black and white beads and she had matching earrings. She'd bought a pair of black and white patent shoes with a chisel-shaped toe and a lower heel to match. 'Pointed toes are on the way out, I read it in *Vogue*, and this new design has come straight from Italy,' she'd informed her sisters knowledge-ably.

'Everything will go like clockwork, you wait and see,' she said firmly now. 'We have covered every single detail; nothing has been overlooked. It will be the success story of the year, and twelve months from now the Green Angel will be the place *everyone* will want to buy their clothes from. You see, we'll be every bit as trendy as London, maybe more so. This city is leading the world in music and fashion and we're going to be right up there with the best of them.'

Lizzie had agreed. 'That's the spirit. We'll stop them dead in their tracks. You wait and see, Angela.'

Part IV

Chapter Twenty

———◆———

Liverpool, 1965

ANGELA LEANED ON THE rail of the upper deck of the ferry and gazed down into the turgid blue-grey waters of the Mersey. Sunlight caught the wash, turning it to a gold-coloured froth and a dredger moved slowly off the starboard bow. The ferry wasn't crowded at that time of the day, it wasn't the rush hour when workers from both sides of the river were returning home, but she had attracted one or two admiring glances. Her pale pink sleeveless dress with its short pleated skirt looked fresh and crisp. She wore low-heeled white patent shoes with a squared toe and over her shoulder was a matching bag.

The July sun was hot on her neck and shoulders and she felt more relaxed than she had done for months. It had been an incredible year, she thought. Roz had been correct; they had taken the city's fashion scene by storm. The show had been an unqualified success and the press had really done them proud with full-page articles and photographs and interviews. The fashion conscious youngsters of city had flocked to the Green Angel Boutique and now her designs could be seen in the clubs and coffee bars, in the shops and offices and on the streets of the city. It had been so successful that they were opening another boutique in Birkenhead, the city across the water to Liverpool. It was the reason why she was crossing the river this afternoon. She had just finished inspecting the shop and discussing the opening with the staff employed to work there. The interior was exactly the same as the Liverpool shop, designed by the same art students, and the garments in stock were identical too. It hadn't been her idea, it had been Lizzie's.

'Why shouldn't they have a boutique over there too? Why should people have to traipse across the river to buy decent clothes? In fact we could think of opening Green Angel Boutiques in some of the surrounding towns. Warrington, St Helens, Southport, even Chester,' she had enthused.

'You'd need a full-scale factory operation to cope with the demand and I think that would be too much for you,' her father had warned. 'Besides, your designs are proving so popular that the big stores are starting to catch on and stock similar lines and you can't compete with the mass market. They will always be able to undercut your prices.'

Lizzie had set her chin stubbornly. 'Cheap imitations. Our clothes are of much better quality and finish.'

'When have quality and finish ever mattered to you young ones? They don't intend to keep them for years like their mothers did. What they want is cheap and cheerful. No, open one in Birkenhead by all means but leave it at that.'

Angela had agreed with Mr Henderson. 'At the moment I suppose we are a big fish in a small pond but if we go branching out like that we'll be a small fish in a very big pond – the mass market. We're doing well, our profits are healthy and we enjoy what we do, Lizzie,' she'd urged. Despite being disappointed Lizzie had acquiesed and helped her find the small but central premises off Hamilton Square.

Looking back over the months Angela realised just how far they'd come and what they'd achieved. If someone had told her on the night of the Valentine's dance that she would now have two shops selling her clothes and that she would have a healthy bank balance she would never have believed them. She had had a serious discussion with Mr Henderson about the money he had invested and she had been adamant that she start to pay him back immediately. She really wanted to make a success of this business, *her* business. She didn't want it to be a side interest of Mr Henderson's. Hopefully in a couple of years' time she would have paid back every penny. They had agreed to a set amount each month and he had advised her to try to put money aside to invest for the future and she had agreed, she trusted his advice. Not that it was all plain sailing: after all the euphoria of the show and the opening of the Green Angel had died down she had come to realise that it was time consuming and extremely hard work, especially for her. She hadn't realised that the fashion industry worked so far ahead. Almost at once she had had to start designing an autumn/winter collection, followed by this year's spring/summer collection and then this year's autumn/winter, and when the Birkenhead boutique was up and running it would be time to think of new ideas for next spring. It was a constant merry-go-round that sometimes caused her to worry that one day she would just run out of ideas or that fashions would change drastically. You always had to be one step ahead in this business, she'd told Roz. She discussed her ideas for hours with Lizzie, then they would decide together what fabrics, colours and trimmings they would use and Lizzie would place all the orders. They produced a prototype of every garment in the new range and when they were satisfied with them it was always Roz who modelled them for the press photographs. Everything looked great on Roz and she was in so much demand as a model that she now only worked part-time at the salon. In fact she had begun to talk about moving to London which was where the national magazines and the big money was to be found – an idea her parents strongly disapproved of.

The sun was beginning to burn Angela's skin and so she walked across the deck and sat in the shade of the funnel as the *Mountwood* moved towards the Liverpool waterfront. She could have caught a bus or a train. There was a regular bus service that ran through the Mersey Tunnel and a train service that ran under the Mersey from James Street Underground Station, but she preferred the ferry crossing, especially when the weather was fine. She drew Emer's letter from her bag and reread it, smiling as she did so. Emer's letters were always amusing and interesting. Her current boyfriend was someone called Grant and, as was frequently the case, was not approved of by Dinny and for the usual reasons. Not a Catholic, not of Irish descent, did not have a decent job and therefore good prospects and dressed in a style Dinny considered unconventional, which meant that Grant was trendy. Emer said she didn't care, that she wasn't looking for a husband just yet, she was enjoying herself. Angela remembered the letter Emer had written after she had received the two dresses Angela had sent her. Dinny had been outraged at the 'indecent' length of the skirts and had said he didn't know what Angela O'Rourke had been thinking of and had forbidden Emer to wear them, even though Joy had approved. There had been a huge row over that and Emer had argued that young people all over

America had minds and ideas of their own and were starting to rebel against what they called 'the establishment'. There were protest marches against the Vietnam War and for civil rights. In fact young Americans who didn't agree with the war were refusing to join the army and were going on the run to Canada. Now Emer had pointed out to her elder brother that Grant only dressed like the Beatles and hadn't the Queen of England awarded them all the MBE? That must mean that *she* didn't think they dressed 'unconventionally' so did he now think he was on a higher level than Herself? She wrote that Dinny had retorted angrily: what Irishman was at all interested in what the Queen of England thought or did? Now, if it were the Irish President it would be a different kettle of fish. As far as Angela could make out it appeared to be an on-going battle but her friend didn't seem too perturbed and was continuing her liaison with this Grant. Joy, it seemed, was always the mediator in these arguments.

She folded the letter and replaced it in her bag, thinking that her aunt's reaction to the press cuttings and photos she'd sent had been very similar to Dinny Cassidy's. Mary had written that she understood young girls loved 'a bit of style', but to go flaunting your legs like that, putting yourself in danger of exposing your stocking tops to the public view, was downright immodest. She wasn't trying to take the shine off everything Angela had achieved, it all seemed a great success, but she was sure no good would come of these new fashions and she prayed it was just a fad and would soon pass. She wrote that Liam had said young girls were only asking for trouble going around half dressed. There would be a huge increase in assaults and then there would be an outcry and whose fault would it be? And it was a well-known fact that the English didn't cultivate a sense of modesty in their young people and it was a sign of the moral decline that was setting in over there. While Mary wouldn't go so far as to agree with all that she wondered was it really *wise* for Angela and the Henderson girls to go on promoting such styles?

Angela grimaced to herself, thinking of the Henderson girls' reaction to that.

'Immodest! What is immodest about showing your knees? Look at all those Hollywood film stars who go around with their bosom falling out of their dresses. That's immodest! And anyway there will be no stocking tops on view, not now we have these new "tights"!' Lizzie had cried, outraged.

'And what your uncle is saying is that *you* are to blame if someone gets assaulted because you designed the dress! That's the most ridiculous thing I've ever heard!' Roz had added. 'Did you see how short Jean Shrimpton's skirt was at the Melbourne Races? And she's a top model!' she'd finished. Jean Shrimpton was her idol.

Angela had shrugged. Liam would come up with something like that. It was just an excuse and a lame one at that. He was an out-and-out hypocrite giving out about a 'moral decline'.

The ferry had drawn alongside the Landing Stage and she went down to the lower deck to disembark, pushing the comments of her aunt and uncle and Dinny Cassidy from her mind. She was going to call into the Mathew Street boutique to see how things were going and to discuss with Abbie, the manageress, the forthcoming sale to clear the summer stock ready for the new autumn lines.

She got off the bus in Victoria Street and was walking through Temple Court when she heard her name being called. She turned around to see a tall lad with blond hair waving to her. She frowned, trying to think where she had seen him before.

'Angela! Angela O'Rourke!'

She still couldn't place him but he obviously knew her.

'It's me. Danny. Danny Fielding. Don't you remember the Valentine's dance at the Grafton?'

She smiled up at him. 'I do so. I still have the card you gave me, it's in my purse.' She did indeed still have it, tucked into the back of her purse, but she had forgotten all about him.

He gave a wry grin. 'I was dead disappointed that you didn't get in touch.'

'I've hardly had time to catch my breath since then,' she laughed as he fell into step beside her.

'You took my advice though and you've done well. Everyone is wearing your clothes. The Green Angel is *the* place to shop. Where are you off to now?' He'd thought a great deal about her and followed her career in the newspapers and magazines but he hadn't seen her since that night. She looked great, he thought. Very trendy but now there was an air of confidence about her that hadn't been there that night.

'To the Green Angel. I've some things to discuss with Abbie.'

'Will that take long? Will you have time for a coffee afterwards?'

She nodded. It wouldn't hurt to take a bit of time for herself and she did like him. 'I'll be about an hour. Is that all right?'

'Great. I'll meet you at the bottom of Bold Street, we'll go up to El Cabala, it's the smartest. Don't go standing me up.'

'I wouldn't do a thing like that. If I say I'll meet you I will.'

She was finished earlier than she had anticipated and so she walked slowly through the city centre to the bottom of Liverpool's most expensive and exclusive shopping street. He was waiting for her, clutching a large bunch of flowers.

'I was coming through Clayton Square past the flower ladies and I thought, Hey, why not get some for the Green Angel? So these are for you.'

She smiled, feeling her cheeks flush. No one had ever bought her flowers before. 'They're gorgeous, thanks.'

He grinned at her and pushed his fringe of blond hair back, his blue eyes dancing. 'I did feel a bit of a fool, like, waiting here with a bunch of flowers in my hand but . . .' He shrugged and they walked up the street to the coffee bar which was at the top end.

She had been there once or twice before and liked the way it was decorated with carved African masks and palm-like plants in big tubs. They sat at a table by one of the plate-glass windows and he ordered Danish pastries and espressos.

She tweaked a curl forward on to her cheek. 'And how is your business doing? Marketing, wasn't it?'

He looked pleased with himself. 'Great, just great. I'm thinking of buying a car. One of those Minis. It would be just the thing for nipping around town.'

'Really?' She was impressed. He must be doing well if he could afford to spend over six hundred pounds on a car and he was well dressed in the height of fashion.

The coffee and pastries arrived and they talked about the music scene and their favourite television programmes, such as *Ready Steady Go* and *The Avengers*, and the Beatles first film *A Hard Day's Night*.

'And are you still working as hard?' he asked, fiddling with a teaspoon.

She nodded. 'We're about to open another Green Angel boutique in Birkenhead.'

He looked at her with open admiration 'There's no stopping you, is there? You'll have a fashion empire one day, I'll bet. Do you have any time to yourself?'

She wiped her mouth with the corner of the paper serviette and shook her head. 'Not much.'

'You know that old saying, "All work and no play . . ."? How old are you, Angela?'

'I was twenty last birthday. And you?'

'Twenty-two next week, so will you come out with me to celebrate it? It's no fun celebrating on your own.' He put his head to one side and put on an expression of exaggerated sadness.

She couldn't help but laugh and she felt completely at ease with him. There seemed to be a sort of spark between them. 'Stop that, you eejit. Of course I will, as it's your birthday.'

He became serious and reached across the table and took her hand. 'As soon as I saw you at the Grafton I thought, That's the girl for you, Danny lad. I mean it. We'll have a great time. We'll go for a good meal with a bottle of wine and then on to a club. Where will I meet you?'

She shrugged. She did like him, he was fun to be with and no one had bought her flowers or asked to take her for a meal before. Perhaps it was time she started to enjoy herself a bit. She hardly ever went out. 'You choose, after all it will be your special day.'

He squeezed her hand and smiled. 'It will be special now. Next Tuesday and I'll meet you at seven o'clock where we met today at the bottom of Bold Street.'

'I'll be there, Danny. I promise,' she replied, preparing to gather up her handbag.

He got to his feet. 'Are you going home now?'

She nodded.

'I'll walk you to the bus stop. Then I've got someone to see.'

He paid the bill and then held the door open for her and as they walked out into the street he caught her hand and held it. She smiled shyly at him, thinking that, unlike Emer, she'd never had a boyfriend but maybe it was the right time and maybe he was the right one?

Chapter Twenty-One

❦

A NGELA HAD WONDERED WHAT to buy him for a birthday present and had sought the advice of George and Tom. They had said not to go for a tie as it was a well-known fact that when it came to choosing ties girls were useless, even if they were fashion designers, and lads liked to choose their own. But what about a trendy set of cufflinks? Most of the jewellers were stocking a good range now and would even wrap them for you, so she had settled on a pair in silver shaped like dice with coloured stones set into them.

The fact that she was going on a date caused a stir of excitement when she confided in Roz that night. Roz's own romance with Stefan had been short-lived but they were still friends.

'Well, it's about time you went out and enjoyed yourself. What's he like?' Roz demanded, applying Vaseline to her eyelashes which she swore made them grow thicker overnight but which her mother said entirely ruined the pillowcases.

'Don't you remember him? He was at that Valentine's dance.'

'That was ages ago and there were dozens of lads there!' Roz protested.

'He's tall with blond hair and blue eyes and he has his own business. Danny Fielding is his name.'

'Oh, that one. I do vaguely remember him. Didn't he give you his business card?'

Angela nodded. 'He has his own flat in Faulkner Square.'

Roz swivelled around on the dressing stool and frowned. 'It used to be a very posh area but now it's terribly run down. He hasn't asked you to go there, has he?'

Angela looked a little perturbed. 'No. I'm meeting him at the bottom of Bold Street.'

'Oh, I suppose if he doesn't live at home he can't afford to pay a high rent and pay all his bills too. I wonder why he doesn't live at home?' Roz pondered.

Angela smiled at her. 'Not everyone does, Roz. I haven't lived at home since I was six years old. He's probably got a reason.'

Roz bit her lip. 'Oh, God! Trust me to put my big foot in it.'

'It's OK, honestly. If I get a chance I'll ask him.'

'No, don't. He might think you're prying,' Roz advised.

'Well, maybe not on a first date,' Angela agreed.

Roz brightened. 'What are you going to wear? If you are going for a meal and then on to a club it better be something that will look good for both and still make you stand out in the crowd.'

'I don't think I really want to stand out.'

Roz had wagged a finger at her playfully. 'You've got your reputation to think of. You can't be seen to be looking "streelish", as you say.'

They had gone through Angela's wardrobe, which, considering she made her living from clothes, wasn't exactly overflowing. Roz had discarded three outfits as not at all suitable and they had finally settled on a scarlet trouser suit made of a cotton and Terylene mix. It was a shade that suited Angela's colouring. The trousers were flared at the bottom and the tunic top was hip length and had three-quarter sleeves that also flared at the cuff.

'If you wear some chunky beads and big earrings it will look great. Our Sal's got just the thing, she won't mind lending you them. That material won't crease when you are sitting to have the meal and it will be cool enough for a club. They get really warm and you don't want anything that's going to stick to you. What shoes will you wear?'

'I've got those black ones with the low heel and the big petersham bow on the front and I've got my black bag.'

Roz nodded her approval. 'Let me do your make-up. I'm getting really good at it – all those tips from the professionals – and treat yourself to a manicure and a good trim.'

Angela agreed. Her hair did need trimming and she would have her nails painted with a frosted polish. 'But no false eyelashes! Sure, I don't want one falling off into my dinner and making me look a right eejit!'

Roz raised her eyes to the ceiling. 'You're not dressed without eyelashes!'

'Maybe *you're* not but I'll be just grand with mascara. Now I want to get this letter finished to Emer.'

'She'll be that excited you've finally got yourself a boyfriend that I shouldn't be at all surprised if she persuades Dinny to let her phone you, just to see how it went.'

It was Angela's turn to raise her eyes to the ceiling. 'He'd never agree to that. It would cost an absolute fortune!'

*

Again he was waiting for her. 'You look gorgeous!'

She smiled her thanks, glad now that she had taken such care with her appearance. 'Happy birthday!'

He took her hand. 'It's going to be the best birthday I've had for years. I've booked a table for us at a really nice Italian restaurant just around the corner. It's very trendly but it won't be too crowded at this time so we won't have the evening spoiled by noisy crowds.'

She was relieved to hear that for she had never been to a restaurant before and was a little apprehensive. The last thing she wanted was to make a show of herself in front of crowds of people.

It was lovely, she thought as they were ushered to their table. It was small and intimate and not very brightly lit. There were flowers on the table and a candle in a raffia-covered wine bottle. On the walls were posters of different Italian cities, Rome, Venice, Florence and Milan. There were plenty of other couples dining but the waiter had considerately seated them on the far side of the room where it was a little less crowded.

She let him choose for her because, after reading the menu, she had to admit to him that it was a bit daunting, she'd not tried Italian food before. He said that the spaghetti carbonara would be a good choice and that he would have the same and they'd start with some garlic bread with mozzarella. He ordered a bottle of Chianti.

When the waiter disappeared she took the cufflinks from her bag and passed them to him. 'I bought you these, I hope you like them, but if you don't they said they would change them.'

He looked surprised but pleased. 'I didn't expect you to go and buy me a present.'

'Well, it *is* your birthday and you are treating me to a great night out.'

He opened the box and then reached over and took her hand. 'I think you have great taste so I won't be changing them. In fact I'll treasure them. Only wear them on special occasions, like.'

The waiter appeared with the wine and after Danny had tasted it and nodded his approval, their glasses were filled.

Danny raised his glass. 'Let's have a toast. To a great night and my special girl. You will be "my girl", Angie, won't you?'

She nodded, smiling at him with sparkling eyes. 'No one has ever called me Angie before.'

He raised her hand to his lips and kissed it gently. 'I'm always going to call you that. It will be my name for you and no one else is going to be allowed to use it.'

She had a wonderful night. They talked for ages over the meal and he frequently made her laugh with his anecdotes about his fellow Liverpudlians, especially over the rivalry between the two football teams. The wine brought a flush to her cheeks and she felt a little light-headed: she steadfastly refused a second glass. When they had finished the meal the waiter brought them each a little glass of Sambuca which had a coffee bean floating on the top. It just put the final touch to the occasion, Danny said with a nod of thanks to the waiter. After that they walked to the Pink Parrot club where he insisted on buying her a cocktail.

'You'll be after having to carry me home at this rate, Danny. If I have a drink it's usually only a shandy or a glass of lager and lime.' She had laughed and had resolutely refused to have anything else to drink. The club was quite dimly lit but above the chrome and glass bar was a bright pink neon image of a parrot on a swing. The dance floor was quite small and was made of thick glass blocks illuminated from beneath and was already half full of couples dancing to the music of the live trio dressed entirely in black. They had danced until midnight when she said she really must go or the last bus would have gone and besides she had to work tomorrow.

He walked her to the bus stop with his arm firmly around her. 'Have you enjoyed yourself?' he asked as they reached the bus shelter, which was deserted at this hour on a Tuesday night.

'I have so. It's been a really great night, Danny, thank you.'

He took her in his arms and bent to kiss her and despite herself she flinched and pulled back a little.

'What's wrong? What's the matter? You're not afraid of me, are you? I won't hurt you, Angie.'

She looked up into his eyes. 'Sure, I know that, Danny. It . . . it's just that I had a bad experience . . . once. Oh, I'm just being an eejit!' She put her arms around his neck. She really liked him and she wasn't going to let old memories ruin the night.

He kissed her gently on the cheek. 'I won't rush you. I promise.'

'I . . . I'll tell you about it one day,' she promised, resting her cheek against his. She wanted him to kiss her, she was certain it wouldn't be at all like the time Liam had grabbed her. And she certainly didn't want to lose him.

'That's OK. You tell me when you're ready. When can I see you again?'

She was relieved. 'At the weekend?'

'Great. I'm picking my car up on Friday. Shall I come and call for you and we'll go off and test it out?'

'That would be great. I live at eighteen Yew Tree Road, it's in Walton, further down than the hospital, past

Dunlop's, on the left-hand side. Opposite the library.'

He kissed her cheek again. 'I'll find it. About eight? Here comes the bus, so goodnight, my special girl!'

She kissed him back, on the cheek, and then boarded the bus which was virtually empty.

He watched her and waved as the bus pulled away. He was disappointed and wondered what kind of experience she'd had. He shrugged; he knew better than to force things. She'd come round in her own good time.

She sat thinking about him as she travelled home. He had been so considerate and generous. She knew many lads would have become irritated at being rebuffed like that and she was angry with herself. She really, really liked him and hoped it would become something stronger than just liking as she got to know him better. Why had she stiffened and pulled away like that? She had sworn to herself that she was not going to be a victim. Next time she saw him she would tell him just what had happened; he deserved an explanation.

Roz was still up when she got in. She was wearing a lilac-flowered cotton shortie dressing gown over her baby doll pyjamas, her hair set in big rollers. 'I wouldn't have been able to sleep so I didn't go to bed. Well, tell me everything!'

'It was a great night. We went to Signor Rico's and had Italian food and a bottle of wine, then we went to the Pink Parrot and I had a Blue Lagoon cocktail.'

'Was that fellow trying to get you drunk?' Roz asked pointedly.

'Not at all! He's not like that! Anyway I refused to have anything else. I saw the price of them and he'd spent enough on me already. We danced for the rest of the night.'

'And did he like his birthday present?'

209

'He did so. And then he walked me to the bus stop.'

'And did he kiss you?'

'Honestly, Roz!' Angela protested. 'Wasn't it only a first date?'

'So? You do fancy him, don't you?'

'Yes. He's really nice.'

'I'd have been mortified if a lad I fancied and had spent a great evening with hadn't kissed me goodnight.'

'He did. On the cheek.'

Roz rolled her eyes. 'Oh, very proper.'

Angela laughed, taking off her shoes and Sal's earrings which had started to pinch her earlobes. 'He really is very considerate,' she said, thinking of her reluctance to let him kiss her properly.

'Didn't you want him to snog you then?'

Angela nodded. 'Shall we drop the subject of kissing?' She was tired and didn't want Roz probing any further.

Roz shrugged. 'Are you seeing him again?'

'He's calling here for me on Saturday night. He's bought a car so we're going for a test drive.'

'God! He must be doing well. There are not many lads of his age with their own car.'

'I know. It's a Mini.'

'Mam will be made up he's calling for you. You know what she's like about seeing who we are going out with. If she likes him he'll be expected to come here all the time, like Harry, our Sal's current fellow.'

'I know and I'm sure she'll like him.'

Roz frowned. 'Don't go telling her he's got his own flat.'

Angela was puzzled. 'Why not?'

'She'll think he'll be taking you back there and seducing you. Lizzie went out with a lad once who was in lodgings and she went mad. There were that many rows that in the end

Lizzie gave him up. She said it wasn't worth the hassle and besides she didn't like him that much.'

Angela looked thoughtful. 'Surely she trusted Lizzie?'

'That was our Lizzie's main argument.' Roz got to her feet but there was a mischievous smile on her lips. 'Anyway, if he wants to seduce you he can do it just as well in a car. Be a bit cramped and awkward though. Not that I've any experience, you understand,' she added grinning.

Angela made a swipe at her, laughing. 'Stop giving out about being seduced! I've no intention of letting anyone go *that* far and if your mam hears you we'll both be in trouble.'

'I was only joking. Come on, we both need our beauty sleep, it's nearly one in the morning.'

As they both went up the narrow back staircase, Angela clutching her shoes and bag, Roz giggled in the darkness.

'Now what's amusing you?' Angela whispered.

'I can't wait to see this Danny Fielding and his car.'

'Roz Henderson, if you go making a holy show of me I'll not speak to you again, I swear!' Angela threatened.

'Oh, you know I won't,' Roz replied but she was very curious to meet Danny Fielding. She was determined to find out just what he did that gave him the means to buy a car but yet rent a flat in a very run-down part of the city.

Chapter Twenty-Two

·---·••·---·

By the time Saturday arrived Roz had succeeded in making Angela nervous.

'Honestly, Roz you've gone on so much about Danny this week that now everyone can't wait to meet him,' she said, biting her lip as she checked her appearance in the mirror in her bedroom. She had decided to wear a pair of white trousers with flared bottoms, a navy and white striped top and a short navy jacket.

'So, what's wrong with that? Anyway, Dad and the lads are more interested in seeing his car. Especially our Tom, he wants one, he's saving like mad. Here, tie this to the handle of your bag, it finishes off the outfit.' She held out a red chiffon scarf with white spots on it.

'You'll make him feel desperately embarrassed, as if he's being inspected to see if he's suitable or not.'

Roz looked thoughtful. 'I suppose he is, but not in any kind of awful way. He won't be interrogated. He'll be made welcome, you know he will.'

Angela sighed; she knew Roz was right.

When finally Danny arrived and Angela ushered him in to meet everyone she was relieved that he didn't seem to mind at all.

'Lovely house you've got here, Mrs Henderson. I hope you don't mind me calling for Angie? I've just got a new car so I'm going to take her to Southport.'

Lydia Henderson beamed at him. He was pleasant and had nice manners. 'An evening like this is perfect for a drive to the seaside. There should be a breeze on the Promenade there.'

Roz had raised her eyebrows to Lizzie hearing him call Angela 'Angie'. Roz was quite impressed by the way he was dressed. Well-cut trousers, narrow fitting and without turn-ups and black winkle-picker shoes. A striped pink and white short-sleeved shirt and a fine-knit white sweater was carefully slung over his shoulder. He dressed well and definitely had style.

'Mind if I have a look at the Mini?' Tom asked, unable to contain himself.

'Sure. Come on out, have a sit inside, get the feel of it. They're great cars. Handle really well,' Danny offered.

'Don't be out there talking for hours, the lad's come to take Angela for a drive, not stand out there nattering to you,' his mother chided.

The three lads, accompanied by Mr Henderson, went out to inspect the car and Mrs Henderson advised Angela to go with them. 'Once those two lads start on about cars and engines they'll have him there all night,' she warned.

'I'll go with you and physically drag them back inside if necessary,' Roz offered.

Danny was visibly proud and pleased as the two boys enthusiastically admired his latest acquisition and after answering innumerable questions about horsepower, revs, mileage to the gallon, manoeuvrability and the like he at last extricated himself and opened the door of the smart little red car for Angela.

'I'll have her back safe and sound before midnight,' Danny promised Mr Henderson before sliding easily into the driving seat.

Roz waved as they pulled away. She hadn't had a chance to ask him anything. 'Did he say what kind of a business he has, Dad? He must be making good money from it to be able to afford to buy a brand new car.'

'He said he didn't pay cash for it but he did pay a fair bit as a deposit, to reduce the monthly payments, but he was a bit evasive about the business. "Sort of import–export" was how he described it. Still, no doubt we'll learn more in the future. He seems a decent-enough lad though.'

Roz nodded. 'She really likes him and I suppose that's the main thing.'

Angela enjoyed the drive although it felt as though they were seated very close to the ground, especially when they came close to a van or a lorry, which seemed to tower over them. Danny had laughed when she'd said that and told her she'd get used to it. They drove along the Marine Drive where the flower beds were a riot of colour. It was a beautiful summer evening and many people were taking advantage of the weather, so they drove to the far end and then parked the car. From here you could see across the wide estuary of the river Ribble to Morecambe and even Blackpool. The tower was clearly visible outlined against the dusky blue of the sky. It was almost deserted at this end and they walked hand in hand towards the marine lake. Danny had said that if she felt like it they would take a stroll along the pier later on and if she felt in a giddy mood they could have a ride on the carousel. If not, they would find somewhere to have a drink then maybe some supper. The sea air always made you hungry.

'You don't have to go spending a fortune on me when we go out, Danny. You work as hard as I do, probably harder, and you've the car to pay for now,' she told him.

'I like to spoil you, Angie. All that studying when you were nursing and now running a business. Someone should spoil you, no one else seems to have done so far.'

She looked thoughtful. She didn't want the evening to end the way the last one had done. 'I suppose my Aunt Mary did, in a way. I went to live with her when I was six. My parents couldn't afford to keep me, that was the excuse, although I often think they didn't want to. They kept the baby that came after me.'

He squeezed her hand sympathetically. 'I know how that feels,' he said quietly.

She looked up at him and saw a hardness in his eyes she'd never seen before. 'You do?'

They sat down on a bench facing the lake and he put his arm around her shoulders. 'I've not told many people this, Angie, I . . . I suppose I feel ashamed of it. I never knew who my father was, he was long gone before I was even born, and my dear ma preferred to doll herself up to the nines and go out drinking and dancing, rather than be stuck at home looking after me. So she left me with my granny. I lived with her until she died when I was seventeen. I loved her, my gran, she was more of a mother to me than *that* one. I don't even know where she is now. That's why I live on my own, in Gran's old place. I've no one else. So you see I do understand how it feels to be rejected and ignored.'

She nodded slowly and leaned her head on his shoulder. 'I'm so sorry, Danny. It . . . it hurts, doesn't it, to know they didn't want you, didn't care about you? I can't think of Mam and Da without bitterness but Aunt Mary was good to me and the Hendersons have taken me into their family and made me feel part of it. I had . . . have three brothers and three sisters and the young one who was the cause of me being given away, but I haven't seen or heard from them for years. I don't know where they are and I missed them.'

He kissed her forehead and when she looked up at him the harsh light had gone from his eyes, replaced by sympathy and understanding. 'At least I had no one else to worry about or take care of, just myself, and I seem to have been doing that for years and years. Gran wasn't in the best of health for as long as I can remember. She was a widow and she'd had a hard life.'

'Do you find it very lonely?' At least she had had her aunt and Emer and now Roz and her family, she thought.

He smiled and shook his head. 'Not really. I've got mates. Some of them I ran the streets with when we were younger, some are more recent friends. And I deal with a lot of people day to day and now I've got you, my special girl.'

She snuggled closer to him, watching the ducks and swans gliding across the flat dark surface of the lake. She was glad he had confided in her; she felt that they shared a bond now, that their pasts had brought them closer. She felt she could tell him anything. 'I . . . I said my aunt was good to me and she was, but . . . but my uncle . . .' She paused and plucked nervously at one of the buttons on his shirt.

He kissed her again on the forehead, his eyes narrowing. So, that was it. The bloody uncle had been interfering with her, the pervert! 'You don't have to tell me, Angie, if you don't want to. If it upsets you.'

'It . . . it didn't start until I was sixteen. Aunt Mary couldn't have children of her own and it seemed to sort of drive them apart. He took to the drink and one night . . .'

217

'There's no need to go into detail. I don't want you dragging up bad memories and getting upset.' He didn't want to know just what the dirty old sod had done to her.

'I didn't let him. I wouldn't give in. The last time I fought him, scratched his face and ran out of the house. I wasn't going to suffer in silence. I was going to tell the doctor I worked for but when I got there I found that his wife had just died. I left after that. Came to Liverpool and the rest you know.'

She had spirit, he thought admiringly. 'Didn't you tell your aunt? Didn't she suspect what was going on?'

Angela shook her head. 'No, she knew nothing and I . . . I couldn't tell her. I just *couldn't*! Only my friend Emer knew but she'd gone to America. I told Father Dwyer after the first time but he didn't believe me. He more or less said I was lying, you would have thought it was all my fault the way he carried on.'

'Bloody priests!' The bitterness was back in his voice. 'What do they know about anything? Always laying down the law, telling you what to do or what not to do. Ours was always coming round wanting to know why I wasn't at Mass or at school. Always upsetting my gran, he was. He knew she had nothing but he was always looking for a handout for some charity. As if the Church hasn't got enough money without taking it from a poor old widow. He came round when she was dying but I chased him out. I bloody told him where to get off. Told him to sling his hook and not come back. I've done all right for myself without anyone's help, advice or interference. I've managed well enough without priests and so can you.'

His revelations had surprised her. 'I didn't know you were a Catholic, you never mentioned it.'

'It's not something I'm all that proud of.'

'So you've lapsed.'

'I think I'd describe myself as more "collapsed".' The old cheerfulness was back in his voice.

'I don't feel bitter towards Father Dwyer, I still go to church, but I hate Liam and I'll never go back. What is there to go back for? Aunt Mary doesn't really approve of the clothes I design. I don't think she really understands how well I've done, how lucky I've been, and as for my mam . . . she probably doesn't even know or care where I am.'

'Ah, let's forget all about the past, Angie. We've got a great future in business, both of us, and now we've got each other. Come on, let's go to one of those posh hotels on the promenade and have a drink to cheer ourselves up.' He pulled her to her feet and they walked towards the promenade with their arms around each other.

They had a drink in the bar of the Clifton Hotel and then they strolled back eating fish and chips from a newspaper. She had laughed as she'd wiped her greasy fingers on his handkerchief. 'If my Aunt Mary could see me she would be giving out to me for "eating with my fingers in the public view", a desperate crime!'

He threw the grease-stained newspaper into a rubbish bin. 'Well, she can't so don't even think about it. You enjoyed them, didn't you?'

'The best I've ever tasted,' she replied, smiling.

'They always taste better eaten in the open air and out of newspaper. We'd better be heading back now or I'll be in trouble for keeping you out late.'

He parked the car further down from the house and out of the direct light from the streetlamp. 'They won't expect me to come in, will they?'

Angela shook her head. 'No. They'll probably be in bed.

Mr and Mrs H. are usually up early even on a Sunday. I have a key.'

He grimaced. 'I like my lie-in on a Sunday morning.'

She sighed. 'I've still got some designs to finish – even on a Sunday.'

He took her in his arms. 'I'm glad we had that talk. We understand each other better now and if you're still upset about . . . *him*, I understand about that too.'

She stroked his cheek and then gently brushed back a lock of blond hair from his forehead. 'I think that now I've told you, it will help. I . . . I want you to kiss me goodnight properly, Danny.'

He kissed her very gently on the lips and she didn't flinch or pull away. It was very, very different, she told herself. He knew all her secrets now, things she hadn't even told Roz. A feeling of pure joy washed over her as she kissed him back and she realised that she was falling in love with him. She trusted him. He wouldn't hurt her. She was his 'special girl'.

Chapter Twenty-Three

⟨———⟩

THEY WENT OUT EVERY Saturday night after that and sometimes on a Sunday evening too. Angela would try to see him on weekdays but often either she would be just too busy or he would have to meet someone to set up or close a business deal. It had been easy to fall in love with him, she often thought. She felt so at ease with him, he was amusing and attentive and he seemed to really understand her. He didn't come to the Hendersons' house as frequently as either Lydia or Bernard would have liked but they had to agree that he treated Angela well, she was happy with him, and that they were both very involved in their careers so time was limited.

Angela and Lizzie had successfully launched their autumn/winter collection and they now had a short breathing space. Angela had completed her designs for next season and Lizzie had everything in hand, except for the material for the lightweight summer coat. Skirts had become even shorter and were being worn with lower-heeled shoes or boots that came up to the knee and handbags were much smaller. They now had competition not only from the big stores but from other boutiques that had opened in the city. It was London that was leading the world on the fashion scene with the boutiques in the King's Road and Carnaby Street constantly setting new trends for both young men and women, something Roz was always reminding them of.

'We're not going to go through all that again, are we? You're not going to live in London, your dad has made that quite clear,' Mrs Henderson said emphatically when Roz once again brought the subject up on a damp February evening when they were grouped around the television set in the kitchen. She felt that her youngest daughter would be easily dazzled by the bright lights and fast life in the capital city; she feared for her wellbeing and her husband was in total agreement with her. Roz was too young; let her grow up a bit. The news had just finished and she had been bemoaning the fact that a loaf of bread had gone up and would now cost one and three pence halfpenny which she thought was scandalous. Bernard Henderson had been more interested in the news that Harold Wilson, the Prime Minister, had called an election for the end of March. Bernard was an avowed Conservative and did not agree at all with most of the policies of the Labour Party and had hopes that they would not be re-elected. The news from Vietnam was always depressing, the Americans didn't seem to be making much headway at all against the Viet Cong even though they had launched a massive offensive last month, he thought.

'But I could earn a fortune down there,' Roz protested.

'And it would cost you a fortune to live down there as well. You'd be no better off,' her father replied, getting up to change the channel. He wanted to see an interview Mary Whitehouse was giving on her campaign to clean up TV, something he agreed was decidedly needed.

'But I'm just not getting any further up here,' Roz persisted stubbornly.

Her mother was losing patience. 'How much further do you want to go? You are never satisfied, Rose. And anyway, aren't you getting a bit too old now? That Twiggy is no more than a child, she looks like a child too, and she seems to be in great demand, judging by all the papers and magazines. It's about time you found yourself a decent lad and settled down.'

This was something Roz definitely did not want to hear. 'Mam, I'm not twenty yet! And speaking of Twiggy, do you know how much she earns? Ten guineas an hour! An *hour*! She might look like a little waif but she's no fool, she's earning a fortune!'

'Fortune or not, until you come of age you'll do as I say, young lady.' Bernard Henderson said firmly.

'Angela's courting, so is Emer and our Sal. In fact she's told me that she and Harry might well be getting engaged in the summer.'

Bernard Henderson shot his wife a warning look and Roz raised her eyebrows as she glanced at Angela. 'Great. A wedding might just take your mind off me. I'll settle down when I'm ready, Mam. At the moment I'm more interested in my career.'

'It seems you can have both these days. Look at Angela,' her mother pointed out.

Angela cast a sympathetic glance at Roz. 'Sure, I'm not exactly thinking of getting married.'

Mrs Henderson looked disappointed. 'Why is that? I thought it was really serious between you and Danny?'

'Can we please have an end to this discussion? I'd like to watch this interview. This woman talks a lot of common sense,' her husband said, irritably leaning forward to turn up the sound.

Roz and Angela had no desire to listen to Mrs Whitehouse's views on television programmes and so went into the front lounge.

'It's freezing in here! Switch that electric fire on,' Roz instructed Angela while she drew the heavy velvet curtains, shutting out the mist of needle-fine rain that was falling outside. Both Sal and Lizzie were out.

'So, you're not intending to marry Danny then? I thought you loved him,' Roz probed, flinging herself down in a chair and draping her long legs encased in opaque black tights over the arm.

'I *do* love him and if he asked me, I would marry him. We get on so well together and we want the same things in life, but he hasn't asked yet. I only said that to divert your mam's attention from you, you eejit!'

Roz was mollified. 'Thanks. I think she's let the cat out of the bag about our Sal and Harry. Sal's not mentioned anything about an engagement to me or our Lizzie as far as I know.'

'Maybe she wanted to tell them first, that's only right.'

'He is a bit of a drip though,' Roz commented drily.

Angela laughed. 'Just because he doesn't dress like a mod? He's training to be an accountant, for heaven's sake, just like Patrick Molloy. They have to be more conservative.'

Roz pulled a face. Emer had finally found a boyfriend her brother approved of. Patrick Molloy was the grandson of Irish immigrants from Sligo, a Catholic and a junior accountant in a large firm. Dinny and Joy were actively encouraging the courtship and Emer had written that she really did like him. He was a bit quiet and serious but very nice just the same and this could be the *real* thing. Only time would tell.

'And isn't that a dead boring job?' Roz continued. 'Still, both our Sal and Emer seem happy enough. They're not going to let me go to London though, that's as plain as the nose on your face. I'll have to wait until I'm twenty-one and that's not for another two years.'

'And you intend to go then?' Angela could see huge rows ahead if Roz persisted with this intention.

Roz hesitated before she nodded. 'I think so but Mam could be right. With the likes of Twiggy coming up, well . . . I'm not getting any younger. It's a very short-lived career and I haven't even had a proper stab at it yet, I'm lucky if I get two guineas an hour. It might well be too late for me when I get to twenty-one. I suppose I started too late.'

Angela couldn't help but grin at Roz's woeful expression. 'You'd think you were positively ancient. You are *young*, you eejit, and we'll go on employing you to model our collections.'

Roz's good humour returned. 'Thanks. Well, I'm not going to go and get myself engaged to some dimwit just to keep Mam happy.'

'I wouldn't be after saying that Harry is a dimwit and she wouldn't want you to get engaged just to please her. You have to spend the rest of your life with whoever you marry.'

Roz sighed. 'I suppose one day I'll meet Mr Right, just as you have. Do you think Emer will end up marrying this Patrick Molloy? He doesn't look too bad, not from the photo she sent you.'

'She will if Dinny and Joy have anything to do with it, and her mam is over the moon apparently. Stopping anyone on the street who will listen. Aunt Mary said in her last letter that she couldn't understand why anyone who obviously had the brains to hold such a position would find anything in common with Emer, who isn't the brightest, God help her. I thought that was a bit harsh of her and a tiny bit jealous but then she always wanted me to do better than Emer.'

Roz cast her eyes to the ceiling. 'What is it with parents that they always want you to do better than any of your friends? I would have thought that your happiness was more important than what kind of a job your "future intended" had or what kind of background he came from. Look at all the rows Emer has had with Dinny in the past over boyfriends he didn't consider suitable.'

Angela looked thoughtful. 'I suppose he just wanted what was best for Emer and, anyway, your parents don't put too many constraints on you.'

'Except when it comes to moving to London,' Roz muttered resentfully.

'If you're after starting on that again, I'm going to bed!' Angela warned.

Roz shrugged and sat up. 'So, do you think Danny will ask you to marry him at some time in the future?'

Angela smiled. 'I hope so.'

'Great, I can be a bridesmaid.'

'You'll be bridesmaid to Sal before me.'

Roz nodded. 'I suppose I will. She might well ask you to design her dress.'

Angela shook her head. 'No. I wouldn't undertake anything as important or special as that. Sal is quite "conservative", for want of a better word, I think she'll go to one of the big bridal shops. And don't you go suggesting I do it, she might feel obliged to agree and I don't want that.'

'Oh, well, you can design your own dress, when he gets around to asking you. Would you go and live in that flat?'

'Don't you think it's a bit soon to be after asking me things like that?' Angela replied, avoiding the necessity of a direct answer. She had been to his flat once. It wasn't even a flat, she thought, it was just one room in a big old dilapidated house. She had tried not to show how taken aback she was. The area was very run down, as were all the houses in the square, which overlooked a small park that was overgrown, neglected and full of litter. The paint on the doors and window frames was peeling; panes of glass were broken and cracked, covered over with pieces of cardboard. The hallways, which had once been very grand with intricate plasterwork on the ceilings and cornices – now stained and with chunks missing – were dark and musty and smelled of damp and stale cooking and other even less savoury odours. Some of the spindles on the banister rail were missing and the stairs were devoid of any covering. She hadn't expected him to live somewhere like that and it had been hard to hide her shocked expression. His room had a big, ornate marble fireplace, the chimney flue of which had been boarded up, now a two-bar electric fire stood in the hearth. The carpet that covered most of the floor was old and threadbare, its edges frayed. A single divan stood against one wall, covered with a faded green candlewick bedspread. There was an ancient sofa with sagging springs and one chair. A battered wardrobe and chest of drawers stood against another wall and in the corner by the window there was a gas stove, a small sink with a wooden draining board curtained around the base with grubby and stained red and white gingham. A geyser for heating hot water was attached precariously to the wall above the sink and a shelf holding a few pans and dishes was fastened to the wall alongside it. Newspapers, magazines and what looked like a pile of bills were strewn across a modern coffee table and on a very rickety little table stood a record player with a pile of LPs stacked on a shelf underneath. She had tried not to make any kind of comment at all. He was always neat, clean and smart in his appearance, he didn't appear to be short of money, and he had his car, so she had never expected him to live like this. But then she had

227

remembered what he had said about his gran. She had been a poor widow who had had a hard life, she had probably lived here for years and years and he hadn't seen the need to replace all these old things, most of which had obviously been hers. But no, she certainly was not going to go and live there when she married him.

Mrs Henderson stuck her head around the door. 'Phone for you, Angela. It's Danny. He apologised for it being late but he says it's quite important.'

She went out into the hall and picked up the receiver. 'Hello.'

'Angie, sorry it's late but are you still looking for material for those summer coats?'

She frowned. 'I am so. Lizzie did get some samples but they were too heavy and not the quality we were looking for.' They had wanted a very fine wool mix in pale blue and pale pink for the short, semi-fitted coats.

'I think I can get you just the thing and at the right price. Would you be interested?' He sounded brisk and businesslike.

She considered it. He'd never made an offer like this before. 'I'd have to see it first, Danny.'

'Of course. I wouldn't expect you to buy something you'd not seen. I've got some samples. Could you come up here tomorrow night? I'd have to have a decision quickly as there is another buyer interested.'

She bit her lip. She was torn between the desire to see samples of a material they really did need and reluctance at going to that neighbourhood on a dark winter night. 'Could you not bring the samples here, Danny? It would be a great help if you could.'

'Sorry, Angie, but it's impossible. My contact says he needs an on-the-spot decision, he was reluctant to let me have samples at all but I managed to persuade him. About seven? I'll have to go now, luv, there's the pips and I've no more change. See you tomorrow.'

She replaced the receiver. He'd been calling from a public telephone in a pub or club, there had been noise in the background. She sighed. She would just have to go. He was only thinking of her so she really shouldn't be so reluctant to make the journey.

Chapter Twenty-Four

LIZZIE HAD BEEN DOUBTFUL when she'd told her of Danny's offer.

'We never buy material like that, we always buy from reputable firms,' she'd reminded Angela. 'Not that I'm suggesting that Danny isn't reputable,' she added, seeing a flash of hurt in Angela's eyes.

'I know but we haven't been able to find what we need at the right price. He's trying to do us a favour so the least I can do is go and have a look at it. It might not be suitable either.'

Lizzie had nodded but she couldn't understand why Danny needed an 'on-the-spot' decision. Surely his 'contacts' as he called them could have given them a day or so? Their suppliers sent samples and didn't expect them to order immediately; there was always time for deliberation.

'There is someone else interested in buying it,' Angela had explained.

Roz hadn't been happy about her going to Faulkner Square at night and had said so. 'It's a terrible neighbour-hood, he should get out of there. It's a wonder his car hasn't been stolen. You take care, Angela, and don't be too late leaving.'

'I will. I'm not a child not fit to be let out on my own,' she'd replied with more confidence than she'd felt.

She got a bus into town and then one that fortunately put her off on the corner of the square. Even though it was bitterly cold some of the doors to the old houses stood wide open and groups of children and older boys and girls sat on the steps leading up to the doors. They looked in her direction and fell silent, nudging each other. She was too well dressed for this neighbourhood. She hastened her steps and was relieved as she climbed the stairs to his bedsit.

He opened the door, dressed in jeans and a pale blue sweater, and kissed her, drawing her inside.

He had tidied up a bit since her last visit, she noticed, and the room was at least warm if not very brightly lit.

'Sorry, sweetheart, to drag you all the way up here on a night like this but it couldn't be helped. Here, let me take your coat.'

She slipped off the short cherry-red wool coat and the matching baker boy cap. Underneath she wore a black and white hound's-tooth-check pinafore dress and a black ribbed polo-neck jumper. She stretched out her hands to the glow from the electric fire. He'd carefully hung her coat on a hanger which he'd then hung from the picture rail.

'Sit down, sweetheart. Would you like something to warm you up? I've got a drop of cherry brandy somewhere.'

She sat down on the sofa and smiled up at him. 'No, thanks. Maybe later. I'd better have a look at the samples first.'

'Right, let's get the business out of the way first.' He crossed to the chest of drawers and brought out two folded pieces of material and passed them to her.

She spread them out across her knees and rubbed them carefully between her forefinger and thumb. They were of a very good quality and just the right weight. 'They feel like pure wool.'

He'd seated himself beside her. 'The best. One hundred per cent merino.'

She frowned. 'That's expensive, Danny. Very expensive. I have to keep my costs down, especially now that there is so much competition. I was really looking for a wool mix that would be a reasonable price.' She held the pale blue sample up; in the dim light it was impossible to see the exact shade. 'Have you a brighter light, Danny?'

He brought a table lamp over. 'Is that better? You did say pale pink and blue. My contact says you can have it for three and six a yard and he has enough for you to make the quantity you need, but I'm certain with a bit of bargaining I can get him down to three bob a yard.'

It was a very low price for material as expensive as this. 'How can he afford to accept such a low price?'

'Because he has contacts abroad who buy on his behalf and then bring the stuff in. That cuts out all the middlemen.'

She was still uncertain. 'And when could I have the order delivered?'

'Tomorrow, if you like. I'd arrange to bring it to the workrooms. Oh, and his terms are strictly cash on delivery.'

She bit her lip, still undecided. Such a fast delivery was very tempting, as was the price, and cash wasn't really a problem. The shades seemed to be all right but she wished she could have seen them in daylight.

'He really does need an answer tonight, Angie. I promised I'd ring him later on. It's good stuff at a great price and he's another two buyers ready to snap it up if we refuse it,' he urged, a note of apology in his voice.

At last she nodded. 'Right. Tell him I'll take it if it can be delivered tomorrow.'

He smiled broadly at her and kissed her on the cheek. 'I'll be there with it myself by lunchtime, promise. Now, will we have a drink to celebrate our first joint business venture? It could be the start of something that will benefit us both.'

She drank the sweet liqueur slowly. She didn't really like it, it was rather sickly, but she didn't want to hurt his feelings. 'It's a weight off my mind, Danny, that it is. We were getting worried that if we couldn't get that material soon we'd have to drop the coat from the collection. We're already in production with everything else.'

He put his arm around her and drew her to him. 'I don't want you to worry about anything like that ever again. If you're having problems just let me know and I'll sort something out. Now, no more shop talk tonight, sweetheart.'

His kisses became more and more passionate and he slid his hand down and caressed her breast. She felt a surge of passion. She shouldn't be encouraging him, it wasn't right or fair, and yet she didn't want him to stop. His hand moved down to the hemline of her skirt and he caressed the inside of her thigh then moved upwards and she felt almost weak.

'Stay, Angie, sweetheart? Stay the night and let me love you? I *do* love you, you know that,' he whispered.

With a huge effort she pulled away from him. 'No. No, Danny, I . . . I can't. I'm sorry . . .'

He looked hurt and disappointed. 'You don't love me?'

'I do! Honestly and truly, I do! It's just that . . .' Part of her wanted to stay but her conscience had a stronger voice.

He got to his feet and paced the floor, his hands thrust deep into the pockets of his jeans. 'You're not still clinging on to what the Church teaches, are you? I told you we could both manage quite well without all that nonsense and besides, young people do what they want to now. People don't look down their noses at you the way they used to.'

She gazed up at him pleadingly. She wanted him to understand. 'It's got nothing to do with all . . . that.'

He sat down beside her again and took her hand. 'Then what is it? I won't let anything happen to you. I'll take care, take precautions. You won't get pregnant. The last thing either of us needs right now is a baby.'

She shook her head. That wasn't what she had meant at all and she still wasn't sure about contraception. 'I didn't mean that, Danny.'

He was becoming impatient. She was just being a tease. There was a name for girls like that and it wasn't a very nice one. 'Then what is it? If you love me and I love you and I've promised to be a careful . . . ?'

She was choosing her words carefully; she really didn't want to hurt him. 'I do love you, Danny, but I feel I want to wait until I'm ready . . .'

'You mean "married". Why don't you just say it?'

There was a hard note in his voice and it upset her. 'I'm not trying to force you or trap you into marrying me, truly I'm not! I feel I'm still too young for something as serious but I'm not ready for . . . that. It's got nothing to do with whether the Church says it's right or wrong, it's the way *I* feel. And I couldn't let the Hendersons down, I just *couldn't*.' It was the truth, she thought. How could she face them? She would feel so ashamed.

'So you think more of them than you do of me?' He was openly bitter.

'No! Oh, Danny, it's not a matter of choosing between you or them. If I stayed here with you they would be worried, they would know what I was doing and it would upset them and I respect and admire them too much to disappoint them like that. I do love you, but please, can't we . . . wait?'

He leaned forward, his head in his hands. 'It's a lot to ask, Angie.'

She touched his shoulder gently. 'I know, Danny. I do love you.'

He turned and she was so relieved to see him smile even if it was wryly. 'I know, sweetheart. I shouldn't rush you.'

Suddenly she realised what he meant. 'It's got nothing to do with Liam Murphy! This . . . You are so different . . . so special.'

He nodded slowly. 'Let's not talk about it any more. I think there's still a drop left in the bottle.'

She shook her head. 'You finish it off. I'd better be going. I don't want to be out too late.'

He leaned over and kissed her cheek. 'If you're sure?'

She nodded. She didn't trust herself to stay any longer.

He got up and fetched her coat and helped her on with it. 'I'll walk you to the bus stop then I'll go and make that phone call.'

When the bus arrived he kissed her goodnight and promised he'd see her tomorrow – with the material. 'Lunchtime, Angie.'

She gave him a quick hug. 'I'll be waiting, Danny, and thanks for being so understanding.'

The bus moved off and he walked quickly away in the direction of the nearest phone box.

She sat deep in thought as the bus moved through the cold, dark streets towards the city centre. She felt a little disappointed that he hadn't asked her to marry him even though at this precise moment she didn't feel ready to rush into marriage. She would have felt better if he had suggested they get engaged, then they could have planned their future.

In say a year or eighteen months they could have got married, had a lovely wedding and found somewhere decent to live. She would have been happy to do that. She didn't want it to be a Register Office affair with herself in an ordinary suit or dress and then back to that terrible bedsit. She wanted to be married in a church wearing a long white wedding dress and veil with Roz and Lizzie and Sal as bridesmaids and Mr and Mrs Henderson looking pleased and proud and maybe even Aunt Mary coming over for the occasion. She wanted to do things properly. She didn't want a hole-in-the-corner affair just so that they could make love. Surely that wasn't the sole reason for getting married? It was spending time together, sharing hopes and dreams and the everyday things. Planning a future; caring for each other without selfishness. Even though she was part of this modern generation and was completely comfortable with the music and the fashion and many of the new ways of thinking, there were some things she couldn't bring herself to accept. She didn't want to lose him but she didn't want to compromise the things that were important to her: self-respect, the respect of people she was fond of and, if she were totally honest, the teachings of her Church, even though she might not agree with all of them.

She felt depressed and anxious when she at last arrived home. Lizzie, Roz and Mrs Henderson were up.

Lydia Henderson got to her feet. 'I feel relieved now you're in, Angela. I'll go up to bed. Don't you girls stay up too late.'

'Well? Did you agree to take the material?' Lizzie asked.

Angela nodded. 'It's just what we wanted in both pink and blue. Danny is going to deliver it himself tomorrow lunchtime.'

Lizzie smiled. 'Great! The sooner we get started the

better.' She noticed that Angela didn't seem to be quite as enthusiastic as herself. 'What's wrong? Do we have to pay more than expected?'

Angela sat down in an easy chair and began to pull off her boots. 'No. The price is very good.'

Lizzie looked quizzically at Roz, who shrugged. 'Have you had a row with him?' Roz probed.

Angela sighed heavily. 'Not a row exactly. Just a bit of a disagreement. He . . . he wanted me to stay the night.'

Roz looked a bit taken aback. Of course she knew lots of girls who went to bed with their boyfriends and a couple who indulged in one-night stands but Angela wasn't so easy-going. 'God! What did you say?'

'I told him I couldn't,' she replied flatly.

'And then I suppose he got a cob on and said you couldn't possibly love him otherwise you'd agree?' Lizzie succinctly summed up the situation.

Angela felt weary. 'Something like that.'

'That's as old as the hills. They all try that one,' Lizzie said disparagingly.

'Did he then say it would be all right because you know he's going to marry you – one day?' Roz asked but then, seeing the expression on Angela's face, she carried on: 'They're all the same! They use the same worn-out old clichés and think we'll be fool enough to fall for them!' As soon as she'd said it she could have bitten her tongue. Angela's face crumpled and tears sprang up in her eyes.

Lizzie glared at her sister. 'Oh, don't take it to heart, Angela. I bet he came round in the end?'

Angela nodded and wiped her eyes. 'I tried to explain as best I could that I do love him but I just couldn't do something like that.'

'Of course not. You're a decent girl and he should respect

that. Don't worry about it,' Roz advised, wondering if he had in fact said he'd marry Angela.

Angela tried to take some comfort from her words while Lizzie hoped that he wasn't going to let them down. Was he a fly-by-night they wouldn't see hide nor hair of again – nor their material?

Chapter Twenty-Five

LIZZIE WAS GREATLY RELIEVED when at twelve-thirty Danny appeared driving a small white van. Angela too was relieved to see him for in the dark hours of the night she had been overcome by fear and doubt. Did he really love her? she'd asked herself over and over. What if he didn't and had only wanted her for one thing? Because she had refused would she never see him again? She had woken this morning with a headache.

'Right on time, as promised!' he said cheerily, grinning at them both. 'And how is my special girl this morning?'

'She's got a headache. I've told her she worries too much but now we've got the material we can get going.' Lizzie hurried over to inspect their purchases.

'It's all here,' he informed them, drawing a long roll wrapped in paper from the back of the van.

Lizzie tore some of the paper away, revealing the powder-blue fine wool. 'That's exactly the colour we wanted. Will you bring it all inside, Danny, please?'

'You see, he's all sweetness and light this morning,' she

241

whispered to Angela as they went into the workroom.

Angela smiled with pure relief, wondering why she had worried herself sick all night.

Danny didn't seem to be in a great hurry and inspected the workrooms thoroughly, asking questions and nodding in agreement at the replies.

Angela took him into the office and handed him an envelope. 'There we are, cash on delivery, and thanks again, Danny. You've saved the day.'

He put the envelope into his pocket. 'Are you too busy to come to the pictures tomorrow night? *Darling* with Julie Christie is on at the Gaumont.'

'I've been wanting to see that. I'd love to go.'

'I'll meet you outside at seven and we can go for a drink afterwards. I'd better get back now and pay my man.' He patted his pocket and kissed her on the cheek. 'See you at seven, sweetheart, and don't forget if there is anything else I can help you with, just ask.'

Lizzie had overheard the last of this conversation. 'We might just take him up on that, that wool is gorgeous. Certainly a bargain and it would be a godsend if he could get other materials at those prices. So, where are you off to then with him?'

'The cinema tomorrow night.'

Lizzie smiled at her. 'See. Just like old times. He was just trying it on. They all do.'

Angela nodded. 'I suppose so but I'm definitely not going back to that bedsit – ever. I don't want to go through all that again.'

They were both very pleased to see the coats finally in production and that evening as they described the material to Sal she said they were to save a pale pink one for her.

'I'll need something smart for June,' she informed them.

'Going somewhere special?' Roz probed with an innocent expression on her face.

'You know I'm getting engaged to Harry, Roz. Mam said she'd let it slip,' Sal replied.

Roz grinned. 'We weren't sure if we were supposed to mention it. Congratulations. Can I be a bridesmaid?'

Sal tutted. 'Honestly, Roz, give us time to catch our breath. We don't intend to get married until next year at the earliest. We've got to save up for the deposit on a house. But, yes, I intended to ask you and Lizzie and Angela to be bridesmaids and Harry's sister of course.'

'You really don't have to have me, Sal. I'm not family and I'll understand,' Angela said.

'Nonsense! Of course you are family,' Sal said firmly. 'And I would really like you to design my dress.'

Angela was delighted. 'Oh, Sal, that's great! I thought you'd go to one of the big bridal shops. I didn't expect you to ask me, I told Roz that.'

'She did,' Roz confirmed.

'Why go to one of those places when we have such a talented designer in the family?' Sal had genuinely not considered buying a dress from a shop.

'I won't be after disappointing you, Sal. I've plenty of time to come up with lots of ideas,' Angela promised.

Waiting outside the Gaumont Cinema the following evening it was bitterly cold and frost was already forming on the pavements. There was a queue but it was gradually getting smaller. She wore the cherry-red coat but with black trousers and a black sleeveless tunic and red polo-neck jumper under it. She was glad she had dressed warmly but her feet were beginning to feel very chilly indeed. She started to walk up and down, looking at the posters on the cinema walls. It was unusual for him to be late. She hoped he wouldn't be long. He must have been delayed, she thought a little irritably; her feet were numb. She checked her watch; it was almost fifteen minutes past seven. The programme started at half past and she hated going in late, disturbing people by having to push past to the seats the usherette indicated with her torch. She peered anxiously along the road but there was no sign of him.

By eight o'clock she realised he wasn't coming and walked back towards the bus stop. She felt utterly miserable. He'd never stood her up before. She was freezing cold and tears stung her eyes. She wouldn't believe that he had deliberately left her standing there or even worse that she would never see him again. No, there had to be an explanation. But why couldn't he have got word to her? He could have phoned the box office, a little voice in her head pointed out, but she resolutely silenced it.

When she arrived home she could hear voices coming from the kitchen. They had visitors, she surmised, and the last thing she wanted to do was to have to make pleasant conversation with friends of Mr and Mrs Henderson. She took off her coat and hung it in the cloakroom and then went upstairs to her bedroom. She'd just sat down on the edge of the bed to take off her boots when Roz stuck her head around the door.

'I thought I heard you come in.'

'I'm frozen to the bone, so I am. He didn't turn up,' she informed her friend dejectedly.

Roz came and sat beside her. 'And I know why, Angela. I think you'd better come downstairs with me.'

Angela looked at her questioningly, a puzzled frown creasing her forehead. 'Why? Oh, Roz, nothing dreadful has happened to him, has it?' she asked, panic rising up in her.

'He hasn't had an accident in that car?' She had a vision of him lying in a hospital bed and she shivered. She clutched Roz's arm. 'He . . . he's not . . . ?'

'No. Nothing like that, although *that* would be favourable in the present circumstances,' she finished cuttingly.

'What circumstances? Roz, stop talking in riddles. What's happened?' Angela pleaded.

Roz looked at her with pity in her eyes. She didn't want to tell her but it wouldn't be fair to let the news come from strangers. Poor Angela was going to be devastated. 'That material was stolen. The police are downstairs. They've arrested him and the man he got it from.'

Angela couldn't believe it. She stared at Roz in horror. 'No!'

'It's true. They've been watching them both. They saw you with him the night before last. I thought I should tell you rather than you have to learn of it in front of everyone. But we'd better go down now. They were waiting for you to get back, prepared to stay here half the night if needs be.' What she hadn't told Angela was that she could be arrested too, for receiving stolen goods. Her father had been horrified to learn this and had argued strenuously that Angela had known nothing about it. That she was running a legitimate and reputable business and wouldn't be so foolish as to compromise everything she had worked so hard for by knowingly buying stolen material. They had listened to him seriously but still wanted to interview her themselves.

Angela followed her downstairs in a daze. She couldn't believe this was really happening. Danny *arrested*!

In the kitchen Lydia and Bernard Henderson were sitting struggling to believe what had happened. Lizzie was standing with her back to the dresser, her face white with shock.

'Angela has just come in. She's been waiting outside the

Gaumont for him and when he didn't turn up she came home. I've told her what's happened,' Roz announced.

Angela looked at the two plainclothes policeman with trepidation. They looked like hard, experienced men and she felt they would instinctively know when they were being lied to.

'Miss Angela O'Rourke?' the older of the two asked.

She nodded.

'I'm Detective Sergeant McCauley and this is Detective Constable Armstrong. Sit down.'

She sat at the table opposite him and to her relief Mr Henderson came and sat beside her.

Sergeant McCauley opened a notebook and glanced down at it. Then he looked directly at her. 'You are acquainted with Daniel Fielding of flat three, ten Faulkner Square?'

'I am so. We ... we've been courting for about six months.' The hard grey eyes seemed to bore into her and involuntarily she shivered.

'And you purchased material from him?'

Angela nodded and then informed him of everything that had happened. 'But I swear to God I didn't know it was stolen! I wouldn't have touched it if I'd known. It was the first time we'd ever done something like that. We always buy from wholesalers but I thought he was doing me a favour, helping me out,' she finished.

'You didn't suspect at all? Didn't you think it strange that material of such quality was being sold so cheaply?

'No. I told you what he said when I asked him about that and we ... we needed material desperately. The wholesalers couldn't offer anything at such a price.'

'And now you know why,' came the scathing reply. 'He never mentioned a word about you not knowing the material was stolen. It is a serious crime, Miss O'Rourke, receiving.'

Angela was horrified, realising for the first time that she could be facing criminal charges. She felt physically sick and what made it worse was the fact that he hadn't spoken up for her.

'He must have said something! He wouldn't do this to me! He wouldn't let me be . . . arrested!' she pleaded. He *must* have done, she thought desperately.

The sergeant shook his head. 'Not a word. We've been watching him for quite a while and a few of his associates. Oh, he thinks he's quite a clever lad, does Danny boy. But he's never had a proper job and this last year he's been seen around the clubs in town, very well dressed, throwing money around and driving a new Mini. All very foolish; it arouses suspicion. He never had anything in his flat, we've searched it on a couple of occasions, but we were patient. We watched him and found he's got a lock-up garage. We found plenty of stuff in that. Quite a haul it was. He'll be going down this time.'

Angela shook her head in disbelief. Danny was a thief, an out-and-out thief. That's why he had plenty of money. 'He . . . he said his business was "import – export". He never explained it fully but I believed him. I trusted him.'

Sergeant McCauley believed her. In fact he felt sorry for her. She was obviously just a young and very naive girl who had fallen for that little toe-rag's pack of lies. He had a daughter of her age and Lucy was just as naive and trusting. It was the result of their upbringing. They'd never come into contact with such reprobates as Danny Fielding. He'd dealt with them all his working life. 'He's a thoroughly bad lot, is Danny boy. He's been in and out of trouble since he was eleven. He's got a record as long as my arm for petty crime but recently he's branched out into more serious stuff. Oh, he's very plausible, comes across as honest and quite charming, but that's not going to cut any ice where he's going.'

Angela stared at him. His words had painted a picture of a Danny she didn't know.

Mr Henderson shook his head. 'He took us all in. No wonder he seemed to have plenty of money, enough to buy a car. Believe me, sergeant, this is the first time anything like this has happened. The girls always buy directly from reputable wholesalers. I should have kept my eye on them but they were doing so well that I left them to get on with it. I've my own business to run. We're a respectable family and the girls have worked very hard to get the business off the ground.' He sighed heavily. He was angry with himself for not probing into Danny Fielding's business dealings more deeply. No wonder the young blackguard hadn't come to the house very often, afraid he would have been found out.

Sergeant McCauley closed his notebook. 'We won't be pressing charges against you, but you'll have to give evidence at the trial, Miss O'Rourke, and we'll have to take all the material. It's evidence.'

Despite the relief that she wasn't facing arrest, this was another blow. There was no chance now of them getting anything else to replace it. The coat would have to be dropped from the collection but what was worse was the fact that she would have to give evidence against him. She would have to face him in a courtroom, knowing he had deliberately lied to her, enmeshed her in his criminal activities.

The two men stood up. 'You'll be notified when you will be needed. I'm sorry but let it be a warning to you not to believe everything you're told and not to blindly trust people,' the sergeant said, a little more kindly.

Mr Henderson showed them out, thanking them for their discretion.

Angela covered her face with her hands and began to sob. Roz instantly came and put her arms around her. 'Don't let it upset you, Angela. He's just not worth it,' she soothed.

'I feel such a fool, Roz! I'm such an eejit! I believed him when he told me he loved me!' she sobbed. He hadn't cared for her at all. He had just used her. She wondered too if his tales of a miserable, neglected childhood were all true or if it had just been a ploy to gain her sympathy. He had *known* that material was stolen, that's why he couldn't bring it to her; she'd had the inconvenience of going to his place. Had that been part of the plan to get her into his bed? It was all just too much to bear.

'As Dad said, he took us all in. We all thought he was great; Mam was always going on about his lovely manners. How were any of us to know what he was really like?' Roz looked at Lizzie for support.

Lizzie came and sat beside Angela. 'Roz is right, Angela. How were we to know what a ... a ... con man he was? Thank God we found out in time, we could have bought more stuff from him and then we would have ended up in jail too. You can make a mistake once and it can be overlooked but not twice or three times.'

Angela realised Lizzie was right but it only made her feel worse. He'd known what could happen to her and he hadn't cared. He'd been more than willing to have sold her more stolen goods, hadn't he told her to 'just ask'? And he hadn't even had the decency to tell the police that she'd known nothing about it. That hurt terribly. It really showed that he didn't care for her one little bit. It had all been lies and cheap patter – 'sweetheart' and 'my special girl' – and for what? To make money and to get her into his bed. And she'd trusted him implicitly. She'd told him all her secrets and believed he'd never hurt her. Now she felt as though her heart was breaking.

Chapter Twenty-Six

———◆———

SHE CRIED FOR MOST of the night, sobs that shook her entire body, and nothing anyone could say seemed to help at all. Everyone was upset and thoroughly disgusted by Danny's behaviour. Lydia Henderson kept shaking her head and muttering, 'To think I thought he was such a nice lad!'

'Angela, you're going to make yourself sick. I know it hurts terribly but try to think positively. Something good must come out of it,' Roz urged, casting an imploring look at her mother for help as she sat with her arms around her friend.

'Rose is right, Angela, luv. It's better to find out now. If things had gone on and you'd have got engaged or even married, think how much worse it would have been. You've had a lucky escape, thank God.' Lydia really doubted that things would have gone that far; usually the Danny Fieldings of the world didn't saddle themselves with wives. He might have put an engagement ring on Angela's finger – just to get her into bed – but that's as far as it would have gone. When he'd tired of her he'd have dropped her, but she couldn't say that to the poor girl.

Angela just sobbed harder. She couldn't take comfort from Mrs Henderson's words, not at this minute. All she could think of were the words he had said to her, the terms of endearment, the promises never to hurt her, and her hopes of a happy future with him. Now all that was dust. Oh, how could she have been so stupid as to have believed him? So stupid not to have enquired about his past in greater detail – although no doubt he would have lied to her about that. Every man she had been close to and had trusted had let her down. Her father, Uncle Liam and now Danny. Was she destined never to know the happiness and security of true unselfish love?

In the end they had got her to bed, giving her a couple of aspirin tablets to try to calm her down.

'I wish I had something stronger but there's never been the need in this house before for sleeping tablets or nerve pills,' Lydia Henderson said anxiously. She was worried about the girl. She was taking it very hard but then wasn't that only to be expected? He had deceived them all.

'She'll be all right, Mam. Give her time. It's all come as a terrible shock to her,' Roz answered as they closed the door quietly.

'Time does heal and she's young, it's just that she seems to have had a rotten life, apart from her success with the business, and I know she's not going to take much consolation from that right now but she might do, given time.'

Roz nodded. 'Some people do seem to be born unlucky but surely things can only get better for her? She has had a lucky escape with him, she could have ended up going to jail too and that would have killed her. If she'd married him, she could have been tied to a criminal for the rest of her life. Oh,

I could just murder him! The nasty, selfish, lying little bastard! I hope they lock him up for years!'

'Rose! I know you are upset – we all are – but I won't have you using language like that!'

'Sorry, Mam, it's just that I feel so strongly. I *hate* him!'

'And I think Angela will come to hate him too but she still has to face him in court. I really wish she could get out of that but she is the key witness. It could be months before the case comes to trial and by then, hopefully, she will be getting over it all – but the trial could set her back. Seeing him again and having it all dragged up and listening to his lies – because no doubt he will lie his head off oath or no oath – that will make her feel terrible.'

'I hadn't thought of that, Mam, but I'll be with her when she has to go to court,' Roz promised.

Angela tried desperately to forget him, to put him and everything he had said and done out of her mind, but it was so hard. For days she kept breaking down in tears; she hardly ate and slept fitfully. Lydia and her daughters urged her to throw herself into her work – she had to start on the designs for the autumn collection – but she couldn't concentrate and she had no enthusiasm for it. She did write to Emer, pouring out her heart to her friend and received a letter back, full of sympathy and concern and the promise of a phone call which materialised two days after the letter arrived.

'Angela, come down! Hurry up! Emer's on the phone for you!' Roz shouted up the stairs, having answered the phone. She prayed that this would cheer Angela up.

Angela hadn't really expected her old friend to phone but she was glad she had and ran quickly down the stairs.

'Angela? Is that yourself?' Emer sounded as though she was just next door and for the first time in weeks Angela smiled. It was so good to hear Emer's voice again after so long. Letters just weren't the same.

'Yes, it's really me. I wasn't sure you'd phone.'

'Didn't I say I would? I told Dinny it was an emergency and Joy agreed. How are you feeling? I wish I could come over to cheer you up,' Emer said sincerely.

'I wish you could too but isn't it great that I can talk to you? I'm getting over it, slowly,' she lied.

Emer couldn't contain her anger. 'He's a rat, that's what he is! A nasty, lying, heartless little rat! Aren't you well out of it all? Good riddance to him. I hope they throw away the key. Are you back working yet?'

'Not really. I just don't seem to be able to concentrate, somehow it's not the same now.'

'Sure, that's only to be expected but you *have* to. You can't waste your life and your talent because of *him*! Don't I tell everyone here how great you are?' Emer paused and her tone changed. 'Angela, will you do something for me?'

Angela bit her lip, wondering what Emer would ask. 'If I can. What is it?'

'Will you make me a dress? I've this special occasion to go to with Patrick, it's to do with his work and I want to impress the people in there,' Emer confided.

She sounded a little worried, Angela thought. 'Long or short?' she asked.

'Short, but nothing that will have them all raising their eyes and thinking I'm a bold brat or some kind of hussy. I don't mind what colour, I'll leave that to you.' Emer paused, listening intently. She was hoping that her request would give Angela an incentive to start work again. She had discussed her friend's plight with Joy and they had agreed that she needed something to help take her mind off things. There was in fact a big dinner coming up at Patrick's firm of accountants, so this seemed the perfect excuse.

'Of course I'll do it, Emer. When will you need it for?'

'The end of March, is that enough time? And, Angela, I insist on paying for it – and the postage too. To hell with the expense! Don't I earn good money now?'

'Sure, that's plenty of time and we ... we'll discuss payment later.' She had no intention of taking any money.

'That's grand, thanks, Angela. I'm afraid I have to go now as Dinny said I had to keep it short and he's giving me looks fit to kill. But take care of yourself, I'm thinking of you. And write soon.'

'Bye, Emer, and thanks. Thank Dinny for me too.' Angela replaced the receiver. It had cheered her to actually speak to Emer. She felt a lot better. She wondered if Mr Henderson would let her return the call at some time in the future? She would give him the money for it. Long-distance calls were very expensive.

The following morning she set to work on a dress suitable for Emer's function and Mrs Henderson was relieved to see her take an interest in her work again. Her relief was shortlived, however, for the letter arrived giving the date when the Daniel Fielding's case was to be heard in the Magistrate's Court. It was in ten days' time. She certainly hadn't thought it would be that soon.

Angela was dreading it. Dreading seeing him again, dreading having to get up in the witness box and dreading having her blind, trusting stupidity exposed to a room full of strangers.

Mr Henderson had gone with her when she had had to go and see the prosecuting solicitor. He had gone through it all with her, what she could expect, what she must say and she'd found it helpful. Roz had determinedly said she would go with her to the court and Bernard Henderson was to accompany them. It was going to be an ordeal and he wouldn't let Angela go without moral support.

The morning of the trial they had both dressed with some care for Mrs Henderson had said that Angela should look neat and tidy but well dressed; she was after all a reputable businesswoman. And Roz was not to go looking 'showy' and attracting too much attention, so nothing ostentatious. Angela wore a charcoal-grey trouser suit with a plain white blouse under it and a lighter grey coat over it as it was still cold and blustery. Following her lead Roz wore a dark brown trouser suit with a cream polo-neck jumper under it and a long sleeveless tunic in tan suede over it.

Angela had never been inside a courtroom in her life and was very nervous. She was grateful for the support of Roz and her father. The room wasn't as big as she'd envisaged but it seemed to be full of people. A clerk approached and asked her her name and address and then she was shown to a row of chairs. Roz and her father were to sit further back and her confidence waned as they went to the seats indicated. She saw Sergeant McCauley and Constable Armstrong and the older man smiled and nodded to her. She nodded back but couldn't muster a smile. Butterflies were dancing maniacally in her stomach and her throat felt dry. She clasped her hands tightly together in her lap. They were all instructed to rise as the three magistrates came in and took their seats. Then she heard someone call for the accused to be brought up and she looked determinedly down at the floor. She didn't want to see him.

She heard him state that he was Daniel James Fielding of flat three, ten Faulkner Square. At the sound of his voice she winced involuntarily and closed her eyes for a second, trying not to remember how he used to call her 'sweetheart'. She kept her eyes firmly downcast but she knew it was only a matter of minutes before she would have to face him.

It was like a dream – a nightmare – that was confused and of which she could recall only fragments, she thought as they left the building. She held Mr Henderson's arm very tightly for she was still shaking. She had gone into the witness box, taken the oath and confirmed her name and address. Then she had been asked did she know the accused? She had had to look at him then and pain had torn at her heart. He looked just the same. Not downcast, or afraid, or contrite. Dressed in a dark suit, white shirt and a tie, he was his usual cocky self; he'd even smiled at her. She had felt sick, physically sick, then. He looked so sure of himself, so confident. Was he expecting her to lie for him? She hadn't been able to look at him again as she'd truthfully answered all the questions the prosecution asked. She heard herself described as a young, naive, trusting young woman of impeccable character and morals who had been duped by this hardened criminal into buying stolen goods from him. She had been swayed by the fact that she needed the said material urgently for her business, which, as Their Honours were aware, was a prominent city centre boutique. After that things were hazy. She had gone back to her seat and the police evidence had then been heard. She vaguely remembered hearing him answering questions but all she'd wanted to do was get away from that room as quickly as possible. As far away from *him* as possible. Then she had heard both verdict and sentence: guilty and a jail term of two and a half years. At last she had been allowed to leave.

'Thank God that's all over and done with. Perhaps things can go back to something approaching normal,' Bernard Henderson said with relief as they walked to where he had parked the car.

Roz squeezed Angela's hand tightly. Angela was very pale and she was still shaking. 'I thought you were great. You sounded very calm and sincere.'

'Of course she was sincere, she was telling the truth,' her father rebuked her.

'Dad, you know what I mean. They couldn't *not* believe her. He's got a record as long as your arm and I'm delighted he's going to jail for all that time. He certainly didn't look as smug and as sure of himself when he left the dock as he did when he first came in.'

'He . . . he *smiled* at me. I felt sick,' Angela informed them, her voice cracking slightly.

'The cocky little devil!' Mr Henderson replied. 'Well, let's go home. You must try to put it all behind you now, Angela. It's over and done with.'

She nodded but she felt utterly drained and emotionally exhausted. She would never forget today's experience but maybe in time she could look back on it with some resignation and even satisfaction. Justice had been done.

Part V

Chapter Twenty-Seven

Liverpool, 1966

GRADUALLY AS THE MONTHS passed the pain of Danny's betrayal grew less and Angela threw herself into her work. The dress for Emer's special function and the outfit for Sal's engagement that she had designed and made had been the major turning points. Emer had written saying it was the most gorgeous dress she'd ever had and that it had been greatly admired, especially by Patrick and even his 'battleaxe' of a mother. Angela had smiled at that. Emer had long ago told her that she was viewed by that particular lady as an unsuitable match for her precious son, but of course Emer wasn't going to let that stand in her way.

Sal and Harry had announced their engagement in June. Mr Henderson had insisted that they observe proper etiquette and so a formal announcement was printed in the newspaper. Harry's parents and sister had been invited for tea and they in turn had invited the Hendersons, including herself, out for a meal at the Adelphi Hotel, no less. Roz had commented that they were only showing off, trying to outdo her parents and that really it was quite pathetic on the part of people who were supposed to be 'grown-ups'. Sal had been delighted with the pale mint-green dress and matching coat that Angela had designed. With it she'd worn the double row of pearls her future mother-in-law had given her and pearl earrings. She'd completed the ensemble with ivory pearlised leather shoes and bag and her mother had said she looked every inch a lady and that she was proud of her. Roz had privately said to Angela that she thought Sal looked a bit old-fashioned and staid. The pearls had ruined the effect of the coat and dress, she thought. It would have looked better with a 'pop art' brooch and big, chunky earrings.

'Sure, what else could she do but wear the pearls? His mother would have been upset if she hadn't,' Angela had replied.

Roz had pulled a face. 'Well, I wouldn't have ruined a gorgeous outfit just to please *her*. She's a bossy, domineering old bat!'

Angela had shaken her head in mock despair. 'You sound just like Emer. She wrote and told me that she isn't going to the Labor Day picnic if Patrick's mother insists she wears a dress or skirt. She was planning to wear her new denim jeans and a strappy top. She said, and I quote, "The old battleaxe says it's not 'feminine or ladylike' for girls to wear jeans."'

Roz had laughed. 'Good for Emer!'

But there were times when something would remind her of him: a song, a place, a red Mini hurtling along the road, and then she'd feel the ache in her heart. He was serving his sentence in Walton Prison and that was only down the road, but she wished it was hundreds of miles away. When the bus passed the top of Hornby Road you could see the prison walls and she always shuddered and looked away.

*

August was again hot and humid and she was finding it hard to concentrate on designs for next spring. She tried always to work in the back office of the workrooms so she could discuss things with Lizzie on the spot but the room was small and had only one window which was now open as wide as it was possible to open it. It really wasn't the ideal place for she needed a desk light, which added to the heat. She pushed her sketch pad away and leaned back in her chair. She was debating whether to include a range of garments made in denim: skirts, waistcoats, jackets and flared jeans.

Lizzie came into the room, carrying a sheaf of invoices. 'God! It's like a sauna in here!' she exclaimed.

'Don't I know it? What do you think of denim?'

Lizzie sat down opposite her and pulled the sketch pad towards her. 'It's OK. Hardwearing, not the easiest of materials to work with, but getting popular. I like the skirt and waistcoat. You can wear the waistcoat with the flares too but I'm not sure about the jacket. Would it be a bit too masculine?'

'Unisex is all the rage now,' Angela reminded her.

'I know. Are you thinking of going down that route?'

Angela shook her head. 'Not really.'

Lizzie nodded. 'Good. I for one don't particularly want to go out in something that my brother would wear.' She got up and leaned against the window frame, fanning herself with an envelope. The window looked out into the small yard at the back of the building. 'Not a particularly pleasant view. There's no air in here at all, Angela. You'll give yourself a blinding headache. Why don't you walk back home and have your lunch with Mam? You'd at least get a bit of fresh air and something decent to eat. I'd come with you but I'm expecting a delivery and I want to check they've sent the right stuff this time. If not they can take it straight back and that will be the last order they'll get from us.'

Angela got to her feet. Maybe a walk would do her good. Maybe she could make a decision about the denim on the way. Lizzie was right, she had the beginnings of a headache now.

She did feel much better when she arrived home. All the windows were open, as was the back door, and since the kitchen was at the back of the house and therefore only got the sun early in the morning it was fairly cool.

'Sure, I couldn't stick that office. It's stifling,' she informed Lydia Henderson.

'I don't blame you. Why don't you work here this afternoon? You can sit in the dining room with the French doors open,' she suggested. 'I'm off to one of my tea dances with Florrie McDonald from next door so there will be no one to disturb you. Now, I've a nice bit of salad and some ham. You wouldn't be bothered cooking in this weather.'

Angela set the table as Lydia washed the lettuce and sliced the ham.

'Was that the post?' she called from the back kitchen.

'I'll go and see,' Angela offered.

There were two letters for Mr Henderson and two for herself. The blue airmail letter was from Emer but the other one was from Ireland and it wasn't Aunt Mary's writing. She opened it first when she got back to the kitchen. She went cold. It was from Uncle Liam. Her aunt was ill, he wrote. Very ill. Not expected to live very long and so she should in all decency go back to see her before it was too late, for how would it look if she didn't?

'Angela, what's wrong? You've gone as white as a sheet,' Lydia Henderson asked, coming into the room with two plates of food.

264

Angela tried to pull herself together. 'It . . . it's from my uncle, he says Aunt Mary is very ill. She's not expected to live for very long. Why didn't she tell me? Why? In each letter I've had from her she's told me she was grand. Not a word about anything.'

Lydia Henderson shook her head sadly. Poor Angela, this was yet another shock, another blow, and she was only just getting over Danny Fielding. 'I'm so sorry, really I am. She probably said nothing because she didn't want to upset or worry you.'

'He . . . he says I should go but . . .' She couldn't go back, not with her aunt so ill and *him* there. She would be expected to stay with them; it would be the talk of the place if she didn't.

'Of course you must, luv. We'll sort everything out regarding the travelling and our Lizzie is quite capable of keeping things going while you are away. Don't worry about how long you will need to be gone for.'

Angela looked up at her with despair in her eyes. It would look callous and heartless to refuse to go and she did want to see her aunt again but . . . but how could she explain about her uncle? 'Do you think Roz could come with me?' she pleaded. 'I don't want to go alone.'

'Well, I suppose so but she might feel as though she's in the way, it's not as if it's some kind of holiday. She might feel as if her presence would be resented.' Seeing that Angela was obviously distressed she continued, 'Ask her when she gets in. I'll leave the decision up to her.'

Angela nodded thankfully. Surely after she had told her friend about Liam, Roz wouldn't refuse?

It was almost five o'clock when Roz arrived home, she'd been modelling some knitwear which on a sweltering August day had been far from comfortable and she was hot, tired and irritable.

'Why do you all have to work so flaming well far in advance? I've been strutting up and down all afternoon in knitted dresses and heavy cardigans and jumpers, trying to look cool and elegant. In this heat!' she exclaimed, flopping into a chair and kicking off her shoes.

Her mother handed her a glass of cold lemonade. 'Calm down and drink this. Angela has something to ask you, she's had some bad news.'

Roz took a large gulp and looked enquiringly at her friend. 'What's happened now?'

Angela didn't want to have to explain in front of Mrs Henderson. 'Finish your drink and then we'll sit out in the garden and I'll tell you.'

Roz quickly gulped down the rest of the lemonade and got to her feet and followed Angela into the dining room where the French windows led out on to a very small back garden that was surrounded by a high wall.

Angela carried two of the dining chairs out on to the grass. At least they wouldn't be overheard out here.

'What's wrong, Angela?' Roz asked quietly.

'I had a letter at lunchtime from my uncle. Aunt Mary is very ill, she's not expected to last long. Oh, I wish she'd told me! She's deliberately kept it from me.'

Roz shook her head. 'Probably didn't want to worry you. What . . . what is it?'

'Cancer, he says.'

'Will you go back?' Roz could see her friend was upset and who wouldn't be? But she was sure there was something else.

Angela nodded. 'Will you come with me?'

Roz frowned. She could understand that but she would

stick out like a sore thumb. 'Wouldn't I be in the way? I mean, I'm not family, I'm not even related to you. They don't know me. No one knows me.'

Angela bit her lip. 'I want to see Aunt Mary again, she was good to me, but there is a good reason why I don't want to go back alone and it's the reason why I came to Liverpool.'

'I thought that was to train as a nurse?' Roz looked closely at her friend and could see she was struggling with her emotions. 'Well, go on, tell me. You know you can tell me anything and you can trust me,' she urged.

Haltingly Angela told her, trying to keep her voice steady, and watching as Roz's eyes widened in horror and revulsion and finally anger.

'Oh, you poor, poor thing! And your aunt never knew or even suspected?'

Angela shook her head.

'You should have gone to the police! He deserves to be publicly humiliated and then jailed!' She couldn't begin to imagine what Angela had gone through, nor did she want to, it was just too horrible.

'The Guards wouldn't have believed me. Father Dwyer didn't. It would have been *his* word against mine and everyone would have known and I . . . I . . . just couldn't have stood that. You don't know what it's like to live in a small town, Roz. I'd have been gossiped about in every home and mud has a habit of sticking.'

Roz shook her head in disbelief. 'I can't *believe* that a priest would think you were lying about something like *that*!'

'I know. It really upset me at the time.'

'It's absolutely disgraceful and he . . . he's *disgusting*!'

'So you can see why I don't want to go back alone? If he tried anything I would make a huge fuss about it and this time I'd make sure I was believed, but how could I do that to Aunt Mary?'

Roz could see her point. The poor woman was on her deathbed, the last thing she needed was to learn that her husband was a pervert and for him to be exposed to the entire community as such and probably jailed. 'Of course I'll come with you and if I get the opportunity I'll give that filthy old bastard a piece of my mind!' She squeezed Angela's hand.

Angela shook her head slowly. 'Roz, I'll do that myself. I'm not a sixteen-year-old who is dependent on him for a roof over my head now. I've grown up and I've gained a great deal of confidence since starting the business. Aunt Mary knows how well I've done and she's no doubt told him. I'm not afraid of him now.'

Roz nodded. 'But if you need any support, I'll be right there.'

'I know and thanks.'

'You should have told me, I'm your friend. You told Emer.' She felt a little disappointed that Angela hadn't confided in her but then she told herself she was being childish. She found it hard to understand just why Emer hadn't done something to help Angela; she would have done. She would at least have told her mother and father and demanded something be done about Liam Murphy. Surely Emer's mother would have believed both girls? But then she remembered that Emer had only been sixteen too. Nor did she know what the Cassidy family was like; they might well have believed Liam or this Father Dwyer. And Emer had had to leave Ireland, she'd had no choice, and there was nothing she could do to help Angela from three thousand miles away. Danny Fielding was even more despicable in her eyes now. Angela had explained why she had confided in him and he'd still tried to get her friend to sleep with him. He was a callous, insensitive, self-centred, conniving little rat. She stood up.

'I'll go and tell Mam that I'm going with you and she can start to make the arrangements and we'd better think about packing.'

Angela also stood up, feeling much better. It would certainly help to have Roz with her in the days ahead.

Chapter Twenty-Eight

T HE FOLLOWING EVENING BOTH girls were aboard the Liverpool to Dublin ferry. Lydia Henderson had insisted on booking a cabin for them; she wouldn't hear of them sitting up in all night in a public lounge, as she called it.

'It's a long journey and you'd get no sleep at all and then you'd both be worn out by the time you arrived. And it's far from a pleasure trip and Angela will have the worst part of it to face when she gets there,' she'd stated firmly.

Angela had agreed, thinking that Mrs Henderson couldn't possibly know how bad she would feel when she finally walked through the door of her aunt's house. Despite the fact that her aunt had never expected her to make the long and arduous journey home she now felt she should have made the effort, even if it had been just once or twice.

It had been a calm crossing and they'd got a taxi to Heuston Station and then the train. They seemed to have been travelling for hours, Roz thought, when they finally arrived in Edenderry. She felt tired and grubby but she looked around with interest as they walked out of the station.

'It is only small,' she mused aloud.

'Didn't I tell you it was? We'll have to walk from here but it's not too far. There are no buses or trams and by the time we'd have rounded up the local taxi driver, we could be there,' Angela informed her, looking around. She had never wanted to come back here and nothing seemed to have changed much at all.

It was still warm, sticky and overcast as they walked towards Mary's home. Roz thought everything looked a bit run down and shabby and there were very few cars or vans on the road. To her city-bred eyes the roads were narrow and the shops all looked small, their window displays dull and old fashioned, but she kept her thoughts to herself. At least the town didn't have all the noise and dirt and crowds as the city did, she conceded, and it was surrounded by fields. That was one thing in the place's favour at least.

Angela knew Liam would be expecting her, although he would be at his work at this time of day, but the door would be open. People never locked their doors here, there was no need. Mrs Henderson had insisted on her sending her uncle a telegram. She hadn't wanted to but in the end she'd agreed, although she hadn't mentioned to him the fact that Roz would be accompanying her.

She had been greeted by many people on the walk to Mary's house, all expressing sympathy, and she had thanked them but had kept the conversations as short as possible.

'We'd never be after getting there before teatime if I stopped and chatted to everyone,' she'd answered when Roz had remarked that she seemed to know most of the town, which was something that didn't happen in big cities.

Peg Cassidy was just leaving Mary's house as the two girls walked up the path.

'Ah, Angela, so you've arrived at last! Himself told me this morning you'd be here some time today. You look very well, child.' Peg had quickly taken in the very stylish but also very short dresses both girls wore.

Angela smiled at Emer's mother. 'We got the overnight ferry. This is Roz Henderson, my friend. She was good enough to come with me.'

Roz shook the older woman's hand and smiled. 'It's nice to meet you, Mrs Cassidy.'

Peg had to look up. The girl was very tall and slim, she thought. So, this was the one who was a model, no less; Emer was always mentioning her in her letters, saying how fantastic she looked in the photographs Angela had sent of her 'collections'. She found it almost impossible to believe that young Angela O'Rourke was a well-thought-of fashion designer with her own business, but the girl looked different now. She was very smartly dressed but it was more than that. She had a new air of confidence; she seemed very sure of herself. She sighed. 'Sure, I wish it were under better circumstances, Roz.'

'How is she?' Angela asked tentatively.

Peg Cassidy shook her head sadly. 'Not good, I'm afraid to say. Not good at all, God help her. Hasn't the pain got her destroyed entirely? The doctor has been kindness itself and we've all pitched in and helped out, sure Liam doesn't know how to cope. She waited on him hand and foot, so she did. He was a well-minded man, I can tell you.'

Angela just nodded. At least her aunt was being well cared for by the neighbours, if not by *him*. 'I'm very grateful for all your help and I know Aunt Mary is too. We'd best be going in now.'

'The doctor usually calls at some time in the afternoon and if there's anything you need just come to me,' Peg instructed as she left the girls to make her way home.

Angela looked at Roz and then took a deep breath. 'Well, here goes. This is going to be an ordeal, so it is. I've been dreading it the whole time we've been travelling and I don't know which is going to be the worst thing, facing him or seeing her in so much pain, knowing . . .'

Roz squeezed her arm. 'You've got me to help you out, remember? We'll get through it all together and you won't see him until he's home from his work.'

Everywhere was just as neat and tidy as on the day she'd left, Angela thought, looking around. The neighbours must have worked hard. Had he given up the drink? she wondered. They put their cases down and then Angela went upstairs, followed by Roz. Roz had said she would try to sort out the sleeping arrangements as it wasn't fair to burden Mary with introductions at a time like this. Maybe later on, if Mary felt up to it, she could go and meet her.

Although she had seen people who were dying or were in great pain and distress when she had been nursing, Angela was shocked by her aunt's appearance. Mary seemed to be little more than skin and bone, a tiny shrunken figure in the big bed. Her skin was stretched over her bones and looked like thin parchment. She picked up the skeletal hand and Mary opened her eyes.

'Angela. Angela, child.'

Angela bent and kissed the sunken cheek. 'I came as soon as I could. Don't try to talk, Aunt Mary. Save your strength. You should have told me you were ill, I'd have come at once.'

'You were so busy. You had so much to do with . . . with the business.'

'I was never too busy to come and see you, stay here and nurse you, which is what I'm going to do now.'

Mary inclined her head and closed her eyes again and Angela thought she seemed reassured by her words. She sat beside the bed, holding her aunt's hand and thinking back to the days when she had been a child and had been happy in this house.

After an hour Roz came quietly into the room and shook her head in pity at the sight of Angela's aunt. 'Is she asleep?' she whispered.

Angela nodded. 'I don't think she's got long at all, Roz.'

'Poor thing, it must be terrible for her.'

'I've told her I'll nurse her and I will. The neighbours have been very good but it's not fair to rely totally on them.'

'I'll help out too. I can see to the housework, the cooking and the washing.' Roz frowned; she'd heard a noise downstairs. 'Was that someone coming in?'

'It might be Dr Leahy or one of the neighbours.'

Roz went down to investigate and then returned with the doctor.

Angela had expected to see Dr Leahy but to her surprise it was Dr Emmet who came into the room. She hadn't thought he would stay in a backwater like Edenderry.

'Angela! You managed to get home in time. I begged her to let you know how ill she was but she wouldn't listen to me at all. She kept saying she didn't want you to be troubled, you were so busy, so in the end I told Liam to write to you.'

Angela was touched by his words. 'I'm glad you did. I'll nurse her now and Roz is going to keep the house going.'

Roz had already introduced herself and so he went to Mary's side and checked her pulse and the array of medication on the table beside the bed.

'Mrs Cassidy said you come each afternoon. That's good of you.'

'I like to keep a check on things.' He picked up his bag and walked to the door and indicated that Angela should follow him.

He spoke very quietly. 'You'll have realised that she hasn't got long, Angela. It's the drugs that kill in the end. She's on the highest dosage I can give her.'

She nodded. 'I know that.'

'All that can be done is to make her as comfortable as possible. It's a desperate way to go but I'm sure she'll be thankful that you are here, as will Liam. He's taking it badly.'

'You mean he's drowning his sorrows in Dempsey's every night?' she asked, a harsh edge to her voice.

He heard it and was surprised. 'Not every night, it's his way of trying to cope, I suppose.'

She didn't reply. That was all they needed! Liam falling in drunk.

'Still, I don't think he'll be after calling in to Dempsey's tonight. He knows you'll be here waiting for him. That should cheer him up a bit.'

She set her mouth in a thin, tight line. Oh, yes she would be waiting for him all right.

'I hear you've done very well in Liverpool, but not at nursing,' he said as they went down the stairs.

'I'd never have made a good nurse, my heart just wasn't in it. Oh, I didn't mind the practical side but I found the studying very hard. It was beyond me.'

'James was quite disappointed when he heard but I told him it would be for the best and it certainly was. Don't we get to hear all about you and how talented you are and how fortunate you've been? Mary came up and showed us all the cuttings from the newspapers and magazines. She was so proud of you.'

This surprised Angela. She had thought her aunt didn't really approve of her designs. She smiled at him. 'I'm glad about that, truly I am.'

She had changed, he thought. She'd blossomed. She must

be twenty or twenty-one now and was a very attractive and confident young woman, every bit as stylish as the 'fashion plate' he'd met downstairs. If the pair of them stayed for any length of time they'd have every lad in the area beating a path to their door, although he didn't expect them to stay for long. There was little to hold them in a small country town like this.

'I didn't think you would have stayed,' she said as they reached the front door.

'Just after Dolores died James needed company and support and I get on well with him, so I stayed. There is work enough, we're kept busy and I do like living here. I don't miss the city at all.'

She could understand that. She smiled at him. She had always liked him and now she realised he was quite a handsome young man. She wondered had he found anyone special in Edenderry? Was that why he had stayed? He could only be in his late twenties or early thirties.

'I don't suppose you will be staying on after . . .' he probed.

'No. I am busy. I do have a business to run and it's one where we are always working at least six months ahead. "Next season" seems to dominate my life.'

'I'll leave you to it then. You'll have Liam in looking for his supper before long. I'll call tomorrow but if she worsens send for me, day or night.'

'Thank you, it's a relief to know I can count on you,' she replied sincerely.

Roz had made a cup of tea and had found some biscuits. 'He's very nice. Quite good-looking too. You told me he was old with a shock of grey hair.'

'That's Dr Leahy, it was him I was expecting to see when Mrs Cassidy said "the doctor". Dr Emmet came here as a locum, I didn't think he'd have stayed on. Aunt Mary never told me.'

'How is she? Did he say anything about her?' Roz asked quietly. She wasn't regretting accompanying Angela – how could she have let her friend face *him* alone? – but she had very little experience of death and even less in running a house. Only now was she beginning to realise how thoroughly spoiled she'd been. Her mam did everything for her, for them all.

'He said she hasn't long but can't give her a higher dosage of the drugs. All we can do is make her comfortable.'

'It's going to be very hard for you, Angela. She brought you up. She was like a mother to you.'

'I know and I hate to see her like . . . this.' Angela thought of her mother. Roz was right. Mary had been more of a mother to her than Maura O'Rourke. Would her parents come to Mary's funeral? she wondered. Funerals in Ireland were always well attended. People came from miles away; they made a special effort. If her parents didn't come it would be viewed by everyone as a grave breach of social etiquette and a mark of disrespect to Mary, but they'd never come to Edenderry in all these years so why should they come now?

'Dr Emmet told me *he's* not coping with it very well. In fact his way of coping seems to be drowning his sorrows in Dempsey's pub every night,' she informed Roz.

'Oh, God! That's the last thing we need, a roaring drunk on our hands every night.'

'He probably won't go tonight. He thinks I'm here on my own.'

Roz smiled grimly. 'Well, isn't he in for a shock then?'

Angela nodded. 'And won't he be needing something strong to drink by the time I've finished with him?' she said ominously.

Chapter Twenty-Nine

———◆———

THE TWO GIRLS HAD had their supper by the time Liam arrived home from work. Nearly all the neighbours had called in to see Angela and meet Roz and offer their help and support.

'People are so good and generous here, Angela,' Roz had remarked after Mrs Kennedy had called bringing a home-made fruit cake.

'In small communities we all try to help each other in times of trouble and hardship,' Angela had replied

She had been up to give Mary her medication and to make sure she was comfortable and Roz had washed and dried their dishes and was putting them away in the press when Liam arrived home. His gaze fell first on Roz and he stared at her, trying to puzzle out just who she was and why she was here.

Angela looked closely at him. He seemed to have shrunk, or was it just her imagination? She remembered him as being taller and thinner, but now he was short and stout and his hair was grey. He'd put on weight while her aunt had wasted away.

'We came over on the night ferry; we got here early this afternoon. I'm glad you wrote and told me how sick she is. I'm going to nurse her for the little time she has left,' she informed him, deliberately keeping her voice low but her tone was firm. She had promised herself that there would be no shouting or screamed abuse and recriminations, that she would remain calm and in control of herself, but inside she didn't feel very calm at all.

Liam ignored her words. 'Who's she?' he asked, eyeing Roz suspiciously.

'This is Roz Henderson, my friend. Aunt Mary will have told you I live with the Hendersons,' Angela answered still determinedly holding his gaze.

Liam glanced at the girl again. He was becoming annoyed. A bold young rossi, he thought, with all that make-up and the dress so short it was positively indecent. Angela had no right bringing her here. 'What has she come for? She's not needed and she's not welcome. Aren't you the bold one to take it on yourself to bring a stranger to the house when your aunt is dying?'

Angela had expected something like this but before she could say anything Roz had moved towards him. She glared down at him with contempt.

'I came with her because I wouldn't let her stay here alone with the likes of you, you disgusting, despicable pervert! Oh, I know all about you and what you tried to do to her when she lived here! You should be locked up!'

Liam's face went an ugly shade of puce and a vein in his forehead started to throb. 'You bitch! You stand in my house and call me a pervert! It's a lie! It's a pack of evil lies she's been after telling you! You can get out, the pair of you! You're not wanted here!' He raised his clenched fist to Roz but she held her ground.

'So you're a bully as well? Don't think you can frighten me. Lay one finger on me or her and I'll have you arrested for assault. And won't that cause an almighty fuss? Attacking a visitor to your home? And I'll make damned sure that everyone in this town knows all about you.'

Liam was shaking with anger and the fact that she towered over him and obviously meant what she said only increased his fury. He spluttered, unable to form his words.

Angela pulled Roz away. Inside she was trembling but outwardly she was icily calm. 'You know I'm not lying and neither of us is going anywhere. Aunt Mary needs me and I need Roz to keep the house going. I'm not a sixteen-year-old eejit now. I've made something of myself. I'm successful and I'm someone to be reckoned with. I'm not afraid of you even though you robbed me of my innocence and ruined the last year I spent here, to say nothing of betraying that poor woman lying upstairs. So, you'd better believe me when I say touch me and I'm straight off to the Garda Barracks – and they'll believe me. Everyone will believe me this time – even Father Dwyer – and you'll go to prison, which is no more than you deserve. There is nothing more to be said and I'm not having Aunt Mary's last days destroyed by fights and arguments. She deserves to go with peace and dignity. She deserved far better than she got, especially from you! So, while she's alive you'll come home sober and show her some kindness and respect.'

Now that it was all out in the open and she had con-fronted him she felt drained but she could see that he believed her. All his blustering bravado had gone. He looked drawn and haggard and he couldn't or wouldn't meet her eyes. He turned away muttering that he was cursed with a houseful of she-devils.

'Go up and see her. She's been waiting for you to come home – God knows why!' Angela instructed cuttingly.

'And then you can have the supper I cooked for you,' Roz said coldly. 'And I hope it chokes you!' she muttered under her breath. He was the most repulsive man she had ever had the misfortune to meet, she thought.

When he'd gone upstairs Angela sank down in a chair; her legs seemed to give way under her. Roz immediately went to her side and sat on the arm of the chair.

'Are you all right? You were great. You certainly gave him a piece of your mind and now I think he's afraid of us both, which is no bad thing. He'll think twice about starting an argument or going to the pub. Will I get us something to drink?'

Angela nodded. 'I think there's half a bottle of sherry in a cupboard in the back kitchen.' She needed something to warm her up; she felt cold and numb. The days ahead were going to be an ordeal, both in having to watch her aunt suffer and be under the same roof as her uncle, but once poor Mary had been buried she would go back to Liverpool. There was nothing to hold her here; she didn't even have fond memories to cling to.

They both found the days long and hard. Angela, helped by the neighbours, nursed Mary. They washed her, changed her, turned her in the bed to prevent pressure sores and administered her medication. Angela slept on a mattress beside the sick woman's bed, although she got little sleep. At midnight on the fourth day after their arrival she heard Mary calling her. She got up and gently took the sick woman's hand.

'What is it? I'm here. Is the pain worse?'

Mary was so weak it was difficult to hear her words so Angela bent closer.

'Angela, you know I . . . I've always been so very fond of

282

A Daughter's Journey

you, child. As . . . as fond as if you'd been my own.'

Angela squeezed the thin hand, the tears pricking her eyes. 'I know that, Aunt Mary, and you . . . you've been so good to me. Everything I've achieved so far . . . sure, I couldn't have done it without you.'

Mary managed a smile. 'I . . . I'm so proud of you, child. You've done far better than I ever expected you to. So . . . so talented.'

Angela remembered Ronan Emmet's words. 'Dr Emmet told me you were. He said you took all the press cuttings up to show them.'

Mary nodded slowly. 'He . . . he's such a good, kind . . . considerate young man.'

It was Angela's turn to nod her agreement. 'He's very nice. I've always thought so.'

Mary became agitated and Angela wondered it she wanted to see the doctor. 'What is it, Aunt? Shall I send for him?'

Mary shook her head and tried to raise herself up from the pillows. 'No! 'Tis not that, Angela. I . . . I have to tell you . . . something.'

For a brief, awful moment Angela thought her aunt was going to tell her that she knew all about Liam. 'What's troubling you?' she asked bleakly.

'Oh, Angela, I'm sorry! So . . . very sorry. I . . . I shouldn't have done it. It wasn't right.'

Angela was confused although it was a relief to realise that whatever it was Mary was trying to tell her it had nothing to do with Liam. 'Done what, Aunt?'

Mary fell back on the pillows and in the dim light she looked even more shrunken and skeletal and Angela realised that she had sunk back into sleep, exhausted by her efforts. What could she have been trying to say? Would she have another chance to tell her or would it remain a mystery?

Chapter Thirty

FROM THAT POINT MARY slept almost continuously. When she wasn't asleep, she was confused, which Angela found distressing. There were no opportunities to talk or reminisce, or even comfort. All Angela could do was try to keep her as calm and comfortable as possible.

From the day Angela and Roz had arrived Liam had slept on the sofa. He barely spoke a word to either of them but would sit for an hour beside Mary when he came in from work and then took refuge behind his newspaper.

Roz was finding it very hard work indeed. She was the first to admit that she wasn't the best of cooks and the turf-fired range utterly defeated her. Meals were either undercooked or burned but neither Angela nor Liam complained. There weren't as many labour-saving appliances as she was used to either. The range had to be kept lit not only for cooking but to heat the water which in the August temperatures made the kitchen unbearably hot and stuffy. It had to be raked out each morning, which meant that clouds of fine white ash covered every surface, which increased her workload. She longed for her mam's automatic washing machine for the amount of laundry there was to be done took hours in Mary's twin tub. She seemed to spend every waking hour cleaning, stoking the range, cooking and pegging out or bringing in washing.

Dr Emmet called every afternoon and both girls began to view his visits as an hour's light relief from the grinding toil. Angela in particular looked forward to his arrival. He would sit with her and Mary for half an hour and, since Mary was usually asleep, they would talk quietly about his life here in Edenderry and hers in Liverpool. She now knew he had family and friends in both Galway and Manchester and he realised that she looked on the Hendersons as the family she had lost. Then he would go and help Roz with whatever she was battling with that particular day. One afternoon he had found her on her knees in front of the range, her face covered in smuts and with beads of perspiration on her forehead.

'Is it after giving you trouble?' he'd asked.

'Trouble! That's an understatement! It's gone out again and I can't get it to light.' She'd wiped away the perspiration with the back of her hand, leaving sooty marks across her forehead.

'There's a bit of a knack in getting them lit,' he'd agreed.

'Tell me about it! Why in the name of God does everyone use this damned stuff? What's wrong with coal or electricity or gas?' She'd hurled a sod of turf into the range in sheer frustration, breaking a nail in the process.

He'd taken off his jacket and rolled up his sleeves. 'Here, let me have a go at it. The reason why turf is so widely used is that it's cheap and plentiful. This is a poor country and not many can afford to use electricity for heating. As for gas, there isn't any, and coal is also expensive, it has to be shipped in. Even the power station is run on turf. Bord na Móna means the Board of Turf.' He'd grinned at her astonished expression. 'They ran the trains on turf during the Emergency – the war. Mind, it wasn't a great success, it took hours and hours to get anywhere.'

She'd shaken her head in disbelief. No wonder Angela didn't want to come back here.

'Ah, you get used to it. There now, it's away,' he'd said with some satisfaction.

Roz had thanked him profusely but told herself that they were very lucky that they didn't have to get used to it. There were some benefits to living in a city.

Mary died three days later, a week to the day after Angela's arrival. She went peacefully in the end with Liam and Angela and Dr Emmet and Father Dwyer at her side. Roz had stayed in the kitchen making tea for the neighbours.

''Tis a blessing, Father. She's out of her pain now,' Liam replied to the priest's words of consolation. The two men had gone downstairs together.

Angela stood at the bedside as Dr Emmet covered her aunt's face with the sheet. In this instance she had to agree with her uncle. She dashed away her tears with the back of her hand.

'Angela, can I give you something to make you sleep? It's been an ordeal for you and you're exhausted,' Ronan Emmet asked kindly. He was genuinely worried about her. She was pale and there were dark circles under her eyes and she was obviously upset.

She shook her head. 'Thank you but no. There's so much to do now. There are all the arrangements to be made for the removal and the burial.'

'But surely Liam will see to all that?'

'I'd like to see that everything is done properly, the

way she would want it. She was very particular about such things.' She was well aware that now Liam had the perfect excuse for taking to the bottle again. He could drink himself into the gutter or the grave for all she cared but not until after Mary had been buried and she had gone back to Liverpool.

'Well, if there is anything I can do?'

She'd thanked him and they had gone downstairs. The kitchen was already full of people who had come to pay their respects – news always travelled like lightning in small communities – but Roz seemed to be coping. Mr Harney, the funeral director, arrived to discuss everything with Liam and the parish priest and Angela took the opportunity to explain to Roz how these things were conducted in Ireland.

Roz found it all very strange and was surprised at the speed at which things happened here. Just hours after the death everyone who had known the deceased would come to pay their respects and pray for Mary's soul. Then Mary would be 'removed' from the house to the church where the coffin would lie overnight, and the burial would take place the following day. Roz had only ever been to one funeral, she told her friend, that of her father's oldest brother. Her grandparents were all long dead. Even though the family was Catholic there had been no removal and no wake. Uncle Thomas had been taken to the Chapel of Repose where he'd lain for two days and anyone who wished to do so could go and see him for the last time, but it was in no way compulsory. Her mother had said there was no need for her to go, it was better to remember him as he had been when he'd been alive and well and she'd agreed. Then there had been the Requiem Mass, followed by the cremation and a buffet at an hotel for the mourners. It was all very private and much quieter.

'I suppose it's because people have such large families here and communities are small and close, so everyone has known the person who has died,' she'd said, although privately she'd thought Uncle Thomas's funeral had been a far more dignified affair. There had been less of the public spectacle about it.

It *had* all been very hectic, Roz thought, as they stood in the hallway watching Mary's coffin being carried out. It seemed as though the whole town had passed through the house and were now going to go to the church. They would all walk behind the hearse, there were no funeral cars to take the family, but then it wasn't far. At home quite often the cemetery or the crematorium was miles and miles away across the city from the church. Both she and Angela wore black dresses with short sleeves. Their heads were covered with black lace mantillas and their shoes and bags were also black. Liam had a dark suit, a white shirt and black tie and looked morose, his face blotched and his eyes red and puffy. He hadn't set foot in Dempsey's since his wife had died but there had been drink taken in the house, although he had abstained this morning after Angela had had sharp words with him.

Angela wished it was all over. She was tired and her head was aching with lack of sleep and tension and the stifling heat wasn't helping either. Just a few more hours, she told herself. Just one more night in this house and then they would be on the way to Dublin for the ferry. There had been sharp words over the fact that she had insisted Roz walk beside her to church. Liam had said it wasn't her place. She was a stranger and Mary's sisters would be upset and annoyed, as would his own family, to have your one walking ahead of them in the funeral procession and her so tall you couldn't help but notice her. Angela's nerves were already frayed and she had snapped that she didn't care. Her aunts had never kept in close touch, something that frequently happened in large families when brothers and sisters could be scattered far and wide and were concerned only with their own families. Had any of them come to help out in the last weeks? No, they had not, so they could just put up with it and so could he.

The church bell began to toll and Mr Harney ushered them towards the door and Angela suddenly remembered the last time she had walked behind a coffin to the church. It had been that of Dolores Leahy. She held on to Roz's arm tightly.

She was touched to see that so many people had turned out. Mary would have been pleased that she was so well thought of, she thought sadly. She had ignored the hostile and reproachful looks Mary's sisters had cast in her direction. They were all her aunts but she hardly remembered any of them. When they reached the church she gave brief nods of thanks and recognition to Doctors Leahy and Emmet and Miss Dunne who were in the pews at the back. To Mr and Mrs Cassidy, Mr Hickey the butcher and all the other shopkeepers. Then as they reached the front pews she clutched Roz's arm so tightly that Roz winced and bit her lip to stifle the cry of pain as Angela's nails dug into her flesh.

'What's wrong? Do you feel faint?' Roz whispered looking alarmed for Angela had gone deathly pale.

Angela shook her head, her gaze fixed on the three figures in the front pew who had all turned towards the funeral procession as it approached the altar steps. Her mother and father and the girl she knew must be her youngest sister, although she didn't even know her name. They hadn't come to the house and so she hadn't expected them to make the journey to the church, but they had.

Roz guided her into the pew and as Angela sank to her knees her mother reached across Liam and touched her arm. She felt as though she had been stung and snatched her arm away. Why had they come? It would have been better if they had stayed away.

Chapter Thirty-One

———◆·◆·◆———

SHE COULDN'T CONCENTRATE ON the Requiem Mass at all. Her mind was in turmoil. She had never expected them to come and it had thrown her emotions into utter confusion. She felt as though the eyes of everyone in the church were boring into her which, in a moment of stark clarity, she realised was not the case. She had dragged her shocked gaze away from the tearful but hurt expression on her mother's face. Her father had stared at her as though he had never seen her before in his life and her sister's eyes had been wide with something akin to astonishment. She felt Roz reach for her hand and she gripped it tightly. Why had they come? she asked herself. Why now? Was it just to pay their respects to Mary as convention demanded or had they known that she would be here? After all this time had they wanted to see her? No. That wasn't possible. There had never been a single word from them in all these years. The hurt and bitterness came flooding back. It was as if the years had rolled away and she was six years old again and hearing for the first time that she was to be given away.

'Are you sure you're all right?' Roz whispered. She was worried about her friend. Angela was still very pale and seemed to be in a daze and she prayed that being unexpectedly confronted by her parents, on top of everything else, wouldn't make her ill.

Angela managed to nod. She must try to concentrate on this Mass for her aunt's soul. It was the least she could do for Mary had been good to her. She closed her eyes and fixed her mind on Father Dwyer's voice as he intoned the de profundis.

Maura covered her face with her hands, to all intents and purposes deep in prayer, but her emotions were threatening to overcome her. Angela had changed so much but she would have recognised her anywhere. She had grown into a lovely, confident, elegant young woman and she knew she had Mary to thank for that. Her heart had begun to race with joy when she'd seen Angela but the look of what she could only describe as shocked horror that her daughter had given her before she'd turned away had sent a knife-like pain through her. It was as if Angela hated her. But why, she asked herself? Surely as she had grown she had come to understand the desperate circumstances that had forced Maura to part with her? Mary would have explained, she was certain of it. And didn't Angela realise how very fortunate she'd been? The tears slid down her cheeks and she prayed that when the service was over she would have a chance to speak to her daughter.

Angela felt a little calmer when the funeral was finally over and her aunt had been laid to rest in the churchyard. Everyone had come to shake her hand and Liam's and she had tried to ignore her uncle's comments about what a wonderful wife Mary had been and how much he would miss her. Roz stood a few paces behind her, feeling totally out of place but determined to give what moral support she could and gradually the crowd dwindled as people made their way back home or to their businesses. Angela looked around and immediately Roz was beside her. Only her uncle, her Aunt Olive and her husband, Father Dwyer, Doctors Leahy and Emmet and her parents and sister remained.

'I don't want to speak to them, I *can't*!' Angela was emphatic.

Roz bit her lip. She could see how upset and troubled Maura O'Rourke looked. Both Angela's parents looked old and worn out and had a hesitant, apologetic look about them as if they knew they were viewed as the poor relations. She felt sorry for them. 'I know but . . . but you can't just ignore them,' she urged.

'I can! Haven't they ignored *me* for years? Why did they have to come? Why couldn't they have stayed away?' she hissed.

'Your Aunt Mary was her sister, Angela.'

Ronan Emmet stood beside them, looking concerned. 'Are you two girls all right? You look a bit distraught.'

Angela nodded and swallowed hard. From the corner of her eye she had seen her parents approaching. 'I . . . I want to go back now, please.'

Roz looked appealingly at the young doctor and he nodded. Dr Leahy had told him how and why Angela had come to live with her aunt and uncle. 'Of course you do, Angela, it's been an ordeal for you but I think there are a few people who would like to talk to you first. I'll wait and run you all back to Liam's house in the car.'

Angela felt trapped as both he and Roz turned away and stood a few paces away. Slowly she turned to face the little group, her lips set in a taut line, her eyes hard.

'Angela! 'Tis a fine girl you've grown to be and . . .

and . . . we're proud of you. Mary did a grand job of rearing you.' Martin O'Rourke felt a little in awe of this confident young woman.

Angela couldn't reply. She felt outraged. How could he stand there and say such things? As if it was something commonplace to give your child away to someone else. He had no right to be proud! He had no rights at all, he had forfeited them all years ago.

Maura held back, hurt and bewildered by Angela's silence and her all too apparent coldness.

'We read all about you, Angela. There was a piece in the *Tribune* about you and how successful you are. I cut it out and kept it.'

Angela looked at the young girl who was her sister. She must be fourteen, she thought, and she reminded her of Aoife. She was reasonably well turned out in a shortish grey dress with a white collar and black shoes. Her dark curly hair was taken back in a ponytail, tied with a white ribbon. This one was better dressed than either she or her other sisters had been, things must have improved.

'Madeleine told all the girls in school she was coming to meet you today,' Martin ventured awkwardly, for so far Angela hadn't uttered a word.

So that was what they'd named her. She inclined her head slightly towards the girl.

Maura could stand it no longer. She reached out and laid her hand on Angela's arm. 'Will you come out to the home place and visit us, Angela, please? Maddy wants so much to get to know you, she's so proud of her big sister, and we . . . we've missed you desperately.'

Angela shook her head vehemently. No! No, she would not go and visit them. It wasn't her home and hadn't been for years. They had ignored her for years too. She wanted nothing to do with them. All she wanted to do was go back to Liverpool.

'Please, please don't disappoint us, Angela!' Maura begged with tears in her eyes.

Angela felt the tears sting her own eyes but she shook her head again. 'No. No, I . . . I . . . can't. I'm going back to Liverpool tomorrow. It's all arranged.'

Maura let her hand drop to her side and Angela turned away and walked quickly to where Roz and Ronan Emmet were standing with Dr Leahy.

'Please, I'd like to go back now.'

Dr Leahy looked at her intently for he had heard Maura's words and Angela's reply. They all had. 'Angela, child, will you not reconsider?'

'No. I can't! I just can't! I just want to go home. I don't think I can stand much more.'

Roz put her arm around her. 'Come on, let's go back.'

'I'll drive you both. James is going to take Liam and Father Dwyer.' Ronan Emmet could see that the meeting with her parents had seriously upset Angela and he determined that he would stay with them for a while and perhaps give her something to calm her if necessary.

Roz sighed heavily. She supposed that Liam would take to the bottle once he got home and she wished they were leaving tonight instead of tomorrow.

She made a pot of tea for Angela, herself and Ronan Emmet and after he had had one small glass of whiskey Dr Leahy excused himself, leaving the priest and Liam to sit and talk quietly in a corner of the room over another glass of Jameson's.

'So what time is your train tomorrow?' Ronan Emmet asked. Thankfully Angela seemed to be much calmer.

'Twelve noon. That will get us to Dublin in plenty of time for the night ferry,' Roz answered.

'Morning surgery should have finished so I will pick you both up and drive you to the station,' he offered.

Roz refilled his cup. 'Thanks, it's very good of you.'

Liam looked across at them. 'I was just saying that as you are going back so soon, would you like to go up and see if there is any little thing of Mary's that you would like to have as a keepsake, Angela?'

Angela was about to refuse, thinking bitterly that he couldn't have thought of this himself, but she changed her mind. She would like something that had belonged to her aunt. She nodded. 'I would like something to keep.'

'Go on up then,' Liam urged, pouring himself another drink.

The room was neat and tidy, exactly the way Mary had always kept it. Since her aunt's death her uncle hadn't come in here, he'd continued to sleep downstairs although no doubt that would change once she and Roz had departed. She crossed to the press under the window and opened the top drawer. Mary's underclothes were still there, folded neatly. The other two drawers revealed clothes belonging to both her aunt and uncle. On top of the press was a statue of the Infant of Prague, two small china bowls and her aunt's hairbrush. She glanced around. Mary had had very little in the way of jewellery. She had been buried with her wedding ring and the little gold cross and chain she had always worn around her neck. She crossed to the wardrobe and opened it. Her aunt's clothes still hung there; no doubt Liam would give them to the St Vincent de Paul Society, in time. On the shelf at the top were the two hats and two handbags her aunt had possessed and in the corner was a tin that had once contained fancy biscuits, the sort you bought at Christmas. She pulled it forward; it had a picture of an alpine village in winter on the front. Maybe there would be something in here that she might like to keep.

She sat on the edge of the bed and opened it. Inside there were letters and a few birthday cards, all looking a bit worn and faded. She sighed; there was nothing of interest here. She was about to close it when a word on one of the cards caught her attention. In a shaky, spider-like hand the name 'Angela' had been written. She picked it up. It was a cheap birthday card with kittens playing with a ball of wool on the front. *For Angela on your tenth birthday, love Mammy and Daddy*, she read. With shaking hands she picked up one of the letters. It was years old, judging by the date, and it was from her mother. She read it slowly and carefully and then went on to the next and the next. She had almost read them all when Roz came into the room.

'We were wondering why you were so long so I . . .' Her words died as she caught sight of her friend sitting on the bed, surrounded by old letters and with tears pouring down her cheeks.

'Oh, Roz, I was wrong! I was so very wrong! She . . . they hadn't forgotten me! She wrote all these letters to both me and Aunt Mary and she . . . she sent cards too, birthday cards!' Sobs were making it hard to speak. 'She . . . she begged Aunt Mary to bring me to visit or even just to write. Why didn't she tell me? Why did she keep all these from me? Why did she let me believe they didn't *care*?'

Roz put her arm around her, shaking her head sadly. She couldn't believe it. It was a terrible thing Mary had done, making Angela believe that her parents had forgotten her. And why? 'Maybe . . . maybe she thought it was for the best,' she replied not very convincingly. It was downright cruel in her opinion.

'How could it be for the best?' Angela sobbed.

'Maybe she was jealous?' Roz mused aloud. 'Perhaps she

thought that because your mother had given you to her she had no right to go on loving you. Perhaps she wanted you to love her more than you loved your mother. We'll never know now.'

Angela groaned and collapsed against Roz. 'And I . . . I wouldn't speak to them. I didn't want anything to do with them, I refused to go and see them!'

'Well, that's easily remedied. You can go and see them and explain, take the letters with you.'

'But . . . but we're going back tomorrow, Dr Emmet is taking us to the station. It's all arranged.'

Roz stood up, pulling Angela with her. 'It can be unarranged,' she said firmly. 'In fact I'll go down now and talk to him – to all of them. You dry your eyes and wipe the mascara off your cheeks then gather up all those letters and cards and put them back in the box.'

Angela nodded. She was finding it very hard to understand why Mary had acted the way she had but at least now she *knew* her mother did love her and had never forgotten her. She hugged the box to her, feeling all the hurt and bitterness drain away.

As she went down the stairs Roz wondered if Liam had known about those letters. He must have, she reasoned. Had it been he who had advised his wife to keep them from Angela? Anger filled her eyes. Well, she was about to find out.

'Is she all right? Where is she?' Ronan Emmet asked as Roz entered the room.

'No, she is not "all right"! All her life she's believed her parents didn't care about her, that they wanted nothing to do with her. It hurt her deeply and made her bitter towards them. Well, now she knows it wasn't true. She's found a box of letters from her mother, letters that her aunt kept from her.' She turned to where Liam and Father Dwyer were sitting, staring at her. 'And I suppose *you* knew all about it. You *must* have!'

'Sure, I . . . I knew a . . . nothing!' Liam spluttered, the colour rising in his cheeks.

'Liar! I can see by the look on your face that you did!' Roz shot back.

Father Dwyer stood up. 'Now, young lady, that's enough! I'll not have you calling the poor man a liar in his own home and him just after having buried his wife.'

Roz wasn't going to be intimidated by the parish priest. 'With all due respect, Father, I think he knew and I also know that he had a very good reason for not wanting her parents – especially her father – to get in touch with her.' She glared at Liam, who was looking decidedly sheepish.

'I think you are mistaken in that and, whatever her reasons, Mary would have believed that what she was doing was for the best,' the priest replied, his voice full of conviction.

Roz looked at him in astonishment. 'For the best? You think, Father, that to make a child believe her parents don't love her or care about her is right?'

Father Dwyer wasn't used to having his pronouncements challenged and particularly not by such a bold young rossi as this one. 'I'm not saying that. What I am saying is that Mary, God rest her, took the child in and reared her as her own giving her every advantage in life and—'

'Angela is aware of that and she was always grateful, but that's not the issue here, Father,' Roz interrupted.

The priest was angry. 'I can see they do not teach you respect in England!'

Roz held her ground. 'I was taught respect, Father. I was also taught that respect has to be earned and I cannot respect

301

anyone who thinks it right to deliberately hurt a child the way Angela has been hurt – whatever the reasoning behind it.'

Ronan Emmet could see that this was developing into a full-scale battle. He hadn't known about all this but he agreed with Roz and he admired her for sticking to her guns. 'I think we should all calm down. Nerves are bound to be frayed at a time like this and things are said in the heat of the moment that are often regretted later.'

Roz looked at him questioningly. Was he siding with them? she wondered. But unless she told him about what Liam had done to Angela he wouldn't understand and she had no intention of doing that. 'She'll be down in a few minutes.'

'Good. I'll have a talk to her,' Ronan Emmet replied.

'And if you have any sense, doctor, you'll advise her against causing any more upset and grief in this house,' Father Dwyer said curtly, picking up his biretta from the sideboard, preparing to leave. He had no intention of having Angela O'Rourke and this brazen little madam further insult him. This was what became of living in that increasingly godless country across the water.

Liam had also risen and had shrugged on his jacket. He had no intention of staying either and facing Angela, for he had known about the letters. 'I'll walk with you, Father, and then I'll go and see a few of the lads.'

'Don't bother to rush back!' Roz muttered under her breath as the two men left.

When Angela came down she was much calmer and was relieved to find that both her uncle and the priest had gone for she had heard the raised voices.

Roz sank down in a chair, running her hands through her hair. The room was very warm and stuffy. 'She's upset that she refused to go and visit them because it's all arranged for us to go back tomorrow,' she informed Dr Emmet.

'Arrangements can easily be changed. Do you want to go and visit them tomorrow, Angela?' he asked kindly.

'Of course I do. I was . . . horrible to them! You know I was. But you . . . you know how I missed them!' she answered, a sob in her voice.

'It wasn't your fault,' Roz soothed.

'I'll have a word with James. We'll sort out the morning surgery between us and I'll drive you over. It's Saturday, usually we're not too busy and there is no evening surgery so you can stay for a while.'

Angela smiled for the first time in days. 'I'd be so grateful.' She turned to Roz. 'Will you come too?'

Roz frowned. 'I wouldn't want to intrude on something as private as that.'

'I'd really like you to come, Roz.' Angela felt she might need some moral support. It had crossed her mind that after the way she had treated her parents today, they might not now want to see her.

Roz bit her lip but Ronan Emmet came to her rescue. 'Why not come for the drive? We can go for a walk while Angela sees her parents and then we can all get something to eat on the way back here.'

Roz nodded, looking relieved, then she turned her mind to the practicalities. 'Would it be too much to ask to use your telephone? I'll have to contact the ferry company and my mam. She's expecting us back on Sunday morning and Dad was meeting us off the ferry. You are the only one I know who has a telephone in the house, apart from Father Dwyer,' she finished sharply.

'Of course. Why don't you both come back with me? James won't mind the bit of company and he'll be happy to hear your news, Angela.'

Roz got to her feet. 'Thanks, it's very good of you and I

can honestly say that the least time we have to spend in this house the better. It's been a very strange day altogether and I'll be glad when it's over.'

'I'm sure you both will,' Ronan Emmet agreed as he ushered them towards the door.

Chapter Thirty-Two

B Y MID-MORNING THE FOLLOWING day it was very hot. The fields looked dry and parched and the cattle stood in the shade of the trees and hedges. A haze shimmered over the brown bog land and both girls were glad of the slight breeze that came in through the open windows of Ronan Emmet's car. On her lap Angela held the box of letters and her small handbag. Both she and Roz had gone to bed early to avoid a possible confrontation with Liam but he hadn't come home.

'Probably out cold on someone's sofa,' Roz had remarked cuttingly.

'More likely in a ditch but I couldn't care less,' Angela had replied. The more she had thought about it the more she realised that Roz was probably right, Liam must have known about the letters.

She gave Ronan the directions once they reached the parish of Rahan. It was fifteen years since she'd left but nothing seemed to have changed much, she thought, glancing around as they turned into the narrow bohreen, but as they approached the house she was surprised to see chickens foraging in the yard and at one side of the house there was a vegetable patch. Even the single-storeyed little house looked better than when she'd left. The outside walls had been limewashed and there were even cotton curtains at the windows. A thin spiral of turf smoke rose from the chimney into the cloudless blue sky and the door stood wide open.

Ronan Emmet stopped the car at the top of the laneway. 'I think you should go on by yourself, Angela. I'll reverse back down the lane, it's a bit too tricky to turn in such a narrow yard.' It was going to be an emotional time for them all and he felt his presence and that of Roz would be an intrusion. He grinned at her. 'I'd probably run down half the poultry and destroy your mother's kitchen garden as well and that wouldn't be a great start,' he said by way of an excuse.

Roz caught his eye in the rear-view mirror and nodded her agreement. Angela got out and stood looking at the small house, the box of letters held tightly to her, as the car backed slowly down the bohreen.

Hearing the sound of the engine both Maura and young Maddy had come to the door. Maura's hand went to her throat as she caught sight of Angela standing in the yard. She had cried so many bitter tears since yesterday that her eyes were puffy and her head ached. Maddy too had been upset and very disappointed and now she hung back, clinging to her mother's arm. 'What's she come for, Mam?' she whispered.

Maura didn't answer her but she took a step forward and then another and then Angela began to run towards her. Maura caught her in her arms.

'Oh, Mam! Mam, I'm so sorry! I didn't know! I thought you didn't care about me, I thought you'd stopped loving me! She kept all your letters from me! I only found them yesterday afternoon,' Angela sobbed, clinging tightly to Maura's thin body.

Maura could hardly speak. 'Hush! Hush now, Angela, you're home. You've come back and that's all that matters,' she soothed, stroking the short dark curly hair. 'Come on into the house and we . . . we'll talk. Don't upset yourself, darlin'.'

Angela let herself be guided towards the door where Maddy stood biting her lip, not knowing what to say or do. Angela reached out and took her hand. 'I'm sorry, Maddy, for . . . yesterday.'

Maddy gazed at her sister and her eyes filled with tears. 'It wasn't my fault, Angela. I . . . I didn't ask to be born.'

Her words made Angela feel so dreadfully guilty. She had always blamed Maddy for her being given to Mary and Liam but it was as the girl had said, she hadn't asked to be born. 'I know, Maddy. I'm sorry.'

When they were in the kitchen Maura sat her down and gazed at her, shaking her head in disbelief. She had prayed so hard for this day to come and now that Angela was actually here, sitting in her old home, she could scarcely believe it. 'We . . . we all missed you, Angela, but me more than anyone. Not a day went by that I didn't think about you, pray that you were happy, that I'd done the right thing and that I'd see you again soon. It . . . it was so hard to let you go and then when there was no word I . . . wrote and kept on writing and hoping . . . but then when I heard nothing I began to wonder did . . . did you not want to know about us? I went to Mary's house once. I was so desperate I saved the fare. You were at school but I wanted to wait to see you. She . . . she refused me. She said it would upset and confuse you and make you unhappy and make her position impossible. She . . . she said you thought of her as your mother now, not myself, and it was best to leave things that way. She . . . she turned me away.'

Angela took her hand and squeezed it. 'Oh, mam, I didn't know that. I missed you too, Mam, all of you. I was miserable at first, things were so different, but I got used to it and she . . . she was good to me. I had the best of everything.' She looked at her mother's pale, careworn face now alight with joy and knew that she could never tell Maura about Liam Murphy, her mother had suffered enough. She wouldn't add to that by increasing the burden of guilt Maura already carried. She smiled through her tears at her sister. 'Put the kettle on, Maddy, we've all got a lot of catching up to do.'

Maddy did as she was bid and Angela and her mother sat talking quietly, both brushing away the tears from time to time. Angela told her mother about her early life with her aunt and uncle, her friendship with Emer and her days with the Leahys.

Maddy handed them the mugs of tea. There were so many things she wanted to ask her stylish and successful sister but she would have to wait.

'I never even knew you'd gone to Liverpool,' Maura said sadly, thinking there was so much she didn't know about her own daughter.

'I honestly don't know why she kept everything from me, Mam. What harm would it have done at all? I wouldn't have loved her any the less – and I did come to love her.'

Maura shook her head. 'I can only think that it's as she said to me, she thought it would unsettle you, make you unhappy, make you want to come back.'

'I would have wanted to come and visit, Mam, but . . . but I looked on that house in Edenderry as my home, until I was sixteen and Emer went to New York. That's when I knew I wanted more from life than just being a skivvy. So Dr Leahy helped me to get a place as a student nurse but I just wasn't cut out for it.'

Maddy sat on a stool at her mother's side mesmerised as Angela told them of her meeting and subsequent friendship with Roz Henderson, of how she had given up nursing and gone to live with them and of how she had become a designer and the owner of two boutiques. It was like a fairy story, Maddy thought, but she realised that even though Angela had had such an amazing life, she hadn't really been happy.

'That's when I found out you were in Liverpool. Your da saw the article they did on you in the local paper. We couldn't believe it. Our little Angela so successful.' Pride shone from Maura's eyes.

'Where is Da?' Angela asked, looking around and noticing for the first time that there was more furniture in the room than there used to be. There were also a few ornaments, a mirror above the range and rugs on the floor.

'He's at his work but he'll be home soon. God was good to us, he's had steady work now for a few years. John Devaney's a very old man now and crippled with the arthritis but as stubborn as a mule about going on with the farm. Didn't the young priest talk him into taking your da on full time to help out about the place and I go up a few times a week to clean the house.'

Angela nodded, wishing her father could have got such steady work years ago when they'd needed the money so badly. 'And the others? Aoife and Caitlin and Carmel and the boys? I missed them all, Mam. What's happened to them?'

Maura sighed with resignation. One by one she had seen them all leave. 'Aoife was the first to go. She went to Dublin and was in service for a bit, and then she went to America. She's in Chicago, she's married and has two children. I'm a granny now though I know I'll never see those children. She always sent money home in the early years. Carmel is in Boston.' She smiled. 'She went into nursing and loves it.' A frown furrowed Maura's brow and she paused. 'We . . . we don't hear much from either Jimmy or Peter. They went to Glasgow and we heard there was some trouble.' Maura bit her lip.

'With the police, Mam?'

Maura nodded. It grieved her that two of her sons had gone to the bad and were now in prison.

'They're both in jail,' Maddy informed her sister.

Angela was horrified. 'Oh, Mother of God! What did they do?'

'Got in with a desperate crowd and robbed a bank. It nearly broke your poor da's heart. We were so ashamed.'

'What about Declan?' Angela probed, wanting to divert her mother's mind away from this revelation.

'He's in London. Father Kenny, God rest his soul, got him settled with a good Catholic Irish family in Kilburn and he's a job as a porter in a hospital. He's a good lad, writes every month and sends us what he can spare.'

This was a relief to Angela and she said so.

'But you'll never guess what Caitlin is doing now,' Maddy interrupted her blue eyes full of mischief.

Angela was afraid to ask. Caitlin had always been the one who complained most and caused the most trouble. She wouldn't be at all surprised if she'd set up a house of ill repute.

'She's Mother Mary Immaculate now. She's in a convent in Perth in Australia,' Maddy informed her triumphantly.

'Caitlin is a *nun*!' Angela couldn't believe it. Her outspoken bold brat of a sister was *Mother Mary Immaculate*!

'There was a mission at the church and your da and I were only delighted when she came home and said she wanted to join the Order and they'd promised to have her.'

Angela nodded. It was the desire of every Catholic parent to have a child in Holy Orders, it was something to be proud of.

'It's been a great comfort to us, especially after the lads . . .'

'Have you all their addresses, Mam?'

'I have so and they'll all be delighted to hear from you, but I don't want you to go writing to those two blackguards. It won't do your career any good at all to be associated with the likes of them.'

Angela didn't know what to think about her brothers. It must be terrible for them to be locked up but yet maybe her mother was right. It was something she would have to think more deeply about.

Maura was busy looking for some paper and a pen to write out all the addresses so Maddy seized the opportunity to confide in her sister.

'Don't you have a great life in Liverpool? Sure, you wouldn't want to come back here. I know I wouldn't.'

'It is great but I work very hard. I hardly seem to have a moment to myself.'

'But imagine making and wearing all those gorgeous clothes!'

Angela smiled at her. 'There's a bit more to it than that.'

Maddy glanced towards her mother and, seeing she was fully occupied, she lowered her voice. 'Angela, can I come to Liverpool and work for you? I don't want to be the only one left buried here in the bogs.'

Angela was taken aback. 'I . . . I don't know, Maddy.'

'Please? I'd work very hard, so I would, and I'd be no trouble to you and I wouldn't want much of a wage.'

Angela could understand the girl wanting to get more out of life than she would if she stayed here and she would love the opportunity to get to know her sister better, but did she

want to take on the responsibility of taking care of Maddy?
'Let me think about it, Maddy. You've another two years at school yet.'

'But it would be something to look forward to, Angela,' Maddy pleaded.

Angela didn't want to be drawn into making any promises and she didn't know how her mother would feel about letting Maddy leave home. 'Write to me and I'll write back and keep you up to date with all the latest trends and we'll see.'

Maddy was disappointed but she nodded as the sound of a car coming slowly up the bohreen came to their ears.

Angela stood up. 'That will be Roz and Dr Emmet.'

Maura looked out of the window. 'And isn't your da just coming into the yard too. He'll be delighted to see you, Angela.'

Angela went out to meet him as the car pulled into the yard. Martin stopped dead in his tracks, unable to believe his eyes. 'Angela! Is it yourself?'

She hugged him. 'It is, Da. Oh, I'm so sorry for the way I behaved yesterday. I was horrible to you all, but . . . but Mam will explain everything.'

'Ah, don't worry your head about that, child. It's just thankful we are you came.' Martin's voice cracked with emotion as he held her tightly.

Roz looked at Ronan Emmet helplessly as they witnessed this scene. 'We came back too soon.'

'It certainly looks like it but we can't go off again now, it would look too obvious.'

Angela had turned towards them holding on to her father's arm.

'Should we go away and come back in half an hour?' Roz asked, grinning wryly.

'Not at all. Won't you both come in and have a cup of tea

with the family?' Martin replied, his voice full of happiness. Of course it wasn't the kind of home either of them would be used to but at least these days their circumstances had improved and he knew Maura could provide both tea and a bit of cake.

Roz said they would be delighted for they were both parched, having walked for what seemed like miles beside the canal and now her feet were killing her.

Angela laughed, looking down at her friend's elegant shoes, which were definitely not designed for country walks. 'You never learn, Roz Henderson, do you?'

Roz grinned back. 'A slave to fashion, that's me. Did she tell you how we met? I was wearing four-inch stiletto heels and fell off the bus.' She pealed with laughter, greatly relieved that Angela's visit had obviously been a success. Angela looked happier than she had for ages. As happy as she'd been before Danny Fielding had appeared on the scene.

They had all had tea and currant cake and Maddy had been completely enthralled by Roz who she thought was the most glamorous person she'd ever seen. Roz had complimented Maura on the cake and said that this was a lovely, peaceful place to live.

'You'd die of boredom here within a week, Roz,' Angela had stated.

'Ah, I don't know about that. Wouldn't she have every young fellow for miles fighting over her,' Maura replied, smiling. She would certainly cause a stir, they'd never had anyone as exotic-looking in the parish before.

'And so would Angela,' Martin added.

'Ah, give over with all that malarkey, Da!' Angela laughed, realising with reluctance that Ronan Emmet had glanced at his watch. She stood up. 'I'm sorry but we'll have to go. We've the packing to do when we get back and I don't want to impose on Dr Emmet. I'm sure he's got plans for this evening.'

'It was very good of you to bring the girls out to us, doctor,' Maura said as she handed Angela the piece of paper with the addresses on.

Angela hugged them all in turn and promised faithfully to write regularly, giving them all her news. Roz too hugged Maura and young Maddy and shook Martin's hand. 'I'm so glad everything has worked out so well,' she said sincerely.

They all stood in the doorway and waved and Angela waved back, pushing from her mind the memory of the last time she had been driven away from here in a car. All that was in the past now.

'Are you happy now? They're very nice,' Roz asked.

'I know and I'm happier than I've been for years.'

'Would you ever consider coming back, to live, I mean?' Roz asked.

Angela shook her head. 'I don't think so. Apart from them what is there here for me? And there's the business.'

'You could always open a boutique in Dublin,' Ronan Emmet suggested. 'There isn't one as far as I know.' He had grown to like and admire her in the short time he'd known her.

'And where would I find my customers? The young ones still have to leave Ireland to find work, you know that. Even Maddy has asked me can she come and work for me in Liverpool.'

Roz raised her eyebrows. 'She was quick off the mark. What did you say?'

'That I'd think about it. She's got two more years at school still and I don't know how Mam would feel about her leaving. They'd have no one at home then.'

Ronan Emmet nodded. 'It's desperate that parents should

have to struggle to rear a family, only to see them all go and be left alone in their twilight years. One of these days it will change, it will *have* to, or we'll be a nation of old people.'

Angela nodded her agreement but wondered when or if things would ever change in the country of her birth. But she would be going back to Liverpool in a far more contented frame of mind and she would contact her sisters and her brother. She smiled. She had a great deal to tell Emer now.

Before she followed Roz into the house Angela turned to Ronan Emmet and smiled. 'Thank you for taking me today. You know how much it meant to me. I told you how much I missed them when we used to talk when Mary was dying.'

'I was only delighted to see you all so happy, Angela, I mean that.'

'I know you do.' She felt strangely sad to be taking her leave of him; she had grown closer to him these last few days. Of course she would see him when he ran them to the station tomorrow but this was the last time she would see him alone.

He smiled and took her hand. 'You've been through some difficult times, Angela, but I admire you for the way you've coped with them. You're a grand girl and don't forget if you ever do feel like coming back you could open a shop up in Dublin.'

She smiled but shook her head, remembering the reply she'd given him earlier but wondering, too, if he was saying in a roundabout way that he wanted her to come back? She didn't know him well enough to ask him that. 'I'll see you in the morning, Dr Emmet.'

He grimaced. 'Can you not call me Ronan? Dr Emmet makes me sound as old as James Leahy and I don't call you Miss O'Rourke.'

She laughed. 'I'll see you in the morning, Ronan.'

Chapter Thirty-Three

———⋆———

THEIR JOURNEY BACK HAD been uneventful. Ronan Emmet had driven them to the station and Mr Henderson had met them off the ferry. Both Bernard and Lydia were very relieved to hear that Angela had been reconciled with her parents and sister. Roz was just relieved to be home.

'Everything is so different there, Mam. I mean it's nice and so are the people but well, everything is about twenty years out of date. There aren't even many cars on the streets of Dublin.'

'You mean you felt like a fish out of water,' Lizzie stated.

'What about you, Angela? Did everything feel strange to you?' Lydia Henderson asked.

'Sort of. I've got used to living in a city now. You take so many things for granted.'

Lizzie nodded, looking a little worried. 'Well, one thing we can't take for granted are our designs.'

'Why? Has there been some kind of revolution while

we've been away? Has everyone reverted to wearing clothes similar to their mothers?' Roz asked flippantly.

Angela looked at Lizzie more closely knowing she kept a very close eye on the fashion scene. 'We're going to be all right with our autumn collection, aren't we?'

'I hope so but there have been a few new designs appearing in London. Like ankle-length skirts and coats, "maxi" they're called, and jumpsuits with very wide legs. It's all stemming from "Flower Power" and "Ban the Bomb".'

'I don't think girls will abandon their mini-skirts and not everyone wants to look like a hippy. I *hate* those Afghan coats with all that tatty-looking woolly stuff around the hem and sleeves and I've heard that when they get wet they positively *stink*!' Roz pulled a face. 'You wouldn't want to be in the same room as someone wearing one.'

'That's because they're made from goat skins that haven't been cured properly,' Lizzie informed her sister.

Angela sighed. 'I suppose we'll have to include some jumpsuits and maxis for next spring if we want to keep up with the trends.'

Lizzie nodded her agreement. 'We've got a lot of work to do in the months ahead.'

They did indeed work hard and Roz was dispatched almost immediately to London for a weekend to have a good look at what was appearing in the boutiques in Carnaby Street and the King's Road. She was also to go and pay particular attention to Barbara Hulanicki's boutique Biba. She returned with a great deal of shopping, including two pair of Courrèges boots, one pair in silver, the other in white. They were completely flat and had square toes and came over the knee.

'They're calling them "go-go" boots. Everyone's wearing them to dance in, especially in silver,' she'd informed Lizzie and Angela. She reported that plenty of girls were indeed wearing the maxi length and that she'd seen jumpsuits in all kinds of fabrics, so Angela began to work on designing her own version of the new trend.

Angela's satisfaction with the way her business was going was only heightened when she realised that she had at last paid off her debt to Bernard Henderson.

'It's a huge relief to me that at last I've paid you back. I truly appreciate everything you've done for me but I now feel that the business is *mine*, if that doesn't sound ungrateful?'

He smiled at her across the dining-room table. They often had meetings such as this one when they discussed financial matters and she asked his advice. 'It's not a bit ungrateful, Angela. I'm very proud of what you have achieved. Now you will have more money to invest in the business. Remember, you can't stand still, you will always have to look to the future.'

She nodded seriously. 'I know that and I've been thinking about market research and wondering if I shouldn't do some myself. The London shops seem to be taking the lead now.'

He considered her words and then nodded. 'You need someone based in London to do it for you. Will I make some enquiries or do you want to do that yourself? It is your business now.'

Angela frowned, thinking about it. She had ever less time to spare herself these days. 'I think I would be glad of your help and I don't really know how much I would have to pay for such a service, but I really do have to keep up with the trends.'

'I'll look into it, but you don't want to pay extortionate rates which would seriously eat into your bank balance. You do realise, Angela, that you can now afford to buy a car of your own or a flat? Not that we would want you to leave us, you're part of the family, but if you felt you would like a bit more privacy . . .'

Angela shook her head. 'I like being part of a family but it is nice to know that I can afford such things. I'd not thought about a car, I can't drive and the public transport is good, so I don't think I'll bother.'

'I wish those two lads of mine had the same attitude!' He confided, smiling as they gathered up their bank statements and ledgers.

Angela was used to working six months ahead by now but as she wrapped the Christmas gifts for her parents and Maddy and Emer she still thought it a little strange to be surrounded by swatches of brightly patterned light summer materials and samples of feather boas dyed in all colours of the rainbow. True to her word she kept in regular contact with her mother and she often sent Maddy clothes. Her sister had written to say that she was the most stylish girl in the parish now and that all her schoolfriends were green with envy. Maura told Angela that she was spoiling the child and filling her head with all kinds of ideas about 'going into the fashion business'. Indeed the way things were going the child was in danger of losing the run of herself entirely. Hadn't Father Seamus warned all the young ones – and from the pulpit no less – that he would not allow the Holy Sacrifice of the Mass to degenerate into a fashion parade.

'You're going to have to let Maddy come over when she finishes school, Angela. You'll get no peace otherwise,' Roz had warned and Angela was thankful that her sister still had some time yet at school. Lizzie had commented that when Maddy realised how mundane some of the job was, and how hard she would have to work, she might change her mind. The fashion industry wasn't quite as glamorous as a lot of people thought it was.

'Of course, you could let her come over in the summer holidays and she could start in the workroom, doing the boring jobs everyone has to do when they first start and which they all hate, it would give her a real insight,' Lizzie had added.

'I suppose so, but where would she stay?' Angela had asked.

'Here, of course. Our Sal's announced that she's getting married in June. Harry's grandmother is giving them some money so they can get a house. I'm going to move into her bedroom so Maddy can have mine or you can have my room and Maddy can have yours.'

Angela had given it a lot of thought and concluded that Lizzie could be right. It might just solve the problem of Maddy's obvious infatuation with what she termed the 'fashion business' and if she stayed here she could keep her eye on her sister.

She was thinking about it now as she tied the ribbon on the parcel for Maddy. Inside the box was a set of pale lemon nylon baby-doll pyjamas, overlaid with permanently pleated white nylon. Highly unsuitable for the cold, damp Irish winter and the often damp and chilly Irish summer, but very pretty. After Christmas she would write to her mother and suggest that her sister come and stay for a few weeks in the summer and help out in the workroom. She would also have to discuss with Sal the designs she had come up with for the wedding dress and the bridesmaids' dresses; the material would have to be chosen and ordered before she started on the designs for autumn next year, 1967.

Roz stuck her head around the door. 'Mam said if you've

finished parcelling those things up, she'll take them to the post office for you. And I've brought your post.' She was clutching two letters and a mug of tea and was completely enveloped in a long beige knitted cardigan over brown bell-bottomed trousers and brown skinny rib polo. 'I'm only just getting warm after standing all morning in the park in a lilac and pink flowered jumpsuit with a halter neck and no sleeves and a purple feather boa! Honestly, I sometimes wonder why I do it? In summer I swelter in tweeds, tartan and jumpers and in winter I freeze to death in poly chiffon and cotton.'

Angela grinned at her. 'You know you love doing our photo shoots for us.'

Roz perched on the edge of the table and sipped her tea. 'You've a letter from Emer and one from Ireland, but it's not Maddy's writing.' She had had letters from Maddy herself and knew the girl's handwriting.

Angela opened Emer's letter first, knowing Roz was always interested in Emer's news. She scanned the lines, keeping Roz informed and then she gave a little shriek of delight.

'What! Tell me?' Roz demanded, full of curiosity.

'She's getting engaged at Christmas and they hope to get married in the January after next, nineteen sixty-eight. Patrick will have been promoted by then and they'll be able to afford a place of their own for she says she'd rather live on the streets than with the old battleaxe.'

'That's great news!' Roz enthused then grimaced. 'God! Wait until Mam hears that. She'll start going on at me again, especially now that Lizzie and that Phil Caldwell seem to be getting serious.'

Angela didn't reply, she was concentrating on Emer's letter. Then she looked up at Roz. 'She wants us to go for the wedding.'

Roz's eyes widened. 'To New York? Both of us? Really, me as well?'

Angela nodded. 'Dinny and Joy are going to help his mam and da with the fare so they can go too, so she'll have some family around her on the day. She says it's very good of him because she was sure the battleaxe would make some comment about her guest list. And she says she feels she knows you so well and wants to meet you.' Angela grimaced. 'And there's some comment about me not being seriously *involved* with anyone so I won't be taking a fiancé or husband so it will be nice for me to have a friend to travel with.'

'It's not as if you don't go out and you haven't had offers,' Roz replied.

Angela was thoughtful. She did go to dances and sometimes to clubs with Roz and Lizzie and she had been asked out on dates but there hadn't been anyone she had really wanted to get to know better. Sal was getting married, Lizzie was courting seriously and now Emer too was getting married and it made her feel a little wistful, as though there was something lacking in her life. The memory of Ronan Emmet came back to her. They had written to each other occasionally, newsy and lighthearted letters, but he always ended those letters by reminding her that if she ever did decide to go back to Ireland she would be very welcome in Edenderry.

Roz interrupted her thoughts. 'We *are* going to go, aren't we? You can't miss it. She's your oldest friend and I've always wanted to go to New York!'

'Of course I'll go but do you think your mam will let you?'

'Why not? She can't refuse, not for something as important as Emer's wedding and she won't want you to be travelling on your own. Oh, it's so *exciting*! I've got ages to save up some spending money. I've heard that the shops are *fabulous*!' Roz automatically assumed her father would foot the bill for her trip.

Angela smiled. 'Before she left Ireland we said that if she got rich she would come back to Dublin and we'd stay in the Shelbourne and shop in Grafton Street and that if I got rich I'd go there and stay in the Waldorf Astoria and shop on Fifth Avenue.'

Roz laughed delightedly. 'I can't see us staying at the Waldorf but we can certainly go shopping in Bloomingdale's and from what we saw of the shops in Dublin I'd say you got the better end of the deal. Do you think she'll ask you to do her dress? She knows you're doing Sal's.'

'I don't know but it would cause a bit of a problem with fittings and the like. She would be better going to a bridal shop or I could design it and she could find someone over there to make it.'

Roz was totally absorbed in this unexpected opportunity to visit New York and was already trying to decide how much money she could save in a year. Saving was something completely alien to her nature so it was a few minutes before she realised that Angela had fallen silent.

Angela had opened the other letter and read the contents and had folded it again. It was from Ronan Emmet.

'What's wrong? Who is the other letter from?' Roz asked.

'Ronan Emmet. Liam Murphy is dead,' she stated flatly.

'I can't honestly say he'll be missed,' Roz replied tartly. 'I suppose he drank himself to death?'

Angela shook her head. 'No, although I think the drink may have contributed to it. He . . . he hanged himself.'

'Oh, my God!' Roz exclaimed.

'Ronan says it must have been Mary's death that unhinged his mind and drove him to it.' Angela was trying to feel some pity for him. How unhappy and troubled would he have to have been to do such a dreadful thing? Had he come to regret everything he had done? He must have, she reasoned, and he had been unable to live with the fact.

'More likely guilt about the way he behaved both to you and your aunt.'

Angela nodded. 'At least he didn't do it while Aunt Mary was alive. Ronan wants to know if I will be going over. I'm not. I'm not going to be a hypocrite.'

'What will you tell him? The truth?' Roz asked quietly, all thoughts of New York banished from her mind.

'No. How could I do that and especially in a letter? I'll just say I'm very busy and that it's too close to Christmas. I'll send some flowers and probably Mam and Da will make the effort to go over to Edenderry.'

Angela felt her explanation would make her look cold and heartless but she just couldn't tell Ronan Emmet about Liam's behaviour. Apart from anything else there was a chance he wouldn't believe her. Father Dwyer hadn't.

'Will you ever tell your mother the truth about him?' Roz asked, wondering if Maura O'Rourke would grieve for the man who'd taken her child in.

'No. Why should I go piling more guilt on to her shoulders? If I told her she would never, ever forgive herself for sending me there. It would kill her.' Angela sighed heavily. 'It's over now, Roz. He's dead and he went to his death without being absolved from his sins. That's punishment enough. I have to forget all about him and get on with my life now.'

Chapter Thirty-Four

———◆————

BOTH PIECES OF NEWS had been relayed to the family; that of Liam Murphy's death first. Lydia Henderson had sympathised but had agreed with Angela's decision not to go over. This was not a good time of year to be crossing the Irish Sea, she said, and he had only been related by marriage to Angela and she hadn't seemed to be particularly close to him. It had of course been very different when Mary had died; Angela had been very fond of her, although she still couldn't understand Mary's callous decision to keep all Maura's letters hidden away.

Emer's news had cheered them all up but Lydia Henderson wondered about the wisdom of letting her flamboyant and headstrong youngest daughter go off to a city like New York without any kind of parental control; she realised, however, that there was little she could do about it. Roz would be nearly twenty-one and it was a formal invitation to a wedding, there was no reason why Roz should refuse. They could certainly afford to pay for her trip and Roz was so full of excitement that she hadn't the heart to say she couldn't go. At least Angela had plenty of common sense, she thought. Hopefully enough for both of them.

After their new styles for spring were in the shops and selling well and Sal's wedding dress was in hand, Angela wrote to her mother suggesting that Maddy come over in the summer holidays. She had discussed it with Lydia Henderson first. She had broached the subject late one Saturday afternoon in early April after Sal and her mother had returned from town, Sal having urged her mother to start looking for her outfit for the wedding and not leave things to the last minute as she usually did.

'That one has me worn out trying on dresses and two-piece costumes and hats. There are weeks and weeks yet,' Lydia complained as Angela handed her a much-needed cup of tea.

'Mam, I'm sick to death of telling you that Harry's mother wants to know what colours you are wearing so she doesn't buy the same. She's always asking me, you know what she's like. I'm demented with the pair of you!' Sal complained.

'Oh, if she's that worried tell her to go and get her outfit, then I'll get mine. She fusses about things too much, does that one.'

'Honestly, Mam! You know that's not how things are done and I don't want her commenting that we know nothing about wedding etiquette,' Sal retorted indignantly.

'You sound just like Emer,' Angela said, grinning wryly at Sal. Sal raised her eyes to the ceiling. 'At least Emer would understand!'

'All right, Sal. We'll go again next Saturday and I promise we won't come home until I've bought something. Now, can I have a bit of peace?'

Sal smiled triumphantly and went upstairs, taking the new underwear she'd purchased with her.

'I know that it's not really a good time to be bringing this up but I'd like to ask would it be all right if I write and ask Mam if Maddy can come over and stay for a few weeks in the summer holidays? Lizzie and I think it will be a good idea for her to spend time in the workrooms, show her what working for a living is all about. I wouldn't be after asking her before I'd spoken to you about it.'

Lydia sipped her tea and looked thoughtful. She knew from experience what it was like to have a daughter who harped on and on about something. Roz was always doing it. At least since the advent of this trip to New York no more had been said about going to live and work in London, which was a blessing; but now Sal was getting as bad with all this wedding malarkey. 'I think it's a good idea too and it will give your poor mother a bit of peace and quiet. She's welcome to stay here but will she be all right travelling on her own? She's very young.'

'I suppose I could go over to Dublin and meet her off the train,' Angela mused.

'I've got a much better idea. We'll all be exhausted after our Sal's wedding – you included. She'll be going off on her honeymoon so what I suggest is that we all go over for a holiday and you can bring Maddy back with us. I'll speak to Bernard this evening. Oh, he'll moan a bit about the expense after the wedding but we haven't had a holiday in years and those two lads are quite capable of running the business without him.'

It was a great idea but Angela was doubtful. 'I don't know if I can spare the time for a holiday.'

'Of course you can. A break will do you good and a week or ten days away aren't going to make *that* much difference to your schedules. And it will give our Rose something else to think about other than flaming New York! She's beginning to sound like a cracked record.'

Angela grinned. 'I know. I hope she's not going to be disappointed when we finally get there.'

'That's settled then. We'll take the car over and go touring. I've always wanted to go, my family came from Cork. Tell your mother we'll come back via Offaly and pick Maddy up.'

'Will there be enough room, do you think? There will be five of us without Maddy,' Angela queried.

Lydia looked thoughtful. 'I suppose we could hire a bigger car or even buy one. I fancy one of those Humber Hawks.' She paused, thinking about her husband's reaction if she suggested this expense on top of everything else. 'Or when we get there we could hire a Mini for you girls. Phil is teaching our Lizzie to drive and she's bound to have passed her test by then and our Rose did say there was hardly any traffic on the roads over there so you should be fine following Bernard and me in the Austin. Then our Rose could travel back with us and you, Lizzie and Maddy can come in the Mini.'

Angela laughed. 'I won't be able to do a thing with her. I don't think she's ever been in a car in her life. It will be yet another fantastic experience she'll be able to boast about at school.'

Lydia got to her feet. 'It will if our Lizzie doesn't have you all in a ditch. Now, I'd better get a move on with the supper.'

Angela too got up. 'I'll give you a hand and thanks for letting Maddy stay.'

Everyone had thought it a wonderful idea, except Sal who complained that this forthcoming holiday seemed to be taking precedence in her mother's mind over her wedding.

'Don't be such a killjoy, Sal. You'll have your big day with all the trimmings and then your honeymoon in Spain. Your father is going to organise our little trip so there's no need for

330

you to get upset,' Lydia told her. After some initial pro-
crastination Bernard had agreed that they did need a holiday
and it would be good to have a week touring the peaceful
Irish countryside where the roads were not crowded with
lunatic drivers as they were increasingly becoming here. He
was very thankful indeed, he said, that the government had
brought in this new law to test drivers suspected of being
drunk. It was possibly the only good thing this Labour
government had done so far. He had been deeply disappointed that Harold Wilson's party had been re-elected.

Roz had kept the thought to herself that from what she
had witnessed so far of Lizzie's driving, her sister might well
be classed as a 'lunatic driver'. Still, she was bound to have
improved by the time Sal got married.

Angela had written first to her mother imparting all this
news and asking for permission to bring young Maddy back
with them. Maura wrote back:

*I've been discussing it all with your Da, and he thinks it is
a great idea. Doesn't she have the heart across me wanting
to be a dress designer like you, maybe a bit of hard work will
change her mind, please God, for I can't make her
understand that it's a talent you have. It's not something she
can learn from books. Isn't she mad to get away from here
and have what she thinks is a grand exciting life in a huge
city like Liverpool but my mind will be greatly relieved to
know she's with you and Mrs Henderson and, sure, aren't
we looking forward to meeting Herself and Himself who
have been so good to you. Will you be after writing to the
bold strap yourself or will I be the one to tell her? There's a
very nice bed and breakfast place run by Mrs Hickey on the
canal bank just below Killina. She'll be only delighted to
have you stay on your way back to the ferry. 'Canal View',*

331

the place is called. Your da and myself are looking forward to
seeing you again, acoushla. Will you be able to bring us some
photographs of the wedding when you come?

'Everyone loves a wedding,' Roz commented breezily
after Angela had read this out to her. 'But I'm really looking
forward to Emer's, not that I'm not looking forward to being
a bridesmaid to Sal,' she added.

'Oh, will you stop going on about Emer's wedding! You'll
be after upsetting Sal and you know how touchy she's
getting.'

'So are you going to write and tell young Maddy?'

'I am so but I'm not going to glamorise it all. She's going
to have to work and be paid the same as any young girl
starting out and she's not going to be going off into town by
herself either.'

'Will we stop off in Edenderry on the way back, do you
think?' Roz always threw herself wholeheartedly into things
and if they were going to tour Ireland then they might as well
go and revisit the little town.

'What for?' Angela asked flatly.

'You could go and put some flowers on Mary's grave and
maybe go and see the two doctors. They were both very nice.'

Angela looked at her friend closely but Roz was all wide-
eyed innocence. 'Do you fancy Ronan Emmet, is that the
way of it?' she probed, feeling a little uneasy.

'I do not! He's nice enough but could you see me married
to a country doctor and living in that place? I'd die of
boredom if Miss Dunne didn't kill me first. She was very
disapproving of me when we were up there using the phone.'

Angela laughed. 'I don't think she really approved of me
either. I think she thought I'd got above myself and neither
of us could ever live up to Dolores Leahy in her eyes.'

332

'Ah, so you've been thinking about the young Dr Emmet yourself!' Roz teased.

Angela shook her head and bit her lip. 'I've not heard a word since I wrote saying I wasn't going over. He probably hasn't got a very high opinion of me now and anyway I can't see myself as a country doctor's wife either. Now, I'd better write to Maddy.'

In her letter she tried to play it all down, emphasising that she would be expected to work hard, that the tasks would be boring and her wages low. That she would be expected to help out in the house and keep her room tidy. That she wasn't to think she could be going off to shop in Liverpool city centre by herself and that the journey was tiring, whether by train and ferry or by car and ferry. To her dismay Maddy seemed to ignore everything completely. She wrote back saying she was so excited that she couldn't sleep. She was actually coming to Liverpool on a sort of working holiday and she would be *paid*. She would have real money of her own to spend on herself and she would be staying in the Hendersons fine big house where there was hot and cold running water and a bathroom and all kinds of modern appliances, like a television set. It was going to be a huge adventure for her to be driven around the parish in a Mini by Lizzie and as soon as she was old enough she was going to learn to drive and why hadn't Angela herself taken lessons? Everyone in her class was sick with envy but particularly that hateful Bernie Donnelly who thought she was above everyone else because her da had bought a second-hand car and they now drove to Mass on Sundays.

Angela read all this with despair. 'Oh, Holy Mother! What have I let myself in for?' she confided to Roz.

'I told you you'd do no good with her. Still, it's only for a few weeks, then she'll have to go home.'

'But she'll expect to come again when she leaves school!'

'She might not. She might hate everything: the noise, the traffic, the litter, the work—'

'She'll drive poor mam mad, I know she will.'

'Then you'll just have to bite the bullet and let her stay when she has finished school.'

'Oh, I just don't know, Roz! She'll be my responsibility then.'

'Oh, cheer up. You might enjoy having her here and she might just prove to be as talented as you are.'

It was something Angela had not thought about but somehow she doubted it. Only time would tell.

Chapter Thirty-Five

———•◦◦•———

A S THE WEATHER GREW WARMER and the days became
longer the preparations for Sal's wedding grew more and
more frenetic. Sal was getting herself into a highly agitated
state of nerves and Lydia declared that if things went on like
this they would all end up in the same ward of the local
psychiatric hospital before the big day arrived. Bernard and
his two sons stated that they were glad to go to work for a bit
of peace and quiet.

To everyone's relief Lydia's prediction did not come true
and the day before the wedding Angela insisted they have a
final dress rehearsal so that if there were any minor
alterations needed they could be done that evening.
Everything had been checked and double-checked and at last
Sal felt she hadn't overlooked a single thing.

'I just hope you haven't lost any more weight since your
final fitting. You've worn yourself to a shadow fussing over
everything,' Roz commented flatly to her sister as she did up
the zip in her deep rose-pink satin bridesmaid's dress. It
wasn't a colour she particularly liked but it was Sal's choice.

All the dresses were the same: long and semi-fitted with a scoop neckline and wide bell-shaped sleeves around the edge of which had been sewn pale pink daisies. Their head-dresses were small wreaths of matching daisies.

'Well, if I hadn't double-checked everything myself I really would be a bag of nerves now. Mam can be quite slapdash about things, as you well know, Roz. Look at the carry-on over her hat,' Sal reminded her sister as Angela helped her into her wedding dress.

They were all crowded into Sal's bedroom and the room seemed to be overflowing with tissue paper and boxes and discarded clothes. Lydia Henderson's much disputed hat, resplendent in its box, was on the floor beside the dressing table.

Roz sighed heavily as she slipped her feet into the satin pumps, dyed to match the dress, and looked critically at herself in the long mirror on the wardrobe door. She refrained from grimacing at her reflection. She liked the design of the dress, it was the colour and the trimmings she heartily disliked. Her mother had finally settled on a bronze and green shot taffeta dress and matching coat but had wanted to buy a black, bronze and gold hat she'd seen in the Bon Marché. Sal, Lizzie and Roz had been totally against it.

'Mam, all those colours together will clash horribly! There'll be far too much gold,' Lizzie had protested.

'You'll end up looking like a Christmas tree, Mam!' Roz had warned bluntly.

'And won't my future ma-in-law make some snide remark to that effect!' Sal had added.

'At least Mam won't look like pale blue powder puff!' Lizzie had interjected scathingly for Sal had described the powder-blue coat and dress, liberally edged with pale blue marabou feathers, and the matching hat, similarly embellished, that her future mother-in-law had bought. In the end Mrs Henderson had been persuaded to have a hat made in a moss-green sugar-spun straw that was an almost perfect match to the green in her outfit. The milliner at Val Smith's in Bold Street had suggested it be trimmed with two long bronze feathers and the whole effect was simple but very smart.

At last Sal stood before the mirror in the outfit that Angela had designed for her and gazed at herself critically as Angela placed on her head the pearl tiara to which was attached the long ivory tulle veil.

Lizzie stood back and nodded approvingly. 'You look absolutely gorgeous, Sal! You were right not to have pure white, it made you look drained. Ivory suits your skin tone much better.'

Sal smiled at her sister. 'I wanted something different and I've got it.'

Roz nodded, thinking that no doubt Harry's mother would have some comment to make about it not being 'traditional', for it wasn't. It was a dress and matching coat in ivory duchesse satin. The dress itself was a long, strapless, semi-fitted evening gown and where the panels of the skirt joined the boned bodice it was heavily embroidered with pearls and crystal beads. The coat, which was edge to edge, was also full length with bracelet-length sleeves and a neat round neckline and the heavy embroidery was repeated around the cuffs and neck and down both edges of the front of the coat. Angela had designed it so that it could be worn again for one of the many 'dressy' evening events Sal would be attending with her new husband. If necessary it could be dyed a different colour, she had advised Sal. There would be no problem about the beading, these days it wasn't necessary for dyes to be used with boiling water. There were cold dyes.

'It looks much smarter and more modern than a traditional wedding dress with a very full skirt and long train and yards of lace and ribbon,' Roz said admiringly. 'And you can never do anything else with a traditional dress, it always looks like a wedding dress, even if you have it cut short. At least you can wear that again.'

Angela, her mouth full of pins, nodded her agreement as she adjusted Sal's veil. She was very pleased with the result.

Lizzie glanced around at her sisters. 'Is everyone ready? Do we all look OK? Nothing else to worry about? Nothing needs altering?'

'I don't think so,' Roz replied, hoping that Harry's sister had had the sense to try everything on before arriving here tomorrow morning when it would definitely be too late for alterations. Her shoes were pinching a little but she intended to stuff them with newspaper in the hope that they would stretch a bit overnight.

'I just hope the weather holds,' Sal commented, her eyes going to the window where the last rays of the setting sun touched the glass.

'Of course it will! Nothing is going to spoil your day, Sal,' Roz replied firmly. 'Nothing at all.'

And nothing had gone wrong. The weather had been perfect, Sal had looked radiant and Harry had been delighted with her. There had been the odd comment about her dress being 'unusual' from his mother, which Roz had quickly and firmly stifled with the reply that as it had been especially designed by Angela to Sal's exact requirements, it was indeed unusual and you wouldn't find another one like it anywhere, which was more than could be said for a shop-bought dress no matter how expensive. She personally thought her mother looked very elegant and stylish while Harry's mother just looked over-dressed and fussy.

'It's a wonder all those feathers don't give her a sneezing fit!' she'd commented under her breath to Angela when they'd both first caught sight of Mrs Bradley in the church.

Sal and Harry had gone happily off to Spain on their honeymoon and Lydia and Bernard Henderson heaved a sigh of relief and began to look forward to the first real holiday they had had for years. Angela had decided to go and stay with her parents for the week for she felt she had so much lost time to make up and she preferred to do that rather than go touring around the country. Lizzie was going to drop her off and then pick her up on the way back. Lizzie had passed her driving test at the first attempt, something she was extremely proud of, for both her brothers had had to take it a second time; and when they reached Dublin a Mini had been hired for her by her father.

The good weather held, the ferry crossing was calm and the drive down to Offaly was uneventful with Lizzie adroitly managing the small car as she followed her father's much larger Austin Princess down the narrow, almost-empty roads.

'You are quite sure you don't want to go to call on young Dr Emmet?' Roz asked mischievously as they drove through Enfield, passing a signpost for Rhode and Edenderry.

Angela shook her head. To her disappointment she still hadn't heard from him.

'Stop tormenting her, Roz!' Lizzie chided. 'I have to say it's really great driving over here. There's so much traffic on the roads at home that you have to have eyes in the back of your head. I was terrified the first time I went out on my own. Is it much further, Angela?'

'About another hour. Mam will have something ready for us to eat and you will be glad of a break by then.'

'I'm fine but I suppose Dad will. We're hoping to get to Clonmel by suppertime. He's got us booked into Hearn's Hotel for the night. It's quite famous. I was reading about it. It was where the first Bianconi cars ran from. The first public transport system I suppose you could call it, before the advent of the railways.'

Roz grinned at Angela. 'Quite the little mine of information, isn't she?'

'Well, at least I'm taking an interest in the places we're going to visit,' Lizzie shot back, swerving a little to avoid a small flock of hens that had wandered out on to the road.

When they at last reached the small county town of Tullamore Lizzie went ahead of her father and, following Angela's instructions, it wasn't long before they pulled into the bohreen that led to the O'Rourkes' cottage. Lizzie stopped. 'I don't think Dad will be able to turn his car around, there's not much room. I'd better get out and tell him to leave it on the road.'

Roz looked at Angela quizzically. 'Are you going to be all right here for a week? How are you going to get around?'

'Oh, don't worry about me. I'll borrow a bicycle if I have to but I really don't mind walking.' She meant it, although she was wondering how she would feel sleeping once again in the little room she had shared with all her sisters and which she would now share with Maddy. She had become so used to having her own room and in a house that had every modern convenience. Well, she would just have to get on with it. It wouldn't kill her for a week and there was so much she wanted to talk to her mother about.

Maddy came flying across the yard to meet them, her long dark curly hair tumbling over her shoulders, and for an instant she looked so like the young Aoife that Angela caught her breath.

340

'I've been waiting and watching all the morning for you! I thought you were never coming!' she cried, flinging herself into Angela's arms.

Angela laughed and hugged the excited girl while Lizzie and Roz got out of the car.

'Hello, trouble!' Roz greeted Maddy, smiling broadly.

'Oh, don't you all look just *great*!' Maddy beamed, taking in the stylish wide-bottomed jeans, the bright cotton tops and equally bright matching earrings and bangles all the older girls wore.

Lizzie introduced herself. 'Hello. I'm Lizzie.'

'You're in charge of the workrooms, aren't you? Will I be working with you?' Maddy was like an eager puppy, quite unable to stand still.

Lizzie laughed. 'You will and don't expect me to go easy on you just because you're Angela's sister.'

Maddy was hanging on to Angela's arm. 'I've got some really great ideas, Angela! I was after thinking that we could design a range of clothes especially for girls my age. We all love to look "trendy" too but some of the styles are a bit too old for us. I thought we could call the range "Dolly Rockers"?'

Roz pealed with laughter. 'You see! I told you she might well turn out to be just as talented as you!'

Maura had hurried over to them and had caught the last of the conversation. 'Ah, now, Maddy, stop! Will you not give them all a chance to catch their breath?'

Angela hugged her mother, thinking it seemed so long since she had seen her and although they corresponded regularly, it wasn't the same. 'Oh, it's good to see you again, Mam!'

Maura beamed at her. She had been looking forward to this visit so much. She would have Angela home with her for a whole week. 'Come on inside with you. I've the kettle on. Are your parents not with you?' she asked of Roz.

'Dad's left the car on the road. It's too big for him to turn it around in the yard. They won't be long. Mam's dying to meet you,' Lizzie replied as Lydia and Bernard appeared at the top of the laneway.

'Isn't this a gorgeous place to live, Mrs O'Rourke!' Lydia enthused. 'So peaceful, so quiet.'

'Sometimes it can be a bit too quiet, especially in the winter months,' Maura replied, shaking the hand the other woman had extended.

'Oh, I don't know about that. Bernard was just saying it all makes a lovely change from the noise and the crowds and everyone living on top of each other at home.'

'Will the car be all right on the road? I've pulled it half on to the verge so it's not blocking the path,' Bernard Henderson queried.

'It will be grand. Come on inside now and we'll have a bite to eat. Martin will be back soon. He doesn't normally come home at dinnertime but he wanted to meet you both. We're both so grateful for everything you've done for Angela. Haven't you been goodness itself and now you're to let this bold one here come and stay with you.' Maura beamed at them both, liking them instantly. They were obviously not short of money but there was no side to them at all.

'Well, we've the room now with our Sal gone and what a palaver that wedding was. I'm worn out with it, I can tell you,' Lydia answered, following Maura inside the house.

'Did you bring photographs?' Maddy asked eagerly.

Angela laughed. 'I did so but let us get a cup of tea first.'

She helped her mother to serve the tea and sandwiches while Maddy took her case through into the bedroom.

Martin arrived home and was duly introduced and both families got on well together. After they had eaten Martin went with Bernard to check on the car while Lydia and Maura pored over the photographs Angela had taken of the wedding.

'It will be grand having her back home for a week,' Maura confided after Maddy had persuaded Lizzie to take herself, Roz and Angela for a short drive, she never having been in a car in her life.

Lydia nodded. 'It must have been very hard for you.'

Maura nodded. 'It was and I missed her every single day.'

'Oh, I know I often moan that I'd love a week or two without them all under my feet but I don't mean it. I miss our Sal already and she's only been gone a few days. I was sorry to hear about what your sister did, with the letters, I mean.'

Maura looked uncomfortable; it was something she still hadn't come to terms with.

'Still, it's all in the past now. Angela knows you love her and that's the main thing.'

Maura brightened. 'It is so and we're so proud of her.'

'We all are. She's done very well for herself. Sal's ensemble was beautiful, the photos don't do it justice, and she's designing Emer's outfit. Mind you, it's going to have to be made over there so I hope it turns out well. Angela was doubtful at first, saying she thought it would be best if Emer went to a similar shop just to see what was on offer but Emer wouldn't hear of it. She went and found a dressmaker so Angela agreed.'

'Whoever would have thought she would be so talented? Sure, I don't know where she gets it from.'

'Will she go and see her sisters do you think, while she's over there?' Lydia queried. It seemed such a shame the way Maura's family were all split up.

'I don't know. It's one of the things I'll be discussing with her while she's here. I hope she does. Imagine, those two young ones travelling all that way for a wedding? It was never heard of in my day.'

'Nor mine either but these young ones today have a totally different outlook on life and they've got the money and the freedom we never had. I'm trying not to think about it too much at the moment. Once this holiday is over I know our Rose is going to drive us all mad for the next six months and I just hope Angela has enough common sense to keep her feet firmly on the ground.'

'Ah, she will that, don't you worry about it.'

As the men arrived back, Lizzie pulled deftly into the yard and Lydia stood up. 'Well, we'd better be getting off, Mrs O'Rourke. We've still a fair way to go before suppertime. Thank you for everything and it's been a real pleasure meeting you.'

Angela stood with her parents and sister as she watched Lizzie's little car disappear down the bohreen. Roz had her arm out of the car window and was waving cheerily. Angela smiled as she waved back. It made a change for her not to be the one who was driving away. She was looking forward to the days ahead.

Chapter Thirty-Six

A NGELA FOUND IT STRANGE as she lay beside Maddy in the bed that first night. She could remember vividly the night she'd heard her parents talking, the night when her safe little world had collapsed. She remembered how Aoife had tried to comfort her as the others had slept on; she remembered how cold and miserable she'd been. How things had changed, she thought as she stared at the ceiling. Even this room had changed. Now there was a rug on the floor, curtains at the window, a press for their clothes and a decent mattress and proper bedclothes instead of the old coats that had covered them all those years ago. She remembered her sisters as they had been then. Aoife who had been resigned to a life of poverty until the day came when she could leave to escape it all; Caitlin who had been so unruly and outspoken; and Carmel, the quietest of them all. She had written to them and had received a reply from Caitlin that could have come from a complete stranger, so flat, polite and sanctimonious it had been. Carmel had written a brief note, telling her a little about her life, which appeared to revolve totally around the hospital in Boston. Only from Aoife's letters could she recognise a semblance of the sister she had known and loved.

Maddy stirred beside her and Angela glanced affectionately at her, thinking again how like the young Aoife she looked. Her resentment of Maddy had completely disappeared and she was determined not to lose contact with this sister. She would help Maddy all she could. At last, worn out by the travelling and the events of the day, she fell asleep.

In the days that followed she had plenty of time to talk to her mother as she helped her with the household chores, but the one thing she did regret was the fact that she hadn't learned to drive like Lizzie. She could have hired a car herself which would have made life a lot easier, especially as she had promised Maura they would go into Tullamore later in the week to do some shopping and arrangements would have to be made to find some form of transportation.

'Who has a car in the parish, Mam? I mean apart from the priest and the doctor and Bernie Donnelly's da?' she asked the following afternoon as they sat peeling the potatoes and vegetables for the supper.

'John Devaney has one, wasn't it the same one you went to Mary's in with your da, but he doesn't use it now. Your da says it's just falling to bits in one of the sheds up there.'

Angela looked thoughtful. It didn't look to be that difficult to drive a car; Lizzie had managed it with ease. 'Do you think old Mr Devaney would teach me to drive it? If he isn't using it any more maybe he would let me use it while I'm here, it would make life a lot easier.'

'Mother of God! Would you be up to it, Angela? It looks to be a fierce complicated thing to do.'

Angela laughed at the expression on her mother's face. 'Of course I would, Mam. If Lizzie can do it so can I. I'll talk to Da about it this evening.'

Maura shook her head but she had to admire Angela's spirit. The child was so full of confidence these days, nothing seemed to faze her. 'When you go to New York will you see Carmel and Aoife?' she asked, wiping her hands on her apron and taking the bowl of vegetables to the sink to scrub them.

Angela looked thoughtful as she gathered up the peelings. 'I've already mentioned it to Aoife and she wrote back saying she might try to come. Apparently there is a bus service that is much cheaper than the train, Greyhound I think she said it was called. She said in her letter that if she can get someone to mind the children she would come and stay one night. That's all she can manage. So, it all depends.'

Maura nodded. She would love the two sisters to be reunited, even if it only for a few hours. 'Would you not think of going over to her?'

'I really do want to see her, Mam, but I won't have much time myself. We are only there for five days, and there's the wedding and all that will entail. Emer's expecting me to go with her for her final fitting to make sure her dressmaker has copied my design to the letter, plus I'll have my work cut out keeping Roz from buying so much stuff that we'll not be able to bring it all back on the plane. You have no idea what she's like about shopping!'

'And Carmel?' Maura queried, thinking it must be a grand thing altogether to have as much money as the Hendersons seemed to have.

'She's more or less told me not to expect her to come to New York. She's neither the time nor the money. She seems very dedicated to her job but then she was always quiet and serious. I'm sure she's a far better nurse than I would ever have been.'

'It's a vocation, Angela, and it wasn't what the good Lord intended for you.'

347

As Angela began to trim the meat she thought this would be a good time to broach the subject of Maddy's future. 'I was very fortunate in that respect, Mam, and I'm thinking that Maddy might do as well, with the right training.' She took a deep breath. 'How would you and Da feel if when she's finished school, she came over to me? Hopefully they will accept her into art college to do a design course and in her spare time she could work with Lizzie and learn the practical side of things and then, if everything works out well, you would have two fashion designers in the family.'

Maura sat down at the table and looked intently at Angela. 'You'd do all that for Maddy?'

Angela sat opposite her and reached for her hand. 'She's the only one I seem to have left, Mam. Carmel and Caitlin are like strangers, I don't *know* them any more. I'll see Aoife, I hope, but she's so much older than me and we won't have too much in common. I've become close to Maddy; I want to help her do well. She's dead set on being a designer and I can help her and keep my eye on her too. I . . . I still feel guilty about the way I blamed her for me being sent away.'

'Ah, Angela, don't fret yourself about that. Weren't you only a child yourself at the time and didn't understand and then, well, the way things were with . . . with Mary, God rest her.'

Angela smiled sadly. 'I remember wondering why you couldn't just tell God you didn't want another baby and ask him to take it back.'

Maura too managed a smile. 'Would that it was that simple. But every child is a blessing, as you'll learn one day yourself.'

Angela thought of the conversation she'd had with Roz all those years ago and Lydia Henderson's firmly held view that the matter of contraception was something between your

348

own conscience and God. Her mother would never in a million years understand that, and she didn't have the easy relationship with Maura that Roz had with Lydia and so could never broach this thorny subject. She stood up. 'Not for a long time yet, Mam. I'm too busy and, besides, the one "romance" I had didn't turn out well. You remember I wrote and told you about it all? So I've no intention of repeating the performance.' And Ronan Emmet didn't seem to want to contact her, she added to herself.

Maura looked at her sadly. Angela had obviously been hurt and that upset her but it was all a part of growing up, a part of life. 'You'll change your mind, Angela, when you meet the right one.'

'Maybe. At least Emer has and aren't I delighted for her. So, will you think about what I said about Maddy? Discuss it with Da? It will mean that you will both be left here alone.'

Maura had already realised this. 'Isn't that something your da and meself have come to terms with? We knew Maddy wouldn't stay here – what is there for her at all? She'd have gone up to Dublin or to London or even off to America, like the other two. At least if she goes to you neither of you will be *that* far away and we'll know she's safe and secure.'

'I'll mind her well, Mam, you have my promise on that,' Angela said seriously.

'I know you will. Wasn't it just a pity that the two blackguards of brothers that you have didn't go to Liverpool instead of Glasgow?' Maura finished bitterly.

Angela sighed. She had already given the matter of her errant brothers a lot of thought. 'It *was* a pity, Mam, and I've been thinking that I might just write. There must be a prison chaplain; maybe if I could contact him he could go and see them, see how they are and ask if they would like me to write to them.'

Maura looked perturbed. 'I don't know, Angela. Haven't I said it will do your reputation not a bit of good to be associated with the likes of those two?'

'But it must be really desperate for them, Mam!'

Maura was unforgiving. 'Wasn't it a desperate thing they did? Don't they deserve to be punished? It broke your da's heart. You didn't see the way it hurt and humiliated him.'

'I'm sorry, truly I am, but if they are sorry for their mistakes, wouldn't it be better if when they get out they have some support, rather than go back to crime?'

Maura sighed heavily and got to her feet. 'I don't know, child. I just don't know, but you do what you think is best. Now, we'd better get started on this meal or we'll have both your da and Maddy in on top of us and mad with hunger. Oh, don't I envy the women who have all the modern appliances. I was only after talking to Maureen Reilly the other day and wasn't she telling me she's moving out to Mucklagh to a new house. It's pleasant up there, you can see for miles from the top road. But shouldn't I be grateful to the good Lord for what I have now. 'Tis more than I had years ago.'

The matter of the car was discussed over supper to Maddy's utter delight.

'Won't that be one in the eye for Bernie Donnelly?'

Angela shook her head. 'Isn't it about time you stopped acting like a six-year-old? If you intend to come over to Liverpool to work you'll have to at least act your age. It doesn't matter what anyone else has, there will always be people who have more – that's just life,' she chided. 'Now, Da, what do you think? Will Himself teach me and lend me the car just for the time I'm here?'

Martin was looking a little dubious. 'It will take you more than a couple of hours to learn to drive.'

'Won't I have plenty of time to practise and no one seems to bother about things like licences and tests here.'

'I'll ask him,' Martin conceded.

Angela grinned at him. 'We'll ask him. We'll walk over after supper and take half of that pie as a bit of a sweetener. Maddy will help Mam with the dishes, won't you?'

Maddy nodded enthusiastically. She was right behind Angela in this matter.

To Maddy's delight and Maura's consternation, when they returned Angela was smiling broadly. Old John Devaney had agreed to teach her and to lend her the car, providing it would start and she paid for the petrol. She was to go over next morning for the first lesson. All three of them had pushed the ageing Morris out of the shed and she had given it a bit of a dusting inside and had noted that it seemed to have all the same bits and pieces as Lizzie's Mini had. She was fully confident that she could manage it and there was hardly any traffic on the roads to contend with.

'When you've learned will you drive me to school, Angela, or pick me up? Just the once?' Maddy begged.

Angela wagged her forefinger at her playfully. 'Didn't I tell you to forget about Bernie Donnelly? Well, just the once,' she relented.

'Won't Roz and Lizzie be surprised when they come back?' Maddy said, beaming.

'Probably horrified, more like. It took Lizzie months to learn and now Roz will start pestering everyone to teach her too and probably harp on at me to buy a car of my own.'

'Will you?' Maddy asked.

Angela shrugged. 'I don't know. There's plenty of public transport in Liverpool but I might have a look at something second-hand. After Emer's wedding.'

'Perhaps you could come and see us more often if you had

a car of your own. It would save you having to come down on the train from Dublin and that takes ages.' Maddy suggested, looking hopefully at her mother.

'Don't be an eejit, Maddy. Isn't she too busy to be jaunting over here by the minutes? Hasn't she a business to run and yourself to mind when she gets back?' Maura reminded her youngest daughter.

'I'll never be too busy to come and see you, Mam, so maybe I will buy a car,' Angela replied.

Angela took to driving like a duck to water, or so old John Devaney told Martin. He'd never known a young one who was so confident or so determined. If she did something wrong, she'd go back and do it again until she got it right. He insisted that after two days Angela would be quite competent to manage the car by herself. Of course had she been driving in a city like Liverpool or even Dublin then things would be different, far more complicated, but here you barely saw another car and very few people had tractors or lorries, and the more practice she got the better she would get.

The first time she went out on her own she was nervous and crashed the gears quite a few times but she told herself that she had so much to do before she went back to Liverpool that she simply didn't have the time to worry about her nerves. Living in the small cottage had made her realise just how hard her mother's life still was. Maura had to bring in every drop of water from the pump in the yard and heat it on the range. Even though they had more in the way of comforts now her mother still used oil lamps and candles. She had become so used to all the modern conveniences of the Hendersons' home that she found her mother's acceptance of the hardship of her life unacceptable. Neither of her parents was getting any younger and in the depths of winter it must be terrible to have to live without hot water and electricity. Even worse, the place was damp. She had never noticed it before but she did now and she was determined that she would find them somewhere better to live before she left. Hadn't Mam only said the other day how much she envied the women who had houses with all mod cons?

She had driven into Tullamore after she had dropped Maddy off at school, hiding her smile as her sister – surrounded by a group of astonished girls – had proudly waved as she'd turned the car around and driven away. She had wondered should she drive to Edenderry to see Ronan and maybe Miss Dunne, but realised that with what she was planning there just wouldn't be time. She had found the auctioneers' office and had gone inside.

'Good morning, Mr Keegan. I'm Angela O'Rourke.' She extended her hand confidently to the middle-aged man who had risen from behind his desk.

'Are you the young O'Rourke one who has done so well for herself across the water?' he asked curiously. He didn't get many young, fashionably dressed girls in here. It was mainly older people.

She smiled but came straight to the point. She didn't have time to give him a full resumé of her success. 'I am so. Now, have you anything on your books in Rahan to rent?'

He motioned her to sit down. 'Is it for yourself?'

She shook her head. 'No, for my parents. A small bungalow, something modern, was what I was after thinking would suit.'

'Ah, there's not much like that at the moment, not in Rahan.'

She frowned. 'Have you *anything*?'

He rummaged in the desk drawer and brought out a

folder which he leafed through and at last triumphantly drew out a sheet of paper. 'I have this, it's on the Mucklagh road though. It might be a piece too far.'

She read the details quickly. It was a two-bedroomed bungalow built five years ago on a half-acre plot of land. There was a good-sized kitchen with a modern range, a parlour with a fireplace and a bathroom. It had all amenities, hot and cold water, electricity and outside there was a good-sized turf shed and an outhouse. It wasn't too far from the church at Killina so her parents wouldn't feel isolated and her mother had seemed to think Mucklagh was a pleasant place to live. 'And how much a week is it?'

'Twenty-five shillings,' he answered.

'And is that inclusive of the electricity?'

He shook his head. She was very businesslike for someone so young. 'It is not.'

'Is it available for immediate occupancy?'

He nodded. 'They can move in tomorrow if that would suit.'

She smiled. She could more than afford to pay the rent and if she could see them settled before she left she would be greatly relieved. 'Then I'd like to take my parents to see it, Mr Keegan. Have you the keys? Could I borrow them for the afternoon? If my parents like the house I can promise we'll take it. I'll call in on my way back.'

He rummaged in another drawer and found a set of keys.

'And I assume there will be some kind of tenancy agreement I have to sign? I'll call in tomorrow to finalise everything after I've seen the solicitor.' She picked up the keys and stood up.

'I'll have everything ready, Miss O'Rourke.' He was astounded at the promptness of her decision. Usually there were lengthy discussions over everything from rent, the neighbours and rights of way, the terms of the tenancy agreement and a hundred other things, but she was going to take the advice of a solicitor, which cost money, so she was obviously serious. As she shook his hand and left he sat down, feeling as though a small whirlwind had just come through his office.

It was a vast improvement on the cottage at the end of the bohreen, Angela thought after she had looked around and was driving back. She hoped she had done the right thing for she hadn't discussed it with her parents. She prayed they would be pleased and not be dismayed at the thought of leaving the home they'd lived in all their married life, but she wanted life to be easier for them both now. It was further for her father to go to work but she intended to buy him a bicycle.

Maura was pegging out washing when she arrived back. 'I was getting worried about you, Angela.'

'I went into town, Mam. Come inside and we'll have a cup of tea. I've something to tell you.'

Maura followed her in, wondering whether Maddy had talked her into something else, for Maddy had pleaded to be allowed to stay off school tomorrow to go with them on the shopping trip into Tullamore. She had flatly refused. The child was getting too bold altogether in her opinion.

Angela handed her mother the keys before putting on the kettle.

Maura looked mystified. 'What's this?'

'The keys to your new house, Mam.'

Maura sat down and looked at her blankly. 'New house?'

Angela nodded. 'Neither you or Da is getting any younger and I just couldn't bear to think of you having to drag all the water inside in the depths of winter. Mam, you have no comfort in this house, you never have. You deserve a warm, dry house with modern conveniences. I've been to see it and it's lovely, it's got two bedrooms, a big kitchen with a very up-to-the-minute range, a parlour and a bathroom. And outside there's an outhouse and a turf shed and enough room for a kitchen garden.'

Maura was shaking her head in disbelief. 'And . . . and how much are they asking for the rent?' she finally managed to get out.

'Twenty-five shillings a week.'

A look of horror crossed Maura's face. 'Mother of God! Angela, we can't afford that.'

'I'm not asking you to. I will pay it, I can more than afford it and if you can't manage the electricity I'll help out. I've thought it all out and I'm going to set up some kind of investment account to guarantee it. Mr Henderson will be able to advise me on the best kind and the way to do it. Oh, Mam, you deserve it. If you could see all the things Mrs Henderson has to make life easier – I want you to have an easier life too.'

'Where is it?' Maura was still stunned.

'On the Mucklagh road but not too far from the church. I'm going to get Da a bicycle too, it's too far for him to walk to work and on the occasions you go up to clean I'm sure someone will give you lift.'

Maura covered her face with her hands and her shoulders began to shake and Angela realised she was crying. She rushed to her and put her arms around her. 'Oh, Mam, please don't say you don't want to leave here, that I've done the wrong thing! I was only thinking of you, truly I was! I should have discussed it with you first, I know, but—'

Maura raised her head and Angela was relieved to see that she was smiling through her tears. 'Won't I be delighted to go? I never imagined I'd be so blessed as to live anywhere other than this. Angela, aren't you goodness itself?'

Angela hugged her tightly. 'It's no more than you deserve, Mam. Now, dry your eyes and we'll have this tea and then this afternoon, when Da gets back, we'll go up and see it. We'll pick Maddy up from school and bring her with us.'

Maura smiled ruefully. 'I'll do no good at all with her now, you realise that? A nice new home, you driving her everywhere and then taking her back with you to Liverpool. Won't she have us all demented?'

Angela laughed. 'You leave Maddy to me. It will be quite a rush to get you settled in before I have to leave.'

As Angela drove her parents up to the bungalow she could sense Maura's excitement. When they got out of the car she handed her mother the keys.

'Here, Mam, you go in first.'

Maddy was jumping from one leg to the other in excitement while Martin looked around him with a rather dazed expression on his face. Maura's hands were a little shaky but she opened the door and stood looking around in delight. 'It's all so light and airy!'

'Oh, Mam, just look at this kitchen, sure, it's got *everything*!' Maddy exclaimed, rushing ahead of her mother.

Angela felt so relieved as they went from room to room exclaiming over everything. They liked it and that was what mattered most.

'Ah, Martin, won't we be just grand living here? Won't it be great altogether in the winter?' Maura enthused, holding tightly to her husband's arm.

'We will so, Maura. Thanks be to God we have such a generous and thoughtful daughter.'

'And I'll really work hard and help with the move and then when I'm older and really working with Angela I'll help out with the rent and things too,' Maddy promised.

Martin smiled at her. 'We have two generous and thoughtful daughters. Aren't we blessed, Maura?'

'So, will I be going and telling Mr Keegan that we'll take it?' Angela asked when they'd completed the tour of inspection.

Maura hugged her. 'Ye will indeed and thank you, child!'

Angela and Maddy made innumerable trips in the car and the larger pieces of furniture were taken on John Devaney's farm cart. The outstanding rent on the lease of the cottage had been paid by Angela so by the end of the week her parents were able to settle – blissfully – in their new home. It was a hectic few days but at last Saturday arrived. Maddy was packed ready for her trip to Liverpool. In the end the Hendersons had decided not to stay the previous night at Mrs Hickey's Canal View bed and breakfast but would find somewhere to stay in Birr and drive up early that morning. Angela and her mother drove over to the now empty cottage for there had been no way of contacting Roz or her family to tell them of the change of address. Angela would then drive her mother home and take the car back and Lizzie would pick her up before they left for Dublin and the ferry.

'It looks so different now,' Maura mused, gazing at her old home. 'Sort of lifeless.'

'You've only been gone a few days!' Angela laughed.

'I suppose every house needs a family in it to give it the feeling of life.'

'Well, I doubt there will be anyone else living in it now,' Angela replied.

Lizzie arrived first, accompanied by Roz. Mr Henderson was waiting on the road.

'What happened? Where is everyone?' Lizzie asked, looking around at the obviously now uninhabited cottage.

'We moved. I'll tell you about it later. Now, will you follow us back to the new house to pick up Maddy? I have to take the car back.'

Roz couldn't believe what she was hearing. 'What car? That old thing?'

Angela laughed. 'I was lucky to get it.'

'Don't tell me you learned to drive in a *week*?' Lizzie gasped.

'In a couple of days, actually, but things are much quieter here.' Angela was urging them back towards the Mini.

'Oh, you can say that again! We've been all over the country and I haven't managed to find a decent clothes shop,' Roz complained.

Lizzie rolled her eyes. 'Don't we all know it and it wasn't for the want of trying. Well, we'd better get going, we'll catch up on everything on the way up to Dublin. We can put your case and Maddy's things in Dad's car, all four of us will fit in the Mini but not the luggage.' She grinned mischievously at Angela. 'Do you want to drive up to Dublin?'

'I do not! And I'm not insured to drive that car so don't go saying things like that in front of your dad!' Angela replied.

Chapter Thirty-Seven

TO MADDY THE WEEKS SHE spent in Liverpool with Angela seemed to have just flown and they had been the most exciting in her entire life. Despite having to work hard and finding some tasks very repetitious indeed, by the time she went home she was more determined than ever to follow in her sister's footsteps.

Angela had gone with her but Mr Henderson had insisted that she apply for a provisional driving licence and take lessons and a test before she attempted to hire a car for she would need to be fully insured and no one would insure her without a full licence. She had done as he had advised and, like Lizzie, had passed her test first time. She had only spent the weekend with her parents for as autumn approached she found herself caught up with next spring's collection and Roz's increasing excitement about their trip to New York.

Angela had written to the chaplain of the prison where her brothers were serving their sentences and had received a reply which in part she found disturbing and upsetting. Father McDonald knew them both and he wrote that he held out little hope of Jimmy O'Rourke ever becoming a reformed character. The lad was unrepentant and seemed to be intent on running with a crowd of hard men he referred to as his 'mates'. Regarding Peter he felt there was more hope and the lad had said he would like Angela to write to him. She had discussed it with Mr Henderson and he had advised her to do so, saying it might be just the lifeline Peter O'Rourke needed. So she had written and had received a reply in the hand of Father McDonald who told her her brother had said he wasn't much of a one for the reading and writing, from which she concluded sadly that Peter was virtually illiterate. She had not mentioned any of these facts to her parents for she knew it would only upset them. She intended to keep writing to her brother and hoped to see him when he was finally released.

The letters and the occasional phone call from Emer only added to her worries and the increasingly frenetic pace of life.

'You'll drop from nervous exhaustion if you're not careful, Angela, and then the only place you'll be going is to a sanatorium,' Lydia Henderson warned after Angela had received a phone call from an almost hysterical Emer.

'Oh, Mam, give over, will you?' Roz had replied impatiently. 'What's the matter now? The wedding hasn't been called off, has it?'

Angela had shaken her head. 'She's in a right state because she can't find the right shade for the trim on the hood of the coat and she mentioned it to Patrick's mother in the hope she could help and then there was a row because "the battleaxe" wanted to know why she wasn't having a veil like normal brides, what was she doing with a *hood* of all things?'

'Oh, God! Poor Emer!' Roz had groaned. 'What will she do?'

'I told her to calm down, that I'll get the trimming and send it over. I designed the damned thing after all so at least I do know what's needed.'

'Why do all these old fogies go on so much about "traditional" dresses and veils and the like? Wasn't our Sal's ma-in-law the same?' Roz had said cuttingly.

'Sometimes our generation finds it difficult to accept the styles you girls want to wear these days, especially in the matter of weddings, so we'll have less of the "old fogies", thank you very much!' her mother had shot back.

'Surely it's up to the bride what she wants to wear?' Roz replied, determined to continue the argument.

Angela's head had begun to ache. 'Oh, let's not go down that road, Roz, please?'

'Angela is right. If she sends over the trimmings that will sort out that problem. Everyone gets into such a state over weddings. Myself I think there is far too much fuss made these days and far too much expense. Now, I'll have your dad and the lads in soon and after a hard day the less your dad has to hear about transatlantic family rows the better.' With that Lydia Henderson had firmly quashed any further discussion on the matter.

Christmas that year had seemed something of an anti-climax, Angela thought. Everything was overshadowed by their forthcoming trip. New suitcases had been bought, plus matching vanity cases for their make-up and cosmetics, and there had been further arguments between Roz and her mother about the type of clothing that should be taken.

'Didn't Emer say it's absolutely freezing, so don't go packing anything flimsy,' Lydia warned but to little avail as Roz had protested that Emer had also told them that every-where was centrally heated, even places like airports and bus stations.

Bernard Henderson was to drive them to Manchester Airport in the late afternoon as it was an overnight flight and it was a highly excited pair of girls who checked in at the airport. Neither of them had ever flown before; nor had they ever ventured so far from home. Angela was really looking forward to seeing her old friend again and to her delight Aoife had written telling her that she was coming for an overnight stay and so the two sisters would be reunited, if only for a very short time.

They didn't manage to get much sleep on the plane but by the time they touched down at JFK the following morning their weariness was dispelled by their first sight of New York.

'Oh, it's all going to be just *great*! I know it!' Roz enthused after they had collected their cases. They came through passport control and immigration and Angela looked around at the crowd of people waiting to greet the new arrivals.

'Angela! Angela! Here, I'm over here!' Emer was standing by the barrier literally jumping up and down and waving madly, her face glowing with excitement.

Both Angela and Roz hurried towards her as fast as their luggage would allow. Emer hurled herself at Angela and the two friends hugged each other laughing and with tears of pure joy in their eyes.

'Oh, Emer! I've missed you so much, that I have!' Angela cried. 'And you've hardly changed at all, except that you've let your hair grow.' Emer's hair was still blond but fell around her shoulders in a long bob.

Emer hugged Roz and then stood back. 'God, aren't you tall? I never realised it, not even from the photographs and you look . . . stunning!'

Roz laughed. 'How can anyone look "stunning" after no sleep and being stuck in a cramped space for hours and hours, especially with legs the length of mine?' But she was delighted just the same.

Emer took both their vanity cases. 'Let's get out of here. I remember only too well how tiring the journey is and then there's the time difference to contend with. It will take a day or so to adjust.'

'Oh, we'll be just great. We've got so much to see and do that we can't waste time catching up on *sleep*,' Roz replied as they made their way out. 'Where's the taxi rank? I've always wanted to ride in a yellow cab, they sort of symbolise New York.'

'I'll not have you throwing your money away on one of those things, we'll get the bus,' Emer said firmly.

When they were safely installed in their room which was on the fifth floor of a moderately priced hotel near Central Park, Emer insisted that she leave them to unpack and get some sleep but that she would call back at four and take them to meet Dinny and Joy and of course Patrick.

'Have your mam and da arrived yet? I'm looking forward to seeing them again,' Angela asked.

'They're coming in on the Aer Lingus flight from Shannon tomorrow morning. Joy and I are going to meet them as Dinny has to work and Mam is so terrified of flying that she'll be in a desperate state altogether. Hasn't she got her rosary, a little bottle of Lourdes water and about a dozen reliquaries in her handbag – just in case!' Emer replied, casting her eyes to the ceiling. 'What with Mam fussing over everyone and the battleaxe glowering at everyone aren't I beginning to think it will be a blessing when this wedding is all over.'

'Ah, stop that, Emer Cassidy! It's going to be the best day of your life!' Angela laughed.

*

Angela was hard pressed to restrain Roz from going out shopping the minute they had finished unpacking, becoming quite firm about them having plenty of time for that. She had some important things to do, she reminded her friend, such as going with Emer to make sure the wedding ensemble was just right, to say nothing of meeting her sister Aoife, making time to see Emer's parents and even spending a little time with Emer too. Sightseeing and shopping would have to be fitted in around everything else. Roz was unperturbed as she studied her guidebooks and street maps. She had known Angela had commitments and it would be hugely exciting to wander around this city by herself. Besides, she had an agenda of her own that she had told no one about, not even Angela.

As promised Emer came back to take them to her home. Angela didn't remember Emer's oldest brother Dennis or 'Dinny' as he was referred to but he made her very welcome, as did his wife Joy, whom Angela instantly liked and who Roz thought was quite glamorous for someone who was really middle-aged.

'Have you noticed that some American women of Joy's age are really smart and well groomed? I mean she must be well into her forties but you'd never think so, and what do women of her age look like at home? All tight perms, red lipstick, twin sets and "comfortable" shoes!' she'd said on the way back to the hotel, much to Angela's amusement. They had both liked Patrick, Emer's fiancé. He was tall and his Irish ancestry was evident in his auburn hair and pale skin and he had a great sense of humour.

'Everyone seems more relaxed about things, not so up-tight,' had been Roz's opinion.

The following morning, after Emer had settled her parents in with the neighbours they were to stay with, she was meeting Angela outside Bloomingdale's on 5th Avenue and they were then to go for the final fitting of Emer's wedding outfit. Roz of course had decided that she would 'hit Bloomingdale's in a big way'. Angela had pealed with laughter at this attempt at an American accent.

They had both slept very well and after breakfast had gone out to find a bitterly cold but bright morning. Roz had announced that it was too far to walk and that she was determined to get her ride in a yellow cab.

'Don't go completely mad with the shopping, Roz. Remember we've only just arrived,' Angela warned but Roz just giggled.

When Emer arrived she was well wrapped up against the cold and the two girls walked towards the subway, heading for Greenwich Village where Glenda Osborne, the dressmaker, lived.

'I hope you're going to like it, Angela. I hope she's done it right, after all you're so experienced.' Emer sounded a little worried.

'And I'm sure she is too. Will you stop fretting? Will we have time to get a coffee or a bit of lunch afterwards?' Angela was really hoping to spend a little time on her own with Emer.

'Plenty of time. Mam was so exhausted she'll sleep for hours and I'm not seeing Patrick until about eight.' She pulled a face. 'He's bringing his parents to meet mine and I'm not looking forward to that, I can tell you!'

'Sure, she can't be *that* bad, Emer? Patrick's really nice.'

'He takes after his father! I like his dad. She . . . she acts so superior and I just know Mam will get all fussed and go making a show of herself.'

'Calm down, Joy looks well able to keep things under control,' Angela commented.

Angela could find no fault at all in Glenda Osborne's interpretation of her design or her skills as a seamstress. Emer's dress was of heavy cream brocade with an Empire-line bodice and square neckline. It had short sleeves which would be more comfortable in the centrally heated hotel which had been booked for the reception. For over the dress there was a full-length brocade coat with a hood. The coat was fastened with gold and cream braided frogging and the cuffs and edge of the hood were trimmed with cream fake fur. Emer was to wear cream leather ankle boots laced up the front with cream ribbons and would carry a small bouquet of cream and yellow roses and freesias. Her long hair was to be worn up in loose curls. Angela reminded her that as the coat had long sleeves and a high neck and her head would be covered by the hood there could be no complaints that she was breaching any of the conventions their religion demanded.

'You'll look *gorgeous*! You'll take the sight from the eyes of everyone, including "the battleaxe", as you keep calling her,' Angela told her, holding her friend's hands tightly while the dressmaker laughed at the quaint expressions these girls used.

'Just as long as Patrick thinks I'm "gorgeous" I don't care,' Emer replied, smiling.

'He will!' Angela enthused.

With the ensemble carefully packed in tissue paper in a large box, they left and found a nice little café in the Village that was fairly quiet and ordered coffee while they studied the menu.

'You *are* happy here, Emer?' Angela asked. 'I know you didn't have much choice in the matter in the first place, but you seem to have settled well.'

'I have and I wouldn't go back to Ireland to live now,

Angela. Especially not since I found Patrick.' Emer for once was serious. 'We've got everything to look forward to. A place of our own in Queens which is far enough away from the in-laws, and Patrick's agreed to me carrying on at work which will help us afford all the things we want and then we'll think about starting a family.'

'What if the babies don't wait to be invited?' Angela asked, thinking of her mother.

'Patrick and I have talked about that and I told him I'm not going to be like Mam and every other Mammy I know and produce a baby every year until I'm too old and worn out.'

Angela nodded. 'Roz's mother says it's not a matter for the Church, it's something between your conscience and God.'

'Isn't she a sensible woman for her age? I think she's right and there are a lot of women here who think the same way.'

'Does Patrick agree?' Angela asked, sipping her coffee.

Emer nodded. 'He's not just off the boat – or these days the plane. He was born here; he's American. He's got modern views. And anyway, could you just see Herself's face if I presented her with a grandchild every year? She'd be mortified!'

'I wouldn't go telling your mam about it all, she just wouldn't understand,' Angela advised.

Emer was back to her usual self. 'She would not! Wouldn't I be dragged off to get a lecture from the parish priest? I've often wondered why Mam just didn't say a very firm "No!" to Da.'

Angela grinned. 'Because it wasn't what she was taught! I remember Aoife saying it was a Catholic wife's "duty" or some such nonsense that she'd heard from one of the nuns at school.'

'Sure, she didn't take much notice of that herself, did she? She's only two children, hasn't she?'

Lyn Andrews

Angela nodded and Emer again became serious. 'Angela, I wish . . . I wish I could have been with you to help you cope with Mary's death and finding the letters and . . . and after that business with that rat Danny Fielding.'

Angela smiled at her friend. 'I know but I managed. It took me a while to get over him.'

'You haven't let it put you off altogether?'

Angela shrugged. 'Everyone tells me I shouldn't.'

'Mam always says that for every shoe God made a stocking or some such thing – you know what she's like with her sayings – but I think she's right. There *is* someone out there for you and you'll find him and be as happy as I am with Patrick.'

Angela thought of Ronan Emmet and frowned. It was not lost on Emer.

'Is there someone? I know you too well, Angela. Tell me?' She probed.

Angela sighed. 'There isn't anything to tell.'

'There is!'

'I . . . I . . . did really get to like Ronan Emmet. I'm not saying I'd fallen for him. When Aunt Mary was dying he used to sit with me and we'd talk and then he took me to see Mam . . .'

'And?' Emer pressed.

'He said I should open a boutique in Dublin but I told him it wouldn't work, young people in Ireland don't have jobs let alone money to spend on trendy fashions. But when he wrote to me he always finished by saying if I ever went back I'd be welcome in Edenderry and then . . .'

'That sounds promising. What happened?'

Angela twisted a teaspoon between her fingers. Emer was her oldest friend, she could tell her anything. She was beginning to realise just how much she had missed the

370

contact with Ronan. 'He wrote to me telling me about Liam Murphy's suicide and I wrote back and told him I wasn't going over. I . . . I haven't heard from him since. He must have a terrible poor opinion of me now and . . . and it sort of hurts me.'

Emer looked at her thoughtfully. 'Did you not think to go and see him when you were last home?'

Angela shook her head. 'There wasn't time and anyway what could I have said to him by way of an explanation that wouldn't have involved me telling him about . . . what happened?'

'I think you care for him more than you realise.'

'Maybe I do but there's not much I can do about it now.'

'There is so! When you get back make an effort to go and see him. You don't have to be explicit but just tell him that you and that feller didn't get on. He wasn't very kind to you. He'll understand.'

Angela looked doubtful. 'Maybe it's best if I leave things alone. I don't really *know* how I feel about him and I certainly don't know how he feels about me and, besides, as I told Roz, I couldn't stick being a doctor's wife in a place like Edenderry so what's the point in even thinking along those lines?'

Emer had to agree. She shook her head sadly. She wished Angela would find someone special; she certainly deserved to.

The waiter was hovering so they ordered but when he'd gone Emer leaned across the table.

'Now tell me how your mam and da are getting on in the new house and young Maddy?'

For the next hour and a half they talked, recalling schoolfriends and incidents in Edenderry. Angela told Emer all about her business and her life with the Hendersons and her hopes for Maddy. Emer described her life here and all the dreams she had for the future until Angela said that she would have to go back to the hotel for Aoife was arriving later that afternoon and would stay overnight and that no doubt Roz had probably ignored her advice and bought up half of the contents of every shop on 5th Avenue by now.

Emer laughed. 'Isn't she a *scream* that one? And she really is stunning looking.'

'She is a fantastic model but sometimes she can be a bit of a handful and I know her mam was worried about her coming here. I've promised to keep a close eye on her.'

Emer wound her scarf around her neck, jammed her hat over her long blond hair and reached for the cardboard box that contained her precious wedding ensemble, thinking Angela would have her work cut out with Roz Henderson in a city like New York.

Chapter Thirty-Eight

W HEN ANGELA ARRIVED BACK at the hotel it was to find Roz surrounded by Bloomingdale's distinctive brown paper carrier bags and the two beds strewn with clothes.

'Sure, I might as well have saved my breath! You must have spent a fortune!'

'Not too much but I just couldn't resist some of these things. Just look at this!' Roz held up a short silver and white brocade cocktail dress and a pair of matching silver shoes.

'I hope you don't intend to wear that for the wedding? The one colour a guest doesn't wear at a wedding is white, it's looked on as trying to upstage the bride.'

'Oh, honestly, Angela! Would I do that to Emer? You know I've got that electric blue,' Roz protested. 'Was the outfit all right? No last-minute disasters?'

'It's perfect and she will look gorgeous. They are going to call me from the front desk when Aoife arrives but do you think I could get a cup of tea first?'

Roz put down the dress and shoes. 'I'll ask for room service. Isn't it great you can just pick up the phone and order anything you like? Mind you, I have to admit that the tea isn't as good as at home. The coffee's much better.'

Angela nodded but then looked thoughtful. 'Maybe I'll wait until Aoife gets here, she'll be in the want of some tea after that journey.'

'I've been thinking, Angela. You won't have all that long together and you won't want me hanging around all the time, so I think I'll go and do some sightseeing.'

'It will be dark soon,' Angela reminded her.

'There are plenty of places I can go to that are indoors. I can save places like Central Park, the Statue of Liberty and the Staten Island ferry or the Empire State Building for during the day.'

Angela smiled at her friend. 'Thanks. We do have a lot to catch up with but you don't have to stay out all night – and you do remember which areas Joy warned us about?'

'Of course I do and if I end up anywhere that doesn't look too great I'll get a cab back. I'd better put all this stuff away or Aoife will think she's come to a hand-me-down shop, as you say,' Roz said, beginning to gather up her purchases. 'And I think I'll get changed too. I look a bit of a mess.'

Roz had gone off on what she termed 'a bit of a tour' and Angela stood gazing out of the bedroom window at the skyline. It was so long since she had seen Aoife and she felt a little apprehensive. Would she get on with her sister? she wondered. Aoife was seven years older than she was. Would they have anything in common at all, apart from family news? The shrill ringing of the telephone cut through her deliberations. Aoife was on her way up, she was informed.

She smiled as she opened the door and took Aoife's overnight bag. 'Aoife! I'm really glad you could make it.'

Aoife took both her hands. 'Let me look at you now! You

look grand, Angela, you really do. If it hadn't been for the photos you sent I would hardly have recognised my skinny little sister.'

'It's sixteen years since I last saw you, Aoife. It seems like a lifetime ago.'

Aoife nodded a little sadly. 'A lifetime indeed and it's been a lifetime of changes for both of us.' She took off her heavy winter coat and then smiled and Angela caught a glimpse of the young Aoife she remembered so well. 'Would there be any chance that we could get a cup of tea before we start with the chat? I've photos in the bag of your niece and nephew and your brother-in-law. Wedding photos, christenings, First Communions – the whole lot. I hope you've brought some of Mam and Da and Maddy?'

Angela nodded. 'I'll get some tea sent up.' There hadn't been a huge emotional reunion, no hugs, no tears, but she felt very at ease with Aoife. It was almost as if they had never been separated, as if those sixteen years had been just minutes.

Roz had had no intention at all of sightseeing; she had far more serious things on her mind. Earlier in the day, when she had finally left Bloomingdale's, she had caught sight of a sign on a building and had stopped dead in her tracks, causing chaos on the sidewalk as people had had to push past her. The sign had read 'FACES – No. 1 Model Agency'. And the building didn't look shabby or run down, in fact it looked classy. Roz had intended to look up some of the agencies and make a few appointments to see what chance she stood of getting on to their books. She'd given up on London; New York was a far more exciting proposition. She had put out of her mind completely how her parents would react to the idea that she might stay on in New York and she'd carefully put together newspaper cuttings and photos from various fashion shoots she'd done and had brought them with her. She'd gone into the agency and asked to make an appointment for this afternoon and had been instructed to bring her portfolio. Thankfully, Aoife's visit was preoccupying Angela so much that she had managed to get the slim briefcase out without any questions.

Upon entering the agency she gave her name to the receptionist and was asked to take off her coat and hat. Then she was shown into a light, bright office and told that Miss Lieberman would be with her shortly. She felt nervous excitement bubble up in her as she looked around at the various photographs that adorned the walls. She might be fashion conscious, but she wasn't overly vain about her looks: however, she felt she looked a lot better than some of the girls in those photos. She ran her fingers through her hair for her hat had flattened it a little. If she could get work here even for just a few months it would be great and it would give her more prestige when she went back home to say she'd had experience of working in New York. She'd worry about what her mam and dad would say when the time came.

A small, slim, dark-haired woman, who was immaculately dressed, bustled into the room. 'Miss Henderson?'

Roz stood up, smiling.

'Well, you certainly do have the height and the figure. I take it you have experience?'

'Oh, yes, and I've brought my portfolio.' She handed over the case as Rachel Lieberman sat down and motioned Roz to do the same. She looked carefully at everything Roz had brought and then nodded.

'And you do have a green card, Miss Henderson?'

Roz looked puzzled. 'A what?'

'A work permit.'

Roz decided that honesty was the best policy. 'No. You see I'm only here for a few days. I came over for a wedding but I thought I'd see if there was a possibility that I might be able to get taken on to your books? Perhaps have a couple of trial assignments before I go back? I really do want to work in New York and I'm sure there wouldn't be a problem in obtaining the necessary green card.' She sounded far more confident than she felt.

Rachel Lieberman looked at her closely. She was just what they had been looking for. She would be their 'Face of 1969' but she couldn't employ her without the necessary paperwork. She was thinking rapidly; she didn't want to turn the girl away and probably lose her. If she had some studio shots done of Roz Henderson she could hold on to them. 'Miss Henderson . . . Roz, I'd love to put you on our books, I'm confident you will be a success but I just can't employ you until you have your green card, it's illegal. Now, what I suggest is this. You come in and we'll have some studio shots done; we'll keep them on file. Then when you've got the necessary permit we'll start booking you assignments. I'd like to have a quick word with my associates. Would you mind waiting?' She stood up, still holding Roz's portfolio.

'No, not at all.' Roz was trying not to feel too disappointed. She just wished she'd taken the trouble to find out about this 'green card' before she'd left home. Still, it was promising. Studio shots and they'd keep her on file. She wondered how long it would take for her to get the work permit and where she should go for it. Dinny Cassidy, Emer's brother, would know, he was sure to have one. She sincerely hoped it wouldn't take weeks or even months, she didn't particularly want to have to go home because she was fully aware that there would be a huge row and quite probably her parents would never allow her to come back. If it wasn't going to take too long she could stay on. Perhaps Joy would let her stay with them now Emer was moving out, just until she could start work, of course, then she'd find a place of her own. Well, that was the end of the shopping; she would need every dollar she had left now. Thankfully her father had given her some 'emergency money'. She stood up as Rachel Lieberman returned, accompanied by two other women; they were all smiling.

'Hi, I'm Libby and this is Gloria. Rachel's been telling us all about you, Roz, and we've agreed that we'd really like to sign you up, we're sure we can get you work, green card permitting, and if everything works out, well then, perhaps next year you could be our "Face of 1969".'

Roz gasped with delight. 'Really?'

'We've been looking for someone special and we think you are definitely just that person. Now, let's have some coffee while we discuss everything with you, there is a bit of a problem, I believe, with the paperwork.' Libby motioned that Roz should follow them through into an inner office.

An hour later when Roz left she felt as though she were walking on air. She wanted to dance and sing and tell everyone on the street that she had been accepted by Faces and that if all went well she might be chosen as their 'Face of 1969'. She would apply for her green card and she would ask Joy if she could stay with her until everything was sorted out. She had been assured that it wouldn't take too long, she wasn't what could be called 'undesirable' and she would have work. She was to go back the day after Emer's wedding for the studio shots.

She hailed a cab and gave the address of the hotel thinking that she had better calm down. She couldn't burst in and tell Angela her news for Aoife would still be there, she was staying overnight in the same hotel, and she knew her friend wasn't going to be thrilled about having to go back and face the music on her own. She felt a pang of guilt that Angela would have to be the one to inform her parents of her decision but she was certain that when she found out about the fantastic opportunity that she was being offered, Angela wouldn't be too annoyed with her. It was the chance of a lifetime and she just couldn't turn it down, she *couldn't*. A model's career was a short one so she wouldn't be in New York for ever but she knew her father would be furious and her mother would be worried about her. She pushed the thoughts aside. She would wait until after Emer's wedding before she told anyone.

Chapter Thirty-Nine

———◦•◦•◦———

ROZ HAD MANAGED TO hide her excitement from Angela who had been still chatting to Aoife when she'd got back. There seemed to be photographs everywhere and empty teacups.

'You two seem to have been having a good time,' Roz had laughed, her eyes shining.

'We have. Aoife, this is Roz.' Angela introduced her friend to her sister and then proceeded to point out Marian her niece, David her nephew and Tomasz her Polish brother-in-law from the numerous photographs.

Aoife watched the two girls with some amusement. They seemed to belong to a completely different generation to herself: confident, affluent, carefree, fashionable and not in the least perturbed about flying halfway across the world just for a wedding. She'd been a bag of nerves when she'd first come to this country with only a few dollars to her name, no friends and the address of the cousin of her previous employer in Dublin, who had half promised to help her find work and a place to stay.

'Have you had dinner, Roz?' she asked.

'No. I've been too busy seeing . . . the sights, museums and the like,' Roz answered a little evasively. 'But now you mention it, I'm starving. Will we eat in the hotel or go out?'

Angela looked questioningly at Aoife, thinking she might be too tired after an exhausting day to go out. Aoife had been up at the crack of dawn and hadn't even unpacked yet, and it was bound to be freezing cold outside. Maybe she would prefer to stay in the hotel?

'Why not? It's not often I get to take a trip away from home and family. I'll unpack and have a bit of a wash and brush-up and then we'll go out and find somewhere for dinner. Haven't I got something to celebrate, seeing my little sister again after all this time?'

Angela began to help her to gather up the photographs, apart from the ones Aoife had said she must keep, while Roz said she would go and brush her hair and put on a bit more lipstick.

'Isn't it a great pity that you can't stay for the wedding? You could see the outfit Angela has designed for Emer. She's going to look fantastic,' Roz said.

'Mother of God! Tomasz would have ten fits if I was away for more than one night, he'd think I'd up and left him for good. And young Eva, she's his sister, would be even worse, she's after minding the kids,' Aoife replied, laughing.

They decided on a Greek restaurant as none of them had ever tried Greek food before and Roz said they should seize the opportunity to try every new experience. Throughout the meal she had been hard put not to let anything slip about her visit to the agency or her future plans, but somehow she managed to keep her secret. They had had a bottle of wine between them and decided when they got back to the hotel to have a nightcap, after which they had all gone to bed.

Aoife's bus back to Chicago left quite early but Angela promised to get up to see her off. Roz was going to have a lie-in for she said she felt exhausted and wanted to look her best for the wedding, and if she had dark rings under her eyes from lack of sleep she certainly wouldn't look good at all.

After she'd waved her sister off at the bus station Angela had returned and they'd gone out to see the sights that Roz said she'd missed. She was very careful not to dwell too much or go into any great detail about the places she was supposed to have visited the day before.

'We still have a bit of time for shopping,' Angela said after a rather hectic day, thinking that Roz would be dying to go and spend more money.

Roz had shaken her head. 'I'm not too bothered. I thought we could spend the day after tomorrow doing that,' she'd replied nonchalantly.

Angela had been surprised. 'That's not like you. Are you feeling all right? I thought you looked a little feverish last night.'

Roz seized on this. 'I did feel as though I was in for a cold last night but I'm fine now. Still, I think we should have an early night. We've a busy day tomorrow.'

'I hope Emer's going to have one too and I hope she's staying nice and calm and not having a last-minute fit of nerves. Her mam can turn her into a nervous wreck with her fussing.'

'Joy's so sensible that she'll calm everyone down. Don't worry, Emer will be great tomorrow.'

The following day was sunny and bright but very, very cold with the temperature below freezing and Roz wished she had a full-length fake-fur coat to wear over her electric blue dress instead of just a jacket. Remembering the times she'd shivered during Mass at the Blessed Sacrament at home during the winter months, she hoped the heating in the church would be more efficient.

Angela thought she had never seen Mrs Cassidy looking so smart or so nervous. 'Wouldn't you think it was her wedding day and not Emer's,' she whispered to Roz as Peg was escorted up the long aisle by one of the ushers.

'Hasn't Joy done a great job on her though?' Roz whispered back, glancing at Patrick's mother who looked very smart in what was quite obviously an expensive outfit. She could see now why Emer called her 'the battleaxe'. From the way she kept glancing at Emer's small family contingent it was obvious that she considered them to be far inferior to her own much larger party of friends and relations. But the lovely golden-brown velvet dress, with a short matching jacket that boasted a real fur collar, suited Emer's mother's colouring. Peg had a small, very fashionable pillbox hat with a small veil in gold with matching gloves and clutch bag. Her shoes matched the dress. It was also obvious that she had paid her first-ever visit to a beauty parlour, at her daughter-in-law's insistence.

Angela nodded, thinking that Peg's friends and neighbours in Edenderry would hardly recognise her. Joy was matron of honour and Patrick's two sisters were bridesmaids and Angela knew they were all wearing burgundy-coloured velvet dresses. Roz nudged her as the organ burst into life and Emer began her walk to the altar on her father's arm, looking radiant in the brocade coat and dress.

The room that had been booked for the reception was very grand, Angela thought as she and Roz found their places at the beautifully set-out table. The theme was peach and cream and great pains had been taken to make sure that everything matched: napkins, table flowers, the huge swathed bows of ribbon that decorated the room, even the satin bows that decorated every chair.

Roz too was very impressed. 'Don't they do things on such a big scale over here? Would you look at this gorgeous little box, we all seem to have one at our place settings.' She carefully inspected the small peach and cream embossed box decorated with tiny artificial flowers and ribbons. 'There's something inside,' she whispered to Angela.

One of Patrick's cousins, who was sitting opposite, smiled and leaned across. 'There're sugared almonds inside, they're called "favours". Don't you have them at weddings in England?' she asked.

Roz shook her head. 'There are quite a lot of things we don't have at weddings in England that you have over here. My sister was married recently and we thought that was a grand occasion and very stylish but it's nothing compared to all this. Everything here is so . . . modern and different and innovative. I love New York!' She couldn't quite hide the note of excitement in her voice and Angela shot her a questioning look, but Roz was already engaged in conversation with the young man on her right.

Angela's gaze went to Emer who was positively glowing with happiness as she sat beside her new husband. She had taken off the brocade coat and Angela was very pleased to note that the dress seemed to suit the glamorous room setting perfectly. She hadn't let Emer down on this her special day, she thought with some pride, but would she herself ever have her 'special' day? Were Mrs Cassidy and her quaint sayings right? Was there someone out there for her? Oh, she knew she was very fortunate. She had her career, she had a loving family and she had good friends but she still felt there was something missing. She looked across the room and her gaze settled on one of the waiters who was serving the first course of the meal. He reminded her of Ronan Emmet and she suddenly wished he was here with her. She would have liked to have shared this day with him, she mused.

Roz's voice broke into her reverie. 'I just was telling Claire, Patrick's cousin, that you designed Emer's dress and she thinks it's fantastic! She thinks you could really make a fortune if you opened a boutique here, you should think about it, Angela.'

Angela smiled at Patrick's cousin. 'Maybe one day in the future,' she replied.

They had had a wonderful day, everything had gone so smoothly that the new Mrs Molloy had whispered to Angela that not even 'the battleaxe' could find fault, and when they returned to the hotel that night they were both exhausted. When they were being driven back in the cab Roz had become very apprehensive, knowing that she would have to tell Angela her news before they went to bed as tomorrow she was to go for her studio shots.

Angela kicked off her shoes as soon as they got to their room. 'I think that was every bit as grand as Sal's wedding and I've been danced off my feet.'

Roz threw her jacket on the bed and sat down to remove her shoes. She wasn't looking forward to the next half-hour. 'Angela, I've got some news and I have to tell it to you now.'

Angela looked curiously at her. 'What?'

As briefly as she could and without getting too excited about her new career, Roz told her.

Angela's eyes slowly widened in horror as she grasped the fact that Roz intended to stay in New York. 'God in Heaven, Roz! You're never expecting me to get off that plane in Manchester and tell your dad that you're . . . that you've stayed here? He'll kill me, so he will! And your mam! I

386

promised her I'd keep my eye on you! I promised her faithfully!'

'I know! But it can't be helped!' Roz cried.

'Roz, you can't do this to me! You *can't*! Don't you see that they'll blame me? Emer is my friend. It was only through me that you got to know her. You'd never met her before we came over.' She raised both hands to her cheeks. 'They'll say it's all my fault and in a way they'll be right!'

Roz was becoming distraught. 'Angela, I'm truly sorry but can't you see what a fantastic opportunity it is for me? I'd never have been offered anything like *this* back home, you know I wouldn't! It's *New York*! It's a real chance of success.'

'Have you mentioned this to Joy?' Angela demanded.

'No! How could I with the wedding? I haven't told anyone. I *wouldn't* tell anyone before I'd told you.'

Angela was beginning to calm down a little but she was furious with her friend for putting her in this predicament. She gazed at Roz with grim determination in her eyes. 'You are going to make a phone call first thing in the morning.' She glanced at her watch. 'It's too late – or rather too early in the morning at home to do it now.'

'Who to?'

'Your mam and dad. *You* are going to explain all this to them. It's just not fair to expect me to do it and it's not fair on them either.'

'Oh, God!' Roz exclaimed.

'At least when your dad gets to the airport he'll *know* you won't be with me. If he sees me arrive alone the shock could give him a heart attack and neither of us wants that on our conscience.'

'But he'll get a shock when I tell him!' Roz protested.

'Not if you put it the right way. Don't go blurting out, "Dad, I'm not coming home. I've got a job. I've been signed up by a top model agency here in New York and I could even be their 'Face of the year' next year.'"

Roz was biting her lip but she was thinking about it. 'If I say I've been offered a fantastic opportunity and had to give a quick decision . . .' she pondered aloud.

Angela nodded. 'That's better. Then go on to tell him all about it and the fact that you're hoping to stay with Joy and Dinny and that it won't be for ever.'

Roz was feeling a bit better about it now. 'Then I can tell him that you will explain it in more detail when you get back.'

With some resignation Angela nodded her agreement. At least Roz was taking responsibility for her actions and that was the right thing to do but she was fully aware that this news wasn't going to be met with any kind of approval by Bernard Henderson. Neither of them was going to get much sleep tonight, she thought.

Roz had gone over and over it all during the hours when she'd tossed restlessly. She looked tired and anxious, she thought next morning as she looked into the mirror in the bathroom. She'd have to apply her make-up carefully for the photos she was to have taken later on.

Angela had shut herself in the bathroom while Roz made her call, promising that if Roz's father insisted on speaking to her she would do her best for her friend. She couldn't hear a great deal of what was going on but when at last Roz put her head around the door she was very thankful to learn that she hadn't been summoned to the phone.

'How did he take it? What did he say?' Angela asked as she emerged.

'He wasn't happy – that's the understatement of the year, but at least he didn't roar, "You come home at once or I'm coming over to fetch you!" He said he was shocked and . . . and very disappointed in me. He said the right thing to do would have been to have gone back and told them in person. But Angela, I couldn't have done that. They'd never have let me come back and besides by that time the agency might have found someone else. I've to go at once and ask Joy and Dinny if I can stay and if they agree then I've to let him know.'

'And if not?' Angela asked.

'Then I've to go home with you. He said he won't allow me to stay here with no one to supervise me,' Roz replied.

Angela nodded. 'That's fair enough. Your mam is going to worry herself sick about you as it is, without thinking you have nowhere decent to stay. What kind of parents would they be, Roz, if they weren't worried about you?'

'I know,' Roz answered in a small voice. She was praying that now she could persuade Emer's brother to let her stay with them but she was hopeful that once she'd explained everything Joy would be amenable to the idea. 'He did say that I'm to use the emergency money though and I said I was sorry he would be out of pocket, he's paid for this whole trip for me after all.'

Angela stood up. 'We'd better get over to see Joy and Dinny and hope that Dinny hasn't too much of a hangover and that Joy isn't too exhausted. Then I'll have to do a bit of shopping. I want something for Maddy and I think I'll be after needing some "peace offerings" for your mam and dad. I'm not going to escape the fallout from all this entirely.'

Chapter Forty

———

To EVERYONE'S PROFOUND RELIEF, AFTER a little persuasion, Dinny agreed that Roz could move in with them on a short-term basis. Joy said that she had loved having Emer's company and would miss her, a young person livened the place up, so she would be quite happy to have Roz to stay. A delighted Roz had duly phoned her father who had asked to have a few words with Joy who then told them that Bernard Henderson, although still angry, was more resigned to the situation. After this Roz had gone off to the agency and Angela had gone to do some last-minute shopping and then her packing. When Roz returned, full of excitement, Angela had helped her pack and move over to the Cassidys' apartment.

'I'll come to the airport to see you off, it's the least I can do,' Roz had promised.

'I should think so too,' Angela had replied but she had been smiling.

After Angela had checked in Roz hugged her before she went through the gate. 'I'll miss you and I really am sorry.'

'You won't have time to miss me but please do take care of yourself, Roz. I know I sound like an auld biddy but don't get carried away with everything, remember this is a much bigger city than Liverpool. And don't go upsetting Joy and Dinny after they've been good enough to take you in.' She really was happy that Roz seemed to be on the brink of a fantastic career but she was also worried about her friend.

'I'll try and call you but until I actually start to get paid I'll have to watch my spending. I can't promise I'll write but at least I can send postcards.'

'You'd better try and write at least one letter to your mam, she'll be like a cat on hot bricks until she's heard from you and she deserves more than a postcard.'

Roz nodded. 'I'll do it tonight. You'd better go on through. Take care and keep me informed of all the news.'

Angela hugged her again and then walked on, turning to wave before heading for the departure lounge.

When she had settled herself in her seat she leaned back and closed her eyes. People were still boarding so it would be a while before they took off. It had been a very short but eventful trip. In some ways she was glad to be going home, in others she was sorry. She was sorry not to have been able to spend more time with Aoife; she would have liked to have gone and met Tomaz and young Marian and David. She was sorry not to have seen Emer's new home in Queens and spent more time with her old friend, and she was sorry she couldn't stay to keep her eye on Roz, but then she told herself Roz Henderson was nearly twenty-one and should therefore be able to look after herself. She wasn't particularly looking forward to explaining to Roz's parents either. But she was glad to be going home because even though the trip had been short, she had missed everyone. She had gifts for her sister and her parents and she would go over and see them as soon as she could. She had 'peace offerings' too for Lydia and Bernard and souvenirs for Sal and Lizzie. She was also quite relieved to escape the freezing temperatures. It could be cold and damp and miserable at home but at least it didn't get *that* cold and she had found that the constant heat in all the buildings gave her a headache and a dry throat. She also had dozens of ideas buzzing around in her head for designs for her future collections and she'd concentrate on them when she got home.

It was an uneventful flight and Angela managed to sleep for most of the way but when at last they landed and she left the plane and walked towards passport control, she felt very apprehensive at the thought of facing Bernard Henderson.

He was waiting for her just beyond the barrier in the arrivals hall and waved to attract her attention. To her relief he didn't have a face like thunder.

He took her case from her. 'Welcome home, Angela. You look tired. It's a long flight.'

She gave him a quick hug. 'I'm so very sorry about Roz. Really I am.'

Bernard grimaced. 'I don't suppose there was very much you could do. I know only too well how headstrong and stubborn she can be. I'm angry with her, but I feel I can at least trust Emer's brother and sister-in-law to keep an eye on her. Her mother is taking it very badly though.'

Angela nodded. 'I feel I've really let Lydia down. I promised I'd look after Roz.'

'Well, I'm sure that after Lydia has had a good chat with you, she'll feel better,' Bernard replied.

Angela sincerely hoped so.

When they finally arrived home both Lizzie and Lydia

Lyn Andrews

Henderson demanded to be told *everything* about Roz's decision.

'For heaven's sake, put the kettle on, Lizzie, let's have a cup of tea first. We're both cold and Angela is worn out with the travelling and the worry of it all,' Bernard said, a little sharply.

When they were all settled with tea Angela knew she was in for at least an hour of close questioning from both her friend's upset and anxious mother and her irate sister.

As she finished the very detailed story of Roz's first trip to the modelling agency and the subsequent events she was very relieved to see that Lydia was looking far less upset and worried. She had put a great deal of emphasis on how well Dinny and Joy had looked after Emer and had also tried to impress on them that it was a fantastic opportunity for Roz.

'Well, I suppose when you put it like that we shouldn't be too angry with her, and Dinny and Joy are very good,' Lydia replied.

'And a model's career doesn't last for ever. When the work gets scarce she'll come home,' Lizzie added. She really wasn't that annoyed with her sister; you had to grasp every opportunity in life. It was the way Roz had gone about the whole affair and the fact that she had upset their mother that had been hard to take.

'I'm sure she will,' Angela agreed.

Lydia decided to hold that fact firmly in her mind and not to worry herself sick over her youngest daughter. 'You're both right, and she really isn't a child any longer. It might even do her some good to have to stand on her own two feet for a change. Well, I suppose now it will be "nose to the grindstone" again for you, Angela?'

'I have got a lot of new ideas for the future but I thought

394

I'd go over and see Mam before I start work again. I've got photographs and some gifts.'

Lydia frowned. 'I don't know. It's not a good time of the year to be travelling.'

'Oh, Mam! Hasn't she just come three thousand miles across the Atlantic?' Lizzie reminded her, grinning.

'Oh well, it's your decision, Angela. I'm sure they'll be delighted to see you but you'd better take a day or so to get over this trip,' Lydia advised.

Three days later, after Bernard Henderson had booked the ferry and Angela had hired a small car, she set off for Ireland. It was very cold with a sharp frost but there was no wind.

'You take care on the roads when you get over there,' Lydia had said as she'd waved her off.

The night before, she'd lain awake for a while, as her sleep patterns were still a little erratic. She knew her family would be delighted to see her and hear all her news. Maddy would be agog at Roz's latest escapade and her mam would want to hear all about her meeting with Aoife and about Emer's wedding. Angela had smiled to herself thinking that both her sister and her friend were happily married, as was Sal. Lizzie was courting seriously too; an engagement had even been mentioned. That had made her think about herself and where life was taking her and then she'd thought about Ronan Emmet. Should she take the time to go to Edenderry and see him? She was still pondering on this when she finally fell asleep.

She drove carefully along the dark, frosty and virtually deserted road to the Midlands and decided to talk over the matter of going to see Ronan with her mother.

Maura was waiting for her. The kitchen was warm and cosy and the kettle was boiling on the range.

'You've arrived safe and sound, thanks be to God! We've

had a fierce hard frost overnight and I was after worrying about you,' she confided as she hugged Angela. 'Your da has already gone to his work but Maddy's not up yet so I have ye all to myself for a little while.'

Angela took off her coat and placed it over the back of a chair. Then she put the gifts she had brought with her on the table.

'I brought you some things from New York and something for Maddy too.' She looked around and felt a glow of satisfaction that her family was not spending this winter in the old cottage.

'Aren't ye very good to us? I'm delighted to have you home, child.' Maura looked closely at her daughter. 'Is there something troubling you, Angela? Or are you just tired?'

Angela smiled. 'I am a bit tired, all the travelling I suppose. There is something I'd like to talk to you about though, Mam, but later, after I've taken Maddy to school.'

Maura nodded as she poured the tea. 'Ye spoil that one. It won't harm her to walk – 'tis not far, and haven't ye done enough driving for one day?'

'It's all right, Mam. I don't mind and doesn't she walk every other day?'

'She does so. Ah, I suppose it will do no harm,' Maura conceded.

Maddy had been very excited to see her sister and had asked question after question until her mother had told her she was giving them both a headache and that she would be late getting to school if she carried on like this.

'Mam's right, Maddy. I promise I'll pick you up from school and then I'll spend the rest of the day answering all your questions showing you the photos and telling you *everything* about New York and Roz's new career.'

Maddy clapped her hands together while Maura raised her eyes to the ceiling. 'Then won't we all be up until midnight!' she muttered as she cleared away the breakfast dishes.

After Angela returned from driving Maddy to school, she found her mother with her coat, hat and scarf on.

'I thought we'd go for a bit of a walk. It's a grand morning. Cold but bright and sunny and the fresh air will do us both good. It might put some colour in your cheeks, Angela.'

Angela nodded and pulled on a bright red TamO'Shanter then tucked a matching scarf into the neck of her heavy navy maxi coat. It *was* a lovely morning, she thought, as they left the kitchen and crossed the small yard. The sky was a clear blue and the sunlight sparkled on the frost on the bare branches of the trees and hedgerows and the air was sharp and clean.

'Now, what is it that is upsetting you?' Maura asked when they were out on the lane.

'It . . . it's not *upsetting*, Mam. More *unsettling*. I was thinking last night about . . . about the future, my future. Aoife, Emer and Sal are married and Lizzie is getting engaged soon and I . . .' she shrugged.

Maura nodded. 'Are ye feeling that there is no one "special" in your life, Angela? We none of us know what the future holds and sometimes that's a blessing, so it is, but ye have plenty of time.'

'I . . . I was thinking about Ronan Emmet.'

Maura looked at her closely. 'That young doctor from Edenderry?'

Angela nodded. 'I never heard from him again after I refused to come over for Liam Murphy's funeral.'

'And?' Maura probed gently.

'And I was wondering if . . . if I should go over while I'm here?'

'Are ye fond of him?'

Angela looked confused. 'I don't know.'

Maura thought she understood. 'Are ye afraid to trust another man after the last one? Is that the way of it? Put all that behind you, child. There are good men out there and from the little I saw of that young doctor I'd say he wouldn't let you down. Go over to see him. Tell him you drove me over to put some flowers on Mary's grave and thought you'd call in, being in the area. Sure, what harm would it do?'

Angela nodded. She would go and see him. Maybe it would help.

Chapter Forty One

———◆———

A s Maura had predicted, it had been very late when
they all finally got to bed and Angela had been too tired
to think much about Ronan Emmet.

They drove over to Edenderry the next morning. It was
much milder, but it was a grey and dismal morning with a
steady cold drizzle falling from dark, lowering clouds. When
they reached the town Maura insisted on buying a bunch of
early daffodils while Angela sat in the car, thinking how little
the small town had changed from the last time she had visited.

'I'll drive you to the churchyard and then I'll go up to Dr
Leahy's house,' Angela informed her mother as she returned
to the car.

Maura nodded. 'Don't be rushing back for me. I'll go into
the church and say a few prayers for poor Mary's soul.'

Angela still found it hard to understand how her mother
could be so forgiving. Maura always referred to her sister as
'poor Mary'.

'I won't be too long,' Angela promised. 'Sure, you'd be
chilled to the bone in this weather, even in the church.'

The house looked the same, except that it had obviously had a fresh coat of paint fairly recently. The side door was closed because morning surgery was over and Angela hoped Ronan wouldn't have already left to go on his rounds. A young girl who was unfamiliar to her opened the door in response to her knock.

'Do you think it would be possible for me to see Dr Emmet?' Angela asked.

The girl looked at this stylishly dressed and confident young woman a little nervously. She'd only been working here for two weeks. 'Will I go and ask, Miss?'

Angela nodded, but before she could volunteer her name, the girl disappeared. She stepped into the porch to wait out of the rain and at length the kitchen door opened and Miss Dunne appeared, looking thinner and older and frowning in the way Angela remembered so well.

When Miss Dunne caught sight of the visitor the frown disappeared. 'What a surprise! Angela O'Rourke!'

Angela smiled. 'It's lovely to see you again, Miss Dunne. I'm afraid the girl didn't wait for me to give my name.'

Miss Dunne looked pained. 'And who is it that's after coming to the door, I asked her? Of course she didn't know, not having had the sense to ask! Come inside out of the cold, Angela. That one is the latest in a long line of incompetents! I don't know what the young ones want these days but it's certainly not to do a decent day's work. We haven't had anyone with the diligence, consideration and manners yourself had when you were here.'

Angela followed her into the kitchen. 'I drove Mam over to visit Aunt Mary's grave so I thought I'd call in and see how everyone is.'

'That was very thoughtful of you. Ah, I can't complain. I'm not getting any younger, but then who is? Even you are quite the grown-up young businesswoman now, and I hear that Emer Cassidy has married an American accountant, no less.' Miss Dunne managed a rare smile. In her way she was quite proud of what young Angela O'Rourke had achieved in life. She still had the pretty handkerchief case the girl had made for her. 'I'll go in myself to see if the doctor is back, for that Rosie will get everything confused. Sure, she hasn't the sense she was born with!'

Angela hoped Ronan was in. 'I don't want to put you to any trouble.'

''Tis no trouble,' Miss Dunne replied.

In a few seconds the housekeeper returned, followed by James Leahy, who was still wearing his heavy overcoat.

'Angela! Isn't this a great surprise and a welcome one! Come on through to the library. Miss Dunne will send young Rosie in with some tea and then you can tell me all about how the fashion business progresses in Liverpool. We're very proud of you and you are looking very smart and stylish yourself, I have to say.'

Angela followed him into the small and rather gloomy room where she had first broached the subject of a career in nursing with him. He was looking older too, his hair was now almost white and he seemed to have become a little stooped. 'This is very kind of you, but I don't want to take up too much of your time. I know both you and Ronan are busy.'

He looked at her closely as he took off his overcoat. She hadn't been back to Edenderry since Mary had died. 'Not so busy these days. I'm retiring, and there's a new man taking over. As for Ronan, well, I've just taken him to the station.'

'He . . . he's gone?' Angela felt confused and disappointed. 'Has there been . . . some trouble?'

James Leahy sat down in his old leather chair and motioned her to sit in the small chair opposite him. He shrewdly deduced from her voice and expression that she had really come to see Ronan.

'Not at all. As I said, I'm retiring and I persuaded him that he is too young and bright to remain in a backwater like this. He's off to Manchester. Much better prospects.'

Angela didn't know what to say. She just sat staring at him, twisting her hands in her lap.

James leaned forward. 'It was Ronan you came to see, Angela, wasn't it?'

She nodded.

'I always thought he had a soft spot for you, child, but when there was no further contact after Liam died . . .' He shrugged.

'I . . . I . . .' She faltered.

'Angela, are you fond of him?' he asked bluntly.

'I . . . I don't know how I feel, and that's the truth.'

He got to his feet. 'Go on up to the station, there's still time. He sent me home. "No point in waiting in the cold, James. There's a while yet until the train arrives, if it's on time, which I doubt," he said. Go on up there, Angela, and at least talk to him.' He took her hands, pulled her to her feet and ushered her to the door.

Hoping that her mam was keeping warm in the church, she drove as quickly as she could to the station and, after abandoning the car in the yard, hurried to the platform.

'Has the Dublin train gone?' she called to the station master.

He stuck his head out of the office door. 'Gone is it? Sure, it hasn't even arrived in Ballyporeen yet! Are ye looking for someone?'

She breathed a sigh of relief. 'Dr Emmet.'

He grinned. 'Isn't he keeping himself warm in the waiting room?'

To her dismay the small room was crowded but as she caught his surprised gaze she smiled, and he pushed his way toward her.

'Angela!'

'I thought I'd missed you. I called up to the house and . . .'

Ronan took her arm and led her outside on to the platform. He was surprised but delighted to see her. She looked well, he thought. Still very attractive and appealing but with a bit less confidence than he remembered.

'As usual, the train is late but now I'm glad it is.'

She smiled. 'So am I. I drove Mam over to visit Aunt Mary's grave and I thought I'd call and see everyone. I'm on a short visit. I've just returned from New York. My friend Emer got married over there.'

Ronan smiled at her. 'Didn't the whole town hear about Emer Cassidy's wedding? How are your parents?' He was genuinely interested, remembering the reunion.

'They're grand, and so is Maddy. She came over to stay with me for the summer holidays last year and, while I was in New York, I managed to see my eldest sister again. Mam and Da have moved into a new bungalow, they have all the mod cons now. I couldn't bear to see how hard Mam's life was so I found them somewhere better.' Angela felt she was gabbling and fell silent as they walked slowly along the length of the platform.

Ronan nodded. She was a kind and generous girl and she was often in his thoughts. He'd been disappointed when she'd written to say she wasn't coming to Edenderry after Liam's death. He'd wished she had but he hadn't thought it right that he write back and urge her more forcefully to come. When there had been no further letters from her he'd concluded that she didn't want to keep in touch and that had saddened and disappointed him.

Angela felt she should at least try to explain why she had refused to go back to Edenderry. 'I was sorry I didn't come over after . . . after my uncle died but I was very busy and Mrs Henderson advised me against it. The crossing can be very rough at this time of year.'

'Angela, you don't have to explain. Sure, I wasn't after sitting in judgment and besides, it was a tragic affair. He really seemed to go downhill after your aunt's death and you went back to Liverpool. James and I both warned him about the drinking but it had little effect. We're of the opinion it was the drink that was to blame. He wouldn't have done such a thing if he'd been in his right mind.'

She nodded, not looking at him, and he sensed that she was holding something back. She had never seemed as fond of Liam as she had of Mary and she had been decidedly cold towards him at Mary's funeral. And he hadn't forgotten how she had arrived at the Leahys' house in a terrible state the night Dolores had died. He'd assumed there had been some kind of a row which was why he'd walked her home.

'You didn't seem to have much time for him?' he probed gently.

'I didn't. It was something that happened, but it's all in the past now,' she replied, a sharp edge to her tone.

Ronan said nothing. She was telling him not to dig any further and he wondered whether Liam Murphy had had something else on his conscience other than his wife's death. Was that why she had been so distraught that night? Had she been coming to James for help? It wasn't unheard-of. In his profession he had come across abuse more than once. He decided to change the subject. 'And how is your glamorous friend Roz?'

Angela was relieved that he wasn't pressing the matter although she had seen the quick flash of understanding in his eyes. She grimaced and then smiled. 'Don't talk to me about *that* one!'

'Why?'

'Because she came to New York with me but she stayed there. She got a job with a big modelling agency. She's going to be famous and earn a fortune. I was supposed to keep her feet on the ground and not let her lose the run of herself entirely, I promised her mother I would, and then she goes and does something completely mad and leaves me to tell her parents!'

'That wasn't entirely fair, but she always looked too exotic to stay in an ordinary job.'

'I made her call her parents and tell them.'

Ronan nodded. 'She always struck me as being headstrong and a bit spoiled.'

'She's both, but I suppose that's partly her mam's fault. Deep down, she has a heart of gold. I suppose she'll come back home one day. A model's career doesn't last long.'

'And what about your career?' he asked as they re-traced their steps up the platform and the station master appeared to inform them that the train would be there directly, or maybe even a bit sooner.

'Great. I came back from New York with lots of ideas. And now I hear you are off to Manchester.'

'I am. James is retiring and he urged me not to waste my time in a small place like this. He said I should be more ambitious, that I have a great deal to offer. So I thought about it and decided I could see his point. I'm off to a large practice in Manchester. It will be a big change but a challenge too.'

Angela realised that there wasn't very much time left before the train arrived, but also that Manchester wasn't that far away from Liverpool. It wasn't beyond the realms of possibility that she would see him again. He seemed to like her and she really did like him. He had been kind and thoughtful toward her when she had most needed it. There was nothing dishonest about him, unlike Danny Fielding. Her mam was right, she should put that experience behind her and she felt she could safely trust Ronan Emmet with her heart.

Ronan had been thinking about the distance between them too. 'And of course, Manchester isn't a million miles away from Liverpool. There are trains, which probably do run on time, and we can both drive. I'd like to see your boutiques, Angela, not that I'm a great expert on fashion.'

Angela smiled with pure joy. 'I'd like that, Ronan, really I would.'

The other passengers emerged on to the platform and the train came to a halt beside them.

'I have your address. I'll write to you, Angela,' Ronan promised.

'We have a phone too. It's Aintree four six six nine.'

He smiled and bent to kiss her cheek before he boarded the train. 'Then I'll phone you. Take care, Angela. I'll see you soon.'

She smiled back at him and Emer's words returned to her. 'Mam always says that for every shoe God made a stocking.' Had she at last found hers? she wondered. Only time would tell, but Angela felt far more confident about the future now.